GREEK BACHELORS: TEMPTED TO A FLING

ELIZABETH **POWER**

JACKIE **BRAUN**

MARIE **DONOVAN**

Published in Great Britain 2017
By Mills & Boon, an imprint of HarperCollins*Publishers*
1 London Bridge Street, London, SE1 9GF

GREEK BACHELORS: TEMPTED TO A FLING © 2017 Harlequin Books S.A.

A Greek Escape © 2013 Elizabeth Power
Greek for Beginners © 2013 Jackie Braun Fridline
My Sexy Greek Summer © 2009 Marie Donovan

ISBN: 978-0-263-93193-8

09-0318

MIX
Paper from
responsible sources
FSC™ C007454

This book is produced from independently certified FSC™ paper to ensure responsible forest management.

For more information visit: www.harpercollins.co.uk/green

Printed and bound in Great Britain

A GREEK ESCAPE

ELIZABETH POWER

*For Alan – and all those wonderful sandwiches
that kept me going!*

Elizabeth Power wanted to be a writer from a very early age, but it wasn't until she was nearly thirty that she took to writing seriously. Writing is now her life. Travelling ranks very highly among her pleasures, and so many places she has visited have been recreated in her books. Living in England's West Country, Elizabeth likes nothing better than taking walks with her husband along the coast or in the adjoining woods, and enjoying all the wonders that nature has to offer.

CHAPTER ONE

'THAT'S IT! THAT'S the one we want! Stop wasting time, you idiot, and take it!' The camera clicked the second before the bird took off from its rock and flapped away over the crystalline water. 'Didn't think I'd let you get away, did you?'

From her vantage point on the rocky hillside overlooking the shingle beach Kayla Young swung round with a swish of long blonde hair, embarrassed that someone might have overheard her. There was nothing but a warm wind, however, passing over the craggy scrubland, and the relentless sun beating down from a vividly azure sky, and Kayla's shoulders drooped in relief.

She wasn't sure when she had first started talking to herself. Perhaps coming away all by herself to this lovely island wasn't doing much for her sanity, she thought, grimacing. Or perhaps it was a defence mechanism against the knowledge that today, back in England, the man she had thought she'd be spending her life with was an hour away from marrying someone else.

The wounds of betrayal were no longer so raw but the scars remained, and in defiance of them Kayla brought the SLR's viewfinder to eye level again. Only her clamped jaw revealed the tension in her as, silently now, she appraised the beauty around her.

Misty blue mountains. Translucently clear water. Surprisingly hunky Greek…

She'd been following a line inland, coming across the deserted beach, but now Kayla brought her viewfinder back to the shoreline in a swift doubletake.

Bringing her camera down, she could see him clearly without the aid of the zoom lens, and she found herself homing in on him with her naked eyes.

Black wavy hair—which would have been way past his collar had he been wearing one—fell wildly against the hard bronze of his neck. In a black T-shirt and pale blue jeans he was pulling fishing tackle from the wooden boat he had recently beached, and from the contoured muscles of his arms, and the way the dark cotton strained across his wide muscular chest, Kayla instantly marked him as a man who worked with his hands. A battered old truck was parked close to her rock, on the road just above the beach, and as the man started walking towards it—towards *her*—Kayla couldn't take her eyes off him.

For some reason she couldn't quite fathom she lifted her camera to zoom in on him again, and felt an absurd and reckless excitement in her secret survey. A few days' growth of stubble gave a striking cast to an already strong jaw, mirroring the strength in his rugged features. They were the features of a man toughened by life—a man who looked as fit as he was hard. A man not much more than thirty, who would probably demand his own way and get it—because there was determination in that face, Kayla recognised, as well as pride and arrogance in the way he carried himself, in the straight, purposeful stride of those long legs.

A man one definitely wouldn't want to mess with, she decided, with a curious little tingle down her spine.

She could see it all in every solid inch of him—in the curve of his tanned forehead and those thick winged brows that were drawing together now in a scowl because...

Dear heaven! he was looking up! He had seen her! Seen her pointing the camera straight at him!

As her agitated finger accidentally clicked the shutter closed she realised the camera had caught him—and, as he shouted something out, she realised that he was aware of it too.

She stood stock-still for a second as he quickened his stride; saw him moving determinedly in her direction.

Oh, my goodness! Suddenly she was pivoting away with the stark realisation that he was giving chase.

Why she was running, Kayla didn't know. Surely, she thought, it would have been better to stand her ground and brazen it out? Except that she hadn't felt like brazening anything out with a man who looked so angry. And anyway, what could she have said? *You caught my eye as I was sizing up the view and I couldn't stop looking at you.*

That would really have been asking for trouble, she assured herself, with her blood pounding in her ears and her legs feeling heavy. She darted an anxious glance back over her shoulder and saw the man was gaining on her now, along the stony uphill path that led to the safety of the villa.

And why had she been looking at him anyway? she reprimanded herself. She had had enough of men to last her a lifetime! It could only have been because he had an interesting face; that was all. Apart from that she wouldn't have looked twice at him if he had rowed across that water accompanied by a fanfare. She had learned the hard way that men were just lying, cheating opportunists—

'Ooooh!'

Tripping over a stone, she struggled to keep herself upright, hearing her pursuer's footsteps bearing down on her.

Too late, though. She came a cropper on the hard and dusty

path and lay there for a few moments, winded and despairing, but surprisingly unharmed.

She heard the pound of his footsteps and suddenly he was there, standing above her. He was breathing hard, and his tone was rough as he tossed some words at her in his own language.

Utterly awestruck by the speed at which he must have run to have caught up with her, Kayla raised herself up on her elbows, her hair falling like pale rivers of silk over her shoulders.

Having little more than a few words of Greek to get by with, she quavered, 'I don't understand you.' Like him, she was breathless, and shaken by his anger as much as her fall.

He said something else that she couldn't comprehend, while a firm hand on her shoulder—bare save for the white strap of her sun top—pulled her round to face him.

Up close, his features were even more arresting than she'd first imagined. His cheekbones were high and well-defined under dark olive skin. Thick ebony lashes framed eyes that were as black as jet, and his brooding mouth was wide and firm.

'Are you hurt?' His question, delivered roughly in English this time, surprised her, as did that small element of concern.

'No. No thanks to you,' she accused, sitting upright and brushing dust off her shorts, trying to appear less intimidated than she was feeling.

'Then I will ask you again. What do you think you were doing?'

'I was taking photographs.'

'Of me?'

Kayla swallowed, fixing him with wary blue eyes. 'No, of a bird. I snapped you by accident.'

'Accident?' From the way one very masculine eyebrow lifted it was clear that he didn't believe her. His hostile gaze raked over her the pale oval of her face. 'What is this...*accident?*' he emphasised pointedly.

His anger hadn't cooled. Kayla could feel it bubbling just beneath the surface. Despite that, though, his voice had a deep, rich resonance, and although his English was heavily accented his command of her language was obvious as he demanded, 'Exactly how many did you take?'

'Only the one,' she admitted, her breathing still laboured from that chase up the hillside. 'I told you. It was an accident.'

'Well, as far as I'm concerned, young woman, it was one accident too many. Exactly who are you? And what are you doing here?'

'Nothing. I mean, I'm on holiday—that's all.'

'And does the normal course of your holiday usually include sticking your nose into other people's business? Spying on people?'

'I wasn't *spying* on you!' From the way those accusing ebony eyes were studying her, and from the suspicion in his voice, Kayla began to experience real fear. Perhaps he was on the run! Wanted by the police! That would go some way to explaining his anger over being photographed. 'My camera…?' Trying to hide her misgivings, she glanced anxiously around and spotted the expensive piece of equipment lying in the scrub nearby.

Stretching out in a bid to reach it, she was dismayed when the man leaped forward, snatching it up before she could.

'Don't damage it!'

He looked angry enough, she thought. But her camera was something she treasured. A gift to herself to replace her old one after she had discovered Craig was having an affair. Some women comfort-ate. She went out with her camera and snapped anything and everything as a form of therapy, and over the past three months she had needed all the therapy she could get!

'Give me one good reason why I shouldn't?'

Because it was expensive! she wanted to fling back. And

because it's got every photograph I've taken since I got here yesterday. But that would probably only make him more inclined to wreck it, if his mood was anything to go by.

'Perhaps I should simply keep it,' he contemplated aloud, his gaze sweeping over her still pale shoulders and modest breasts with unashamed insolence.

'If it makes you happy,' she snapped, needled by the way he was looking at her. But there was something about that gaze moving over her exposed flesh that produced a rush of heat along with a cautioning tingle through her blood. After all, she didn't have a clue who he was, did she? Supposing he really was wanted by the police?

A bird swooped low out of the pine forest above them, its frenzied shriek making her jump before it screeched away, protesting at the human intrusion.

For the first time Kayla realised just how isolated the hillside was. Apart from a cluster of whitewashed fishermen's houses, huddled above the beach at the foot of the mountain road, there was no other sign of human habitation, while the nearest village with its shop and taverna was nearly three miles away.

As she was scrambling to her feet a masculine arm shot out to assist her.

The sudden act of gallantry was so unexpected after all his hostility that Kayla automatically took the hand he was offering. It felt strong and slightly callused as he pulled her upright, bringing her close to his dominating masculinity. Disconcertingly close.

Her senses awakened to the outdoor freshness of him, to the aura of pulsing energy that seemed to surround him, and to an underlying masculine scent that was all his own.

Swallowing and bringing her head up—in her flat-heeled pumps, she still only reached his shoulder—she took a step back and said in a voice that cracked with an unwelcome tug of unmistakable chemistry, 'I'm not afraid of you.'

'Good.' His tone was terse, and still decidedly unfriendly. 'In that case you won't mind me telling you that I don't like interfering young women depriving me of my privacy. So if you want to enjoy your so-called "holiday",' he emphasised scornfully, dumping the offending camera into her startled hands, 'you'll stay out of my way! Is that clear?'

'Perfectly! And I can assure you, Mr... Mr...No-name,' she went on when he didn't have the decency to tell her. 'I've certainly got no wish to deprive you of anything. Least of all your privacy!' Deciding now that he was probably nothing more dangerous than a bad-tempered local, she pressed on, 'In fact you have my solemn promise that I'll do everything I can while I'm here to see that you maintain it.'

'Thank you!'

Kayla bit back indignation as he swung unceremoniously away, striding back down the path without so much as a glance back.

A few minutes later, coming up through the scrub below the modern white villa where she was staying, she heard the distant sound of a vehicle starting up, and guessed from the roughness of its engine that it was the truck she had seen parked at the head of the beach.

Kayla was still smarting from the encounter as she fixed herself a microwave meal that evening in the villa's well-equipped kitchen. With open-plan floors, exposed roof rafters above its galleried landing and spectacular views over the rolling countryside, the villa belonged to her friends, Lorna and Josh. Knowing how much she needed a break, they had offered Kayla the chance to get away for a couple of weeks.

She had barely met a soul since the taxi driver had dropped

her off here yesterday, so why did the first person she bumped into have to be so downright rude?

Slipping the dish into the microwave oven, she stabbed out the settings on the control panel, her agitated movements reflecting her mood.

Still, better that he was rude than charming and lying through his teeth, she thought bitterly, her thoughts straying to Craig Lymington.

How easily she had fallen for his empty promises. She had believed and trusted him when he'd professed to want to be with her for life.

'He'll break your heart. You mark my words,' her mother had advised unkindly when Kayla had enthused over how the most up-and-coming executive at her company, Cartwright Consolidated, had asked her to marry him.

They had been engaged for two months, and Kayla had been deliriously happy, until that night when she'd discovered those messages on his cell phone and realised that she wasn't the only woman to whom he'd whispered such hollow and meaningless words...

'All men are the same, and the high-flying company type are the worst of the lot!' her mother had warned her often enough.

But Kayla hadn't listened. She'd believed her mother was simply embittered and scarred by her own unfortunate experience. After all, hadn't her own husband—Kayla's father—been a company executive? And hadn't he deserted her in exactly the same fashion fifteen years ago, when Kayla had been just eight years old?

Because of that and her mother's warnings she had grown up determined that the man she eventually decided to settle down with would never treat her in such an abominable way.

But he had, Kayla thought. And she had been rudely awakened and forced to admit—to herself at least—that her mother was right. They *were* the worst of the lot! It was a realisation doubly enforced when she had had to suffer the demeaning overtures of one or two other male members of management who had tried to capitalise on her broken engagement.

After leaving the company where she'd worked with Craig, trying to put the pain and humiliation of what he had done behind her, she might have been able to pick up the pieces of her life if she had been allowed to. But her mother's condescending and self-satisfied attitude—particularly when she'd heard that Craig really was getting married—had made everything far, far worse.

Consequently when Lorna had offered her the chance of escaping to her isolated Grecian retreat for a couple of weeks Kayla had jumped at the chance. It had seemed like the answer to a prayer. A place to start rebuilding her sense of self-worth.

But now, as she took her supper from the bleeping microwave and prodded the rather unpalatable-looking lasagne with a fork, it wasn't thoughts of Craig Lymington that troubled her and upset her determined attempts to restore her equilibrium. It was the face of that churlish stranger she'd been unfortunate enough to cross this morning, and her shocking awareness of him when he'd pulled her to her feet and she'd felt the impact of his disturbing proximity.

Leonidas Vassalio was fixing a loose shutter on one of the ground-floor windows, his features as hard as the stones that made up the ancient farmhouse and as darkly intense as the gathering clouds that were closing in over the mountains, warning of an impending storm.

The house would fall down if he didn't take some urgent steps to get it repaired, he realised, glancing up at the sad state of its terracotta roof and the peeling green paint around its doors and windows. The muscles in his powerful arms flexed as he twisted a screw in place.

It was hard to imagine that this place had once been his

home. This modest, isolated farmhouse, reached only by a zig-zagging dirt road. Yet this island, with its rocky coast, its azure waters and barren mountains, was as familiar to him as his own being, and a far cry from the world he inhabited now.

The rain had started to fall. Cold, heavy drops that splashed his face and neck as he worked and reflected on the whole complicated mess his life had become.

To the outsider his privileged lifestyle was one to be envied, but personally he was tired of sycophants, superficial women and the intrusion of the paparazzi. Like that interfering slip of a girl he'd caught photographing him on the beach this morning, he thought grimly, ready to bet money that she was one of them. For what other reason would she have been there if she wasn't from some newspaper? He had had enough of reporters to last him a lifetime, and they had been particularly savaging of late.

He had always shunned publicity. Always managed to keep a low media profile. Anyone outside of Greece might not instantly have recognised him, even though they would most certainly have recognised the Vassalio name. It was his brief involvement with Esmeralda Leigh that had thrust him so starkly into the public eye recently.

Nor had it helped when a couple of the high-ranking executives he had trusted to run one of his UK subsidiaries, along with an unscrupulous lawyer, had reneged on a verbal promise over a development deal and given the Vassalio Group bad press—which in turn had brought his own ethics into question. After all, as chairman, Leonidas thought introspectively, the buck stopped with him. But he had been too tied up at the time to be aware of what was going on.

That ordinary people had been lied to and were having their homes bulldozed from under them didn't sit comfortably on his conscience. Nor did being accused of riding roughshod over people without giving a thought to their needs, breaking up communities so as to profit from multi-million-pound sports arenas and retail/leisure complexes and expand on Vassalio's ever-increasing assets. The fact that everyone affected had been compensated—and very well—had been consigned only to the back pages of the tabloids.

He had needed to get away. To forget Leonidas Vassalio, billionaire and successful businessman, for a while and sort out what was important to him. And to do that he had needed to get back to his roots. To enjoy the bliss of virtual anonymity that coming here would offer him. Because only one other person knew he was here. But now it looked as though even that might have been too much to expect, if that nosy little blonde he'd caught snooping around today had lied about why she was here.

And if she hadn't, and she really had been photographing birds, why had she been standing there taking a picture of him? Had she just fancied snapping a bit of local colour? One of the peasants going about his daily business? Or could it be that she'd just happened to like the look of him? he thought, with his mouth twisting cynically. In other circumstances he would have admitted unreservedly to himself that he hadn't exactly been put off by the look of *her*. Especially when he'd noted that she'd been wearing no ring.

But bedding nubile young women wasn't on his agenda right now. Heaven only knew the physical attributes he'd been endowed with acted like a magnet on the opposite sex, and he'd never met one yet that he'd wanted to bed who hadn't been willing, but, no, he determined as he oiled a hinge. Whatever her motives were, and no matter how affected she'd been by that spark of something that had leaped between them and made her pull back from him as though she'd been scorched when he'd pulled her to her feet, that girl certainly hadn't had bedroom games in mind.

She had to be staying in one of those modern villas that

had sprung up further down the hillside. That was the direction she had been heading in when he'd caught up with her. He wondered if there was anyone with her, or if she was staying there alone. If she was, he deliberated with his hackles rising, then she had to be here for a reason. And if that reason was to intrude on his peace and solitude...

Finishing what he was doing, annoyed at how much thought he was giving to her, he rushed inside, out of the rain.

She was going to find out the hard way that she couldn't mess with *him!*

CHAPTER TWO

THE THREE-MILE drive to the main village to get provisions had seemed like an easy enough mission, particularly when last night's storm had caused a power cut and made her fridge stop working.

Unless the thing had broken before then, Kayla thought exasperated, having come downstairs this morning to a cabinet of decidedly warm and smelly food.

But the polished voice of the car's satellite navigation system had let her down badly when it had guided her along this track. And now, having parked the car in order to consult the map and try and work out where she was, the little hatchback that her friends kept here for whenever they visited the island refused to start.

She tried again, her teeth clenched with tension.

'Come on,' she appealed desperately to the engine. 'Please.'

It was no good, she realised, slumping back on her seat. It had well and truly packed up.

Lorna had given her the name of someone she could call in an emergency who spoke relatively good English, Kayla remembered, fishing in the glove compartment for the man's number. But when she took her cell phone out of her bag she discovered that she didn't have a signal.

Despairingly tossing the phone onto the passenger seat, she looked around at a Grecian panorama of sea and mountains and, closer to hand, pine woods and stony slopes leading down to this track.

Beyond the open windows of the car the chirruping of crickets in the scrub and the lonely tugging of the wind only seemed to emphasise her isolation. She didn't have a clue where she was.

Glancing back over her shoulder, she recognised way below the group of rocks that ran seaward from the beach where she had seen that surly local yesterday, and that smaller island in the distance, clear as a bell today beneath the canopy of a rain-washed vividly azure sky.

With the sun beating relentlessly down upon her, with an unusable phone and only a broken-down car for company, Kayla glanced wistfully towards what looked like a deserted farmhouse, with a roof that had seen better days peeping above the trees at the end of the track.

Fat chance she had of making a call from there!

Or did she?

Sticking her head out of the window and inhaling deeply, she caught the distinct smell of woodsmoke drifting towards her on the scented air.

With her spirits soaring, she leaped out of the car, grabbed her precious camera and set off at a pace, her zipped-back sandals kicking up dust along the sun-baked track.

It was the truck she recognised as she came, breathless, into a paved area at the front of the house. A familiar yellow truck that had her stopping in her tracks even before she recognised its owner.

Wild black hair. Wild eyes. Wild expression.

Oh, no!

Coming from around the side of the house, the surly Greek was looking as annoyed as he looked untamed.

And justifiably so, Kayla decided, swallowing. She had invaded his territory again—unintentionally though it was—

and she would have run like the wind if she had realised it a second sooner. As it was, she was riveted to the spot by the sheer dynamism of the man.

In blue denim cut-offs and nothing else but a dark tan leather waistcoat, exposing his chest and muscular arms, he exuded strength and raw, virile masculinity.

'I thought I told you to stay away from me,' he called out angrily to her, his long, purposeful strides closing the distance between them. 'What do you want?' As if he didn't know! Leonidas thought, his scowling gaze dropping to the camera clutched tightly against her ribcage. 'Didn't you get enough photographs yesterday?'

He looked bigger and distinctly more threatening than he had the previous day, Kayla decided, unnerved. If that were possible!

'I...I just want to use your phone,' she informed him, ignoring his accusation and annoyed with herself for sounding so defensive, for allowing him to intimidate her in such a way.

'My phone?'

She could feel her body tingling beneath the penetrative heat of his gaze. Her T-shirt and shorts felt much too inadequate beside such potent masculinity.

'You *do* have one?' she asked pointedly, trying not to let his unfriendliness get to her. From the way he'd queried her request she might have been asking him to give her a mortgage on Crete! 'My car...' She hated having to tell him as she sent a glance back over her shoulder. 'It's broken down.'

He peered in the direction she'd indicated. But of course he couldn't see it, she realised, because it was way down the track, hidden by trees and scrub. And all she could focus on right then was the undulating muscles of his smooth and powerful chest, which was glistening bronze—slick with sweat.

'Really? And what seems to be the trouble?' he enquired with the sceptical lifting of an eyebrow. He looked at her with such disturbing intensity that Kayla felt as if her strength was being sapped right out of her.

Beneath the thick sweep of his lashes his eyes were amazingly dark, she noticed reluctantly. His nose was proud, his cheekbones high and hard, his mouth firm and well-defined above the dark, virile shadow around his jaw. As for his body…

She wanted to look at him and keep looking at him. *All* of him, she realised, shocked. She was even more shocked to realise that she had never been so aware of a man's sensuality before. Not even Craig's. But he had asked her a question, and all she was doing was standing here wondering how spectacular he would look naked.

Trying to keep her eyes off that very masculine chest, she uttered with deliberate vagueness, 'It won't go.'

That glorious chest lifted as he inhaled deeply. 'Won't move or won't start?' he demanded to know.

Entertaining a half-crazed desire to needle him, Kayla answered with mock innocence, 'It's the same thing, isn't it?'

Now, as those glinting dark eyes pierced the rebellious depths of hers, she realised that this man would know when he was being taken for a fool, and warned herself against the inadvisability of antagonising him.

'Does the engine fire when you turn the ignition key?' he asked, his sweat-slicked chest lifting again with rising impatience.

'No. Nothing happens at all,' she told him, frankly this time. 'So if you could just let me use your phone—if you have a signal—or if you don't…if you have a landline…' A dubious glance up at the house had her wondering if it had fallen into the state it was in long before telephones had been invented.

'It's Sunday,' he reminded her succinctly. 'Who are you going to call?'

She shrugged. 'The nearest garage?' she suggested flippantly, hoping the man whose name she had been given for emergencies would be at home. In fact Lorna had said to call *her* if she needed any help or advice, and right now Kayla felt she'd get more help from her friend back in England than the capable-looking hunk standing just a metre away.

Suddenly, without another word, he was walking past her.

'Show me,' he said over his leather-clad shoulder, much to her surprise.

She virtually had to run to keep up with him.

When they reached the car he held out a hand for the key and Kayla dropped it onto his tanned palm, noticing the cool economy with which he moved as he opened the driver's door and leaned inside to start the ignition.

It fired first time.

'I don't understand...' She turned from the traitorous little vehicle to face the man who had now straightened and was standing there looking tall and imposing and so self-satisfied that she could have kicked him—or the car. Or both! 'I tried and tried,' she stressed, with all the conviction she could muster, because scepticism was stamped on every plane and angle of his hard, handsome face.

He reached into the car again, switched off the engine and, dangling the key in front of her, said in his heavily accented voice, 'Perhaps you would care to try again?'

She jumped into the car, keeping her defiant gaze level with his, almost willing the little hatchback to refuse to start for her. Because how on earth was he going to believe her if it did?

It did.

She flopped back against the headrest, her eyes closing with a mixture of relief and rising frustration.

'There, you see. It's simple when you know how.'

There was no mistaking the cool derision that drifted down to her through the open door, and suddenly Kayla's control snapped.

'It wouldn't start! I couldn't make it! And if you think I

made it all up for some warped reason, just to come here and annoy you, then, believe me, I've got far more important things to do with my time! My phone won't work! My sat-nav's up the creek! And Lorna's fridge has broken down and ruined all the food I bought. And all you can do is stand there and accuse me of lying! Well, I can assure you, Mr... Mr...'

'Leon.'

She looked up at him askance, her blue eyes glistening with angry tears. 'What?'

'My name is Leon,' he repeated. 'And who is this Lorna you mention? Your travelling companion?'

'No. I'm here on my own,' Kayla blurted out without even thinking. A totally frustrating morning had finally taken its toll. 'Lorna owns the villa where I'm staying.' Lorna who—with her husband Josh—had miraculously come to her rescue by offering her a post in their interior design company after Kayla had found it too distressing to stay on at her old job.

'And you say the fridge has broken down?'

'Big-time!' What was he going to do? Drive down and check that she wasn't lying about that as well?

'Have you eaten?'

'What?'

His hand came to rest on the roof of the car as he stooped to address her through the open door. 'I know I'm Greek and you're English, but you seem to be having great difficulty in understanding me. I said, have you eaten?'

'No.'

'Then drive up to the house,' he instructed. 'I'll be along directly.'

What? Kayla nearly said it again, only just stopping herself in time.

He was offering her hospitality? Surely not, she thought, amazed. He was hard, unfriendly, and a perfect stranger to boot.

Well, not perfect, she decided grudgingly. Only in appearance, she found herself silently admitting. Whatever else he was, he was lethally attractive. But some masochistic and warped urge to know more about him—along with the thought of all that festering food she was going to have to throw away—motivated her, against her better judgement, into doing what he had suggested.

He had almost reached the paved yard by the time Kayla put her camera in the boot, out of the sun, having decided it was for the best since it seemed to offend him so much. Involuntarily, her gaze was drawn to his approach.

Unconsciously her eyes savoured the whole sensational length and breadth of him, from those wide shoulders and muscular arms to that glistening bronze chest and tightly muscled waist, right down to his narrow denim-clad hips. Very masculine legs ended in a pair of leather sandals, dusty from his trek along the track.

There was a humourless curl to his mouth, she noticed as he drew nearer, as though he were fully aware of her reluctant interest in him.

'Around the back,' he advised with a toss of his chin, and waited for her to go ahead of him.

That small act of courtesy seemed oddly at variance with his manners on the whole, she decided, preceding him around the side of the rambling old farmhouse.

Don't talk to any strange men. Never take sweets from a stranger.

Wondering what she was doing, ignoring all those clichéd warnings, Kayla realised her mother would have a fit if she could see her now.

'So…are you going to tell me something about yourself?' Leon whoever-he-was enquired deeply from just behind her.

'Like what?' she responded, still walking on ahead.

'Your name would be a good start,' he suggested incisively.

They had come around to the rear of the house, where weed-strewn shady terraces gave onto an equally overgrown garden.

'It's Kayla,' she told him, following his example and deciding that last names were superfluous.

'Kayla?'

Despite his overall unfriendliness, the way he repeated her name was like the warm Ionian wind that blew up from the sea, rippling through the tufted grass on the arid hills. An unexpected little sensation quivered through her. Or was it the sun that seemed to be burning her cheeks? The warm breeze that was lifting the almost imperceptibly fine hairs on her arms?

'Come.' He gestured to a rustic bench under a canopy of vines. Nearby were some smouldering logs within a purpose-built circle of bricks. Resting on a stone beside it was a grid containing several small plump, freshly prepared fish, their scales gleaming silver in the late morning sun.

'Did you catch those yourself?' She'd noticed a rod and fishing tackle in the back of his truck, and wondered if he went out every day to fish from the boat she'd seen him unloading the previous day.

'Yes, about an hour ago.' He was squatting down, repositioning a log on the fire. 'What's wrong?' he enquired, looking up at her when she still stood there, saying nothing. 'Are you vegetarian?'

She had been silently marvelling at how only this morning those fish had been in the sea—how he had already been down there, brought them back and prepared them for his lunch—but there was no way she was going to tell him that.

'No,' she replied, watching him place the grid on the bricks over the glimmering logs.

'Then sit down,' he commanded, before he turned and strode back into the house.

Left alone, Kayla took a few moments to study its sadly neglected exterior. With its ramshackle appearance, and the odd wild creeper growing out of its walls, it seemed almost to have become part of the hillside that rose steeply above it on one side. She wondered if it might just be a place he had found where it was convenient for him to shack up, and then looked quickly away as he emerged from inside with plates and cutlery and several different kinds of bread in a hand-painted bowl.

'Do I take it that you don't want any?' he called out, noticing that she was still standing where he had left her.

The fish were starting to cook, skins bubbling, their aroma drifting up to her with the woodsmoke, tantalising and sweet.

'No,' she refuted quickly, sitting down on the bench, and earned herself the twitch of a smile from that mocking, masculine mouth as he set the plates and cutlery down on a small, intricately wrought iron table that looked as though it had seen every winter for decades. 'So, why are you asking me to lunch if you want to be left alone?'

'Good question,' he responded without looking at her. He was using a fish slice to turn their lunch. Spitting oil splashed onto the glowing logs, making them sizzle. 'Perhaps it's the best way of keeping an eye on you,' he said when he had finished.

'Why?' She fixed him directly with eyes that were as vivid as cornflowers. 'Why are you so worried about my bothering you? Why do you think I need keeping an eye on?' she queried, frowning. 'Unless...'

'Unless what?' he urged, calmly setting the fish slice aside.

Her heart was beating unusually fast. 'You have something to hide.'

Squatting there, with his hands splayed on his bunched and powerful thighs, he was studying her face with such unsettling intensity that for a few moments Kayla wondered if her original supposition about him was right. He really was on the run from the law. Why else would he object so strongly to being photographed?

Leonidas made a half-amused sound down his nostrils. 'Don't we all?' he suggested through the charm of a feigned smile, and thought, *Particularly you, my scandal-mongering little kitten.*

For a moment he saw tension mark the flawless oval of her face. What was it? he wondered. Excitement? Anticipation? The thrill of getting some juicy snippet about him to pad out some gossip column she couldn't fill with the misfortunes of some other unsuspecting fool?

'Does valuing my personal space necessarily mean I have to be hiding something?' he put to her, a little more roughly, and saw her mouth pull down as she contemplated his question.

It didn't. Of course it didn't, Kayla thought in an attempt to allay her suspicions about him.

'No,' she responded, pushing her hair back behind one ear, wondering why she was finding it so easy to let herself be persuaded.

Disconcertingly, those midnight-black eyes followed her agitated movement before he swung away from the fire, went back into the house.

'What about you?' he quizzed, after he'd returned with a couple of chunky glasses, which he also set down on the table before returning to the makeshift barbecue.

'What *about* me?' Kayla enquired, noticing how the muscles bunched in his powerful legs as he dropped down on his haunches. Her mouth felt unusually dry.

'You're here on your own,' he remarked. 'Which can mean only one of two things.'

'Which are?' she prompted cautiously, watching him wield the fish slice and slide some fish onto one of the earthenware plates he had brought from the house. He handed it to her, before dishing out another portion for himself.

'You're either running away...' He put his own plate down on an upturned fruit crate opposite the bench and retrieved the rustic bowl from the table.

'Or...?' she pressed, swallowing, feeling his eyes watching her far too intently as she took a chunk of the wholesome-looking bread he was offering her.

'Or...you're chasing something.'

'Like what?' she invited, frowning, feeling as though those keen dark eyes were suddenly giving her a mental frisking. She had the feeling that behind that casual manner of his lurked a blade-sharp brain that was assessing her every reaction, and that every word and response from her was being systematically weighed and measured.

Leonidas's mouth compressed. 'Dreams. A good time.' He moved a shoulder in a deceptively nonchalant way. *Another sensation-charged story to smear the Vassalio name.* 'So which is it for you, lovely Kayla?'

With her pulse doing an unexpected leap at the way he had addressed her, Kayla viewed him with mascara-touched lashes half-shielding her eyes.

How could he be so perceptive? So shrewd? He was living here like a gypsy. Whether he was alone or with someone she couldn't tell—although from what he had said she would have put money on it that there wasn't anyone else in residence. A man close to nature, who wasn't afraid of hard work, yet with a keen mind behind all that physical strength and potent energy. And a comprehension of human nature that even Craig with his university degree and his boardroom ambitions hadn't possessed.

She had no intention, however, of telling this unsettling hunk that his first assumption was right. That she *was* running away, and that she hadn't fully realised it until now. Her broken engagement and her recently bruised heart weren't things she wanted to discuss with anyone—least of all a man she had only just met, who didn't really want her there…even if he obviously felt obliged to share his lunch with her.

Looking down at her plate, and the mouth-watering meal she was tucking in to, she shrugged and said, 'I've been doing some temporary work since leaving a job I'd been in for five years. I thought it would be a good idea to come somewhere quiet and have a think about what I want to do if I have to move on.' *If Lorna's company folds and I have to apply for something more permanent,* she thought, and prayed for Lorna and Josh's sake that it wouldn't come to that. Though they *had* been facing a lot of problems recently.

He nodded, whether in approval or simply in response to what she had said she wasn't sure. Positioning himself on the crate from which he had retrieved his plate, he said, 'You mean you're…what is it you call it…?' He pretended to search for the word. 'Freelance?'

Brows drawn together, Kayla said hesitantly, 'Loosely speaking.' Filling in for Josh and Lorna when she'd been at her worst, after their bookkeeper had suddenly taken off with someone she'd met on the internet, was simply helping two people she cared about a great deal.

Leonidas reached around him for a stoneware vessel that was standing on an old tree stump beside him, hooking his thumb through the handle and bringing it over his shoulder like some ancient warrior at a feast before offering some to Kayla.

A hunter, she ruminated. Like those warring Greeks who had fought to keep their lands from invading Romans. Clever. Living by his wits. Untamed.

'It's homemade and non-alcoholic. Try it,' he invited smoothly, thinking that if 'loosely speaking' meant skirting around the truth then the local wine would have been much better at loosening her tongue to his advantage. However, she was driving, and he had to maintain some responsibility for that. 'What were you doing in your job?' he persevered after she'd nodded her assent, reining in the desire to curb the small talk and cut straight to the chase.

'Accounts. I'm a qualified bookkeeper,' she answered, taking the glass he had filled for her and trying a sip. It tasted zesty and refreshing, with lime and other citrus juices blended with something that made it fizz. 'Why are you smiling like that?' If one could call that curious twist to his mouth a *smile*, Kayla thought.

Because that's about as unlikely as my being a nightclub singer, Leonidas considered, amazed and amused by what he decided must be barefaced lies.

'You don't *look* like a bookkeeper,' he remarked, studying her unashamedly in view of the yarn she was spinning him. Beautiful long hair and captivating features. Elegant swan-like neck, small but alluring figure. What he didn't expect was the hard desire that kicked through his body, mocking his efforts to remain in command even as he acknowledged her reaction in the colour that stole across her fine translucent skin.

'What's a bookkeeper supposed to look like?' she queried with a betraying little wobble in her voice, feeling his gaze like a hot brand over her scantily clad body and bare legs.

'Not blonde, beautiful and way too intrusive for her own good.'

She laughed nervously at his double-edged compliment, feeling a stirring in her blood that had nothing to do with the zesty punch, the good food, or the way the warm wind was sighing through the silver leaves of an olive tree that stood at the edge of the shady terrace above the overgrown garden.

'What about you?' she asked quickly, to try and stem the ridiculous heat that was pulsing through her veins. 'I thought this place was derelict. How long have you lived here?' She glanced up at the house, which she had believed was uninhabited. Most of it was in a serious state of disrepair, but one wing of the old building looked as if it had been renovated in recent years. 'I take it you *do* live here?'

'For the time being,' he said uncommunicatively, adding after a moment or two, 'I thought it would be as good a place as any to…what is the expression…? Bed down for a while.'

'You mean…you're just bumming around?'

Leonidas laughed, showing strong white teeth, and through the thick fringes of his lashes he surveyed the young woman sitting opposite him with guarded circumspection, wondering how far she was planning to carry this little charade. Yesterday she had displayed all the characteristics of an opportunity-grabbing undercover reporter, and again this morning, when she had wandered in here with that infernal camera—even if she *had* seemed genuinely distressed when she'd leaped into that hot, angry tirade about her phone, her fridge and her supposedly broken-down car. But if his suspicions about her were right—and he had little reason to doubt that they were—then from the questions she was asking and her response to the answers he was giving he had to admit that she was one hell of a good actress.

'I prefer to call it opting out,' he stated laconically.

'So…do you work?' Kayla enquired.

'When I need to.' Which was twenty-four-seven a lot of the time, he thought grimly. If she was here intent on making a killing out of the Vassalio name, then she would know that already.

And if she wasn't…

If she wasn't, he thought, irritated, refusing to give any credence to that possibility, then she shouldn't have inflicted herself upon him in the way she had.

'And what do you do? For a living, I mean?'

She was still treading cautiously, still playing the innocent.

If she'd been trying for an Oscar, Leonidas thought, she would have won it hands-down.

'I'm in construction.' *As you probably well know,* he tagged on silently.

'A builder!' Kayla interpreted, realising her assessment of him was right. He *was* a man who worked with his hands.

'Loosely speaking.' Deliberately Leonidas lobbed her own phrase back at her. Playing along with her whatever her game was, he thought with increasing annoyance. And suddenly he was fed-up with pussyfooting around.

Slinging his plate onto the table, he stood up, thrusting his hands into his pockets, intimidation in his stance and every hard inch of him as he said grimly and with lethal softness, 'OK, Kayla. This has gone far enough.'

'What has?'

He had to hand it to her. She looked and sounded perplexed. He might even have said shocked.

'The charade is over, sweet girl.'

'What charade?' Kayla didn't have a clue what he was talking about. 'I don't understand...'

'Don't you?' He laughed rather harshly. 'Do you think I don't know what your little game is? Don't know why you're here?'

'No.' She had leaped to her feet and stood facing him now with her hands on her hips, her eyes wide and contesting. 'You've obviously got me mixed up with somebody else! I don't know who you think I am, but whoever it is I'm not the person you were expecting.'

'I was hardly *expecting* anyone—least of all another bloodsucking female with her own self-motivated agenda! Unless you're going to tell me you've come all this way by yourself to slap a petition on me as well!'

'No, I haven't!' Kayla riposted, wondering what the hell he was talking about. 'And whatever your problem is—whoever it is you've come here to escape from—I'd appreciate it if you didn't take it out on *me!*'

She was gone before he could utter another word.

CHAPTER THREE

IT WAS THE crash that woke her.

Or had it been the rain and thunder? Kayla wondered, scrambling, terrified, out of bed. She had been tossing and turning in a kind of half-sleep for what seemed like hours, although it might only have been minutes since the storm began.

Now, as she pulled open her bedroom door, the full force of the gale made her cry out when it almost blew her back into the room. In the darkness she could see an ominous shape lying diagonally across the landing and a gash in the sloping roof, which was now open to the wind and the driving rain.

Kayla gasped as lightning ripped across the sky, so close that the almost instantaneous crash of thunder that followed seemed to rock the foundations of the house.

Fumbling to turn on the light switch, she groaned when nothing happened.

'Oh, great!'

Finding the chair where she had folded the jeans and shirt she had travelled in two days ago, with trembling hands she hastily pulled them on over her flimsy pyjamas, and then groped around for her bag and the small torch she always carried on her keyring.

Debris was everywhere as she moved cautiously under the fallen tree-trunk. Twisted branches, leaves, twigs and pieces of broken masonry and plaster scrunched underfoot as she picked her way carefully downstairs.

It was as if the whole outdoors had broken in, she thought with a startled cry as another flash of lightning streaked across the sky. The crash that followed it seemed to rock the villa, causing her to panic at the torrent of rain that was coming in on the raging wind.

And then she heard another sound, like a loud hammering on the external door to the villa, and mercifully a voice, its deep tone muffled, yet still breaking through to her through the tearing gale and the rain.

'Kayla! Kayla? Answer me! Are you in there? Kayla! Are you all right?'

The banging persisted until she thought the door was caving in.

Reaching it and tugging it open, she almost cried with relief when she saw the formidable figure of Leon standing there, his fists clenched as though to knock the door down if it wasn't opened. Rain was running down his face and his strong bronzed throat in rivulets.

It took all her will-power not to sink against him as he caught her arm and shouted something urgently in his own language.

'Get out of here! Quickly!' he ordered, reverting to English. 'There's been a landslide further up the mountain. This house might not be safe to stay in.' And as she hesitated, casting an anxious glance at her belongings, 'We'll come back for your things in the morning!' he shouted above the wind and the lashing rain. 'You're coming with me!'

Petrified, rooted to the spot by the sound of splitting timber somewhere close by on the riven hillside, Kayla felt herself suddenly being whipped off her feet. She was only pacified by the realisation that she was in a pair of strong, powerful arms, being held against Leon's sodden warmth as he ran with her to the waiting truck.

He had left the vehicle's lights on, and after he had set her quickly down on the passenger seat Kayla saw him race around the bonnet with his head bent against the storm, his purposeful physique only just discernible through the rain-washed windscreen.

He opened the driver's door, his long hair dripping, and as he climbed into the cab beside her and slammed the door against the wind she noticed that his shirt, which was unbuttoned and hanging loose, like his jeans, was soaked through and clinging to his powerful torso.

'Thank you! Oh, thank you!' Dropping her head into her hands as the truck started rumbling away, Kayla couldn't think of anything else to say. 'I didn't know what was happening!' she blurted out when she had recovered herself enough to sit up straight and turn towards him. 'I woke up and thought the world was coming to an end!'

'It would have been for you,' Leonidas stated with grim truthfulness, 'if that tree had fallen on you.'

But it hadn't, she thought gratefully. Nor was she now exposed to the damage it had caused. Thanks to *him*, she realised, and wondered how she would have coped if he hadn't been passing right at that moment.

'What happened?' she queried, baffled, as she began to gather her wits about her. 'Did you just happen to come by?'

'Something like that,' he intoned, without taking his attention from the zig-zagging mountain road. The truck's wiper blades were barely able to cope even at double-speed with the torrential rain.

At half-past one in the morning?

For the first time noticing the clock on the dashboard, Kayla realised exactly what the time was. Had he been out late, seen what had happened as he had driven past? Or had he been in bed? Had he heard the landslide and driven down especially?

Of course not, she thought, dismissing that last possible scenario. No man she knew of would be so gallant as to risk his own safety for a girl he didn't even know let alone like. And it was patently obvious from her two previous meetings with him that he clearly didn't like her. Or *any* of her sex, if it came to that!

'Why are you doing this if you think I'm someone who's out to make trouble for you?' she enquired pointedly, her hair falling, damp and dishevelled, around her shoulders.

'What would you have preferred me to do?' Every ounce of his concentration was still riveted on the windscreen. 'Leave you there to swim? Or worse?'

Kayla shuddered as she interpreted what 'worse' might easily have meant.

'Is it always like this on these islands?' she queried worriedly, staring out at the truck's powerful headlights cutting through the sheets of rain.

'If you come here in the spring it's a chance you take,' he returned succinctly.

Which she had, Kayla thought, deciding that he probably thought her stupid on top of everything else.

'What's likely to happen to the villa?' she asked anxiously, watching the gleaming water cascading off the hills and filling every crack and crevice on the rugged road. 'That tree came right through onto the landing.'

'We'll go down and inspect the damage in the morning.'

'But the furniture and furnishings. And my things,' she remembered as an afterthought. 'Everything's going to get wet.'

'Only to be expected,' he answered prosaically, changing gear to take a particularly sharp bend. 'With a hole in the roof.'

A hysterical little laugh bubbled up inside of her. Nerves, she decided. And shock. Because there was certainly nothing funny about the havoc this storm had wreaked upon the little Grecian retreat her friends had worked so hard for.

'What am I going to say to Lorna?' She was worrying about how she was going to break the news to her, thinking aloud. 'She and Josh have got enough problems as it is.' And then it dawned on her. 'Oh, heavens!' she breathed, still shaking inside from her ordeal. 'Where on earth am I going to stay? Tonight? Tomorrow? At all?'

'Well, tonight you're going to stay with me,' he told her in a tone that was settled, decisive. 'And tomorrow, when you've telephoned your friend to let her know what has happened, we'll think of something else.'

We, he'd said, as though they were in this thing together. Which they weren't, Kayla thought. Yet strangely she gleaned some comfort from it—along with a contradictory feeling of being indebted to him, too.

'Like what?' She didn't know where to begin, or even if the island had any other suitable or affordable accommodation. Lorna had offered to let her stay in the villa rent-free, and although Kayla had insisted on paying her, it was still only a nominal amount. The alternative was that she could fly home...

'There are three hotels on this side of the island. One of them—the largest—is closed for refurbishment,' Leon was telling her, 'but I'm sure as it's out of season one of the other two will be able to accommodate you.'

'I can't stay with you tonight,' she informed him. 'It's such an imposition, for one thing.' She didn't even *know* him! And from what she had seen of him over the past couple of days neither did she want to. 'You said yourself you wanted to be left alone.'

'Which you've failed to acknowledge since the day you arrived,' he told her dryly. 'So why break with tradition?'

'I'm sorry.' Now she felt even worse. 'You don't have to do this. I'm only making a nuisance of myself…'

'What would you prefer me to do?' he asked. 'Put you out into the storm?' He laughed when he saw the anxiety creasing her forehead. 'Relax,' he advised. 'You're coming back with me. So, no more arguments to the contrary—and definitely no more apologies. Understood?'

Uneasily, Kayla nodded.

'I didn't hear you,' he stated over the rumble of the engine and the jaunty rhythm of the wiper blades trying to keep pace with the interminable rain.

'Understood!' she shouted back, and kept her gaze on the windscreen and her hands in her lap until he brought them safely off the road and onto the paved area of the old farmhouse.

The part of the house he led her into was remarkably clean and tidy. It was surprisingly well-furnished too, even though most of the furniture looked worn and in need of replacing, and the tapestries on two of the walls, like the once colourfully striped throws over the easy chairs, were faded from the sunlight and with age. But with its whitewashed walls and cool stone floors it had an overall rustic charm that offered more comfort than she had imagined from the outside.

She was too tired and weary from her experiences to take too much interest in how he was living, and said only after a cursory glance around her, 'I'm really not happy about this.'

She didn't know anything about him, for a start, even if he *had* just rescued her from a house that might possibly be unsafe. He was still a stranger, and up until now a decidedly hostile one.

'I'm afraid you've no choice,' he told her, opening a cupboard and pulling out towels and spare bedlinen, 'because I've no intention of trying to find you a hotel tonight. No hotelier would welcome you turning up at this hour—even if it were safe enough to do so. And if you really don't profess to know me—' He broke off, his speculative gaze raking over her as if, by some miracle, he was at last beginning to believe her. 'I'm not a criminal,' he stated. 'Unless, of course, the police want to charge me with some driving offence I don't yet know about.'

Kayla smiled, relaxing a little, as he had intended her to.

Clever, she thought. Clever and probably very manipulative, she decided, but was too tired to worry about that tonight.

After she had declined his offer of any refreshment, and the room he showed her into was rustic but practical, with the same weary air about its furnishings. Like downstairs, the walls looked as though they hadn't been whitewashed in a long time. A big wooden bed took pride of place, and from the few masculine possessions scattered around the room she gathered that *he* had been using it up until now.

'I'm afraid it isn't five-star, but it's warm and dry and the sheets are clean.' They looked it too. Crisp and white, if a little rumpled, and there was a definite indentation in the plump and inviting-looking pillow. 'Well, I was only in them for half an hour,' he enlightened her, with his mouth tugging down at one side.

So he had been to bed and got up again—which could only have meant that he must have driven down in the storm especially.

'Think nothing of it,' he advised dismissively as their eyes clashed.

Kayla wanted to say something, to thank him at the very least for deserting his bed in the middle of the night to come and see if she was all right. But his manner and all that had gone before kept her mute.

'What will *you* do?' she enquired, glancing down at the bed he'd given up for her. Suddenly worried that she might have given him the wrong idea, quickly she tagged on, 'That wasn't meant to sound like…'

'It didn't,' he said, although the way his gaze moved disconcertingly over her body did nothing to put her at ease. 'Don't worry about me.' He'd started moving away. 'There's a perfectly adequate sofa in the living room.'

Adequate, but not comfortable. Not for his manly size. She had noticed it on the way through and thought now that it wouldn't in any way compensate for losing the roomy-looking bed he'd imagined he would be occupying.

'I really feel awful about this.'

'Don't,' he replied. 'I'm sure you're used to better. As I said, it isn't five-star.' His tone, however, was more cynical than apologetic, and a little dart of rebellion ran through her as their eyes met and locked.

She didn't tell him that she had had a taste of luxurious living and it wasn't something she was keen to get back to. Not when it had meant accompanying Craig to company dinners and luxury conference weekends where she had watched her ex paying homage, she realised now, to people he merely wanted to impress—people he knew could further his corporate ambitions—without really liking them at all.

'I'm more than grateful for—' A sudden vivid flash, accompanied by a deafening crack, had her cutting her sentence short with a startled cry.

'It's all right,' he said. His voice came softly from somewhere close behind her as the thunder seemed to reverberate off the very walls. 'This house might look as though it's seen better days, but I can assure you, Kayla, the roof is sound. No tree is going to fall in on us, I promise you.'

Her visible fear had brought him over to her. She only realised it as she felt his hands on her shoulders through the thin fabric of her shirt, warm and strong and surprisingly reassuring in view of his previous attitude towards her.

'I'm all right.' She took a step back and his hands fell away from her. She wondered what was most unsettling. The storm—or the touch of this stranger whose bedroom she was unbelievably standing in.

'Of course you are,' he said. 'But get out of those damp clothes. And get a good night's rest,' he advocated, before leaving her to it.

He was right about her clothes being damp, she realised with a little shiver after he had gone. Just the short journey from the villa to the truck and then from the truck to this house had been enough to soak her shirt and jeans. She was grateful to peel them off.

There were a few moments in the king-sized bed when she wondered what she was doing there, unable to keep her thoughts from the man who must have been lying there not more than an hour before. Had he been lying here naked? She felt a sensual little tingle, and her nostrils grasped the trace of a masculine shower gel beneath the scent of fresh linen. But it was only for a few moments, because when she opened her eyes again the tearing winds and driving rain had ceased and a fine blade of sunlight was piercing the dimly shaded room through a slit in the shutters.

Scrambling out of bed, Kayla went over and flung them back, feeling the heat of the sun on her scantily clothed body as it streamed in through windows that were already open to the glittering blue of the sky.

The bedroom overlooked the front yard, the dirt track and the rolling hillside that descended so sharply, with the mountain road, to the blue and silver of the shimmering sea.

She could see the truck parked there on the flagstones, where Leon had left it in the early hours.

A surge of heat coursed through her as she thought about how he had come to her rescue last night, and how helpless she had felt in those hostile yet powerful arms as they had carried her to that truck when she had been too shocked and too bewildered to move.

'So you're awake.' A familiar deep voice overlaid with mockery called out to her as if from nowhere.

Startled, Kayla realised that he had been doing something to his truck. She hadn't noticed until he had pulled himself up from under it.

Uncertainly she lifted a hand, mesmerised for a moment by the shattering impact of his hard, untrammelled masculinity.

With his hair wild as a gypsy's, and in a black vest top and cut off jeans, he looked like a man totally uninhibited by convention. Self-sufficient and self-ruling. A man who would probably shun the constraints that Craig and his company cronies adhered to.

But this man was looking at her with such unveiled interest that her stomach took a steep dive as she realised why.

She was wearing nothing but her coffee and cream lace-edged baby doll pyjamas and, utterly self-conscious, she swiftly withdrew from the window, certain she wasn't imagining the deep laugh that emanated from the yard as she hastily pulled the shutters together again.

The bathroom was, as she'd discovered last night, clean and adequately equipped. Some time this morning a toothbrush, still in its packaging, had been placed upon two folded and surprisingly good-quality burgundy towels on a wooden cabinet beside the washstand. Impressed, silently Kayla thanked him for that.

Fortunately her hairbrush had been in her bag when she had made her hasty exit from the villa last night, along with a spare tube of the soft brown mascara she had remembered to buy before leaving London.

Never one to wear much make-up, she had nonetheless always felt undressed without her mascara. A combination of pale hair and pale eyelashes made her look washed-out, she had always thought, and Craig had agreed.

A sharp, unexpected little stab of something under her ribcage had her catching her breath as she thought about Craig, but surprisingly it didn't hurt as she reminded herself that what Craig Lymington thought wasn't important any more.

Leon was in the large sitting room off the hall, locking something away in a drawer, when Kayla came down feeling fresh and none the worse for her experiences of the previous night.

He was superb, she thought reluctantly from the doorway, noticing how at close quarters the black vest top emphasised his muscular torso, how perfectly smooth and contoured were his arms, their hair-darkened skin like bronze satin sheathing steel. She was pleased she'd put mascara on, and that when she'd brushed her hair forward and then tossed it back, as she always did, it had looked particularly full and shiny this morning.

He looked up and his gaze moved over her. He was clearly remembering what she had looked like at the window earlier.

'I've been trying to ring Lorna but I can't get a signal,' she said quickly, hoping he hadn't noticed the way she'd been ogling him. 'Is it all right if I use your landline?'

'You could—if it was connected,' he returned. He took his own cell phone out of his pocket and handed it to her as she came into the room. It felt smooth and warmed by his body heat, reminding her far too easily of how *she* had felt being held against his hard warmth the previous night.

'As soon as it's a respectable enough time,' she began, while trying to deal with how ridiculously she was allowing him to affect her, 'and after you've dropped me off at the villa, do you think you could point me in the direction of the nearest hotel?'

'One thing at a time,' he advised her. 'The first thing is not to plan anything on an empty stomach.'

'Is that your philosophy on life?' She struggled to speak lightly, which was difficult when there was so much tension in her voice.

'One of them,' he answered, with his mouth tugging down at one corner.

She wondered what the others were, but decided against asking. For all the hospitality this man had shown her, he didn't welcome too much intrusion into his personal life, and Kayla certainly felt as though she had intruded enough.

Surprisingly, she got through to Lorna's office on the first try. Gently, Kayla broke the news to her about the storm and the tree coming down, wanting to spare her friend as much distress as she could. Lorna and Josh had been trying for a baby for quite some time, and Lorna had had two miscarriages in the past two years. Now she was well into the second trimester of another pregnancy, and Kayla regretted having to cause her any more stress as she concluded, 'I haven't had a chance to look at it in daylight, but we're going down after breakfast to assess the damage.'

'We?' Lorna echoed inquisitively, so that Kayla was forced to gather her wits together in order to avoid any awkward questions.

'Someone from a neighbouring property. They took me in for the night,' she explained, taking care not to even suggest that 'they' was really 'he'. She wasn't ready to be bracketed with another man in her life just yet.

'Then tell them that I can't thank them enough for taking care of my friend.' True to character, Lorna seemed more concerned about Kayla than about the tree crashing down on her precious villa. 'I'm so glad there was someone else there! What would you have done otherwise?'

My thoughts exactly, Kayla mused, unable to keep her eyes from straying to Leon's superbly broad back as he moved lithely out of the room while her friend made plans for what she intended to do.

'Lorna's parents are going to come over and sort out what needs doing,' Kayla reported to him a few minutes later, having found him in the huge and very outdated farmhouse kitchen at the end of the hall. It contained a dresser and a huge wood-burning stove over which Leon was busily wielding a frying pan. A large pine table stood in the centre of the room, already laid for one. Two large-paned windows faced the front of the house, offering stupendous views of the distant sea, while two more on the other side of the room looked out onto the terraced gardens. 'Lorna and Josh have their own business and don't have much free time,' she explained, handing him back his phone, which he casually slipped into the back pocket of his jeans.

Unlike you, Kayla thought, and for a moment found herself envying his flexible lifestyle. His free spirit and total autonomy. The complete lack of binding responsibility.

'Have you always been so self-sufficient?' she asked, watching him cutting melon, which he put on the table beside a plate of fresh pineapple slices. She wondered if he had already eaten or just wasn't bothering.

'I like to think so,' he responded, without looking at her. 'I've always believed—' and found out the hard way, Leonidas thought, his features hardening '—that if you want something done properly there's no surer way but to do it yourself.'

'Another of your philosophies?' Kayla enquired, her hand coming to rest on the back of one the pine chairs and her head tilted as she waited for an answer, which never came.

No man was an island, so the saying went. But Kayla had the distinct impression that this man was—emotionally, at any rate. He seemed more detached and aloof from the rat race and the big wide world than anyone she had ever met. Uncommunicative. Guarding his privacy like a precious jewel.

'Who did you think I was when you accused me of playing some game with you yesterday?'

'It isn't important,' he intoned, moving back to the stove.

'It seemed to be very important at the time,' Kayla commented, still put out by the names he had called her. 'The things you said to me weren't very nice.'

'Yes, well…we can all make mistakes,' Leonidas admitted, adding freshly chopped herbs to the sizzling frying pan and beginning to accept that he might have made a gross error of judgement in treating her so unjustly. 'I came here to relax. I didn't expect some uninvited young woman with a camera to be taking secretive photographs of me. When you realised I'd seen you on the rocks and you ran from me I decided that you must definitely be up to no good.'

So he had charged at her like an angry bull, Kayla thought, wondering what he'd thought she was hiding that had incensed him so much.

'Yesterday,' he went on, 'when I invited you to lunch, it was to try to find out why.'

'You accused me of spying on you,' she reminded him, folding her arms in a suddenly defensive pose as she bit back the urge to remind him that she hadn't been trying to photograph him on that beach. 'What did you imagine? That I was some sort of secret agent or something?' she suggested with an ironic little laugh. 'Or a private investigator, hired by a jealous wife—?' She broke off as a more plausible possibility struck her. 'A wife who's taken you to the cleaners and who's still hoping to uncover the hidden millions you haven't told her about that you've got stashed away somewhere? Gosh! Is that it?' she exclaimed, when she saw the way his dark lashes came down over his unfathomable eyes, wondering if she'd hit the nail on the head. 'Not about the millions. I mean…'

'About the wife?'

She nodded. Why else would he have referred to her as a blood-sucking female yesterday? He must be licking his wounds after a very nasty divorce.

'Nice try,' he said dryly, the muscles in his wonderfully masculine back moving as he worked. 'I'm sorry to have to shoot down such a colourful and imaginative story, but I'm not married. And since when did a man simply wanting to protect his privacy mean there's an avaricious and avenging wife in tow?'

'It doesn't,' Kayla answered, wondering why the discovery of his marital status should leave her feeling far more pleased than it should have. 'It just seemed a little bit of an overreaction, that's all,' she murmured, feeling her temperature rising from the way he was looking at her—as though he knew what baffling and unsettling thoughts were going through her head.

'So how did you know about this house?' she asked, since it was apparent now that it wasn't just a deserted building he'd happened to stumble across.

'I was born on this island,' he said, in a cool, clipped voice. 'I have the use of this place when I want it.'

'Who owns it?' she enquired, looking around.

'Someone who is too busy to take much interest in it,' he answered flatly, suddenly sounding bored.

'What a pity,' Kayla expressed, looking around her at the sad peeling walls. 'It could be nice if it was renovated. Someone must have treasured it once.'

Once, Leonidas thought, when its warm, welcoming walls had rung with his mother's beautiful singing. When he hadn't been able to sleep for excitement because his grandfather was taking him fishing the following day...

'Obviously the current owner doesn't share your sentimentality about it,' he remarked, and found it a struggle to keep the bitterness out of his voice.

'You said you were born on this island?' Kayla reminded him, feeling as though she was being intrusive again, yet unable to stop herself. Even less could she envisage him as a helpless, squalling infant. 'It's idyllic. What made you leave?'

His features looked set in stone as he tossed two slices of bubbling halloumi cheese onto slices of fresh bread, topping them with rich red sun-dried tomatoes before he answered, 'I believed there was a better life out there.'

'And was there?'

Again he didn't answer.

But what sort of satisfaction was there in never settling anywhere? Kayla wondered now. In just drifting around from place to place?

'Eat your breakfast,' he ordered, putting the meal on the table in front of her. 'And then we'll go down and inspect the storm damage.'

CHAPTER FOUR

THE STRUCTURE OF the villa had sustained less damage than Kayla had feared. However, after Leon had helped her to clear up the debris and mess caused by the falling tree, it was still a far cry from what it had been when she had arrived.

'I'll have to look for somewhere else,' she accepted defeatedly, trying to sound braver and less anxious than she was feeling as she dropped the last packet of ruined food into a refuse bag.

'My very next step,' Leonidas assured her, taking his phone out of his pocket.

He had changed into a pale blue shirt and jeans before leaving the farmhouse earlier and, looking up from the bag she was tying, Kayla noticed how his rolled-up sleeves emphasised the dark olive of his skin and the virility of his strong arms.

'I think you've done quite enough already,' she reminded him. Not only had he rescued her from a terrifying situation last night, he had given her food and shelter, driven her back here, and then refused to leave when it came to the clean-up operation. 'I'm indebted enough to you as it is!'

'If that's all that's worrying you—forget it,' he drawled. 'I'm not likely to be extracting payment any time soon.'

'That's not funny,' she scolded, still unhappy about being in his debt. Or was it that mocking glint in his eyes that affected her more than his hostility?

Whatever it was, she thought, he unsettled her as no man had ever unsettled her in her life. Not to this degree anyway, she realised. And there was more to it than just the danger of getting too involved with a man whom, until the day before yesterday, she had never even met. It was the potent attraction this man held for her, purely physical in its nature and stronger than any she had felt before. Which was illogical, she decided, when she had been engaged to Craig and fully intending to spend the rest of her life with *him*.

But Leon was already taking the necessary steps to get her fixed up with an alternative place to stay.

Listening to that deep voice speaking in Greek to some hotelier on the other end of the line, Kayla realised how much more difficult it would have been for her if she had been left to find accommodation herself. There would have been the language barrier to overcome for a start.

Now, though, as he came off the phone, Kayla saw him shaking his head. 'I'm afraid they're fully booked for the next three weeks.'

There were three hotels on the island, he had informed her, one closed for refurbishing, and he was now ringing the second one on his list. But again he was shaking his head as he finished speaking to their last possible hope. 'They said they would have had a room if you had telephoned yesterday, but they've had to close this morning because of flooding in part of the hotel last night.'

She could tell that he was almost as dumbfounded as she was.

'Well, that's that, then,' she said, swinging the bin bag up off the tiled floor. 'I'll just have to make the best of it here until Lorna's parents arrive tomorrow.' And after that... She gave a mental shrug as she crossed the tiny kitchen. Who knew?

Watching the determined squaring of her shoulders as he

tried to relieve her of the bag, Leonidas felt his heart going out to her.

'Don't be ridiculous,' he said as she opened the door to the garden. 'You can't stay here.' The tree was leaning across the landing at a precarious enough angle to be a safety hazard. Also, because of the galleried landing, the ground floor was open to the elements, as well as to any more debris from the fallen tree.

'No?' Kayla said, coming in from dumping the bag outside. 'And I suppose you can come up with a better idea?'

'Yes, I can,' he stated pragmatically. 'You will stay with me.'

Not can. *Will,* Kayla noted, which marked him as a man who usually got his own way.

'With you?' He was leaning against the sink with his thumbs hooked into his waistband, looking very determined, and a little bubble of humourless laughter escaped her. 'Now look who's being ridiculous,' she accused.

'If you think I'm leaving you here, with that tree likely to come down on you at any moment,' he said, with an upward toss of his chin, 'you can think again.'

'I'm not your responsibility or your problem, Leon,' she stressed trenchantly. 'Anyway, I came here to be alone.'

'Why, exactly?' Leonidas was regarding her with hard speculation. 'What is a girl like you doing on her own in a quiet and remote place like this when you could be enjoying the company of other people your age and living it up somewhere like Crete or Corfu? And don't tell me that you are simply soaking up the sun while considering your next career move, because you could have gone anywhere to do that.'

'Perhaps I don't want to be "living it up",' Kayla replied, feeling pressured by his unwavering determination. 'I came here for peace and quiet. Not to share with anyone else.'

'So did I,' he reminded her, in a way that suggested that the best-laid plans didn't always turn out as one would expect.

'Exactly! And the last thing you want is a…what did you call me? Oh, yes—a "blood-sucking female with her own self-motivated agenda" dumped on you!' she quoted fiercely, with both hands planted on her denim-clad hips. 'Well, believe me, this *isn't* on my agenda!'

'All right. So we didn't get off to a very good start. I shouldn't have said those things to you,' he admitted, coming away from the sink. It seemed to constitute some sort of apology. 'But the fact remains that as things stand this place is a potential hazard, and—my responsibility or not—if you think I am going to stand by and let you risk your safety just because of a few ripe phrases on my part yesterday, then you still have a long way to go in assessing my character. I carried you out of here last night and I'll do it again if I have to.' His features were set with indomitable purpose. 'So, are you going to be sensible and swallow your pride and accept that there isn't an alternative?' he asked grimly.

'There's always an alternative,' Kayla said quickly, refusing to accept otherwise—although the thought of him manhandling her out of there when she wasn't being distracted by falling trees and a possible landslide was far too disturbing even to contemplate.

'Like running away?'

Those jet-black eyes seemed to be penetrating her soul, probing down into her heart and digging over her darkest and most painful secrets.

What right did he have to accuse her of running away? Even if she was, it was none of his business! Yet suddenly everything she had suffered over the past weeks, and everything that had gone wrong since she had been here, finally proved too much.

'Who says I'm running away?' she flung at him grievously. 'And if you think that just because I chose to come on holiday by myself, then I could just as easily wonder the same thing about you! And those weren't just a few ripe phrases you used. You were taking out all your woman problems—whatever they are—on *me!* Do you want to know why I'm here on my own? Then put this in your pipe and smoke it! Saturday was supposed to be my wedding day—only the groom decided he'd rather marry somebody else instead! He just kept the same date and the same time at the same church with the same photographer for *convenience*.' She couldn't keep the bitterness out of her voice.

'Because he wanted to marry her in a hurry, although he *did* have the decency to let me know she was pregnant before I broke off our engagement three months ago. And if that wasn't enough we all worked at the same company, which is why I had to leave. I live in a small community, so the whole neighbourhood knew about it as well, and I just couldn't stay there and face the humiliation. So if running away because I'm not thick-skinned enough to stand there and throw confetti over my ex-fiancé and his pregnant secretary is wrong, then I'm sorry!' She uttered a facetious little laugh. 'I'll just have to toughen up in future.'

'Forgive me.'

Leonidas's face was dark with contrition. And shock too, Kayla decided, almost triumphantly.

'The man's a...' He called him something in his own language which she knew wasn't very complimentary. 'I spoke without knowing the facts.'

'Yes, you did.' Now she had got it all off her chest she was beginning to feel a little calmer. 'Anyway, it's all history. Water under the bridge. I'm over him now.'

'Are you?'

'Yes, I am,' she asserted, her mouth firming resolutely. 'He kept to everything we'd planned for us—for our day...'

Strangely, that was what had hurt the most in the end. 'Even down to the guest list,' she uttered with another brittle little laugh. 'Well, most of it anyway,' she said. 'It's funny how when you're a couple you seem to have a lot of friends. Then when you break up you realise that they weren't really your friends at all. Most of them were Craig's. Acquaintances, really. He didn't have any real friends. They were all company people. People he'd met through his job. Sales reps. Customers. His management team and their wives. The office hierarchy that he liked us to socialise with.'

'You don't sound very enamoured,' Leonidas remarked.

Kayla glanced up to where he was standing with his hands thrust into his pockets, listening with single-minded concentration to all she was saying. 'I'm just angry with myself for not knowing better.'

'How could you?' Those masculine brows came together in a frown. 'How could anyone prepare for something like that happening?'

'Oh, I had a good tutor, believe me. Dad did the very same thing to Mum—ran off with his secretary. So it wasn't as though I wasn't forewarned. I just wouldn't listen. I thought it could never happen to me. But now I know never to get mixed up with that type of man again.'

'And what type is that?'

'The type with a nicely pressed suit and a spare clean shirt in the office closet. The type who's always late home because his workload's so heavy. The type who thinks every reasonably attractive female colleague is only there to boost his ego.'

Leonidas's dark lashes came down over his eyes, but all he said was, 'I thought that kind of male chauvinism went out with the nineteen-seventies.'

'Oh don't you believe it!' Kayla returned censoriously. She was mopping water from the fridge with all the venom she felt towards Craig Lymington and his kind. 'There's something that happens to a man when he gets behind a desk, gets himself a secretary and has his name on the door. Something he thinks sets him outside the boundaries of accepted moral behaviour. But I'm not going to bore you with that. It's my problem and I should have known better. I didn't want to know and I paid for it. End of story.'

Leonidas doubted somehow that it *was* the end of the story, and reminded himself never to tell her what he really did for a living.

'You've had a tough time,' he accepted, deciding that this damsel in distress who had been so badly treated by her fiancé would probably feel nothing but contempt for him if she knew more about him.

She would instantly bracket him with the type of man she despised. And if for one moment he did let on who he was, he had learned enough about her already to know that she would want nothing to do with him. She would refuse his help—no matter how desperately she needed it—which would do nothing to get her out of the predicament she was in now.

'However,' he continued, 'the most pressing problem you have right now is where you're going to sleep tonight. As I've already said, I wouldn't dream of allowing you to talk yourself into thinking it's all right to stay here…' No matter how far outside the boundaries of morality she might think he was if she knew about his desk and his secretary and the spare shirts he kept in his Athens and London offices. 'Which means you either sleep out in the open or you come back with me. Unless, of course, you're thinking of returning home?'

Almost imperceptibly Kayla flinched. With the villa unusable and nowhere else to stay, it did seem the most feasible thing to do. But if she did, what would she be going back to? Her mother's smugness over having been right about Craig? The neighbourhood's silent sympathies? The whispered comments behind her back? What would everyone say if they realised that not only had her proposed wedding turned out to be non-existent but also that the holiday she had been determined to take on her own had turned into a disaster as well?

'If it's your modesty you are worrying about, and you're thinking I might try and—what is the phrase you English use?—"take advantage" of you,' Leon said, remembering, 'then I must assure you that I wouldn't contemplate trying to seduce a girl who is on the rebound.'

'I'm *not* on the rebound,' Kayla denied hotly. But then, realising that he might take that to mean she wanted him to take advantage of her, she added quickly, 'I mean…' And then ran out of words because she didn't know how to phrase what she was trying to convey.

'I know what you mean,' he said, making it easy for her, although there was a sensual mockery on that devastating mouth of his that had her wondering just how pleasurable his taking advantage of her might be, if she were so inclined to let him.

'So what's it to be, Kayla?'

Her name dripped from his lips like ambrosia from the lips of Eros, although she doubted that even the Greek god of love could have harboured the degree of sensuality this man possessed.

She didn't want to go home, that was for sure. Yet neither did she want to be indebted to a total stranger—even if he did look like the answer to every woman's darkest fantasy! That didn't alter the fact that he was a stranger, and no woman in her right mind would agree to stay with a man she didn't even know. So where did that leave her? she asked herself. On the ground outside?

Very quietly, Leonidas said, 'Pack a bag and come with me.'

'You know I can't stay with you.'

'I'm not going to try and talk you into it. Pack a bag,' he

instructed again, without offering her any idea of what his plans were. 'I'll finish mopping up here.'

Leon had asked her to follow him in the car. The little hatch-back coughed a few times when Kayla tried to start it, which brought him over from the cab of his truck to investigate.

The engine fired into life just as he was approaching the bonnet.

Looking up at him through the car's open window with a self-satisfied glint in her eyes, Kayla asked, 'Do you believe me now?'

That masculine mouth pulled to one side, although he made no verbal response. Perhaps he was a man who didn't like being reminded of his mistakes too often, Kayla thought, unable to help feeling smug.

'It needs a good run,' he said, speaking with some authority. 'It's probably been standing idle for too long, which isn't good for any car.'

Following his truck down the zig-zag of a mountain road, Kayla was tempted to stop and take in the breathtaking views of the sea and the sun-drenched hillsides. But she kept close behind Leon's truck, envying his knowledge of every sharp bend, admiring the confidence and safety with which he negotiated them.

After guiding her down past a cluster of whitewashed cottages, he pulled up outside another, with blue shutters and, like the rest, pots of gaily coloured flowers on its veranda.

'Since you refuse to stay with me, I will have to leave you in the capable hands of Philomena,' Leon told her, having come around the truck to where Kayla was just getting out of the car.

'Philomena?'

'A friend of mine,' he stated, moving past her. 'There is one small snag, however,' he went on to inform her as he swung her small single suitcase out of the boot.

'Oh?' Kayla looked up at him enquiringly as he slammed the lid closed.

'She doesn't speak any English,' he said.

'So why would she want me staying with her?' Kayla practically had to run after him. It was obvious that he wasn't going to allow that rather large drawback—to Kayla's mind, at any rate—to interfere with his plans.

'Her family have all grown up and moved away,' he tossed back over his shoulder. 'Trust me. She will be very glad of the company of someone else—especially another woman.'

'But have you asked her?' Kayla wasn't sure that anyone—no matter how lonely they might be—would welcome a guest turning up unexpectedly on their doorstep.

'Leave the worrying to me,' he advised, and uneasily Kayla did.

He had said Philomena was a friend, but as he brought Kayla through to the homely sitting room of the little fisherman's cottage without even needing to knock, she calculated that the woman in dark clothes who greeted them with twinkling brown eyes and a strong, character-lined face was old enough to be his grandmother.

Her affection for Leon was clear from the start, but suddenly as they were speaking the woman burst into what to Kayla's ears sounded like a fierce outpouring of objection. The woman was waving her hands in typically European fashion and sending more than a few less than approving glances Kayla's way.

'She isn't happy about my staying here and why should she be?' Kayla challenged, taking in the abundance of framed family photographs and brightly painted pottery and feeling as much mortified as she felt sympathetic towards the elderly woman.

'She's happy, Kayla,' Leonidas told her, breaking off from a run of incomprehensible Greek. He started speaking very quickly in his own language again, which brought forth another bout of scolding and arm-waving from a clearly none-too-pleased Philomena.

'I'm sorry,' Kayla apologised through the commotion, hoping the woman would understand as she picked up her suitcase and starting weaving through the rustic furniture towards the door.

'No, no! No, no!' A lightly restraining hand came over Kayla's arm. 'You stay. Stay Philomena, eh?' The look she sent Leonidas shot daggers in his direction. Her voice, though, as she turned back to Kayla, was softer and more encouraging, her returning smile no less than sympathetic as a work-worn, sun-dappled hand gently palmed Kayla's cheek. 'You come. Stay.'

A good deal of gesticulation with a far warmer flow of baffling Greek seemed to express the woman's pleasure in having Kayla as her guest.

'You see,' Leonidas remarked, looking pleased with himself as Philomena drew her gently away from the door. 'I said she would want you to stay.'

The appreciative look Kayla gave her hostess turned challenging as she faced the man who had brought her there. 'Then what were you arguing about?' she quizzed.

'Philomena has no one to scold nowadays, so she likes to scold me.' His mouth as he directed a look towards their hostess was pulling wryly. 'Philomena bore seven children, but her one claim to fame, as she likes to call it, is that she delivered me. I'm eternally grateful to her for introducing me to this universe,' he expressed with smiling affection at Philomena, 'but she does tend to imagine that that gives her licence to upbraid me at every given opportunity.'

'For what?' Kayla was puzzled, still not convinced.

One of those impressive shoulders lifted as he contemplated this. 'For leaving the island. For coming back. For not coming back.'

Kayla noted the curious inflexion in his voice as he made that last statement. Her smile wavered. 'And what about just now?'

'Just now?'

Leonidas looked at the woman who had pulled him screaming into the world. She had been there—never far away—throughout his childhood. A comfort from his father's strict and sometimes brutal regime of discipline, his rock when his mother had died.

'I don't think she's happy with the way I've turned out,' he commented dryly to Kayla, and thought that if it were true he wouldn't blame Philomena. There were times lately, he was surprised to find himself thinking, when he had been far, far from happy with himself.

'Oh?' Kayla clearly wanted to know more, but he had nothing more to offer her.

Gratefully he expressed his thanks to Philomena, adding something else, which brought Kayla's cornflower-blue eyes curiously to his as he started moving away.

'I've told her to take care of you,' he translated, with a blazing smile that made Kayla's stomach muscles curl in on themselves. And that was that. He had gone before she could utter another word.

Kayla settled in to her new accommodation with remarkable ease, and as she had suspected, despite the language barrier, she found Philomena Sarantos to be a warm and generous hostess.

She wondered what Leon had meant about Philomena being unhappy with the way he had turned out. Had he meant because of his lifestyle? Not having a steady job? Because he seemed content to drift from place to place?

Two days passed and she saw nothing of him. But then, what had she expected? Kayla meditated. Hadn't he made it clear from the beginning that he didn't welcome intrusion into his life? And, although he had invited her to stay with him at the farmhouse the morning after that tree had come down, she wondered if it hadn't been merely a hollow gesture on his part. He'd known she would refuse, so he'd been perfectly safe in offering her his roof over her head.

What did it matter? she decided now. She'd had enough to occupy her time without bothering herself about Leon over the past couple of days.

The previous day she had driven up to the villa after Lorna's parents had texted her with the estimated time they would be arriving. They had brought some local men with them who were arranging for the removal of the tree, and someone else who, having inspected the building, pronounced the place off-limits for the time being.

After arranging with the men for the necessary works to be carried out, her friend's parents had been extremely concerned as to where Kayla would stay. But having satisfied them— just as she had done with Lorna, over the phone the previous day—that she had found suitable alternative accommodation, she had seen the couple off to spend a few days on Corfu and—in their own words—'make the whole trip worthwhile'.

Now, with the sun having just risen and another glorious day yawning before her, Kayla traversed the dusty path that led from Philomena's cottage and gasped with delight when it brought her down onto the sun-washed shingle of a secluded cove.

Striding down through the scrub, Leonidas came to where the beach opened out before him and stopped dead in his tracks.

Kayla was wading, shin-deep, in the translucent blue water,

moving shorewards. She was looking down into the water and hadn't spotted him yet.

He would have considered the fine white cotton dress she was wearing with its sheer long sleeves and modest yoke demure in any other circumstances, because it made her look almost angelic with her loose blonde hair moving in the breeze. But she had evidently—perhaps unintentionally—allowed the sea to lap too high to preserve her modesty, for now the garment clung wetly to her body, so that the gold of her skin and her small naked breasts were clearly visible beneath.

As she waded forward the sun struck gold from her hair, illuminating the lustrous gold of lashes that lay against her cheeks as her interest never wavered from the water.

Transfixed by her beauty, he noticed the grace of her movements, the way her progress changed the light, making her breasts appear indistinct one moment and then tantalisingly defined the next. A virginal siren, tantalising enough to set his masculine hormones ablaze as his gaze swept the length of her tunic, which only reached the tops of her slender thighs.

She looked up—and when she saw him she put her hand to her mouth in shock. Then her bare feet were running lightly over the shingle towards the white floppy hat he had only just noticed lying discarded nearby.

'I didn't see you,' she called out, snatching up the hat that had been covering her ever-present camera and the rest of her things lying there on the shingle.

'Evidently not.' He couldn't contain the slow smile that played across his mouth as he noted the purposeful way she covered her wet top with the hat, her own smile feigning nonchalance, as though she didn't care.

'Have you been standing there long?'

Not nearly long enough, Leonidas thought, struggling to keep control of his unleashed hormones and the effect she was having on him. He was glad he hadn't simply worn bathing shorts, as he'd been tempted to do, and instead had donned linen trousers with a loose, casual shirt.

She had probably had enough of men lusting after her for their own primeval satisfaction—including that fiancé of hers—without having to endure the same kind of treatment from him.

'You shouldn't go bathing like that without a chaperone,' he chided softly, the dark lenses of his sunglasses revealing nothing of his thoughts.

'I didn't mean to.' Beneath the pale swathe of her hair a modestly clad shoulder lifted almost imperceptibly. 'The sea was beckoning me while I was paddling and I just got carried away.'

'It has a way of doing that, and before you know it—' He made a gesture with his hand like a fish taking a dive. 'It's nature drawing us back to itself.'

He saw her golden head tilt and was struck by the vivid clarity of those cornflower-blue eyes as she surveyed him. 'What a beautiful thing to say.'

Leonidas laughed. 'Was it?' He found himself swallowing and his throat felt dry. He had been accused of expressing himself in many ways in his time, he recalled, but beautifully had never been one of them.

She had turned round to gather her things and was starting to pull on white cropped leggings.

'How are you getting on with Philomena?' he asked.

Thrusting her feet into flip-flops, Kayla retrieved the hat she had momentarily discarded and turned back to face him, keeping its wide brim strategically in place across her breasts.

'She's great.' Her face lit up with genuine warmth. 'She reminds me of my gran.'

'That's good.' He knew he was looking self-satisfied as he flipped open the notebook he'd taken out of the back pocket of his trousers. 'And what does your grandmother think of your being here alone?' He was in danger of sounding distracted, but it was vital he got something down. Something he'd forget if he didn't consign it to paper this very instant. 'Isn't she afraid you'll fall prey to some licentious stranger?'

'No.' Picking up her camera and sunglasses, which she slid onto her head, Kayla pushed a swathe of golden silk back off her shoulder with the aid of the sunscreen bottle she was holding. 'She died. A few months ago.'

The sadness in her voice required nothing less than Leonidas's full attention. 'I'm sorry.'

'Yes. So am I,' Kayla responded, reaffirming his suspicion that she had cared a great deal for her elderly relative.

'You were close?' He didn't even need to ask.

She nodded. 'Mum and I never really were. And after Dad left he was never the loving father type whenever I got to see him, so we just drifted apart over the years. But Gran—Mum's mum—she filled the void in every way she could.'

She was looking over her shoulder out to sea but Leonidas knew that she wasn't seeing the white-crested waves and the indigo blue water. She was hiding emotion—nothing more— because she was embarrassed by it.

'So you lost your fiancé on top of losing a grandmother?' he commented, with a depth of feeling he wasn't used to. 'That's rough.'

She shrugged. 'At least I had Lorna,' she told him with a ruminative smile. 'On both counts she was there for me. She helped me through.'

'Tell me about her,' he said somewhat distractedly Kayla thought as she started walking casually a step or two ahead of him, because he was busy scribbling in a notebook.

But she told him anyway, about the friend she had known from her first day at school who had come to mean as much as a sister to her. About the interior design work that Lorna and her husband were involved in, and how brilliant they were at what they did, but how, with the state of the market and then losing their biggest customer, things had become extremely difficult for them recently. She even went on to tell him how she might find herself looking for another job if things didn't improve.

He wasn't really listening, she decided, relieved, feeling that she had gabbled on too much.

'What are you writing?' She stopped on the shingle, turning to him with her chin almost resting on the hat she was still clutching to her beneath her folded arms.

'Just jotting down a few things I don't want to forget.' He had snapped the notebook closed and was stuffing it into his back pocket.

'You were sketching.' Suddenly it dawned. 'You were sketching *me*.'

'Leave it, Kayla.' His words were laced with a warning not to pursue it.

'You were sketching me. Oh, no!' Kayla hid her face in the wide brim of her hat. How could he? With the ends of her hair all lank and dripping, and she wasn't even wearing any mascara, let alone a bra! 'I look like a drowned and lashless rat!'

'You look like an angel,' Leonidas told her, voicing his earlier thoughts.

'You can't be serious!' Kayla protested, bringing her head up, clinging to her crushed hat as her only defence against those shaded yet all-seeing eyes.

'I never joke about beauty. Particularly the beauty of a woman,' he said, in a voice that seemed to trickle with pure honey.

And you would have known scores of those! Known just what to say to make them feel like you're making me feel now, Kayla thought hectically. Weak-kneed and breathless and wanting so much to believe that all he was saying was true!

She pulled a face, and in spite of everything managed to say with a tremulous little laugh, 'Does that line usually work?'

The firm masculine mouth compressed, and she couldn't seem to drag her gaze from it as he prompted, 'Does it work in what way?' Now that mouth took on a mocking curve. 'In getting you into my bed?'

Kayla felt heated colour steal into her cheeks. Which was ridiculous, she thought. She was hardly a novice to male attention. She'd been planning a wedding, for heaven's sake! Yet there was something about this man that was more exciting and more dangerous to her than any other man she had ever met.

'Isn't it customary?' she returned somewhat breathlessly in answer to his reference to getting her into bed.

'Possibly,' he acceded, 'but not in this case. And not with someone who has been made to feel so unsure of herself that she blushes at the mere mention of a man and woman finding pleasure in each other. Or a man taking any interest in her. There's really no need to hide from me, Kayla.'

Perhaps there wasn't. But when he took the hat she was clutching to her like a shield and his hand accidentally brushed the sensitised flesh above her modest neckline she realised that it was herself that she was afraid of. Of feelings that were too reckless and wild to think about. Purely physical feelings that had surfaced the moment she had first seen him standing on that other beach a few days ago.

Now, with her wet top doing nothing to protect her from his gaze, she could feel her blood starting to surge and the peaks of her breasts tightening in response to his hot regard, so that all she could think about was that hard masculine body locked in torrid sensual pleasure on some bed. And not just any bed. On hers!

'Are you saying that your interest is purely aesthetic?' she queried, her voice croaking from her shaming thoughts and the knowledge of how her rapidly rising breasts were betraying her to him.

'No.' He had removed his sunglasses and was hooking them onto the waistband of his trousers. Now she could see his eyes clearly.

They were dark and heavy-lidded beneath the thick swathe of his lashes, and glittering with such intensity of purpose that her every nerve went into red alert as he closed the screaming distance between them.

CHAPTER FIVE

HIS MOUTH OVER hers was like an Olympic torch blazing into life, setting her insides on fire and sending molten sensations of light searing through her blood.

His kiss was passionate, yet tender. Dominant, yet testing. And the mind-blowing expertise with which he lured her mouth to widen for him was the technique of a man who had studied and understood women—a far cry from a man who had such a laid-back attitude to life. A wanderer. A drifter. Without purpose or design.

He smelled of the earth and of the pines that clad the higher slopes of the hillsides. He was burning with everything wild and unfettered, unrestrained. And yet she felt his restraint—a purposeful holding back—as he held her loosely within the exciting circle of his arms.

That was until the hands that were still clutching her camera and the sunscreen bottle against his wide, cushioning shoulders suddenly slid around his neck. Then, with a groan of defeat, his restraint fell away, leaving only raw passion in its wake as he tossed her hat aside and pulled her hard against him.

Kayla heard a gushing in her ears and wasn't sure whether it was the heavy pounding of her blood or whether she was being captured and submerged beneath the relentless power of the sea.

She could feel the whole hard length of his body—every last inch of it—and she could feel her own responding to the drugging hunger of his mouth.

His back was firm and muscled, and she wished she wasn't encumbered by her possessions so that she could slide her eager hands across it. There was no such encumbrance though in the way her body locked with his. His chest was a wall of thunder, crushing her aching breasts, while the potent evidence of his hard virility was making her pulse with need.

When he put her from him, holding her at arm's length, she uttered a strangled murmur of breathless shock and disappointment.

'Why did you do that?' she quavered. Why had he kissed her when he had just claimed he had no intention of trying to get her into bed?

He was breathing as heavily as she was, and a deep flush was staining the olive skin across the strong, hard structure of his cheeks.

'Because you were wondering what it would be like if I did.'

Still trembling, and perturbed by how easily he could not only read her mind but also by how easily he could bend her to his will, she challenged brittly, 'So why did you stop?'

'Because, as I told you before, I have no intention of taking advantage of a woman on the rebound,' he reminded her, even though his breathing was still laboured and his strong face racked from the passion he was struggling to keep in check.

'And—as I told *you* before—I'm not on the rebound,' Kayla protested adamantly, shamed by her response when he was showing such self-control, and when she seemed to have relinquished all of hers in one experimental kiss!

'Aren't you?' he disputed, although there was a wry smile tugging at one corner of his mouth that softened his challenging remark, before he went on to add, 'You had a relationship with him, didn't you?'

'Well, of course I did,' Kayla returned. 'Of sorts.'

'Of sorts?' He tilted his head, his brows drawing quizzically together. 'How am I supposed to interpret *that*?'

'Any way you like!' Kayla tossed back at him, too embarrassed to tell him that Craig's enthusiasm for her had seemed to go off the boil for several weeks before their break-up, and that she was ashamed of herself now for not suspecting the truth. She had believed him when he had blamed work overload for his not showing enough interest in her. When he'd assured her that things would be different when they were married. When he had got the precious promotion he'd spent all his time working for.

'Were you living with him?'

'No.'

'Why not? If I ever set my mind on a woman I want to become my wife, then she will be firmly in my life—and my bed—before I even ask her.'

'I didn't want us to move in together. Not until we were married,' Kayla emphasised. 'And Craig was in full agreement with that.'

'Really?' Mocking scepticism marked that hard masculine face. 'You could do without each other *that* much?'

'Not that it's any concern of yours,' Kayla pointed out, hating having her relationship with her ex scrutinised so closely by this man she scarcely knew, 'but we wanted to start married life properly. In a place that was our own. I didn't want to just move into his flat. Anyway, there's more to a relationship than jumping into bed with each other at every given opportunity,' she stressed, unconsciously wiping her mouth with the back of her hand. Her lips still felt bruised and swollen and, like her susceptible body, burning from Leon's wholly primal, earth-shattering kiss.

'Is there?' he asked, and she could feel those perspicacious eyes following her involuntary action, mocking her, disconcertingly aware.

'Yes!' She was trembling, knowing that the way she had just behaved with him made nonsense of everything she was saying. And the worst thing was he knew it too. 'The type of man I let myself get involved with doesn't just give in to basic animal lust.'

He chuckled under his breath. 'Is that what I was doing? Then you must forgive me if I fail to live up to the constraints of the type of man you are obviously used to. Although I *could* hazard a guess that your relationship was sadly lacking in what was required to make a lifetime commitment, and that the lack of passion between you could have been why he was getting his satisfaction elsewhere.'

The reminder hurt, stinging her pride and giving rise to that same feeling of inadequacy she had felt after she'd got over the initial blow of Craig's betrayal—especially coming from someone who oozed the sort of sexual potency that this man did.

'I'm sorry,' he murmured, surprising her suddenly. 'I didn't mean to rub it in.'

'Didn't you?' she accused, hiding her hurt pride and dignity beneath the burnished gold of her lowered lashes.

'Well, all right.' A self-effacing smile touched that mouth that had the power to drug her. 'I did. But until it stops hurting, Kayla, you aren't ready for an involvement with any other man. And even if you were, the last thing a sensitive girl like you would want is an involvement with a man like me.'

Why not? Crazily, she heard the mortifying question spring to her lips and was half-afraid that she had actually spoken it. Wasn't he just the type of man she needed right now to drive the bitter after-taste of Craig and all his shallow-minded smart set out of her mind?

'Believe it or not, I'm not looking for one,' she responded, to assure herself as much as Leon. Well, she wasn't, was she? Wasn't she better off—as her mother had always claimed to be—on her own?

'Sensible girl,' Leonidas drawled and, stooping to pick up her hat, deposited it gently and unceremoniously on her head.

'Thanks.' Kayla pulled a wry face. 'Perhaps you'd like to sketch me like this?' she challenged broodingly, relieved, nevertheless, that the disconcerting subject of her love-life had finally been swept aside.

What wasn't so easy to sweep aside, however, was the memory of what had transpired between them a few moments ago.

Why had she responded to him so shamelessly if, as he'd suggested, she was still affected by what Craig had done? Was she so wanton? So desperate for a man? Any man? she wondered. Might she have let this virtual stranger take her here on the shingle without a thought for how it might leave her feeling afterwards?

'I won't be sketching you at all,' he said dismissively. 'For the simple reason that you are wrong. I'm no artist. But if I were, and if I had to keep looking at you looking like this...' His gaze slid over her tantalisingly wet top, making her quiver inside from the powerful impulses generated by the naked need in his eyes, 'then—old boyfriend or no old boyfriend—I definitely would wind up taking you to bed.'

The climb up through the scrub to Philomena's cottage was hot and hilly, and Leonidas walked ahead of Kayla, protecting her from the dense and thorny vegetation that was encroaching on the narrow path, thriving in the rough terrain.

He had had an exacting morning, sorting out a problem that had arisen back in his London office—a case of divided opinion between a couple of members of his board, which his second-in-command had apologised for bringing to his attention.

They said it was tough at the top, he reminded himself

with a grimace. And they could say it again, because no matter how much he needed to escape the rigours of the office for a while, he still needed to keep his finger on the pulsing heart of his business.

Shopping malls, leisure complexes and housing developments didn't build themselves, and after the flak he had taken from the press over the neglect of local residents with last year's bitter fiasco he needed to ensure that no loopholes were left for mercenary lawyers and unprincipled members of his team to make unscrupulous deals over.

Being labelled 'ruthless', 'unscrupulous' and 'a profiteer' by the media wasn't something he wanted repeated any more than he wanted further episodes like the one with his publicity-hungry bed-partner Esmeralda Leigh. He had a reputation to uphold—one that he valued—both in his corporate and his private life, and he would protect and defend it with every shred of his power and his unwavering principles. But he hadn't got where he was today without treading a path that had made him tough, hard-nosed and uncompromising, and he had no intention of wavering from that path. Of allowing himself or anyone else to imagine for one moment that he was going soft. Not even this infernally beautiful girl...

Hearing her breath coming shallowly some way behind him, he stopped and waited for her to catch up. She was clutching her bottle of sunscreen lotion, the bulky camera dangled around her neck, and with her white leggings, her tunic top and that huge floppy hat she looked like an overgrown child who had just raided her great-grandmother's attic. He was happy to notice—for his own sake—that her top had nearly dried.

'Here. Let me carry that.' He could see her cheeks were flushed and that she was finding it a struggle keeping up with him, and he held out his hand for the camera, which she happily relinquished. Silently he extended his other hand.

Realising his intention, Kayla hesitated briefly, and saw a mocking smile touch his sensational mouth.

'It's all right. It doesn't constitute a tacit agreement to let me into your bed,' he advised her dryly.

Of course it didn't, she thought. But an impulse of something so powerfully electric seemed to pass between them when she took his hand that it certainly felt like it.

'Thanks,' she uttered tremulously, hoping that he would think it was the uphill climb in the heat over the rough ground that was making her sound so breathless. Not that every cell was leaping in response to her physical awareness of him just as it had when he had kissed her down there on the beach.

'Where did you learn to speak English so proficiently?' she asked, needing to say something—although she *was* genuinely interested to know.

'When I work, I work mainly in the UK,' he informed her. 'And my grandmother was English, so I had a head start while I was still knee-high to a cricket.'

'Grasshopper.'

'What?' The way he was looking down at her, with such charismatically dark eyes, sent a sensually charged little tingle along Kayla's spine.

'It's knee-high to a grasshopper,' she corrected him, contemplating how well the backdrop of the rugged coast and the meandering hillsides served to strengthen the ruggedness of this man who had been born part of them. But she'd picked up on what he'd just said about *when* he worked. So his employment definitely wasn't regular, she thought, reminded of the recent slump in the building trade and how difficult it had made things for a lot of its workers. Perhaps that was why he'd chosen to 'opt out', as he'd put it, for a while.

'How old were you when you left the island?' She found herself wanting to know much more about him.

'Fifteen.'

She remembered him saying that he'd left to find a better life. 'On your own?' she queried. 'Did you leave to go to college?' she asked, when he didn't answer her question. What else could possibly have taken him away at such a young age?

He laughed at that—a sound without humour. 'No college. No university. I did have hopes of furthering my education, but my father wouldn't hear of it.'

'Why not?' Kayla asked, amazed.

'He wanted me to get out into the world, like he had, and "do an honest job" as he called it.'

'Really?' Kayla sympathised. 'And what did *he* do?'

'He eked a living out of this land,' he told her, with an edge to his voice that had her looking at her curiously.

'And where are they now? Your parents?' She couldn't believe they could still be living on the island, otherwise why would he be staying here alone in some absentee owner's sadly neglected house?

'My parents are dead,' he told her as he walked half a stride ahead of her. There was no emotion now beside that surprisingly hard cast to his mouth.

'I'm sorry,' Kayla murmured. She had discovered during a conversation in the villa with him the other day that he, like Kayla, was an only child.

'One learns to get over these things,' he replied.

From the harshness of his tone, however, she wondered if he had. Or was there some other reason, she pondered, for that inexorable grimness to his features?

'Still…you have Philomena,' she said brightly, hoping to lighten the mood. She couldn't understand why down there on the beach he had behaved like an exciting lover and yet now seemed as uncommunicative as ever.

Was it by chance that he had just happened to come across her down there? Or had he come looking for her especially?

A sharp little thrill ran through her at the possibility that he had.

'Did she tell you where I was?'

His disconcerting glance at her took in what she knew was her thoroughly dishevelled appearance, and a lazy smile curved his mouth, instantly transforming his features.

'Are you suggesting I asked her?'

Mortified that he would even think she might have wanted him to, Kayla tried to tug her hand out of his, and sucked in a breath when he refused to let it go.

'Yes, I did,' he admitted easily, without any of the embarrassment that was burning Kayla's cheeks. 'I came down to Philomena's to check on you. You've had a bad experience. I didn't like to think of it ruining your holiday.'

He actually cared?

Well, of course he was concerned for her, she thought, mindful of the lengths he had gone to in rescuing her the other night, and then not only helping her to clean up the villa afterwards but also bringing her to Philomena's as well.

'It hasn't. Thanks,' she offered, grateful to him, and was warmed by a flash of something closely resembling admiration in his eyes.

She wondered if he had a girlfriend or a partner. It certainly seemed he'd had a stormy affair, judging by the way he had referred to her when he had been generalising about her sex the other day.

'Why were you so unfriendly to me when we met those first couple of times?' she queried, suddenly needing to know. 'You still haven't told me.'

She started as he suddenly stopped dead, pulling her round to face him on the path.

'Do you *never* stop asking questions?' he demanded, his face a curious blend of impatience and amusement.

'No.' She gave him a sheepish little look and shrugged her

shoulders. 'I'm afraid it's a fault of mine. Apparently, according to my star sign, I was born on "the Day of Curiosity",' she quoted with a little giggle.

'And do you really believe all that stuff?'

Seeing the scepticism marking the strong and perfectly sculpted features, she laughed and said, 'No. But they've got that part of me right!'

'You can say that again,' he remarked dryly. 'And as a matter of interest exactly when *is* this illustrious day?' He made a half-amused sound down his nostrils when she told him. 'So you've just had a birthday?' he observed. 'And how old are you, Kayla?'

'Twenty-three.'

'Old enough to know when a man doesn't welcome any more probing into his private life.'

And that told her, Kayla thought, feeling suitably chastised. This time when she tried to pull her hand away she was even more disconcerted when he allowed her to do so.

They had reached the top of the path that ran up alongside Philomena's cottage. There was an area at the back, with a lime tree and a couple of orange trees, where Philomena also grew aubergines and sweet peppers, and where chickens foraged freely in the open scrub.

'How's the car going?' Leon asked, noticing it parked against the side wall of the cottage.

Still feeling put down, but relieved to be speaking on a much less personal level with him, Kayla murmured, 'Fine.' And suddenly, with tension causing a little bubble of laughter to burst from her, she proclaimed, 'Which is more than can be said for yours!'

His truck was parked on the edge of the dirt road just behind the little hatchback, and she could see that one of its tyres was completely flat.

'Oh, dear!' She tried not to giggle again as he thrust the

camera at her and, swearing quietly under his breath in his own language, went to deal with changing the wheel.

Leaving him to it, Kayla wandered into the garden, where Philomena was pegging out some washing, sending a couple of chickens scrambling, clucking noisily.

'A flat tyre.' Kayla made a gesture to indicate what she meant and Philomena nodded, rolling her eyes.

Which meant what? Kayla wondered, curious. Had Philomena hoped that the boy she had brought into the world thirty-odd years ago might be doing better for himself by now? Was that what Leon had meant when he'd said she wasn't happy with the way he had turned out?

Dismissing it from her mind, she moved to help Philomena, but her hostess waved her aside with a warm but incomprehensible protest, pointing to the reclining seats in the welcoming shade of a sun umbrella. Not wishing to offend, Kayla went inside and donned a bikini with matching red and white wrap, which she tied, sarong-style, just above her breasts, before coming back outside into the now deserted garden.

A short time later Philomena emerged from the house with two glasses of something cool and refreshing—juice for her, Kayla realised gratefully, and something a little stronger for Leon.

'I'll take it out to him,' she volunteered, putting her glass down on a nearby table and leaving a thankful Philomena hurrying back inside, because the telephone had started ringing inside the house.

Her discarded wrap had fallen down behind the chair, and wasn't very easy to reach, so with a little sliver of excitement Kayla left it where it was and proceeded to take the glass to Leon as she was.

For the last twenty-minutes or so her ears had been tuned to every sound coming from the dirt road—from the slamming down of a boot to the chink of metal being laid down on sun-baked stones. Now, as she rounded the corner of the house, Kayla's heart kicked into overdrive.

With his shirt removed, and faded blue jeans having replaced his linen trousers, Leon was crouched down, securing a nut on the spare wheel, and for a few moments Kayla could only stand there, watching him unobserved.

His body was beautiful. The bronzed skin sheathed muscles that were flexing as he worked, revealing the tension in his straining biceps and across his wide shoulders, in the tapering structure of his strong and sinewy back.

'Philomena thought you'd like something to drink,' Kayla told him, dry-mouthed, noticing before he turned around how his hair waved below the nape of his neck like jet against burnished bronze.

He dropped the spanner he was using and stood up, his movements cool and easy. That knowing curve to his mouth suggested that he was well aware of her reluctance to let him think that it was entirely her idea.

'That's very good of her.' His answer and his lopsided smile assured her that two could play at that game. His eyes, however, were tugging over her scantily clothed body in a way that was making her feel naked.

'You've been a long time. You should have let me help you,' Kayla remarked, handing him the glass. The accidental touch of his fingers against hers sent a sharp little frisson through her.

'And do you think I would have achieved much with you looking like that?'

Kayla swallowed, watching him drink, trying not to make it too obvious that she was having difficulty staying unaffected by *his* state of undress.

In fact she was finding it impossible not to allow her gaze free rein over his superb body—from the contoured strength of his smooth chest, with its taut muscles and flat dark nipples, to the black line of hair that started just above his navel and ran down inside the waistband of the denim that encased his flat stomach and narrow hips.

He was like a beautiful sleek stallion. All leanness and rippling muscle, with the power to dominate and excite, to control and to conquer using the pulsing energies and surging potency of his body.

'Do you see what I mean?' he taunted softly.

Yes, she did, and she could feel those energies transmitting their sensual messages along her nerve-endings, tugging shameless responses from every erogenous zone in her body.

Beneath the satiny white cups of her bikini her burgeoning breasts throbbed, sending a piercing arrow of need to the heart of her loins.

He was so raw, so masculine, and so shamelessly virile. She wanted to know what it was like to have a man like him filling her, taking her to the wildest edges of the universe with him while she lay beneath him, sobbing her pleasure, in glorious abandon to his thrilling and governing hands.

Shocked by her thoughts, she tried to shake them away, feigning an interest in his truck to try and restore some sense of propriety in herself, grappling for equilibrium.

'Did this thing come with the house?' she queried in a tight, strained voice, slapping the grimy, battered bonnet. 'Or did you have to buy it?'

'It's mine,' Leonidas answered, taking a breath from quenching his thirst and watching her from under the thickness of his dark lashes.

'Perhaps it's time you bought a new one,' she suggested cheekily, amused, deciding that it wasn't only the tyre that needed changing. The bodywork looked as if it wouldn't object to a lick of fresh paint either.

'Perhaps it's time you stopped having a laugh at my expense.'

Was that what she was doing? 'I'm sorry.' Seeing his eyes darkening, quickly Kayla strove to suppress her mocking banter. After all, he probably couldn't afford anything better, she thought. Not like Craig, with his company Jaguar and his inflated expense account. This man would have no such perks. 'I didn't mean to laugh about it—honest.'

'Didn't you?' He had emptied his glass with one final long draught. Setting it aside, he came to where Kayla stood with her hand resting on the top of the radiator grid, as though in apology to the vehicle itself. 'I suppose you measure a man's status by the type of car he drives, huh?'

'No.'

'What would you prefer? A Porsche? Or a Mercedes?' he asked roughly.

'Well, both would be nice…' Her voice tailed off when she noticed how forbidding he looked, and she realised that she wasn't just imagining that hardening in his voice. 'I wasn't making fun of you. Not really,' she tagged on, suddenly afraid that he might think less of her if he thought she had been. 'I suppose I was just getting my own back.'

'For what?'

'For embarrassing me earlier. Making me feel awkward. When you said I was being too inquisitive about your private life.'

He laughed very softly then, his strong implacable features suddenly losing some of their austerity. His eyes, however, were disturbingly reflective as they rested on her face.

'And I thought you were doing it just to prompt some reaction from me,' he murmured silkily, with no apology for silencing her earlier.

'Prompt some reaction from you?' Kayla's throat contracted with heightening sexual tension. 'Why would I want to do that?'

'Because I'm probably one of the only men you've met who

isn't instantly falling over himself to respond to your temptingly sexy signals.'

'I'm not giving off *any* signals!' Kayla breathed, mortified. 'And I'm certainly not trying to get your attention.'

'Aren't you?' Those shrewd eyes tugged over her flushed, indignant features, regarding, assessing and stripping her of her deepest and hottest secrets. 'You wouldn't have come out here looking like this...' an all-encompassing glance took in breasts thrust tantalisingly upwards by the shaping of the cups and skimpy briefs barely skimming her abdomen '...if you weren't.'

Shamefully, she wished she had bothered to retrieve her cover-up before flaunting herself in front of him like this. Because that *was* what she had been doing, she admitted silently. Flaunting herself.

She wanted to say something to redeem herself. Or simply to run away. Anything but stay there and face him like this.

She wished she had run when he suddenly reached up and cupped her cheek, his broad thumb playing across the softness of her pouting lips.

'If I made love to you, Kayla,' he said huskily, 'it would be a fleeting moment's pleasure. That's all. No commitment. No strings. And I don't think you came here to let some man with his own issues to sort out use you like that. A girl like you needs something more than anything I could offer you. Something more meaningful. Not a brief fling to try and forget the man who cheated on you with a few hours of what I can't deny would be sensational pleasure.'

He was deadly serious, but even his words were exciting her. Or was it his thumb, tracing the curve of her plump lower lip, forcing her to close her eyes against the reckless desire to taste him? To inhale his musky animal scent mingling with the smell of grease and metal and everything that made this man exciting to her?

'Who said I want you to make love to me?' she murmured in pointless protest, her eyes inky beneath lashes still half-lowered against his gaze.

'You're inviting it with every denial you utter,' he breathed hoarsely, his voice overlaid with desire. 'And you're not so naïve as not to realise that you're making me as hard as a rock.'

'You're wrong!' she argued breathlessly, and in the only way she knew of saving face she pulled away from him, almost tripping over her own feet in her flip-flops as she virtually ran back to the house.

Upstairs, away from Philomena's shrewd eyes, she went into the shower-room and peeled off the bikini that seemed to be sticking to her.

Why on earth was she so attracted to him? she berated herself under the cool jets of the shower, trying to lather away the sensual heat from her body and that elusive scent of him that still clung to her skin where he had briefly touched her.

He had admitted himself that he was a man with issues.

Woman issues! Which was why he had shut her up, coming back from the beach today.

Well, what did she care? His business was his business. As far as she was concerned, he was simply a man who had helped her out of a difficult situation. Nothing more. It was just that she couldn't seem to stop making a fool of herself when she was with him, let alone concentrate on anything but him when she wasn't!

She tried to think about the past couple of months. Her ex. What had driven her here. Tried to stir up some other emotions to blot out the crazy, reckless feelings she was experiencing for Leon.

But, try though she did, feeling bitter suddenly seemed like a wasted emotion—because Craig and what he had done didn't seem to matter so much any more.

CHAPTER SIX

KAYLA DIDN'T SEE Leon the next day, or the day after that, and when he did come down to the cottage again, looking stupendous in a white T-shirt and light, hip-hugging trousers, it was only to deliver logs to Philomena.

'So you're still roadworthy, then?' Kayla remarked, almost coyly, when he came into the sitting room after offloading and stacking the logs beside the huge indoor oven, still embarrassingly mindful of their conversation the last time they had met.

'Just about,' Leonidas reassured her with a self-effacing grimace. 'And I see that you're just about as cheeky as ever.'

'No, I'm not,' Kayla asserted, thrilled nevertheless by the sensual gleam in those midnight-black eyes that seemed to promise some delightful retribution if she didn't stop. Wildly she wondered if he had been right the other day, and she *had* been taunting him solely for his attention. Because despite all he had said about no attachments and no strings, she wanted that attention now—like crazy! 'We were wondering why we hadn't seen you,' she said, as nonchalantly as she could.

'We?' He picked up on her deliberate choice of pronoun—and on the little tremor she couldn't keep out of her voice. Obviously, from the way his mouth compressed in mild amusement. 'Are you saying you missed me?'

'No.' Kayla was glad that Philomena had left the room—though not before she'd noticed how the woman had laid a grateful hand on Leon's arm for the work he had just done. The unspoken affection the two of them shared touched Kayla immensely.

Yet she *had* missed him, she thought, and Leon knew it too—evidently from the way he laughed in response.

'In that case you won't object to spending the day with me,' he said, deliberately misinterpreting what she had said. 'Philomena told me you were asking one of her neighbours about the little island the other day—about if you could book a trip across there.'

He meant that dark mass of land she could see jutting out of the sea from practically every aspect of this hillside.

'She also mentioned that you spend far too much time worrying that you aren't doing enough to help her around the place. She wants you to enjoy your holiday—so do I—and as there are no organised trips to that island I'll be happy to take you over there myself.'

Even as he was suggesting it Leonidas told himself that he was being unwise. He had assured Kayla—as well as himself—that he wasn't prepared to have any sort of relationship with her, but try as he might he just couldn't keep away. Yet if he spent time with her, he warned himself, he would be deceiving her with every word he uttered. And if he didn't…?

If he didn't then he'd go mad thinking about her, he admitted silently, feeling the thrust of his scorching libido flaring into life just from sparring with her, not to mention from the scent of her, which was acting on his senses as powerfully as if he'd just opened the door on some willing wanton's boudoir.

Her appearance wasn't helping his control. She was wearing white shorts, which showed off far too much of those deliciously creamy legs, and a sleeveless lemon blouse tied under her breasts. It revealed just enough of her shallow cleavage to make him want to see more, and left her gradually tanning slender midriff delightfully bare.

'Thanks, but I think I'll give it a miss today,' she said, disappointing him.

'Suit yourself,' he muttered, turning away. He was relieved that the decision had been made—especially since he had been entertaining the strongest desire to tug open that tantalising little blouse and mould her sensitive breasts to his palms until she sobbed with the pleasure.

'Well…'

Her sudden hesitancy stopped him in his tracks. Battling to control his raging anatomy, he didn't turn around, his breath locking in his lungs as he heard her tentative little suggestion behind him.

'If you could just give me a minute…?'

He swung round then, his desire veiled by his immense powers of self-control. His eyes, as they clashed with hers, were smouldering with a dark intensity and he saw an answering response in the darkening blue of hers that was as hungry as it was guarded.

Almost cleverly guarded, he thought, but not quite enough. She was as on fire for him as he was for her, he recognised, regardless of any feelings she might still be harbouring over that louse who had let her down.

Kayla, as she stood there, captured by the powerful hold of his gaze, felt a skein of excitement unravelling inside her and knew that a watershed had been reached. That with one look and one inconsequential unfinished sentence a silent understanding had somehow passed between them. She had crossed a bridge that was already burning behind her and she knew there could be no turning back.

'No rowing boat today?' Kayla remarked, surprised when, after driving them to a beach further along the coast, Leon guided her towards a small motor boat moored alongside a wooden jetty. 'I didn't think you'd be seen dead in anything less than fifty years old!' she said laughingly.

'Didn't you?' he drawled, with a challenging and deliciously sensual gleam in his eyes as he handed her into the boat. 'Contrary to your thinking, *hrisi mou,* I can...' he hesitated, thinking of the words '...come good when circumstances demand.'

'And *do* circumstances demand?' she enquired airily, in spite of her pulse, which was racing from his nearness and his softly spoken endearment.

'Oh, yes,' he breathed with barely veiled meaning. 'I think they do.'

It was a day of delight and surprises.

With effortless dexterity Leonidas steered the boat through the sparkling blue water, following the rocky coast of his own island to begin with, and pointing out coves and deserted beaches only accessible from the sea.

Having a field-day with her camera, Kayla lapped up the magic of her surroundings whilst using every opportunity to grab secretive and not so secretive shots of this dynamic man she was with: at the wheel, in profile, with his brow furrowed in concentration, or turning to talk to her with that sexy, sidelong pull of his mouth that never failed to do funny things to her stomach. She captured him looking out over the dark body of water they were cutting through, his T-shirt pulled taut across his broad muscular back, his black hair as windswept as hers from the exhilarating speed at which they were travelling.

She'd need to remember, she realised almost desperately, wondering why it was so important to her to capture everything about this holiday. This island. These precious few hours. This man.

Suddenly aware, he glanced over his shoulder and, easing back on the throttle, said challengingly, 'Don't you think you've taken enough?' She was about to make some quip about it being her 'fix', but he cut across her before she could with, 'What are you going to do? Put them on the internet?'

With a questioning look at him, not sure how to take what he'd said, she pretended to be considering it, and with a half-tantalising, half-nervous little giggle, answered, 'I might.'

'You do that and our association ends right now.' His contesting tone and manner caused her to flinch.

'If you're that concerned, then keep it,' she invited, holding the camera out to him. She hadn't forgotten what a private person he was. 'I promise I'm not going to publish them on the web, but take it if you don't trust me not to.'

For a moment her candour made Leonidas hold back. How could he demand or even expect integrity from her when he wasn't being straight himself?

Briefly he felt like flinging caution to the winds and telling her the truth. Only the thought of the repercussions that could follow stopped him.

She would be angry, that was certain. But he had come here seeking respite from all the glamour and superficiality that went hand in hand with who he really was, and he wasn't ready yet to relinquish his precious anonymity. It didn't help reminding himself that it was primarily because of trusting a woman that he had felt driven to take some time out. Because of being too careless and believing that a casual but willing bed partner would share the same ethics as he.

Not that this girl was in any way like the mercenary vamp with whom he had unwisely shared the weekend that had proved so costly to his pride and reputation. But his billionaire status and lifestyle still generated interest, despite his best attempts to keep it low-key—and never more so since his unfortunate affair with the media-hungry Esmeralda—and Kayla was only human after all. What a boost it would be to her bruised ego after being ditched so cruelly by her fiancé for news of her liaison with a man whose corporate achievements weren't entirely unknown to filter back to the world press. One text home to this Lorna might be all it would take to bring the paparazzi here in their droves.

'It's stolen enough of your time from me for one day,' he said, smiling. Yet he still took the camera she was offering and stowed it away in a recess beneath the wheel.

They had lunch on the boat—a feast of lobster and cheeses, fresh bread and a blend of freshly squeezed juice. Afterwards there were delicate pastries filled with fruit and walnuts, and others creamy with the tangy freshness of lime.

Kayla savoured it all as she'd never savoured a meal before, and there was wonder mixed in with her appreciation.

'This must have set you back a fortune,' she couldn't help remarking when she had finished.

'Let me worry about that,' he told her unassumingly.

'But to hire a boat like this doesn't come cheap...' Even if only for a day, she thought. 'And as for that lunch...' She wondered if he would have eaten as well had he been alone and decided that he wouldn't, guessing that he must have been counting on her being unable to resist coming with him today.

'What are you concerned about, Kayla?' he asked softly, closing the cool box that had contained their picnic before stowing it away. 'That I might have spent more than you think I can justifiably afford? Or is it finding yourself in my debt that's making you uneasy?'

'A bit of both, I suppose,' she admitted truthfully. After all, she'd always been used to paying her way when she was with a man, to never taking more out of a relationship than she was prepared to put in. Emotionally as well as financially, she thought with a little stab of self-derision as she remembered how with Craig she had wound up giving everything and receiving nothing, coming out a first-rate fool in the end.

'Don't worry about it,' Leonidas advised. 'I promise you

I'm not likely to starve for the rest of my holiday. As for the boat, I hired it to take myself off exploring today. Your coming with me is just a bonus, so there's no need to feel awkward or indebted in any way. If you want to contribute something, then your enjoyment will suffice,' he assured her, and refrained from adding that most women he'd known would have taken his generosity as their due.

The island, when they came ashore, was beautiful. Lonely and uninhabited, it was merely a haven for wildlife, with only numerous birds and insects making their voices heard above the warm wind and the wash of the sea in the cove where they had left the boat.

There was no distinct path, and the climb through the surprisingly green vegetation was hot and steep, but the feeling of freedom at the top was worth a thousand climbs.

It was like standing in their own uninhabited world. In every direction the deep blue of the sky met the deeper blue of the sea. Looking back across the distance they had covered, Kayla saw the hulk of mountainous land they had left with its forests and its craggy coastline slumbering in a haze of heat.

There were huge stones amongst the grass—sculpted stones of an ancient ruin, overgrown with scrub and wild flowers, a sad and silent testimony to the beliefs of some long-lost civilisation.

'You said you came to sort out some issues?' Kayla reminded him, venturing to broach what she had been dying to ask him since they had left that morning. 'What sort of issues?' she pressed, looking seawards at the waves creaming onto a distant beach and wondering if it was the one where she had first seen him over a week ago. 'Woman issues?' she enquired, more tentatively now.

He was standing with his foot on one of the stones that had once formed part of the ancient temple, with one hand resting on his knee. The wind was lifting his hair, sweeping it back off features suddenly so uncompromising that he looked like a marauding mythical god, surveying all he intended to conquer.

'Among other things,' he said, but he didn't enlarge on the women in his life or tell her what those 'other things' were.

Kayla moved away from him, pulling a brightly flowering weed from a crack in what had formed part of a wall. She was getting used to his uncommunicative ways.

She was surprised, therefore, when he suddenly said, 'I used to dream of owning this island when I was a boy. I used to sit on that hillside...' he pointed to a distant spot across the water, indiscernible through the heat haze '...and imagine all I was going to do with it. The big house. The swimming pool. The riding stables.'

'And dogs?' Kayla inserted, her eyes gleaming, following him into a make-believe world of her own.

'Yes, lots of dogs.'

So he liked animals, she realised, deriving warm pleasure from the knowledge. Contrarily, though, she wrinkled her nose. 'Too costly to feed.' Laughingly she pretended to discount that idea. 'And too much heartache if they get sick or run away.'

'They couldn't run away,' Leonidas reminded her. 'Not unless they were proficient swimmers.'

'Haven't you ever heard of the doggy paddle?' She giggled, enjoying playing this little game with him. Her eyes were bright and her cheeks were glowing from an exhilaration that had nothing to do with their climb. 'So you were going to build a house with a swimming pool? And have horses? Racehorses, of course.'

He shot her a sceptical glance. 'Now you're wandering into the realms of fantasy,' he chided, amused.

'Well, if you can own the island and have a house with lots of dogs, I can have racehorses,' Kayla insisted light-heartedly.

'They'd fall off the edge before they'd covered a mile,' he

commented dryly. 'I was talking about what seemed totally realistic to a twelve-year-old boy.'

Tugging her windswept hair out of her eyes, Kayla pulled a face. 'But then you grew up?'

'Yes,' he said heavily. 'I grew up.' And all he had wanted to do was run as far away from these islands and everything he had called home as he could possibly get.

'What happened?' Kayla asked, frowning. She couldn't help but notice the tension clenching his mouth and the hard line of his jaw.

'My mother died when I was fourteen, then my grandfather shortly afterwards. My father and I didn't see eye to eye,' he enlightened her.

'Why not?'

'Why do we not get on with some people and yet gel so perfectly with others? Especially those who are supposed to be closest to us?' He shrugged, his strong features softening a little. 'Differing opinions? A clash of personalities? Maybe even because we are too much alike. Why aren't *you* close to your mother?' he outlined as an example.

Watching a lizard dart along the jagged edge of the wall and disappear over the side, Kayla considered his question. 'I suppose all those things,' she admitted, rather ruefully. And then, keen to shrug off the serious turn the conversation had taken, she said, 'So, are you going to sketch me a picture of this house?'

'No.'

'Why not?' She had seen him scribbling in his notepad again, when he had been waiting for her in the truck outside Philomena's, and wondered what he could possibly have been doing if he *hadn't* been sketching. He'd also been speaking to somebody on his cell phone at the same time, Kayla remembered, but had cut the call short, leaning across to open the passenger door for her when he had seen her coming. She'd wondered if he'd been speaking to a woman and, if he had, whether it was the woman at the heart of his 'issues'.

'It isn't what I do,' Leonidas said.

'No son of mine is going to disgrace the Vassalio name by painting for a living!'

Leonidas could still hear his father's bellowing as he ridiculed his talent, his love of perspective and light and colour, beating it out of him—sometimes literally—as he destroyed the results of his teenage son's labours and with them all the creativity in his soul. Art was a feeling and feelings were weakness, his father had drummed into him. And no Vassalio male had ever been weak.

So he had channelled his driving energies into creating new worlds out of blocks of clay and concrete, in innovative designs that had leaped off the paper and formed the basis of his own developments. Developments that had made him rich beyond his wildest dreams. And with the money it had all come tumbling into his lap. Influence. Respect. Women. So many women that he could have had his pick of any of them. Yet he hadn't found one who was more disposed to him personally than she was to the state of his bank balance. Not beyond the pleasures of the bedroom at any rate, he thought with a self-deprecating mental grimace. In that it seemed he was never able to fail.

'So what about you, Kayla? Didn't you have any aspirations?'

'I suppose I did but not like yours,' she said, twirling the stalk of a pink flower in her fingers. 'I think I was always practical and realistic. Besides, I was brought up with the understanding that if you don't expect you can't be disappointed.'

'And because of that you never allowed yourself to dream?'

He was sitting on one of the larger stones, one leg bent, the other stretched out in front of him, and Kayla tried to avoid noticing how the cloth of his trousers pulled tautly over one muscular thigh.

'Of course I did,' she uttered, wondering why she suddenly felt as if she needed to defend herself. 'But I've never been one for mooning over things I can't have. Especially things which are totally out of my reach.'

He leaned back and crossed his arms, his muscles bunching, emphasising their latent strength. 'And you don't believe that everything is within your reach if you jump high enough?'

He made it sound almost credible, which seemed quite out of kilter, Kayla thought, with his laid-back attitude to life.

'If you jump too high you usually fall flat on your face. Anyway, you're one to talk,' she commented, still hurt over his refusal to give her a glimpse into even the smallest area of his life. 'You don't even have a steady job.'

'I get by.'

'But nothing that offers real security or fulfils your potential?'

'And why is it so important to fulfil my "potential"?' he quoted. His eyes were dark and inscrutable, giving nothing of his thoughts away.

'Because everybody needs a purpose. Some sort of goal in life,' Kayla stressed.

'And what is your goal, *glykia mou?*'

The sensuality with which he spoke suddenly seemed to emphasise the isolation of their surroundings, and with it the fundamental objective of each other's existence.

'To be happy.'

'And that's it? Just to be happy?' He looked both surprised and mildly amused. 'And how do you propose to achieve this happiness?'

Cynicism had replaced the mocking amusement of a moment ago. She could see it in the curling of his firm, rather cruel-looking mouth—a mouth she was aching to feel covering hers again.

'By staying grounded and true to myself, and not ever attempting to be something I'm not,' she uttered—croakily, because of where her thoughts had taken her. Afraid that she was in danger of sounding a little bit self-righteous, she added, 'By appreciating nature. Things like this.' She cast a glance around her at the wilderness of the island. At everything that was timeless. Untrammelled and free. 'By creating a happy home. Having children one day. And animals. Lots of animals.'

'And that's all it's going to take?' Again he looked marginally surprised. 'Setting up home and having babies?'

'It's better than being a drifter,' she remarked, knowing she was overstepping the mark yet unable to stop herself, 'without any ambition whatsoever.'

'You think I don't have ambition?'

'Well, *do* you?' she challenged, aware that she had no right to, as she pulled her hair out of her eyes again, yet driven by the feeling that he was mocking her values and finding them wanting.

'You'd be surprised. But just for argument's sake, what do you see me doing?' How would *you* have me realise this ambition?'

'You're good with cars,' Kayla remarked, ignoring the mockery infiltrating his question. 'You could be a mechanic. You could even start your own business. With the prices they charge for servicing and repairs these days you could make a comfortable living.'

'If I were a mechanic I wouldn't be able to take time off to come to places like this for weeks at a time.' His mouth compressed in exasperating dismissal. 'And I certainly wouldn't have met you.'

It was there in his eyes—raw, pure hunger. The same hunger that had been eating away at her ever since they had met and which now was taking every ounce of her will-power not to acknowledge.

'You could save enough to be able to buy your own garage,' she went on in a huskier voice. 'Put a manager in. Then you could take time off once in a while.'

'You think it's that simple? A steady job? A mortgage on a business and—hey! You're rich! That isn't how it works, Kayla.'

'How do you know if you don't try? Anyway, it was only a suggestion,' she reminded him, noticing how snugly his T-shirt moulded itself to the contours of his chest, the way his whole body seemed to pulse with unimpeded virility. 'You have to have drive and determination too.'

He laughed. 'And in that you think I'm sadly lacking?'

'You said that, not me,' she reminded him sombrely. 'I was only trying to help.'

'For which I'm very grateful,' he said, with that familiar mocking curl to his lips. 'But that sort of help I'm really able to do without.'

'Suit yourself,' she uttered, moving away from the ruin and gasping at the speed with which he leaped up and joined her as she came onto a plain of shorter grasses, interspersed with tall ferns and flowering shrubs.

'And now you're looking and feeling thoroughly chastened,' he remarked laughingly, catching her hand in his while his fervid gaze played with dark intensity over her small fine features, coming to rest on the pouting fullness of her mouth.

'You're very perceptive,' she breathed, hardly able to speak because of the wild responses leaping through her from his dangerous and electrifying nearness. 'And for a man without ambition you certainly believe in getting what you want.'

'You'd better believe it,' he asserted softly.

Even in a whisper his voice conveyed a determination of purpose that none of the self-important types she had known had ever possessed, and it sent little skeins of excitement un-ravelling through Kayla's insides.

'As for my lack of ambition… As I said, you'd be sur-prised. But what might *not* surprise you right now is to know that my most burning ambition is to feel you lying beneath me and to taste those sweet lips again, *agape mou*. To make love to you slowly and thoroughly until you're crying out for my length inside you. And I think at this moment you want the same thing—regardless of how unfulfilled or goalless you think I am.'

She wanted to protest but it would have been pointless, Kayla realised. She was already melting the moment his mouth came down over hers. She responded to it hungrily—greed-ily—her arms going around his neck, pulling him down to her as if she could never have enough.

Their kissing was hot and impassioned—a passion demand-ing only to be fed as, mouths fused, they sank together onto the sun-warmed grass. And Leonidas did as he'd wanted to do since he had arrived at Philomena's house that morning: tugged firmly on the ties of Kayla's blouse.

He gave a sigh of satisfaction when it fell open, revealing the pale lace and satin of her bra.

Slipping a finger inside, he revelled in the warmth of her soft skin before he pulled down the lace, releasing one mod-est-sized breast from its restraining cup.

Small, he measured, moulding the soft pale mound to his work-roughened palm, yet perfectly in proportion to the rest of her and more than satisfyingly sensitive, he realised as he caressed the pale pink areola into burgeoning arousal.

She moaned softly from the excitement of what he was doing to her. She arched her back, aching for his mouth over the swollen nipple, and almost hit the roof when he suddenly dipped his head and granted her wish.

There was no one and nothing around them. Nothing except

the wash of the waves on the beach below them and the wind that was teasing her hair into the finest strands of spun gold, inviting him to touch it, caress it, lose himself in the perfume that was all woman, all her own.

His lips were burning kisses over her breasts, her throat, the tender line of her jaw, finding and capturing her mouth again with the dominant pressure of his.

'Leon…'

She breathed his name into his mouth, saying it as no one had said it in a long, long time. No one called him Leon these days. Only Philomena…

Far away from this idyll, back in London, in Athens and on the corporate world stage, he was known only as Leonidas. Leonidas Vassalio. Hard-headed businessman. Decisive. Practical. Ruthless…

The reminder almost dragged him back to his senses, but not quite.

Her hands had ripped open his shirt, and he gave a deep guttural groan at their caressing warmth over his bared chest, but they were travelling downwards—down and down—in a quest to drive him wild, break his control.

He sucked in his breath, every nerve flexing like tautened wire, until finally, when she touched that most intimate part of him, even through his clothes, he was lost.

He wanted to stop this madness. Come clean about who he was. Because how could he justifiably do this with her if he didn't?

But as if sensing his reticent moment she was begging him not to stop, and her whimpers of need were all it took to bring about his final undoing.

If he told her who he was now he would be inviting her anger, and he couldn't face that, he realised in meagre justification. Couldn't ruin the mood and her artless belief in him no matter how much he knew he should.

It took little effort to remove her shorts, with her lace-edged briefs following them to where he'd cast them aside.

She was beautiful. A natural blonde, he noted with a soft smile of satisfaction as her legs parted before him and she lifted her body in a sobbing invitation for him to claim his prize.

It would be so easy, Leonidas thought, to remove his own clothes and take all that she was offering, assuage the fire that was burning in his groin. Just one thrust could take him to paradise…

He was hotter and harder than he had ever been in his life just from thinking about such damning pleasure, but through the torment of his stimulating thoughts a shred of sanity—of principle—remained.

He couldn't do it. Couldn't abuse her trust like that. Not while he still felt it necessary to deceive her. And yet she was slick with wanting, sobbing her need and her craving for release from this passion he had aroused.

She was lying with her face turned to one side and her arms above her head in a gesture of pure surrender. An angel, he thought, inviting him to share heaven with her. Or Eve, tempting him among the grasses of her sensuous Eden.

With torturous restraint he dipped his head and pressed his lips to the heated satin of her pulsing ribcage, his mouth moving with calculated precision over her slender waist to the flat plane of her abdomen and beyond. Very gently he parted her legs wider and slipped his arms beneath her splayed thighs.

Feeling his mouth against that most intimate part of her drew a shuddering gasp from Kayla. That dark hair brushing the sensitive flesh of her inner thigh was a stimulation she couldn't even have imagined.

It was the most erotic experience of her life. She had been intimate with a man before, but it had never felt like this. This abandoning of herself so completely to a pleasure that promised to drive her wild.

He knew just how to tease and titillate, just where and how to touch, employing his lips and the heat of his tongue to start a fire building in her as he tasted the honeyed sweetness of her body.

She thought she would die from the pleasure of it, and her body tautened in breathless expectation as flames of sensation licked along her nerve-endings and produced a burning tingle along her thighs.

Her juices flowed from her body, mingling with the moistness of his, anointing his roughened jaw with everything she was—until the mind-blowing sensation proved too much and she cried out as the fire consumed her in an orgasm of pulsating, interminable throbs.

Her sensitivity increased until she couldn't take any more pleasure, and she clamped her thighs around him, trapping him there, holding him to her in a sobbing ecstatic agony of release until the last embers of the fire he had ignited finally died away.

After a while, Kayla looked up at him where he lay beside her, propped up on an elbow. 'Why didn't you...?' Crazily, even after the intimacy they had shared she was too embarrassed to say it.

'Why didn't I what?' Leonidas leaned across her, tracing the curve of her cheek before picking a small windblown flower out of her hair. 'Take what I wanted?' he supplied, helping her.

She nodded, closing her eyes against the exquisite tenderness of his touch.

'Because I don't think you're a girl who indulges in casual sex, and you wouldn't have thanked me for it tomorrow.'

'Because you think I'm on the rebound?' Suddenly self-conscious of her nakedness, when he hadn't even undressed beyond his gaping shirt, she sat up to retrieve her clothes. 'I'm not—I promise you,' she said resolutely, wriggling into her panties.

She was well and truly over Craig now. But perhaps there were other reasons for Leon not taking their lovemaking the whole way. Perhaps he was remaining faithful to someone, she thought uneasily. Someone who moved him to anger and roused his passions in a way she might never be able to do...

'Did you bring *her* here?' She couldn't look at him as she started fastening her blouse.

'Who?'

'The woman you won't talk about?' she said grievously.

He laughed—a deep, warm sound on the scented air, mingling with the drone of insects and the mellifluous birdsong. 'You really are a very imaginative little lady.'

'Not as imaginative as you, with your island mansion and your racehorses,' she accused, kneeling up to tug her shorts on.

'Uh-uh,' he denied. 'The racehorses were your idea,' he reminded her with a hint of humour in his eyes, although the slashes of colour across his cheeks were evidence of the passion that still rode him. 'And now I really think it's time that we started back.'

'I'm being serious,' she stressed, wishing he wouldn't continue to evade the issue, wondering if he was only doing it because there really was someone else.

'So am I,' he breathed heavily, getting up and pulling her with him, and this time his determination brooked no resistance.

CHAPTER SEVEN

LOOKING BACK, LEONIDAS wasn't sure how he had managed to stop himself making love to Kayla that afternoon. Heaven knew he had wanted to. A fact not made any easier by the knowledge of how much she had wanted him, too. But there were ethics to be observed, and there was no way that he could have taken all she had been offering when he wasn't being straight with her. It had all boiled down to guilt, he decided shamefully. Guilt because he wasn't telling her the truth.

But the truth was that he had come here to be alone. Not to indulge in any social or sexual entanglements with a girl who could carry him along with her ridiculous yet infectious sense of make-believe. Well, make-believe to *her,* at any rate. Because he could afford that island, had it been for sale—and a dozen like it, did she but know it. But it seemed like a lifetime since he had indulged in that childish game, and he had found it oddly refreshing.

In the world he moved in there was no room for fantasising or dreaming. Only for cold hard facts and figures. Securing deals. That was living the dream. Or so he had thought.

Until now, though, he hadn't begun to realise how deeply and for how long his dreams had been buried. Firstly by his father, and then more recently beneath the weight of his own responsibilities. He had been so busy making money—reaping the benefits of all he had worked for during the past decade or more—that he hadn't taken the time even to question where those dreams had gone. And now this little nobody had come along, making him question his values. He was annoyed with himself for allowing her to get under his skin to such a degree. But that didn't change the fact that he wanted her more than he had wanted any woman in a long time—much less one who would have been in her own marriage bed right now if things had worked out as they should have.

A hard possessiveness kicked in as he imagined her naked with the faceless, double-crossing character who had betrayed her—he could only temper his indignation at the thought of the two of them together by imagining himself in Kayla's bed. And that brought other problems as his body hardened in response to imagining her sobs of pure pleasure directed at him and him alone as he made himself master of her body.

But things couldn't go on as they were. He was either going to have to come clean at some stage, he decided grimly, or end their relationship before it went any further. Neither prospect filled him with any pleasure.

He knew exactly what she thought about company men, and after the experience she had had with that lowest of the low fiancé of hers—not to mention her father—she'd be blameless for thinking he was no better. Yet staying away from her wasn't an option he welcomed either. He was just relieved that his secretary had e-mailed him with some plans that needed his urgent attention, so that for today at least he didn't have to think about how he could come clean with Kayla. However he chose to tell her, he knew she wasn't going to welcome finding out...

When Leon didn't put in an appearance that day, and didn't come down the next morning, Kayla jumped at Philomena's suggestion that she drive up to the farmhouse with some bread Philomena had just baked.

She'd scarcely given a thought to her ex since Leon had taken her over to that island, she realised, noticing how it seemed to shimmer in the morning sun. She couldn't help marvelling at the difference between the two men and wondering what she had ever seen in Craig.

Had her love for him been so shallow that the first man who came along could make her forget him and the hurt he had caused her so completely? But then Leon wasn't just any man, she reminded herself, with a sudden tightening of her breasts and that familiar stirring of heat at the very heart of her femininity. He made her feel like no other man had ever made her feel.

A throbbing excitement leaped along her veins at the memory of their afternoon on that islet, when he had driven her crazy for him, playing with her like a love-toy, winding her up only to let her run wild with delirious sensation as he had taken her to heights her mental and physical being had never scaled before.

She had wanted him so much! And it had been patently obvious that he wanted her. So why hadn't he taken their love-making to its ultimate conclusion? Was it because there was someone else? But he had called her imaginative when she had broached the subject with him, so perhaps it was simply that he didn't think she was ready to embark on a relationship with him—in which case, she decided with a delicious little shiver, it was up to her to show him that she was.

When she arrived at the farmhouse her heart gave a little leap when she saw the truck parked outside.

So he was in! She wondered if she was being too presumptuous in coming. Supposing he didn't want to see her? Or she'd disappointed him in some way?

Feeling queasy in the stomach just from entertaining that possibility, she tripped lightly round to the glass-paned peeling doors at the back of the house. One creaked open at her less than confident knock.

When she called out there was no reply, and so gingerly she moved inside, still calling his name. He wasn't in the sitting room, and nor did he emerge from the kitchen when she moved enquiringly towards it.

Perhaps he'd gone for a walk, she mused, standing there in the hall, wondering what to do.

About to take a look outside, she heard a sudden thud on the boarded floor above. She dumped her carrier bag with the bread she'd brought on an old pine chest just inside the door. 'Leon?' she called out, and when there was still no response, unthinkingly she raced up the stairs.

His bedroom was in shadow, with semi-closed shutters, but a quick glance towards the bed revealed him lying there on his back, still drugged from sleep, groping blindly for something on the floor on the other side of the bed.

Kayla moved over and, picking up a chunky little clock, replaced it on the cabinet beside the bedside lamp.

'Are you all right?' she asked, knowing what an early bird he usually was. It was already after ten and she'd obviously woken him, she realised, guessing he'd reached for the clock and knocked it over when he'd heard her calling him.

'I must have crashed out,' he mumbled, drawing an arm across his forehead. His eyes were heavy with sleep and his hair was dishevelled and, like his unshaven jaw, satanically dark. 'What are you doing here?'

'I brought you some bread. I thought you were out, but the door was open,' Kayla responded with a nervous gesture of her hand. She was aware that she was gabbling, but it was difficult to do anything else when faced with the sight of his bronzed body, naked save for the fine sheet that barely covered his hips and certainly left nothing to the imagination. 'Aren't you pleased to see me?'

'What do you think?' he drawled, in a voice thickened by sleep and by the involuntary response of his anatomy.

Heated colour touched Kayla's cheeks and yet she couldn't keep her gaze from straying to his potent virility. Driven by something more powerful than her own reasoning, she dropped down onto the bed.

'I think you must be overjoyed,' she whispered, touching kisses to the warm, undulating muscles of his chest, using the pale, sensuous fountain of her hair to caress him as her lips moved over the tautened flesh of his tight lean waist and her hands dealt tremblingly with the sheet.

He let out a deep shuddering gasp of anticipation. 'Why did you come?' he asked heavily.

'I just thought that one good turn deserved another,' Kayla whispered, feathering kisses over his tightly muscled abdomen. She didn't know where she was finding the courage to seduce him like this. She only knew by instinct alone that he was a man who liked his women confident and worldly, not wimpish and nursing the old wounds of a previous relationship.

'Close your eyes,' she ordered softly, getting up.

Leonidas's heart seemed to stop, and then thundered into life when she came back to the bed and straddled him. She was wearing a white top with a little red skirt that swirled about her thighs, and his mind whirled in a vortex of conflicting thoughts as he realised that she had obviously removed what she had been wearing underneath.

'Kayla. Stop this…' He wasn't sure whether he'd spoken the words or whether they were just buzzing feverishly through his brain.

'Why? Is it too early for you?' Kayla teased, excitement driving her even as her mind raced with interminable doubts.

Was she carrying things too far? Didn't he like a woman taking the initiative? He was more down to earth and unfettered by convention than any man she had ever met. He didn't want a woman who was anything but what *he* was. Not someone weighed down with emotional baggage; someone who didn't know her own mind.

Beneath her Leonidas shivered as he felt her sliding down his body, the moist heat of her searing his skin like a molten poultice.

'Dear—!' He swallowed the profanity, his breathing laboured, his body on fire. He had to stop this! But as her soft mouth took possession of him his senses spun into chaos.

He had never felt so powerless, and yet at the same time so shamelessly empowered. His body was a temple of pleasure at which this amazing woman was worshipping.

He felt his size increase and harden like burning, quivering steel. His body was taut as a bow, holding back the flaming arrow it needed to release before it consumed him in its raging inferno.

He fought to contain it, the struggle almost overwhelming him. And just when he thought he had won the battle she slid along his length, positioning herself above him to take him into her.

He tried to pull back, but he was powerless to do anything but push against her slick hot wetness, groaning in defeat as he allowed himself the freedom to let her do whatever she would.

Looking down at him, Kayla registered the rapturous agony on his face, that line of pained pleasure between his closed lids. It lent him a vulnerability she hadn't seen before—one that called to everything in her that was soft and feminine and tender—and yet she felt powerful too. She was in control and glorying in it, dominating the pace and the depth and the rhythm. That was until she heard the guttural masculine groan when he suddenly clamped his hands over her hips and pushed harder and more determinedly into her.

The depth of penetration dragged a small cry of ecstasy

from her lips. She felt the explosion of his seed deep within her and started to climax almost instantaneously.

It was the most fulfilling experience of her life.

They were both breathing heavily when she collapsed, wet and gasping, against the warm damp cushion of his chest, and then he was rolling her round so that she was lying pressed close to his side.

'What was all that about?' he quizzed, as soon as he could speak again. His breathing was still heavy and laboured.

Kayla wasn't sure whether there was disapproval in his husky tones. 'Didn't you like it?' she enquired, almost diffidently.

'Of *course* I liked it!' he shot back, his voice incredulous. 'But right now I'm not sure whether to applaud you for your resourcefulness or to paddle that pretty bare bottom of yours and send you packing back to Philomena's.'

'Why?' An uneasy line pleated Kayla's brows as she lay facing him with her hair wildly dishevelled. 'Do Greek men always have to be the dominant partner?' She was beginning to feel hurt and embarrassed.

'No. But whoever chooses to be should take responsibility for what they're doing. Is there any chance that you could be pregnant after that delightful little escapade?'

'Of course not! I'm not that stupid!' she snapped, trying to sit up and failing when he kept her anchored to his side. She didn't feel it was necessary to add that she was taking the pill. She had tried to come off it after her break-up with Craig, but her periods had gone so haywire that her doctor had suggested it might be best for her to keep taking it until her emotions were on a more even keel.

'So what happens now?' Leonidas asked, his breath seeming to shiver through his lungs.

'What do you mean?' Blue eyes searched the midnight-darkness of his for some sign of tenderness—the tenderness that had been stirred in her by seeing him so vulnerable while she had been making love to him—but there was none.

'We've just become lovers and you don't even know who I am.' Something he was going to have to rectify—and as soon as possible, he realised, floundering. It was a feeling that was alien to Leonidas Vassalio.

'Yes, I do. Or as much as I need to,' she murmured, feeling his powerful body tense as she applied a trail of butterfly kisses over the slick warmth of his heavily contoured chest.

'I'm trying to be serious, Kayla.'

'Why?' she breathed against the velvety texture of his skin, delighting in the way his breathing was growing more and more ragged from her kisses.

But as her fingers trailed teasingly along the inside of one powerful thigh his hand suddenly clamped down on hers, resisting the temptation to let it wander.

'Because I don't believe you're the type of girl who does this without knowing what sort of man she's getting herself involved with and without demanding some degree of emotional commitment.'

And he wasn't offering any. She couldn't understand why telling herself that caused her spirits to plummet the way they did.

'I'm not demanding anything,' she uttered, knowing that the only way to save face was to get the hell out of there. 'And I'm sorry if I offended you!'

Scrambling out of bed, managing to shrug off the hand that tried to restrain her, she heard his urgent, 'Kayla! Kayla, come back here!'

She didn't, though. Her wounded pride propelled her into the adjoining bathroom, her mind focussed only on tidying herself up and getting out.

Stung with regret for upsetting her, momentarily Leonidas flopped back against the pillows. He hadn't intended her to take what he had said in the way she had. He had been trying to explain, in a roundabout way, what he should have told her long before, but procrastinating had only made an awkward situation far more difficult. After what had just happened he didn't know how or where to begin. He only knew that he couldn't let it happen again before he told her the truth—and all he'd managed to do was let her believe she'd offended him...

Offended him! He couldn't stop a lazy smile from touching his mouth.

She'd blown his mind, he thought, when she'd woken him up from a deep, deep sleep and dragged him straight into a cauldron of sizzling pleasure. He hadn't had time to catch his breath—let alone think! And he wouldn't have been caught so off-guard, still in bed, if he hadn't been up practically all night trying to get round one last hitch with those amended plans...

The plans!

He shot up in bed just as Kayla was emerging from the bathroom.

He'd left all his paperwork spread out over the kitchen table with his laptop—incriminating evidence of who he was! It had been late, and he'd obviously crashed out on the bed after he'd come up here and showered!

'Kayla, come here!'

The authority in his voice would have stopped a lesser mortal, but she ignored it as she moved around the bed, frowning, tugging at the draping folds of the bedlinen.

'Are you looking for something?' he asked, knowing he had to act quickly.

Kayla made a grab for the red briefs he was holding up, which only succeeded in bringing her across the bed and against his disturbingly masculine body as he withheld them, effectively securing what he wanted.

'You haven't offended me. You were wonderful,' he murmured, his warm breath a delicious sensuality against her hairline. 'Now, come back to bed. I want to talk to you,' he said, and just as an incentive slipped his hand under the tantalising little skirt and let his fingers play along the outer curve of one taut, silky buttock.

Kayla groaned, weakening beneath his mind-boggling powers of persuasion. She felt vulnerable and incredibly sexy with no panties on, but she despaired at herself too, at how easily and effortlessly he could bend her to his will.

Whatever he had to say, she had the strongest suspicion that she wasn't going to like it. He didn't want commitment. Of course he didn't. And anyway she wasn't ready for another serious relationship yet. Yet neither was she ready to let him have it all his own way.

Catching him in an unguarded moment, reaching round to adjust the pillows behind them, she managed to wriggle out of his arms and snatch her underwear from his grasp, saying, 'I can talk better over a cup of coffee,' as she ran giggling out of the room.

'Kayla, come here!'

She was in the hall, pulling her panties back on, when he raced down the stairs, still fastening his robe, but darted off again laughingly as soon as she saw him coming.

'Will you just stand still and let me talk to you?' he called after her as she grabbed the carrier bag she'd left on the chest and headed for the kitchen. He had to break it to her gently. She'd be angry, it was true, but not as angry as she would be finding it out for herself.

'Go and sit down,' he commanded softly when she turned around. He was pointing to the sitting room. 'I will make the coffee.'

'Fine,' she agreed airily, pivoting away again, 'but I'll keep you company while you're doing it.'

'In the sitting room,' he breathed, in one last attempt to prevent her from seeing all his papers.

She turned in the kitchen doorway, her chin lifting in playful challenge. 'And since when did you suddenly start issuing so many orders?'

'Since I thought you were running out on me without finishing what you started.' One purposeful stride brought him over to her, his mouth a sensuous curve. But inside he was a heaving mass of turmoil.

He had to keep her out of the kitchen—stop her going in there before he had a chance to explain. He cast a surreptitious glance over her shoulder at the table in the centre of the room, heaving with incriminating evidence. He should have told her before. Should have kept her in bed…

'Kayla…'

The way he spoke her name never failed to turn Kayla's bones to jelly.

'Say it again,' she murmured huskily.

'What?' He looked tense, she thought, and mystified too.

'The way you say my name.'

'Kay-lah.'

She groaned her satisfaction and nestled against his chest above the gaping V of his dark satin robe. His skin smelled of the lingering traces of shower gel overlaid with a sensual musk.

'It should be censored—or at least X-rated,' she purred, with her tongue coming out in a provocative caress of that bared skin. It felt silky and tasted slightly salty…

Dear heaven!

Leonidas dragged in a breath, at a loss for the words he needed to say. He didn't know what powers this girl used to bewitch him, but even as he struggled to engage his normally incisive brain his body was responding with an urgent message of its own. It was taking all the mental strength he possessed not to rip down her panties, lay her down right here on the marble floor and enjoy the pleasure of having her beneath him, with himself in the driving seat this time. But he *had* to get her out of this room!

Swiftly his mouth swooped down over hers in a bid to distract her enough to manoeuvre her back into the hall. But he hadn't reckoned on how distracting her soft mouth would be to him.

Feeling her warm body against his, he could only respond to it in a kiss that went on and on, until they both came up for air and her head dropped back against his shoulder.

A few moments later, lifting her head, she murmured, 'What is that?'

Leonidas's spine pulled into a tight, tense rod. All he had succeeded in doing was turning her round, so that their positions were reversed, and she was now looking at the plans he'd set up on an easel. Allowing her to pull out of his arms, he felt the slaying blow of defeat.

Stepping down into the kitchen and dumping the bread bag on the table, bewildered, Kayla couldn't take it in. There were papers. Lots of papers. A laptop and a memo pad. And what she had thought were sketches looked like some sort of plan...

'What is it?' Her eyes skittered from the easel to the table and then the briefcase standing open on the floor. 'Is it something you're working on? Some building work...?'

Leonidas took a step towards her. 'Kayla, I can explain.'

'Explain?' She looked at him with confusion in her questioning blue eyes. 'Explain what?'

What was he doing with what looked like a whole set of plans for some development scheme? And a big, *big* development scheme by the look of it, she realised, when her gaze swept back over the table. Something proposed by the Vassalio Group—a big, *big* developer. She knew that much as her eyes took in the recognisable black and gold logo at the top of the plan she was staring at.

'I don't understand…' Why had his cosy farmhouse kitchen taken on the look of some executive's pad? Why was he looking so serious?

At that moment his cell phone rang from somewhere, shrilling across the sudden pregnant silence.

He pulled it out of the pocket of his robe, his eyes never leaving hers as he intoned incisively, 'Vassalio.' And then the penny dropped.

It was like an unashamed declaration directed specifically at her, Kayla thought, realising she had started to tremble.

Vassalio. Leon. Leonidas Vassalio. She knew the name. Of course she did! She'd heard it often enough in the media, seen the company logo on billboards and advertising for commercial developments, but she'd never taken much notice of it until now.

'You lied to me,' she accused in a virtual whisper when he cut the call short, feeling so shocked and betrayed that it was almost painful to breathe. 'You've lied to me ever since I got here!'

'Misled,' he corrected as he dropped his phone back into his pocket.

As if it made a difference!

'Most of it was what you assumed.'

'Hah! Like I assumed I knew who you were when we were doing what we were doing just now?'

Leonidas Vassalio. The man she had just taken advantage of—and who had let her!

'How could you do it?' She was referring to the sex, shame creeping over her, scorching her already flushed cheeks. What a laugh he must have been having—and at her expense!

'You didn't give me much choice,' he reminded her dryly.

'You could have stopped me any time you wanted to!'

'Really?' A sceptical eyebrow arched sharply. 'You think I'm that superhuman?' His mouth twisted in hard self-derision. 'Show me any red-blooded man you think would be capable of resisting being dragged out of sleep by a sex-goddess with no panties on.'

He made her feel cheap, and she wished fervently that she could turn back the clock instead of just standing there, hating herself for feeling the burn of desire stir deep down inside her where she was still moist and slightly tender from their spontaneous and unrestrained coming together.

'If it makes you feel any better,' he said, running fingers through his long dishevelled hair, 'I didn't intend for things to go as far as they did.'

'Oh, really?' she shot back, her features distorted with self-disgust. 'What a bonus it must have been for you when they did!'

'It wasn't like that.' He sounded defensive, exasperated—angry, almost. 'Why the hell do you think I didn't take things to their natural conclusion the other day on that island?'

'Because it was more fun stringing me along.'

'That isn't true.'

'Isn't it? And what about just now? You wouldn't have thought twice about doing it again.'

'That wasn't my motive,' he stated decisively. 'I was trying to coax you into the sitting room so that I could break it to you gently who I am without it flaring up into the mess we find ourselves in now.'

'You mean instead of me finding out for myself what a rotten lying cheat you really are?'

'If that's what you want to believe,' he rasped, grim-mouthed. 'But it was never my intention to deceive you.'

'Why?' It was a small cry from somewhere deep down inside of her. 'Why should I believe anything you say?'

'All right. I deserve that,' he accepted with no loss of dignity. He clearly wasn't a man to grovel or to eat humble pie. 'Look, I apologise for not telling you before now,' he continued. 'But I didn't know who you were when you first arrived. For all I knew you were a snooping journalist on a mission for a story, and I came here for some privacy. To get away from all the media attention and publicity that's been dogging me over this past year. I wasn't going to risk losing all that for a girl I didn't even know. Apart from which, I found it rather refreshing being with someone who wasn't playing up to me because of the size of my bank balance.'

'So you used me!' Kayla breathed. 'Just for your own amusement.'

'That isn't what I'm saying. But if you want to think that, then there's nothing I can do to stop you.'

'You could have trusted me enough to tell me the truth!'

He made a self-deprecating sound down his nostrils. 'A man in my position can't afford to trust.'

'Which just goes to show the type of people you mix with,' she tossed back, refusing to give any quarter. He had lied to her. Deceived her. And, though it was killing her to acknowledge it, that made him no better than Craig.

'I can't argue with that,' Leonidas conceded. 'But I don't suppose it would make any difference to tell you that you don't fall into their category.'

'You mean because none of the others have been such a push-over as I've been?' Near to tears, it came out almost on a sob, but there was no way in a million years that she was going to let him see that. Forcing aggression into her voice, she uttered, 'A builder. Hah! You must have been laughing up your exclusive designer sleeve!'

Ignoring that last remark, he said, 'That was your interpretation when I said I was in construction—which, as you can see...' he gestured to the plans on the easel, the others on the table '...I *am*.'

'And you let me think it! That's worse than lying! That's…'

'Kayla, stop it!' He made a calming gesture with his hands. 'I can understand how you must feel.'

'Can you?' Her eyes were dark and tortured, and her mouth was twisted in wounded accusation. No wonder he'd got nasty about her taking photographs of him in the beginning!

'I've said I'm sorry, haven't I?'

'And you think that makes it all right? An apology from the great Leonidas Vassalio!' Her bitter little laugh made him visibly wince.

'No, it doesn't make it all right.' Beneath the robe his tanned chest fell in hopeless frustration. He hadn't intended it to sound as dismissive as it had come out. 'I was constantly aware that I was going to have to tell you sooner or later.'

'Oh, really?' Kayla shot him a look of pure incredulity. 'Like when, exactly? After we'd had sex again?'

'Kayla, stop it!' He was moving towards her, but she backed away.

'So how did you imagine I'd respond?' She'd come up against a chair, the one where she'd sat that morning after he'd rescued her from the villa, but she didn't want to think about that now. 'By being grateful to you?'

'Which is exactly why I've never said anything,' Leonidas admitted raggedly.

'Because it would have spoilt your fun!'

'Because I didn't want to hurt you.'

'Oh, you wouldn't have hurt me, Leon!' Hadn't she been hardened by Craig? And before that her father? she reflected bitterly, before tagging on with painful cynicism, 'I'm sorry. *Is* it Leon? Or should that be Leonidas now?'

The emphatic distaste she placed on the name everyone knew him by made him flinch. But he couldn't blame her, he thought. He had misled her, and then been stupid enough to imagine he might be let off lightly when he came clean and admitted it. But she had been hurt too deeply before and he should have known better, he realised. It was crass of him to have thought she would be anything but angry and bitter, especially after finding out in the way she had.

'You wouldn't have hurt me, Leonidas,' she reiterated, in an attempt to ease the pain of another betrayal—and by a man she had believed was different from men like Craig and her father and all the others. A construction worker who'd come here to fish and sketch and live rough for a while because he valued his solitude and his privacy. Except all the time she'd been naïve enough to imagine he'd been sketching he'd been controlling his multi-billion-pound empire! 'I just wouldn't have touched you with a bargepole.'

But she had, she thought bitterly, remembering just how eagerly she had touched him—with her mouth and her hands and her whole reckless and stupidly trusting body. Tears stung her eyes as she thanked her lucky stars that she hadn't quite succeeded in giving him her heart as well.

'Kayla...' He made another move towards her, but she backed away again, knocking the chair into the table this time and pushing some of his papers askew. 'I'm still the same person I was when you were driving me wild for you upstairs.'

'No, you're not! You're as bad as every other *company man*—' she breathed it with venom '—I've ever met. Only worse. Because you've arrived! And to think I was trying to suggest things you could do to make life better for yourself!' She couldn't believe she could have been so stupid. Such an unbelievable fool!

'Which I found very endearing,' he added earnestly.

'Don't touch me!' She made a small panicked sound as he took another step towards her, the thought of what his lips and hands could do to her exciting her in a way that made her feel sick with herself. 'You know exactly what I think about men like you!'

'Then we've both been misguided,' he concluded, his shoulders drooping, suddenly seeming to give up trying to placate her. 'You for taking everything at face value, and I for imagining I could get away with letting you. I just wanted to believe that for a while at least my name and my money weren't the most important things about me.'

There was something in his voice that had her silently querying the inscrutable emotion in that strong, rugged face. 'Is that supposed to make me feel bad?' she challenged. 'Because it doesn't.'

'No. I've already told you,' he persisted. 'It wasn't my intention to hurt you, or to let things go as far as they did.'

'And what about Philomena?' Her gaze had fallen to the bag with the loaf the woman had lovingly baked for him. 'Does *she* know?' she threw at him, hurting, remembering how eagerly she had driven up here to see him, with nothing but making him want her on her mind. 'Does she know what a fool you've been taking me for? Or didn't you risk telling her?'

Thick black lashes came down over his incredibly dark eyes. 'I've never taken you for a fool,' he stated, exhaling deeply. 'As for Philomena…she knows I had my reasons.'

'And she went along with them?' She couldn't believe that of the gentle yet down-to-earth Philomena.

'What do you think?' he said.

She remembered the argument that had ensued the day he'd first taken her down to the cottage, the remonstrations by Philomena since, which seemed to leave him no more than mildly amused.

'You're despicable,' she breathed, as a fragment of memory tugged at her consciousness in relation to something he had said about having had a trying year.

Unscrupulous. Ruthless. Riding roughshod over people. Those were words she had heard in connection with the name Leonidas Vassalio. And then she remembered. It was that stunning American model turned actress—Esmeralda Leigh. She'd publicly named him as having fathered her child. It was she who had called him unscrupulous, when he had challenged the proof of his paternity—though there had been no close-up photograph of him in the article Kayla remembered reading. Just a long shot of him leaving his office, looking rather different from how he looked now, which had been inset in a full-colour spread of Esmeralda lounging in the drawing room of her exquisitely and expensively furnished Mayfair home.

'Esmeralda was right. You *are* unscrupulous!'

'And if you had read the outcome of that fiasco you would have the sense to realise that anything the woman says is fabricated. Her claims were proven to be totally untrue.'

'Well, she wasn't the only one who was good at lying, was she?' Kayla reminded him grievously, realising now what he'd meant that day when he'd referred to a petition being slapped on him. 'Was it because of her that you decided to get your own back when you met me? Were you afraid if I knew who you were I might try and get pregnant so I could use you as a ticket to an easy life? Well, stuff your money! And stuff *you!* Not everyone puts as much value on money as on truth and integrity! I might not be in your league when it comes to material wealth, but at least I can hold my head up and know that what you see is what you get. That everything about me is real. You wouldn't understand that if it was scrawled all over one of your concrete eyesores, and as far as I'm concerned, Mr Vassalio, I never want to see you again!'

CHAPTER EIGHT

'I HAD HOPED your time in Greece would make you feel better,' remarked Yasmin Young, an abrupt and artificially blonde forty-five-year-old to Kayla, who had just come downstairs and declined her mother's offer to cook her breakfast. 'But ever since you've been back you haven't eaten properly. You're too thin. And you've been going around like someone who's lost a shilling and found sixpence. I was right when I said you were unwise, cutting your holiday short like that. I've told you before,' she reiterated, going over what seemed to Kayla like a mantra from her mother these days. 'He isn't worth wasting any more time over, you know. None of them are.'

She was talking about Craig. Kayla hadn't told her mother anything about meeting anyone while she had been away. But the maternal advice applied equally to how she was feeling about Leonidas—and had been ever since she'd returned to the UK on that wet and windy mid-May morning, hurting and feeling so gullible and betrayed. And all because she had been stupid enough to get herself emotionally involved with a man right out of the same mould as Craig, her father and all the others. Because she *had*, Kayla thought, berating herself—even if she had only realised it when it was too late.

'I know,' she responded now, even managing to feign a smile as she poured herself a hasty cup of coffee. She shook her head at her mother's concerned suggestion that she should at least try and eat some toast.

'I'd better go or I'll be late,' she said, rushing out of the door without bothering to finish her coffee.

At least she wasn't out of work and dependent upon her mother to help support her, she thought in an attempt to brighten herself up as she sat in heavy traffic on her way to work. At least she still had a job. And it promised to be a potentially permanent one if Josh and Lorna managed to land the huge contract they had been hoping to secure for the past few weeks.

It would be the break they needed and they were both beside themselves with excitement—particularly as their potential client was Havens Exclusive, a company that provided luxury homes and apartments for the higher end of the market. Kayla was keeping her fingers crossed for them both.

Without her having to worry about things like whether Kendon Interiors would still be trading this time next year, Lorna might have a chance with her pregnancy this time, she thought, hoping fervently that her friend would be able to carry this baby to full term. And being busy again could only be good for *her* too, Kayla decided, because apart from the satisfaction of being able to stay in a job she enjoyed, it helped keep her mind off Leonidas.

She hadn't heard from him since that morning she had stormed out of the farmhouse. Not that she'd wanted to, or even imagined that she would. He didn't know where to find her, for a start.

She'd wasted no time in leaving the island after driving back to Philomena's that last morning, having discovered that there was a ferry leaving that day.

'Leon…he good man,' Philomena, having guessed what had happened, had tried to tell her gently. He could act stupidly sometimes. Like most men! At least that was what the woman had seemed to be saying with her gestures and a world-weary rolling of her eyes.

Well, he hadn't shown any evidence of his virtuous qualities with *her!* Kayla seethed, still hurting from the way he had deceived her, even though it was more than six weeks on. She tried not to think about how he had rescued her that night in the storm and helped her with the clean-up operation the following day. Nor did she want to think about the affection he'd shown towards Philomena. Remembering just filled her with longing, and with such an aching regret that things couldn't have been different that at times it almost took her breath away. He was a rat when all was said and done. She didn't need him or want him! And she certainly never intended to be so taken in by anyone again! So why did she spend every waking moment trying not to think about him? Why did the thought of never seeing him again leave her feeling so down and depressed?

Fortunately the buzz around the office kept any further disturbing introspection at bay, since one of Havens' senior management team was coming in to meet with Josh and Lorna the following day.

'They've already been through our history and our previous trading figures, and now I think they just want to give us the once-over,' Lorna remarked anxiously. Her mid-length bobbed hair was coming out of the clips she had tried to fasten it with as she despaired of her devoted but untidy husband's muddle of an office. Like Kayla, she was blonde and petite—apart from her burgeoning middle—which was why they had often been taken for sisters, Kayla reflected fondly, knowing she couldn't have cared more for Lorna if she *had* been her sibling.

Consequently, having worked late to help tidy up Josh's office and prepare the conference room for what they hoped would be the final meeting, Kayla was getting ready to go home when the telephone rang in her office.

'Hello, Kayla.'

She almost froze, recognising Leonidas Vassalio's deeply accented voice at the other end of the line.

'How did you find me?' Stupid question. A man with his money and influence would have ways and means, she realised, her pulses leaping. Or had she told him where she worked? She couldn't even think clearly enough to remember.

'How have you been?'

She didn't answer but, aware that Josh and Lorna were still around somewhere in the building, moved over and closed the door. She'd been too hurt and ashamed of herself even to tell them that she had met someone in Greece, and she didn't want them finding out about it now.

'What do you want?'

'I'd like to see you.'

'Why?' she asked, breathless from the dark and sick responses suddenly surging through her.

'I would have thought that was obvious after the way you ran out on me that day,' he remarked dryly. 'So suddenly. Without a word.'

'What did you expect me to do?' she asked pithily, in spite of the way her heart was thudding. 'Stick around so you could make an even bigger fool of me?'

'It was never my intention to make a fool of you.' His voice had dropped a semi-tone to become almost caressing, reminding her of how treacherously it had excited her when she'd been deceived into believing he was someone else.

'No?' It came out sounding more wounded than she'd intended. 'I'd like to know what you'd have done if you'd really been trying.'

'Yes, well…'

His words tailed away on a heavily drawn breath while

Kayla pictured him, wherever he was, his hair wild and untamed, looking as casual as he sounded in his automatic assumption that she would even consider seeing him again.

'I know you're still angry....'

'Whatever gave you that idea?' It came out on a shrill little laugh.

'Have dinner with me,' he suggested, amazing Kayla with his unerring confidence.

Even so, her heart leaped traitorously in response.

'Why?'

In the moment's silence that followed she imagined a masculine eyebrow tweaking at her challenging response.

With more composure than she was managing to retain, he answered, 'Because we have things to discuss.'

'Oh, really? Like what?' She could hear Lorna and Josh still working in the conference room above—moving chairs, closing windows for the night—as she pushed her loose hair behind an ear with a shaky hand. 'Like why you made a complete idiot out of me in Greece? Like why you pretended to be somebody you weren't when I was in trouble and needed help? And why you kept pretending even when I was taken in by you and offered you suggestions of what you could do with your life to improve your lot? Or is it the other thing you want to apologise for? For having sex with me when you were lying through your teeth and thinking I'd simply forgive you if I found out? Because *you're* the idiot if you think I'd go anywhere and discuss anything with you after what you did.'

'And that's all you have to say?' His voice was toneless now, devoid of any emotion.

'Why? Do you really want to hear some more?' She could feel the bite of tears behind her eyes but she willed them back. She couldn't cry. Couldn't let him hear how brutally he had hurt her and make an even bigger fool of herself into the bargain. 'Because there's a whole barrelful where that came from!' Resentment defended her from the pain he had inflicted upon her, the hurt to her pride, her trust and her emotions.

'I think I get the message,' he rasped under his breath. 'As the saying goes, see you around.'

He had rung off before she could even regain her wits.

Kayla was at the office early the following morning, to prepare the conference room for the important meeting. She had slept very little for thinking about Leonidas, but she hid her tiredness behind a bright façade as she put out pens and paper, tumblers and a jug of water, arranged fresh flowers for the centre of the long table and generally helped Lorna to stay calm.

Her friend was flitting around in a state of anxious excitement. Worried for her, Kayla insisted that she sat down and took a few deep breaths before the man from Havens arrived.

'Supposing after all this they don't think we're solid enough and change their mind about giving us their business?' Lorna said worriedly. 'Or they think we don't have enough expertise and decide to go with a company that's bigger and better?'

'Bigger, maybe—but not better,' Kayla assured her, meaning it. 'Anyway, you said yourself the contract's as good as in the bag. This meeting's only a formality, so stop worrying,' she advised gently. But secretly she *was* concerned.

Lorna was nearly six months pregnant now, and Kayla knew how much this coming baby meant to her and Josh. Lorna had to stay free from stress if this pregnancy wasn't to end in the same traumatic way as her previous two pregnancies had, and getting overwrought about anything was bad news.

Havens had said that they might require some extra financial information, and Kayla was pleased, therefore, that as their bookkeeper she had been asked to attend the meeting. It would help take the pressure off Lorna.

'You'll also serve as our charm offensive,' Josh had joked. Consequently, when he rang down to her office at ten o'clock sharp and asked her to join them, Kayla slipped her charcoal-grey tailored suit jacket on over her sleeveless blue blouse and, checking the French pleat she'd carefully styled her hair in that morning, took the lift to the first floor, prepared to charm the Havens man for all she was worth.

'Come in, Kayla.' A quiet-voiced Josh—mousy beard neatly trimmed and looking unusually smart today in a jacket and tie—was standing at the top of the table. Lorna was sitting on his right. But it was the man who had been sitting opposite her and was now getting to his feet that made Kayla feel she'd suddenly been gripped by some hideous hallucination. Until Josh said, 'Kayla, this is Mr Vassalio. Mr Vassalio, this is our invaluable bookkeeper, Kayla Young.'

She wasn't sure how she managed to walk around the table to take the hand Leonidas was holding out to her. She felt stiff-backed and winded, and in the four-inch heels she hadn't given a second thought to wearing that morning, suddenly in danger of over-balancing.

'Miss Young.'

She didn't know what automatic response gave her the emotional strength to take his hand in the outward appearance of a formal handshake, or whether he could feel the way her fingers were trembling as he held them in his warm palm a fraction of a second too long.

'Mr Vassalio.' It came out as a croak from between lips that felt as dry as kindling, while flames seemed to be leaping through her blood—not just from the shock of his being there, but from his devastating appearance too.

Since she had last seen him he seemed to have changed his whole persona. The designer stubble was gone, as was the long, unruly hair. Now expertly cut, the jet-black layers waved thickly against a pristine white collar, although the mid-grey suit he wore, with its fine tailoring, could do nothing to tame the restless animal energy of the man beneath.

Clean-shaven, he looked harder—and even more dynamic, if that were possible. The evidence of the high-octane lifestyle he had disguised so well on the island was emblazoned on every hand-sewn stitch of his designer clothes. She had often thought him totally out of place in the run-down environs of the farmhouse. Today he was exactly where he belonged. Here, in the halls of business, he cut a figure of formidable power in his dress, his manner, and in the overwhelming authority he exuded.

Kayla couldn't think, paralysed by the dark penetration of his gaze and the mockery touching his stupendous mouth. When she did eventually manage to drag her gaze from his it was with a confused look at Josh, and she blurted out the first thing that came into her head.

'Not Mr Woods…?'

It was the wrong thing to say, and she realised it when she saw the dismayed look on Lorna's tense and nervous features. But it was with a Mr Woods that the appointment had been made.

'Woods couldn't make it.'

Leonidas's response drifted down to Kayla as though through a thick fog. She was hot and perspiring. Her clothes, so fresh and cool only minutes before, now seemed to be sticking to her.

'Mr Vassalio's the main man. Havens Exclusive is one of the companies within his group. He wanted to see us for himself,' Lorna told her. 'Isn't that right, Mr Vassalio?'

'Leonidas, please.' The smile he gave Lorna could have melted a polar ice-cap, and Kayla saw her friend visibly relax.

'Leonidas.' Smiling up into the perfect symmetry of his dark masculine features, Lorna repeated the name as if it was some sort of coveted trophy. She was positively glowing in the man's effortless charm, Kayla realised, wondering what her friend would say if she told her what a cheat he was. What a liar!

'Perhaps Miss Young would sit here…' he was already pulling out the chair beside his '…and fill me in on anything I might need to know.'

It was all purely a formality. Like his handshake, Kayla thought with a little shiver. She knew he would already have had Havens suss out their financial credibility and their ability to meet their commitments before he'd let one of his companies consider investing a penny.

But was this just a bizarre coincidence? Or had he specifically arranged for Havens to take advantage of Josh and Lorna's expertise, armed with the knowledge that she, Kayla, worked at Kendon Interiors? Had he known when he'd telephoned her last night that he'd be coming here today? If so, why hadn't he said so? Or had his intention been to give her the shock of her life? To get his own back for refusing to have dinner with him? Because if it had, he had succeeded. And how!

She couldn't stop her eyes from straying to him as he began talking business with Josh and Lorna. She couldn't help noticing how richly his hair gleamed in the light of the window behind him. Nor could she keep her ears from tuning in to the resonant tones of his voice, any more than she could stop the subtle spice of his aftershave lotion acting on her nostrils like some exotic aphrodisiac.

His hands were a magnet for her guarded yet brooding gaze—long, tapered hands that had made her cry out with their tender and manipulative skill. The dark silky hairs that peeped out from under an immaculate shirt cuff were an all too painful reminder of his dark and dangerous virility.

He had been stupendous before. Now he was no less than sensational! A man who would turn heads with his dynamism and that air of unspoken authority. A man who was wealthy

and ruthless and powerful. She'd known that before she'd left
the island. But this man she didn't know at all.

Seeing him in full corporate action, power-dressed and
dominating everyone else in the room, she couldn't believe
that this was the man she had taken the initiative with and
pleasured so uninhibitedly that last morning, and it left her
feeling as mortified as if she had tied him up first and chained
him to the bed.

Except that this man could never be chained or domi-
nated...

Heat suffusing her body, she looked up and met his eyes
just as he was finishing saying something to Josh about the FT
Index. From the smouldering burn of his gaze as it dropped
to her fine blouse she knew he had guessed what she was remembering, and from the discreet curve of his mouth she
knew, with shaming certainty, that he was remembering it too.

She was glad when the meeting was over, the terms of the
contract finalised, and he was preparing to leave. Being polite and courteous for Josh and Lorna's sakes was beginning
to tell on her nerves.

At least he would go now, she thought. And hopefully after
today, after he gave Havens the go-ahead to start the process
for the contract rolling, she would never have to see him again.
She didn't know why that prospect failed to satisfy her as it
should. In fact it left her surprisingly down-spirited.

She just wanted to get back to her office. Get stuck into
spreadsheets and invoices and try to forget that Leonidas Vassalio had ever existed.

He was talking to Lorna about the baby, asking her when it
was due. Seeing she was no longer needed, Kayla seized the
opportunity to excuse herself, and was heading for the door
when she heard deep Greek tones request, 'Could I presume
upon you, Josh, to spare your Miss Young for a little while

longer? There are one or two things I need to run through with her, if she'll be good enough to walk with me back to my car.'

Go to hell! Kayla wanted to toss back as she pivoted round. But of course she had to be on her best behaviour for her friends' sake. There was no way she was going to let them down.

'Take all the time you need,' she heard Josh saying amiably, unaware of the conflict going on inside her.

Leonidas was holding the door wide for her, his arm outstretched so that she had to duck underneath it, and her startling response to his raw and overpowering masculinity made her voice falter even as she sniped in a hostile whisper, 'Does everybody *always* jump over themselves to please you?' She was breathing shallowly, trying to shrug off her involuntary reaction to him, how the heady, tantalising scent of him affected her.

'Not everybody.' Amusement laced his tones, but there was something about the look he gave her which excited her even as she rebelled against the way it seemed to promise, *but you will.*

'Why didn't you tell me yesterday?' she remonstrated as soon as they were in the corridor of the modern office unit, keeping her attention on a large potted fern that was benefiting from the light from the wide windows.

'Tell you what?'

As if he didn't know!

'That you were coming here today.' She was acutely aware of him walking beside her.

'You didn't give me the chance.'

'Really?' Her head swivelled round from the view across the landscaped business park. 'I don't seem to recall you trying to bring it into the conversation.'

'For what other reason were you imagining I wanted to take you to dinner?'

Colour burned her cheeks at the hard edge to his voice. He was an executive now, Kendon Interiors' biggest client—or would be when that contract was signed—and with that remark he was reminding her of it in no uncertain terms.

'Then you should have made your motives more obvious.'

'Like you're doing now, in bringing me along here instead of using the lift?'

'I always prefer to use the stairs.'

'As you did on your way up?'

Of course, Kayla thought, realising that she had walked right into that one. She should have known that his keen brain would have been attuned to every sound that had heralded her approach. He would have heard the ping of the lift and the door gliding open only seconds before she had come into the room.

'What's wrong, Miss Young?' His deliberate use of her surname seemed mockingly incongruous with the electricity that was crackling between them. Even the light click of her heels against the comparatively sturdy tap of his over the polished floor seemed to stress the glaring differences in their sexualities. 'Don't you want to chance the two of us being alone together in a lift?'

Kayla's heart seemed to stop when he opened the glass fire door onto the next level and her jacket brushed his sleeve as he let her through.

'Why are you flattering yourself that I'd let that bother me?'

'Because if you could read my mind, Miss Young, you'd know that I have the strongest urge right now to rip that prim little suit off your body, followed by your blouse and then your—'

'Do you mind?' Her heels clicked more agitatedly at all he was suggesting as they came down onto the ground floor. From behind her desk the young receptionist smiled at them as they passed, her eyes feasting appreciatively on Leonidas.

'Modesty, Miss Young?' Though his mouth was twitching

at the corners, he kept his eyes on the external glass doors, which slid open to admit them into the morning sunshine. 'I hadn't noticed any of that when you were bouncing up and down on my bed.'

'Stop it!'

'Why? Can you dismiss it that easily?' he tossed at her, sounding more impatient now. 'Because I can't. Or are you saying you've forgotten just how much pleasure we gave each other?'

'I thought there was something you particularly wanted to discuss with me?' she parried huskily as her memory banks seemed to burst with erotic images of their time together before she'd found out who he was, that he had lied. 'If there isn't, then I'll get back to my office. I do have things to do, you know.'

'So do I.' His words came out on a harsh whisper.

They had reached his car: a sleek dark monster of a thing that put every other vehicle in the car park into the shade. This statement of his wealth and importance was something Kayla should have expected. Nevertheless, it still managed to knock her metaphorically sideways.

Stupidly, when he had phoned her last night, she had half envisaged him calling from his truck. But the truck belonged to Leon. Leon the drifter, who chopped logs and caught his own lunch and made sketches of her on a whim like some carefree, exciting bohemian. Or pretended to, she remembered, hurting. But this piece of expensive machinery belonged to Leonidas, Chief Executive of the Vassalio Group. International tycoon. The grandest player in the company man's arena.

'You look pale,' he commented in a surprisingly soft voice, his eyes tugging over features she knew looked sallow beneath her tan, taking in the dark smudges under her eyes. 'And thinner. Have you been overworking?'

'Not particularly,' she answered, and felt his dark scrutiny reawakening every aching hormone in her body. *I've just been lying awake at night, wondering how I'm ever going to forget you!*

His gaze had dropped to her middle and a cleft appeared between his eyes. 'You aren't…?' His meaning was obvious.

'Pregnant?' Kayla quipped curtly.

A furore of emotions seemed to cross his strong features and for one crazy moment she wished she could tell him that she was. Not because she wanted his baby. Or did she? The thought came like a bolt out of the blue. Surely she couldn't…?

She pushed the notion aside, refusing even to go there.

No. She would have just liked to see him rocked off his axis. Taken down a few degrees from his arrogant assumption that he could come here and—what? Take up from where they had left off? But she couldn't lie, couldn't deceive or hurt anyone the way he had deceived and hurt her.

'No, I'm not. Foolish though you might have thought me, I wasn't *that* foolish. Or mercenary,' she tagged on after a moment, thinking of the adverse publicity he had been subjected to by the famous Esmeralda. And to what end? To try and hang on to a man she couldn't bear to let go?

Was that relief in those spectacular eyes of his? She couldn't be sure. Nor could she understand why she felt such a bone-deep emptiness inside as she watched him open the passenger door of the car with one inconsequential movement of the remote control mechanism.

'Get in,' he commanded softly.

'No.' She was trembling from his nearness and everything his determination implied. But he was standing between her and the door he had just opened, and with the car in the next bay effectively blocking her route she couldn't escape without causing a scene.

'I said get in,' he rasped. 'Or, so help me, I'll start ripping off those clothes of yours here and now and make love to you in front of this whole blasted building! So what is it to be, Miss Young?'

She wanted to call his bluff. To resist getting into his car and falling victim to her own weakness for him, which would leave her hating herself for letting him use her as Craig had used her, for continuing to let him take her for a fool. She had a worrying suspicion, though, that if she did he would be quite capable of carrying out his threat. And so, reluctantly, with her heart beating wildly, she complied.

CHAPTER NINE

As LEONIDAS GOT in and started the car Kayla's nerves were stretched to breaking point.

Where was he taking her? As he put the car in motion she was so dangerously drawn to his dark magnetic presence that she didn't know how she would respond if he intended to do all he had threatened.

There were trees and bushes throughout the business park, separating units identical to the one that Kendon Interiors occupied. Kayla shot an anxiously challenging look at Leonidas as he brought the car around the trees to the last unit, which was still unoccupied, and cut the engine, leaving her tense and rigid at their screaming privacy.

'Tell me this is just some bizarre coincidence,' she implored him, her voice shaking. 'Your coming here today.'

'If you're asking if your friends approached my company with their business, then I'd like to say yes. But as it was my not being entirely honest with you that created a situation where I've had to virtually kidnap you to get you to talk to me, then I have to tell you that we brought our business to them. When you unintentionally made me aware of what Kendon Interiors were about it interested me, and I wanted to find out more. The company whose custom they lost because of the economic downturn are an old established company and well-known to me, and I knew they wouldn't have been dealing with your friends' business if what they had to offer wasn't a cut above the average in their field. Havens needed a new design company, and having had Kendon Interiors vetted over the past few weeks I liked what I saw and recommended them to my directors at Havens.'

'And you knew I'd still be working for them, of course?'

'With what amounted to a virtual rescue package in the shape of a potential and very valuable client on the table, your redundancy seemed pretty unlikely,' he drawled.

So he *had* been listening to her that day on that beach when he'd seemed preoccupied with what he had been scribbling in his notebook—and had acted on it! Nothing would escape this man.

'So you used what I told you about Josh and Lorna's difficulties and deliberately set out to get them on your books just so you could get to me? That's stalking!' she accused heatedly.

'I prefer to call it a good corporate move,' he corrected. 'And while you drove me nearly insane in the bedroom, Kayla, I think you should be aware right here and now that I never let passion of any kind rule my head. Do you really think I'd let a company of mine waste money on a product they didn't need? A product that wasn't going to be of enormous benefit to me financially? I'm a businessman, Kayla, first and foremost. And while I can't deny that advising Havens to use Kendon Interiors' skill and expertise does generate some secondary benefits, my corporate interests are what concern me over and above anything else.'

'If by "secondary benefits" you mean getting me back into bed, forget it!' Kayla retorted, with her pulses racing.

'I was referring to the benefits to Kendon Interiors,' he returned phlegmatically.

Why did she have to open her mouth and put her foot in it again?

Abashed, Kayla sank back against the cushioning black

leather with her eyes pressed closed, her hair a pale contrast against the headrest.

'You never cease trying to make me feel uncomfortable, do you?' she expressed in a censuring whisper.

'Quite unintentionally, believe me,' he answered, almost as softly. 'I think it's this unnatural denial by you of everything there is between us that is responsible for it.'

'There's *nothing* between us,' she refuted, knowing that in doing so she was guilty of doing exactly what he was accusing her of. Everything that was feminine in her was craving those strong arms around her again.

'No?' he queried, with such a wealth of meaning that her eyes flew open in guarded challenge.

He was looking at her without restraint, his eyes glittering with dark desire as they touched on the fullness of her trembling mouth. She felt her breathing grow shallow, felt an excruciating need at the very core of her as his heated gaze slid down to the silvery blue of her blouse, and her breasts rose and fell sharply in traitorous betrayal of her emotions.

'Leonidas…'

It was the first time she had spoken his full name without penetrating sarcasm. It was a breakthrough, he thought, even if she did sound like an accused prisoner who had just realised that any further denial of her crime was useless. Or perhaps she couldn't fight this thing that was making her so tense and cagey, that was driving him almost insane with the need to have her.

Scarcely daring to trust himself, he trailed a finger lightly along the silky texture of her jaw and heard her breath shudder brokenly through her lungs.

'Is that a plea?' he enquired huskily, feeling the ache in his body intensify in throbbing response.

No, it isn't! Kayla wanted to cry out in protest—except

that the feelings he was arousing were preventing her from saying a thing.

'What do you want?' she asked falteringly at length, not daring to look at him. If she did then she'd be lost, she realised, despairing at herself. And she couldn't lose herself to him again—not after the last time. Not after the way he had treated her.

'I want us to finish what we started,' he said, amazing her with his arrogance and yet making her go weak in spite of everything. But at least he wasn't touching her any more.

'Why? Did you fall madly in love with me in Greece and realise you can't live without me?' she suggested with bitter poignancy.

There was a far too lengthy pause before he answered.

'Only fools and adolescents fall madly in love,' he responded dismissively, and his cynicism was stinging even though it was no less than she would have expected from him. 'But I have to admit to having acted entirely out of character with you. You think you know me, but you don't, and I intend to show you exactly who Leonidas Vassalio is.'

'And how do you propose to do that?'

'By asking you to stay with me under my roof for a few weeks. In fact I'm insisting upon it.'

'Insisting?' He sounded so sure of himself, as though he wouldn't take no for an answer, that Kayla viewed him with a guarded question in her eyes. 'You're joking, surely?'

'On the contrary,' he said. 'I've never been more serious in my life. I think it would be a good idea if you move in tomorrow.'

'And if I don't?' It was a breathless little challenge, and one that he didn't take up immediately.

He didn't know why it was so imperative to keep this girl in his life—only that he had to. And if bending her to his will was the only way to do it, then so be it, he determined grimly.

'It would be a pity,' he expressed now. 'Especially as Josh and Lorna imagined we were all getting on so well. But starting a partnership of any kind without total harmony all round doesn't augur very well for future business.'

What was he saying? She wasn't sure, but she had a very good idea.

Though he wasn't actually telling her to her face, she felt sure that he would use Josh and Lorna's difficulties as a lever. The contract wasn't signed yet, and he could use his influence on Havens to get them to withdraw from supplying Kendon Interiors with their greatly anticipated custom. And if that happened...

Mortified, she breathed, 'You'd rescind that contract and see a business go down the drain if I don't do exactly what you're asking?' For what other reason would he have so miraculously sought Josh and Lorna out—regardless of what he'd said—if it wasn't to use their company's problems to his advantage?

His eyes, as she finished speaking, were darkly reflective, giving nothing away.

'Well, since you seem to know me so well...'

He didn't finish. He didn't have to, Kayla thought bitterly, staring with hurt, disbelieving eyes across a patch of manicured lawn to the vacant unit in front of which they were parked. A 'TO LET' sign was pinned to its rendered fascia. The place looked dark. Empty. Soulless.

Like he was, she thought achingly, and knew she had fallen in love with him back there on that island. In love with a man she hadn't even known...

A bell rang in her mind, reminding her of something he had said that last day after they had made love, but she pushed the memory aside. She didn't need anything that threatened to topple the barrier she had been forced to erect against him. Yet when he caught her chin between his thumb and forefinger and turned her head to look at him just the touch of that broad thumb sliding sensuously across her mouth almost broke her trembling resolve.

'Open your eyes,' he commanded softly.

When she did she saw something in his face that for a moment seemed to mirror her anguish—some emotion that burned with a dark and almost painful intensity. But then it was gone, like the extinguishing of a light, and his features seemed only to harden as he leaned forward, tilting her chin higher until there was just a hair's breadth between his mouth and hers.

His scent and his nearness were killing her. She wanted...

Oh, dear heaven! She wanted him! Even knowing what he was like. Even after the way he had deceived her! All she could think about was being naked in his arms and making love with him until...

She pressed her eyes closed to try and blot him out. A traitorous sensual tension gripped her. His breath was warm against her mouth, and the heady spice of his shaven jaw was acting like a powerful drug, stripping her of her will and her power to resist, until without even being aware of it she was leaning into him, her lips parting involuntarily to receive his kiss.

'No.' In an instant he was pulling back. 'Now isn't the time—and this certainly isn't the place.' His breathing came raggedly through his lungs. 'There will be ample opportunity in the future, I promise you. But in the meantime, if you're going to get to know me, *hrisi mou*, somehow I don't think we're going to achieve it like this.'

The sensual snub left her bruised and angry with herself—for feeling such bitter disappointment as well as for allowing him to see how much she still wanted him physically. It just showed him, once again, how he had the power to humiliate her just by turning her into a yearning, quivering wreck.

'I don't need to get to know you, Leonidas Vassalio. I know exactly what you are. You're playing games with me for your own amusement! And you're using my friends to exploit the situation, no matter how you might try to dress it up! All right. I'll go along with your little game.'

If she didn't, and Havens withdrew their offer, Kendon Interiors would be plunged straight back into the difficulties they'd been facing before. And if that happened, if Lorna was subjected to more stress during her pregnancy... Kayla shivered, unable to bear thinking that the safety of a baby's little life might easily be in her own hands.

'I'll move in with you,' she conceded, in a voice clogged with emotion, 'but I'm not sleeping with you, if that's what you're imagining. I'm only doing it for Josh and Lorna's sake, so don't you ever forget that—and don't imagine for one moment that I'm going to enjoy it.'

'I wouldn't be so presumptuous,' he assured her with mockery in his eyes. 'And now I'm going to take you back. Your firm has a proposed contract to fulfil...'

The sudden seriousness of his tone served to remind her of exactly what he was—a typical high-flying executive, ruthless and manipulative, like all the rest she'd known.

'And they're not going to fulfil it if one of their principal staff is out testing her luck by antagonising their biggest client.'

Of course. He had the upper hand and he knew it, Kayla thought, shooting back nevertheless, 'Is that a threat?'

'Why not go the whole hog and call it blackmail?' he suggested smoothly. 'I'm sure you'd prefer to.' When she didn't answer, 'Tomorrow,' he reminded her, as he brought his powerful car around to the front entrance of Kendon Interiors. 'I'll pick you up at eight.'

The pool threw back reflections of the dazzling white mansion. A modern house, built to Georgian design, Leonidas's principal UK home was a breathtaking showcase of large airy rooms, all exquisitely furnished, combining modern with Regency and luxury with unfaltering good taste. A rich man's castle, presided over by a resident staff who catered for this king of enterprise with unstinting respect and affability, as if he was more to them than just the man who paid their wages.

Now, lying beside the luxurious pool in equally luxurious grounds before it was time to get ready for the company dinner to which he was taking her tonight, Kayla was forced to accept, from what she'd observed over her first couple of days in his spectacular house, that the respect shown between Leonidas Vassalio and his staff was entirely mutual.

'Are you ready?' he asked two hours later, as she emerged from the suite of rooms he had assigned to her. It comprised a bedroom with floor-to-ceiling wardrobes, a four-poster bed and a carpet thick enough to drown in, a separate dressing room and a bathroom with a huge sunken tub within a setting of honeyed marble.

'I don't know,' Kayla responded, trying hard not to reveal how just the sight of him standing there at the top of the stairs in a dark evening suit and exquisitely fine shirt was making her blood sing with need. 'I'm your puppet. You tell me.'

He moved towards her like a dark panther, his equally dark eyes taking in every detail of her appearance.

She was wearing a strapless dress with a pale blue bodice that ran into a darker blue, the colour continuing down into purple and then burgundy as it swirled around her ankles. Silver high-heeled sandals gave him a glimpse of burgundy-tipped toes.

She'd twisted her hair up into a knot, leaving a few tendrils to fall softly around her face. Her only concession to cosmetics was a smudge of smoky-blue shading on her eyelids and a burgundy gloss enhancing her lips. Her long lustrous lashes, he was pleased to notice, she'd left naturally gold. Delicate spirals of silver hung from the lobes of her ears, matching the delicately twisted necklace that lay against her softly-tanned skin.

'You look beautiful.' For a moment it was all Leonidas could say. 'And you're not my puppet,' he countered when he had found his voice again. 'You're an independent-minded if not stubborn young woman whom I'm delighted to be accompanying tonight. If I'd wanted a puppet I wouldn't have had to travel too far to find myself a dozen of those.'

No, because every woman he knew would probably leap at the chance to do his bidding, Kayla thought. Whereas *she* was a woman who had walked away from him—said no to him when it had mattered—and that surely had to prove too much of a challenge for a man like Leonidas.

'Then you should have found yourself a dozen, shouldn't you?' she said, smiling brightly for the benefit of a manservant who was passing as they started down the magnificent staircase.

'Perhaps I should have,' he agreed, sounding mildly amused.

From the magnificent staircase to his magnificent car, to dinner in the ballroom of an equally magnificent hotel, Kayla was entranced but at the same time overwhelmed by the world he moved in. It was poles apart from that of the man he had purported to be—a man who had 'opted out', driven a wreck of a truck and bedded down in the run-down environs of a Greek farmhouse.

Here she saw a man at the very pinnacle of his prosperity. A man who lived and travelled in style and circulated with some of the most influential names in society. A man eloquent enough to hold an audience of over three hundred captive as he delivered an after-dinner talk on human complacency towards the state of the planet, leaving his peers congratulating him after a standing ovation that left him remarkably unfazed.

'You were brilliant,' Kayla remarked, unable to resist saying it as the tables were being cleared and couples were beginning to wander onto the dance floor to enjoy the middle-of-the-road music provided by a professional live band. She hadn't had a chance to speak to him since before he'd given the talk, and he'd been surrounded by many guests wanting to speak to him ever since.

'I was just stating fact and emphasising the responsibility that we as professional bodies should engage for the sake of our children and our children's children. We're only custodians of this earth. We don't own it,' he said. 'But am I to assume that I've hit on one topic that you're not going to flay me over tonight?'

With a change of tone he had wiped away her attempt to strike an equal balance with him if only for a few hours. Retaliation was futile, she decided. And anyway a smiling brunette, very glamorous and sophisticated, came up to him at that moment to thank him effusively, ogling him with such a blatant come-on in her sultry green eyes that there was no room for doubt as to exactly what she wanted from him.

'He's so eloquent!' she enthused to Kayla, daring to touch red-tipped fingers to his dark sleeve. 'He made my flesh go all goosebumpy just listening to him!'

'Really?' Kayla responded, trying to look impressed. 'Well, if that makes you goosebumpy then you should take a look at his sketches!' She felt the bunch of muscle in his powerful arm as she slipped hers through it in a gesture of pure possession. 'Of course he's very modest about them, but I'm sure he'd show them to you if you asked him nicely.'

Smiling uncertainly, the woman uttered something that Kayla didn't catch and, realising she was intruding, moved hastily away.

'I know you've got your grievances,' Leonidas rasped, as soon as his admirer was out of earshot, 'but do you have to air them in public? And what was *that* display of play-acting all about?' he queried, locking her arm against the sensuous fabric of his jacket as she would have pulled it away.

'I thought I was supposed to act as though I was enjoying being with you?' she murmured, with a bright smile for anyone who might be watching them.

He made a disapproving sound down his nostrils. 'You're behaving like every woman I went to Greece to get away from.'

Which was why he had been so careful not to tell you who he was, her inner little voice piped up to remind her. But she didn't want reminding, and silenced the voice with the flash of another smile and a clipped, 'How do you *want* me to behave?'

'As Kayla Young. Guileless. Easy to like. And infernally inquisitive.'

'A fool,' she tagged on, all falseness gone. She was only aware then that he was leading her onto the dance floor. 'Guileless. Easy to like. And an infernally inquisitive, easy-to-fool fool!'

'How can I forget it?' he murmured, slipping those strong arms around her. 'You aren't prepared to let me.'

'Any more than I'm prepared to let you forget that I'm here under protest.'

'No, you aren't,' he purred silkily, drawing her close, sending Kayla's senses reeling in shaming response. 'I don't think "protest" can in any way account for the way we're both feeling now.'

This close to him she could feel every steel-hard muscle of his body—in the whipcord strength of his back and shoulders, in his hard hips and powerful thighs, and in the stirring evidence of his arousal. It made her want to press herself against him, and it took every shred of will-power she possessed not to do it.

'You aren't feeling anything. Just a bruised ego and severely dented pride because you can't bear a woman ever saying no to you.'

He laughed very softly, and with his cheek against hers whispered in her ear, 'Not a woman whom I know wants me as much as I want her—no.'

Even his breath was a turn-on against her treacherously pulsing flesh, without the stimulus of his stunning appearance and the way he'd had everyone there tonight eating out of his hand. It made her wish that they didn't have the baggage of the past hanging over them and that she was somewhere else, alone with him, not moving like this under an exquisite chandelier, with three hundred other people in the room.

'In fact, do you want to know what I think you are thinking now?'

The lights spun gold from Kayla's hair as she lifted her head in challenge. 'No,' she dismissed with a saccharine-sweet smile. 'But no doubt you're going to tell me anyway.'

'Well, let's see if I'm right,' he suggested. He was looking down at her and emulating her smile in a way that to anyone watching would have marked them undoubtedly as lovers— hungry for each other, wanting only the privacy of their bedroom. 'I think that right now you would prefer to be back at the house and for me to be slowly undressing you with some soft music playing. And I think you'd like me to remain clothed while I carry you naked up to my bed. There's nothing like the sensuality of cloth to add zest to lovemaking, is there, Kayla? Particularly when the man wearing it doesn't give a fig for how you might abuse it, just so long as he can gratify your desires and make you sob with pleasure.'

It was so close to what she had been thinking that Kayla could scarcely breathe. She could feel her cheeks burning from the shaming imagery. 'You're just indulging in your own un-inhibited fantasies.' she croaked, her throat as arid as a Grecian hillside, and she felt those dark masculine eyes appraising the results of what his mind-blowing words had produced.

'Am I?' he challenged softly, with a knowing smile.

She wasn't even aware that the music had stopped until his arms fell away from her, and then she could see one of the older male guests to whom she'd been introduced earlier beckoning him from the bar.

'I'll be a few minutes,' Leonidas apologised, and left her to flee to the mercifully deserted sanctuary of the powder room.

A flushed-faced, bright-eyed creature stared back at her from the mirror above the luxuriously equipped basins. She felt as though she had just been aroused to fever-pitch only to be left abandoned and wanting. Wanting *him,* she acknowledged painfully, wondering how she still could.

How could she stay under his roof when every time he touched her it was like dropping a firework into a powder keg? When her common sense went up in smoke just at a look from him, even without the X-rated things he'd been saying to her just now?

And yet he hadn't attempted to touch her intimately since he'd brought her to his house—had merely treated her with a detached respect that had kept her awake over the past two nights wondering why he hadn't. Had he finally accepted that he had treated her unfairly and was now doing his best to make it up to her? Or was his plan to wear her down with the sort of earth-shattering sensuality he'd used just now until she was begging for him to make love to her?

She hadn't met a company man yet whose motives weren't entirely self-centred, so why should Leonidas Vassalio be any different? She rebuked herself for her moment of weakness in even daring to hope that he might be. Wasn't he using the plight of two people she cared about purely to satisfy his own selfish demands? And he'd already lived up to the type of man he really was in the way he had lied to her in Greece.

Even so, it was with a sick and building excitement that a little later she sat in the shadowy intimacy of his car, acutely aware of him sitting there beside her, changing gear with an immaculately cuffed wrist as he took a bend, driving them home, his jacket discarded in the back...

Only the hall light was burning on a dimmer switch as they came through the electronically operated gates and he admitted them into his magnificent house. Having watched the way he'd used his security card to open the impressively carved door, Kayla couldn't help comparing this man, with his millions and his discreet surveillance staff and his stringently guarded home, with the one who had slept with his doors unlocked—open to the world—alone on a lonely Greek hillside.

'Thanks. I think I'll go straight up,' she murmured, breathless with anticipation. She wasn't sure how she was managing to drag herself away from him as she started towards the wide sweeping stairs.

'Kayla...'

His soft command stopped her in her tracks, her heart beating a frenzied tattoo. If he touched her...

Dear heaven! She *wanted* him to touch her! To take the decision away from her, carry her up these stairs and drive her wild in the sumptuous luxury of his bed!

She turned round, her legs threatening to buckle under her. 'What?'

'You dropped your wrap,' he said, in a voice that was screamingly intimate.

Even the purposefulness of his tread on the pale marble was a sensuality that made her tense and yearning body throb.

Very softly he moved over and placed the blue and silver sequinned stole which she hadn't even realised had slipped off lightly over her bare shoulders. Then, with heart-stopping gentleness, he turned her round to face him.

He had retrieved his jacket since stepping out of the car,

and the dark cloth now spanning his shoulders was a sensuality she wanted to touch.

It was a replay of all he had tormented her with earlier, and she caught her breath, held in thrall by the scent and warmth and power of him as he stooped and pressed his lips against her forehead.

'You look tired,' he remarked, gazing down with some dark, unfathomable emotion at the naked hunger in her eyes. 'Get some rest,' he advised softly, leaving her excruciatingly lost and aching for him. 'We've got another busy day tomorrow.'

CHAPTER TEN

'WHY DIDN'T YOU tell me you were seeing him?' Lorna gasped, amazed, after Leonidas had telephoned Kayla in the office on Monday morning. 'And don't tell me you aren't, because that phone call certainly wasn't about trading figures! You're going out with him, aren't you?'

Imperceptibly, Kayla tensed. She hadn't told anyone that she was staying with Leonidas. All she had told her mother was that she was spending a couple of weeks with Lorna, and as Leonidas lived within a reasonable driving distance of Kendon Interiors, which meant that she could still come into the office, she had decided not to involve her friend in the lie.

'Don't spread it about,' she implored, reluctant to reveal her secret or to face the awkward questions that people would ask if she did.

What could she tell them, anyway? That she was only with Leonidas because he had made it impossible for her to refuse? That he was as good as blackmailing her to get her to comply with his wishes, and that she didn't intend staying in his house a second longer than after that contract was signed?

'If the paparazzi get wind of it they could turn his life into a circus,' she tagged on as casually as she was able to, although she was aware, from things Leonidas had already mentioned in passing, that they really could do just that.

'I won't. Well, only to Josh, of course,' Lorna stated unnec-

essarily. 'But how did you manage it? No, scrub that,' she put
in hastily. 'You're smart and you're beautiful—he wouldn't
have been worth his salt if he hadn't noticed you the moment
you walked into the conference room last week. Wow! Won't
that be one in the eye for Craig!' she continued, clearly flab-
bergasted. 'Honestly, Kayla! Do you *know* how rich he is?'

*Rich and manipulative and using his power to get exactly
what he wants,* Kayla thought desolately. Because what he
wanted was her, back in his bed. She was certain of that, despite the fact that he was making no advances to her in that
respect, and regardless of how much he had hurt her—was
still hurting her with his calculated plan to use her friends'
precarious position as a lever to get her to fall in with him.

It was for that reason that she still couldn't bring herself to
tell Lorna about meeting him in Greece. Lorna, who always
thought the best of people, would instantly imagine that he
had cast his company's business their way because Kayla had
recommended them. She might even think he was doing it as
a favour to her, Kayla, and she couldn't bear her friend to be
deceived by him as she had, when nothing could be further
from the truth.

'His money doesn't interest me,' Kayla tried to say nonchalantly, which produced a knowing little laugh from her friend.

'Well, no. I can see that there's far more that would interest
you before you even got to his wallet! Gosh! If I wasn't married—and pregnant…'

'Which you are,' Kayla emphasised, managing a smile,
knowing that her friend was only jesting. Lorna adored Josh,
and her one desire in life was to give birth to their healthy
baby. Dropping an almost envying glance to her dearest
friend's burgeoning middle, Kayla decided right there and
then that whatever it took to help Lorna fulfil that desire she
would do, regardless of the cost to her own emotions.

* * *

During that week Leonidas went away on some unexpected business, returning a couple of days later to steal Kayla away early from the office and take her to a charity auction, where canapés were handed round on silver dishes and champagne flowed like water from a spring.

It was an event where the proceeds from the various items on offer went to a tsunami relief fund, and it soon became clear to Kayla that it was because of Leonidas's attendance and his company's support of the event that so many people had got involved.

'Did you enjoy that?' he asked her afterwards, when they were in the car, pulling away. 'As far as you were able to, of course, bearing in mind that your enjoyment level was probably stuck on zero in view of who you were with.'

Like her, he had refused the champagne after the first half-glass, and she was beginning to discover that his driving standards—as with most of what he did—were impeccable.

'Very amusing,' she remarked dryly, turning to look out of the window, secretly admiring the gardens surrounding the grand English country manor his company had hired to host the event. 'What was the object of the exercise in bringing me here today? To show me how charitable you can be?' She'd been surprised when he had paid over the odds for a small and not particularly well done watercolour of one of the local landmarks. 'There are those who might say you can afford to be.'

'You would be one of them, I take it?' When she didn't answer, already wishing she hadn't been so quick to snipe at him like that, he went on, 'It isn't about affording it, Kayla. It's about having enough clout to make others aware of the importance of events like this and bringing everyone together to contribute.'

Which he had done—and very successfully, she accepted, secretly impressed. Although she couldn't bring herself to admit it aloud, privately she couldn't deny that she had enjoyed herself—very much.

He took her to a West End show one evening—one she had wanted to see and for which she had been unable to get tickets. Afterwards, coming out of the exclusive restaurant where he had taken her for a late dinner, they were leapt on by photographers who almost succeeded in trampling her to death before Leonidas got her into the waiting limousine he'd had one of his aides bring to whisk them away.

'How do you cope with all this?' Kayla challenged, and he could tell from the all-encompassing gesture of her small chin that she meant the security and the car and the public demands his billionaire status made upon him, and not just the frightening intrusion of the paparazzi.

'One learns to live with it,' he said in a matter-of-fact voice, and then, more solicitously, asked, 'Are you all right?'

She nodded, but he could see that she wasn't. That anxious line between her eyes assured him that she was anything but happy being there with him. Also, being jostled by those photographers had caused the fine white silk of her dress to tear, and her beautiful hair, which she had styled so elegantly before they had left the house, was coming out of its combs. She looked as if she had been out in a gale—or with a far too impassioned lover.

The thought made him hard, but he steeled himself against it. She wasn't ready to accept him back into her bed just yet.

Consequently, when they reached the house he left her to go to bed alone and went straight to his study, where he spent hours catching up on some pressing paperwork in an endeavour not to give in to the almost overwhelming urge to mount the stairs two at time, rip back her bedcovers and watch her hollow protests dissolve beneath the surging demands of their entwined bodies.

The photographs were emblazoned across the tabloids the

next day, with Kayla caught looking surprised and dishevelled and Leonidas urging her determinedly into the car.

'Have you seen them?' she wailed, ringing him on his mobile, having already spent half an hour on the phone, dodging awkward questions from her mother. She wasn't sure where he was, but her call had been diverted to his secretary first, who had obviously been asked to field his calls.

'Yes, I did, and I'm sorry,' he expressed, sounding annoyed over the publicity.

She was beginning to appreciate why he'd gone off to that island to escape it all for a while. Why he had been so angry when he had caught her supposedly taking photographs of him that first day.

'Say nothing,' he recommended, when she told him that someone from the press had found out where she worked and had been ringing the office to try and get her to talk to them. 'Throw them a crumb and they'll knead it into a whole loaf. If you say nothing it will blow over within a week.' He apologised again before ringing off.

A couple of hours later a large bunch of red roses was delivered to the office as added consolation from Leonidas, much to the excitement of everyone at Kendon Interiors—particularly the female contingent, who had already seen the article and were still drooling over the hard and exciting image of the high-powered tycoon.

As arranged, he picked Kayla up himself from the office that evening, using his car's superior power to roar out of the business park before one lurking newspaperman and a couple of young girls from the office who had rushed out to get a glimpse of him knew what had happened.

'Thank you.' Kayla looked gratefully across at him as he brought the powerful car into the early rush-hour traffic. 'For getting me out of there so fast—and for the roses.' Remembering her telephone call to him earlier, however, and the manner in which she had finally got to speak to him, she asked, before she could stop herself, 'Did you get your secretary to send them for you?'

Wasn't that what company men did? she reflected bitterly, remembering other roses. Before turning their focus on their adoring secretaries themselves?

'I'm not your father, Kayla,' he answered grimly, without taking his eyes off the rear window of the car in front of them, uncannily reading her mind. 'Nor am I your ex-fiancé. When I send flowers I never do it without choosing exactly what I want myself.'

Which put her in her place, good and proper! She didn't doubt that in this instance at least he was telling her the truth.

He was due to fly to the Channel Islands for a conference that weekend. Expressing concern, however, at Kayla being left to the mercies of the press for a couple of days, he instructed her not to stray beyond the boundaries of his home, and made sure she complied by instructing one strong-armed member of his security staff to keep his eye on her.

'What are you imagining I'll do if I go out?' she quipped as he was leaving for the helicopter that was standing, its blades whirring, on the landing pad in front of the house. 'Find some man to impregnate me so I can tell everybody it's yours?'

She regretted it almost as soon as she'd said it.

'You aren't a prisoner, Kayla,' he said, all emotion veiled by the dark fringes of his lashes. 'I'm only thinking of your privacy and your safety.'

And he was gone, leaving her with only the briefest touch of his lips branding her cheek.

As it was a good weekend she swam in the pool and sunbathed on the terrace, catching up with some reading and watching a couple of adventure movies in the mansion's impressive professionally equipped cinema room.

Nothing, though, could compare to her traitorous excitement at hearing Leonidas's helicopter returning on Sunday evening after she had gone to bed—deliberately early so that she wouldn't have to see him. Wouldn't have to battle with this underlying sexual tension that was building in her daily with a terrifying intensity, and which was becoming almost impossible to keep from him whenever he touched her—however casually. And she *had* to keep it from him, she thought, harrowed and racked with frustration. Because wasn't this part of his ploy? To wear her down with wanting him? Just to redeem his indomitable masculine pride? And if she did ever succumb again to her own foolish and weak-willed desire for him, what then?

No, she had to be strong, she determined. Had to resist him at all costs. Just until that contract was signed.

When Leonidas picked her up from the office the following evening it was to take her for an early dinner in a favoured bistro he knew and then, much to her surprise, on to a photography exhibition.

'I thought as you're so attached to that camera of yours,' he said, pulling up outside the small but well-attended little gallery, 'you might appreciate seeing what the professionals have to offer. Of course if you'd rather not...'

'No. No I'd like to,' Kayla put in quickly when he looked in two minds about whether to park or drive away. Craig had hated anything like this, and even Josh and Lorna couldn't understand what Craig had used to call her 'camera fetish'. Just the chance to be among like-minded people for a change was something she didn't want to pass up.

The exhibition, by private invitation only, was being hosted by an acquaintance of Leonidas's, and Kayla could tell as soon as they were inside that he and the gentle grey-haired man were true friends. There was none of the deference or playing up to Leonidas that she had seen among some of the people at the functions she'd attended with him, until she'd wondered how he could ever tell who was really sincere.

'Leonidas tells me that you're quite the enthusiast,' the man said to her, smiling. Leonidas—still dressed, as she was, in a dark business suit—was, with the rest of the twenty or so guests, browsing some of the artwork around the gallery. 'If ever you feel you have something to offer, then you know where to come.'

'It's just a hobby!' Kayla laughed warmly, wondering what Leonidas had been saying to his friend about her. That he had said anything at all gave her a decidedly warm feeling inside.

'So what do you think?' Suddenly he was there beside her, sharing her interest in a waterfall scene with some interesting use of light.

'It's good,' she expressed, enervated by his dark executive image. 'But if it had been mine I'd have toned the light down a little.' She was finding it hard to concentrate when she could feel the power of his virility emanating from him, and her nostrils were straining for every greedy breath of his cologne. 'It isn't subtle enough for me.'

'And you like subtlety?'

Dry-mouthed, Kayla touched her tongue to her top lip and saw the way his eyes followed the nervous little action. 'Every time.' She even managed to smile, but her lips felt stretched and burning.

'Perhaps this will be more to your taste.' They had moved on and he was referring to a landscape captured beneath an angry sky.

'Much too wild,' she dismissed laughingly, and saw the sexy elevation of a dark eyebrow.

'Are you saying you prefer something more…tamed?'

There was sensuality in the way he said it, in that momentary hesitation. Or was she imagining it? she wondered, her heart still racing when he immediately invited her opinion on the technicalities of the photograph—its depth of field, how it captured the eye.

He knew a lot about the subject, and she was impressed.

'I've studied a bit,' he said modestly, when she told him so. 'Unlike you. You're a natural,' he commented, making her glow inside. 'So, what about this one?'

'Too much Photoshop,' she quipped, wrinkling her nose, and he laughed.

For a moment it felt as it had that day he had taken her to that little island and she'd been insisting on racehorses on a piece of land not a mile wide. Indulging in make-believe. Playing games with him. Except that it was different tonight. Tonight the very air around them was pulsating with a dangerous chemistry, and she wasn't with Leon, the man she'd believed to be open and carefree with scarcely two pennies to his name. She was with Leonidas Vassalio, hardened billionaire, powerful magnate and the man who had hurt her—was still hurting her just by being the type of man he was. The type who would use her concern for her friends to get what he wanted.

'My Gran used to say that the camera doesn't lie. But it does,' she accepted, suddenly feeling low-spirited. 'Maybe not in her day,' she went on, 'but in this day and age the emphasis seems to be on how much you can artificially enhance or embellish, and on what you put in or take out. You can't really tell what's real any more and what isn't. There's so much that isn't as it seems.' *Including you,* she thought achingly, and had to glance away, pretending to be temporarily distracted by the other guests milling around them so that he wouldn't see the emotion scoring her face.

'And that means so much to you?'

'Yes, it does,' she said. 'I like the camera to capture things as they really are.' She turned back to him now, her feelings brought under control. 'Men and women. Places. Things. I like them portrayed "warts and all", as the saying goes. I'm not a fan of illusion. Being fooled into seeing something that isn't really there.'

He tilted his head, the movement so slight that she wasn't sure whether she had imagined it or not. His eyes were dark pools of inscrutable emotion and she wondered what he was thinking. That he had done just that with her when he hadn't told her who he was?

'Let's go home,' he said.

He spoke very little to her on the relatively short journey back, while the car ate up the miles in the gathering dusk.

There had been a sporadic press presence at the main gates of the house over the past few days, and Leonidas wasn't taking any chances when they arrived home.

'We'll take the east entrance,' he told Kayla as he turned the car down a quiet lane that stretched for a couple of miles and which, from the manicured trees above the high wall that soon came into view, obviously skirted his property.

Another pair of electronically opened gates brought them past a small lodge and into his home through a smaller and more secluded side entrance.

'Why isn't this part of the house used?' Kayla whispered as they came out of rooms covered in dustsheets which Leonidas had had to unlock to allow them into the main body of the house. She felt like a child creeping around when she should have been in bed. Or a guilty mistress sneaking away from the ecstasies of her lover's bed...

'I had this part converted for my father, but he never came here,' he said, his voice taking on a curiously jagged edge.

'Why not?' Kayla asked, thinking how thick and black his hair was as he stopped to lock the door behind him. It made her want to rake her fingers through it, twist the strong tufts around them as she lay beneath him, crying out from the terrifying pleasure he was withholding from her.

'I believe I told you before. We were never able to get on. I wanted us to try and establish some sort of rapport as he was getting older.' They were moving along a softly lit carpeted passage now. 'To try and forge some sort of bond with him.'

He was so close behind her that if she stopped he would collide with her, Kayla thought hectically, craving the feel of his warmth through her prim little jacket and tight pencil skirt.

'And did you?'

'No. There was too much between us—far too much to even imagine we could repair it. He didn't want to share in my good fortune or the things I could give him. He didn't want anything from me,' he concluded, with something in his voice that she might have mistaken for pain if she hadn't known better.

'Why not? Wasn't he proud of you?' she queried, feeling for him in spite of herself as they came through an archway into the main hall alongside the sweeping staircase. She couldn't believe that any parent with a son like Leonidas—driven, enterprising, so overwhelmingly successful—could possibly be anything else.

'Oh, I think he was satisfied that I'd turned out to be the man he had been determined to mould me into,' he accepted harshly.

Kayla glanced back over her shoulder and saw the rigidity of his features, the hard cynicism touching his mouth. 'And what type is that?'

'The type who understands that sentiment and idealism are for fools and that common sense and practicality are the only two reliable bedfellows.'

'Do you really believe that?' she murmured, with wounded incredulity in her eyes as she stopped, as he had, at the foot of the stairs.

'What does it matter what I believe?' he said.

He meant to her. And yet it did matter, she realised—far too much—and she had to sink her nails into her clenched palms to keep herself from blurting it out.

He was hard and ruthless. She'd realised that even before she'd left Greece. Although she hadn't known how hard and how calculating he could be until she'd seen him in full corporate action, which was how he had managed to climb to the very top of the executive ladder while still only thirty-one. Yet there was an altruistic side to his nature too, reined in beneath that cold and ruthless streak, which could have had her eating out of his hand if she had been weak enough to let it. But she wasn't, she thought turbulently as she found herself battling against a surge of responses to that dark and raw sensuality that transcended everything else about him.

'Thank you for taking me to the exhibition,' she said, in a husky voice that didn't sound like hers. 'It was thoughtful of you. I think I'll go straight up. Goodnight.'

If she had thought he would let her go then she had been fooling herself, she realised too late, when his firm, determined fingers closed around her wrist.

'You might not like the man you think I am—or what I stand for—but it excites you, Kayla.'

How right he was! She felt panicked as he drew her towards him and brought the fingers of his other hand to play along the pulsing sensitivity of her throat.

'*This* excites you.'

'No, don't—please…' It was a hopeless little sound. The sound of one who knew her cause was lost.

'Why? Are you afraid that if for one minute you let your guard down you might just have to acknowledge how much you want me?'

'I don't want you.' Rebellion warred with the dark desire in her eyes. Futile rebellion, she realised when she saw him smile.

'No?'

He was barely touching her, yet every feminine cell was screaming out to the steel-hard strength and warmth and power he exuded. She could feel her breasts straining against her blouse, could feel the moist heat of her desire against the flimsy film of her string.

'You want me and it's driving you mad. It's driving us both mad,' he admitted, and his scent and his nearness and that iron control were electrifying as he tilted her chin with a forefinger—all that was touching her now. 'You want me,' he said huskily, his dark eyes raking over her upturned mouth. 'Say it.'

It was a soft command, breathed against her lips, and it was that excruciating denial of the kiss she was craving, which finally broke her resolve.

'I want you! I want you! I want—!'

His mouth over hers silenced her wild admission in the same moment that she twined her arms around his neck to pull him down to her.

He caught her to him, those strong arms tightening around her.

Kayla wriggled against him, seeking even closer contact with his body, her own a mass of desperate wanting as their mouths fused, broke contact, devoured in a hunger of frenzied need.

He was tugging off her jacket, letting it lie where it fell, ripping buttons in his urgency to get her out of her clothes. But when her hands slid under his jacket and it fell away from those broad shoulders he suddenly swept her up off her feet and mounted the stairs with her as effortlessly as if she were a rag doll.

Of course. The staff.

The thought penetrated her consciousness, but only for a second, because all that mattered was that she was with this man, destined for his bed, and she was going to know the full meaning of his loving her.

In the physical sense...

She shook that thought away, because all she wanted was to have him inside her—anyhow, anywhere and any way it came.

He set her down on her feet before they had even reached his room, pressing her against the wall of the carpeted landing, as hungry for her mouth as she was for the pleasuring mastery of his hands on her body.

He surfaced only to tug off her gaping blouse, pulling her against his hard hips so that he could deal with the back zipper of her skirt.

It slipped to the floor and she was standing there in nothing but a white lacy bra and string and black high-heeled sandals, revelling in his groan of satisfaction as he caught her to him again.

His tongue burned an urgent trail along the shallow valley between her breasts and, clutching his shoulders, she arched against him as his mouth moved ravishingly over a lacy cup.

The fine silk of his shirt was a sensual turn-on under her urgently groping hands, the fabric of his immaculately pressed trousers heightening her pleasure as he suddenly cupped her buttocks and lifted her up and her legs went around him, her fingers tangling wildly in his thick black hair.

It was the culmination of everything he had promised and everything she had dared to imagine, she realised as they finally made it to his room and he dropped her down onto the yielding sensuality of his big bed.

They had been lovers in the spring, but it hadn't been like this, she thought as he came down to her, still fully clothed, and removed the last scraps of her underwear with swift and amazing dexterity. Perhaps he had been right when he'd suggested that his power and influence excited her. Perhaps she was no different from all those other women she'd seen visually devouring him, she thought. Because she had no control over the desires he aroused in her.

Naked, she writhed beneath him, wanting him naked too, wanting the hands that were reclaiming her body never to stop—because she had been made for them. For this…

When he moved away to hastily shed his clothes, she watched with her hair spread like wild silk over the darker sheen of his pillow, her arms arched above her head in wanton abandon to the thrilling anticipation of what was to come.

'I called you an angel once,' he said hoarsely, looking down at her from where he was standing, unashamed and magnificent in his glorious nakedness. 'But I was wrong. You're a she-devil.' It was said with a curious tremor in his voice.

'And you...' she whispered, her body pulsing as he finished sheathing himself—not taking any chances this time—and came back to join her '...are the devil incarnate.'

'Yes,' he murmured, his voice humorously soft against her lips.

But she didn't care, because she was on fire for him, burning up in a conflagration of need and wanting and desire.

Skilfully and with controlled deliberation he slid down her body, anointing her skin with kisses, although his body was taut with his own need and his breathing was as ragged as hers.

Their hunger was too demanding for much foreplay. As he moved above her, positioning himself to take her, Kayla welcomed his hard invasion, her legs opening for him like silken wings for the sun.

His sliding into her was an ecstasy she couldn't have imagined and she lifted her hips to accommodate him, a small cry spilling from her lips.

His penetration was deep, with each successive thrust taking him deeper, until he was filling her, stretching her, turning her into a being of mindless, unparalleled sensation where nothing else mattered but the union of their two bodies.

She was riding with him, being taken to a place where only the two of them existed—a rapturous world of feeling and sharpening senses that grew into a mountain of exquisitely unbearable pleasure, urging her upwards to its summit. And suddenly as she reached the top the mountain started to explode, and she cried out from the pleasure that was bursting all around her. She was falling, tumbling in a freefall of interminable sensation, clinging to the man she never wanted to let out of her arms, part of him, belonging to him, as he tumbled with her through the sensational universe.

When she came back to earth she was sobbing uncontrollably, all her pent-up feelings for him released by the shattering throbs of her orgasm.

Some time afterwards, when her sobs had subsided, Leonidas asked, 'Are you all right?'

She was lying in the crook of his arm and the warm velvet of his chest was damp from her tears.

'Yes, I'm fine,' Kayla murmured, and rolled away from him, unable to tell him why she had wept. If she did, then he would know, and she didn't want to admit it to herself. So she stayed where she was, on her side, with her legs drawn up, not wanting to face the truth or the reality of what had just happened.

Leonidas woke shortly before dawn.

Kayla was still lying with her back to him, as far over on her side of the bed as it was possible to get. With a crease between his eyes, Leonidas slipped quietly out of bed, so as not to disturb her, and went to take a shower.

When he returned, wearing a dark robe, she was still sleeping, but now lying on her back. What little make-up she'd been wearing last night was smudged—either from his over-zealous treatment of her or from crying, he remembered uneasily—and her hair was alluringly tousled from making love.

Unable to help himself, he stooped to press his lips lightly to her forehead. She stirred slightly, her brow furrowing as though her dreams were troubled.

'Leon...'

He wasn't sure, from her soft murmur, whether that was

what she'd said, but if it was it wasn't meant for the man who had made love to her last night. Not Leonidas Vassalio, corporate chairman and billionaire. Not after the way she had cried after they had made love.

She didn't trust him or even like him, and she despised herself for wanting him. Why else would she have shed tears of such bitter regret when she'd been overtaken—as he had—by their mutual passion last night?

It was his fault for thinking in the beginning that he could have a casual fling with a girl like her and that keeping the truth from her wouldn't matter. Nor had he been right in thinking he could bend her to his will in making her come here to try and get her to want him as she had in Greece. She was never likely to. She was hurting, and he had never intended that.

What was that old adage? he pondered distractedly, moving away from the bed. If you loved something, you had to let it go. If it came back to you, it was yours. If it didn't, it never would be.

But what he felt for this beautiful, bewitching girl wasn't *love,* he thought, steeling himself against any emotion. Not as she deserved it. And she certainly wasn't his. So wasn't it time to let her go?

Wearing a silver-grey suit, white shirt and silver tie, Leonidas was perched on one of the high stools, browsing through a newspaper, when Kayla came into the huge, sterile-looking kitchen an hour or so later. Behind him the sky was overcast beyond the panoramic window, and even a myriad lights in the halogen-studded ceiling couldn't detract from the dreariness of what should have been a bright summer day.

'Good morning.' He scarcely glanced up from whatever he was reading in the *Financial Times,* although just that briefest glance from him set her insides aflame as she thought about how intimately and passionately he had pleasured her last night.

After a moment he cast the newspaper aside on the kitchen counter beside him. 'Kayla, we have to talk,' he stated without any preamble, angling his long, lean body to face her on the stool.

'About what?' she queried, with sudden queasiness in her stomach. What was he going to say that lent such a serious tone to his voice?

'I've been a moron,' he told her. 'If that's the correct expression. You were right. I have been trying to keep you in my life for the sake of my own pride—my ego, if you like— because I didn't like my ethics being brought into question in anyone's mind. Particularly the mind of a girl who was very sweet and trusting and whom I treated very unfairly when I was with her in Greece and I needed to put that right.'

'What are you saying?' Kayla queried in a small, broken voice.

'That I've been very selfish and inconsiderate and that you don't need to pander to my fragile ego any longer. Your friends' contract is assured, if that's what you've been worrying about, so you're free to cast me off…if that's what you wish,' he added with some hesitancy, and as though he was picking his words very carefully. 'Whenever you like.'

If it was what she wished?

Pain speared through her so acutely it felt like a knife slicing through the life-force of her very being. She'd never been let down and effectively rejected in such a considerately phrased manner before. But he'd got what he wanted, she thought wretchedly, trying to concentrate on her breathing. It was her total capitulation that he had needed to redeem his pride, and now she had given him that he needed nothing more.

He was just like all the others—right out of the same mould. The type of man she'd vowed never to be attracted to again.

Except that this man was different. This man wasn't even capable of feeling. Not love, she accepted, anguished. He'd practically admitted that to her himself last night. Loving was a weakness—something only fools entertained—and Leonidas Vassalio was anything but weak, and certainly no fool.

'Well…' Her smile felt stretched as she tried to put on a brave face, and she wondered if she was visibly shaking as much as she was trembling inside. It occurred to her then why he'd wanted her kept out of the way of the press while he'd been away last weekend. Because he didn't want anyone thinking she was a permanent fixture in his life. 'I'd better go and start packing,' she said as tonelessly as she was able, and wondered at the unfathomable emotion that turned his eyes almost inky black.

'I have to fly to Athens,' he informed her, consulting his watch, his tone similarly flat.

It was a trip, she'd discovered, which he took on a regular basis, often going back and forth between London and his Greek office. 'If you're keen to go today, I obviously won't try and stop you, but I shan't be able to take you myself. I can, however, arrange for a car to be put at your disposal whenever you wish to leave.'

'That won't be necessary,' Kayla murmured, wanting to get out of there—and quickly—before the tears that were burning the backs of her eyes overflowed and gave her away.

He nodded as though he understood, and somehow she managed to drag herself from the room with her pride intact, safe in the knowledge that he would never know the truth. A truth she only admitted to herself now, as she stumbled over the stairs up which he had carried her so purposefully last night. That she was deeply and hopelessly in love with Leonidas Vassalio.

CHAPTER ELEVEN

MOVING LEADENLY THROUGH the silent cottage, Leonidas was checking each familiar room. He had promised Philomena's daughter he would do that for her, and that he would take anything he wanted. Anything that meant something to him, she had said.

Coming back through the kitchen, he let his glance touch painfully on a cherished oil-lamp, some sprigs of dried herbs, the stack of unused logs beside the huge stove, and his nostrils dilated from a host of evocative scents—rosemary, sage and pinewood, trapped there by shutters which remained reverently closed against the intrusion of the outside world.

There was nothing for him here. He had everything he wanted in the memory of Philomena's presence, her warmth and her voice, often scolding but always wise, and he wished fervently that she was there now, with her affectionate scolding and her wisdom.

He could hear her still, when he had run down here on countless occasions to escape his father's bellowing and his character-moulding brutality.

Be true to yourself, Leon.

But he hadn't been, had he? Not in his hopes and aspirations. In everything he hadn't been able to feel. Not since he'd been a child, or maybe a young adolescent, but certainly not as a man.

Since his mother had died and his father had blamed him for it he had built a hard, impervious shell around himself. A shell that no one, not even he himself, could crack. Only once had he ever—

He slammed the brakes on his errant thinking.

No, he hadn't been true to himself, he realised grimly. But that, like everything about this house, was now part of the past.

Grabbing one final look around filled him with such an ache of grief in his chest that he had to take a minute to steel himself before stepping outside into the bright sunlight and closing the door for the last time.

'I was just going to ring you,' Kayla said brightly as Lorna came through on her cell phone. 'The men have done a great job! The builder's been paid—in fact he's only just left—and the villa looks as good as new!'

She was standing looking up at the rafters above the galleried landing, and at the freshly rendered walls, which now bore no sign of the damage they had sustained earlier in the year. She tried not to think about how Leonidas—or Leon, she amended painfully—had rescued her that night, risking his own life in coming down here and carrying her out to the truck. She wasn't going to think about that. Or anything else about him, she decided achingly, just as she had promised herself she wouldn't when she had stepped off the ferry the previous day.

Josh hadn't been able to leave the business, and as his in-laws were away on an anniversary cruise Lorna had been fully intending to come here and do the inspection herself. But that had been before her doctor had strongly advised that she was in no condition to travel, so Kayla had immediately allayed her friend's anxieties by offering to come instead.

What she hadn't anticipated was how unbearably being here would affect her. She had known it would be painful, but just how excruciating she hadn't been prepared for. All she wanted to do now was lock up the villa, drive down and see Philomena, and then get the hell off this island before the last ferry left that day.

Now, to try and take her mind off the memories that were killing her, in a voice thickened by emotion she asked, 'Is there any news yet on that contract?'

The business that Havens Exclusive were giving them had all been agreed in principle, but the company seemed to be dragging its heels, and the paperwork that would secure it still hadn't come through. Josh and Lorna were on a knife-edge, waiting for the contract to arrive, and Kayla was secretly worried that it never would.

'That's why I'm ringing.'

The anxious note in Lorna's voice told Kayla that it still hadn't arrived.

'I rang Havens yesterday, and they seemed to think it was sent to us two weeks ago. Then today someone else said they didn't think it had been. I tried to ring Leonidas, to see if he knew anything about it, but his office said he was in Greece this week. I know you're not seeing him any more, but as you're already in the country, and as you said things between you only sort of…fizzled out…'

It had been the only way Kayla could describe her break-up with Leonidas to her friend without falling apart emotionally. 'I was wondering…is there anything you can do to get hold of him from your end? To see if you can find out what's happening?'

Lorna sounded in such a state that, although her nerves were already stretched to breaking point at the thought of calling him, Kayla agreed to help.

She knew he made regular trips between the UK and Greece, and with her heart thumping a few minutes later she got through to his Athens office.

'I'm afraid Mr Vassalio isn't here this week,' a thickly accented female voice informed her in nonetheless perfect English. 'You should be able to contact him on his mobile.'

'Thanks,' Kayla said, feeling deflated after it had taken so much courage to call in the first place.

It seemed too personal, ringing his cell phone number. Far, far too intimate... After a few moments, though, for Lorna's sake, she forced herself to do it.

'You have reached the voicemail of Leonidas Vassalio...'

Just hearing his deep tones sent fire tingling through her veins, but with her heart beating like crazy Kayla cut them off in mid-sentence. There was no way she could leave a message without her voice shaking uncontrollably. And then he'd know, wouldn't he?

She'd try him again later, she decided, breathing deeply to steady her pulse-rate. In the meantime she would do what she'd planned to do before Lorna had rung and pop down to see Philomena.

The shutters were closed when Kayla pulled up alongside the cottage, which wasn't that surprising as the late summer sun still burned fiercely here at this time of day, she thought. Even so, the flowers outside in their pots looked neglected and wilting, and there was an ominous air of emptiness about the place.

The door leading from the yard where she had sunbathed in the May sunshine looked securely closed, which was unusual, she realised, and there was no bread baking in the old clay oven, or any spotlessly clean washing hanging on the line.

As she came around the house, looking up at the shuttered windows, a man loading a cart called to her from a little way down the lane. He tilted his head, his weathered face sympathetic, and the expressive little gesture of his hands assured Kayla of what she dreaded most.

Oh, no!

As she wandered numbly around the side one solitary chicken ran clucking across the yard, and the sound only seemed to emphasise its screaming loneliness.

Her heart heavy with grief, Kayla got into the car, fighting back the emotion she could barely contain. But she knew she had to, because if she let it out for just a moment then she'd be swamped by it, she thought. By memories that were so much a part of this place. And Leonidas…

Her cell phone was sticking out of the bag she'd tossed onto the passenger seat, jolting her into remembering that she was supposed to try and contact him again.

Did he know? About Philomena? And then she realised that of course he would know. He would be heartbroken, she thought. In which case how could she ring him and ask him about something so trivial as a contract? She couldn't. Anyway, his office had told her that he hadn't come to Athens. And yet his London office had stated categorically that he had…

Of course!

Her gaze lifted swiftly to the hillside and the invisible ribbon of road that wound up above Lorna's villa. He would have been told about Philomena and he would have come here to be with her family. Because she was *his* family. Or the only person worth calling 'family' that Leonidas Vassalio had. In which case he would be here! Not in Athens! Here! At the farmhouse! Where else would he stay?

She didn't know if the little hatchback would stand up to the punishing drive as she tore out of the lane and took the zig-zagging road up to the familiar dirt track. She only knew she had to see him. She prayed to heaven that he would be there, and that he wouldn't send her away.

The farmhouse looked the same as she swung into the paved yard. Pale stone walls. Green peeling shutters. Its rickety terracotta roof seeming to grow out of the hillside rising sharply above it. The truck was still there too, looking as dusty and as sorry for itself as it ever had.

No one answered when she knocked at the flaking door.

Coming around the back, she noticed how baked everything looked from the hot, Ionian summer, remembering with a sharp shaft of pain how she had sat there on the terrace under that vine-covered canopy, enjoying the fish Leonidas had cooked for her the first time she had come here.

Again, there was no response to her knock, and after several attempts to make him hear she tried the doors. They were locked, just as Philomena's had been.

Everything was the same, but nothing was, she thought achingly, peering through one of the half-open shutters. Supposing he had gone? Supposing he hadn't been here at all? She couldn't bear it if he wasn't. She didn't think she'd ever find the courage to face him again.

She could see papers lying all over the kitchen table, just as there had been on that dreadful morning when she'd seduced him so shamelessly before discovering who he really was. And there was his pinboard with his plans on, propped up against the easel.

So he was immersing himself in work. Was that how he was dealing with his grief? Carrying on regardless with that formidable strength of character? That indomitable will that was such an integral part of the man she had so desperately fallen in love with?

A sound like a twig snapping behind her had her whirling round, her pulses missing a beat and then leaping into overdrive when she saw him striding up through the overgrown garden.

'What are you doing here?' He spoke in such a low whisper that she couldn't tell whether he welcomed seeing her, but his eyes were penetrating and his features were scored with shock.

'I came to check the villa. For the builder. I mean for Lorna.'

She was waffling, but she couldn't help it. Just the sight of him, in a loose-fitting, long-sleeved white shirt tucked into black denim jeans seemed to be turning her insides to mush.

He looked like the old Leon, with his chest half-bared and that thickening shadow around his mouth and chin. But his hair—only slightly longer than when she had seen him last—was still immaculately groomed, and with that air of power that Kayla could never detach from him now he was still very much Leonidas—the billionaire. He looked leaner, though, she decided, and his eyes were heavy, and she remembered in that moment that he was in mourning.

'I—I heard about Philomena.' She made a helpless little gesture. 'Just now. I went down there. I'm so…so sorry—' Tears threatened and she broke off, unable to keep the emotion out of her voice.

He merely dipped his head in acknowledgment. Perhaps he didn't trust himself to speak, Kayla thought.

'I thought you were gone. I wasn't sure if you'd even been here, and I wanted to see. To tell you.' She was prattling on again, but she didn't know what else to say to him. He wasn't making it particularly easy for her.

As he crossed the flagstones, taking his key out of his trouser pocket, she was struck, as she always was, by the grace and litheness with which he moved, and by his sheer, uncompromising masculinity.

'Is that why you came?' He glanced over his shoulder as he stooped to unlock the door.

'Yes,' she answered, because it *was* the only reason. She would never have had the courage to seek him out over anything less.

'And who told you I was here?' He pushed open the door, gestured for her to go inside.

'No one. I just put two and two together,' she said, moving

past him with every cell responding to the aching familiarity of him beneath her flimsy feminine tunic and leggings.

'And came up with four?' He sounded impressed as he followed her in. 'What made you so sure I was in the country?'

'I'd been trying to ring you,' she admitted, and then felt like biting off her tongue. But the atmosphere of the ancient farmhouse, with its familiar rusticity and evocative scents, was so overwhelming that she hadn't stopped to think.

'Oh?' His tone demanded more as he guided her into the sitting room. It looked the same, with its jaded walls and tapestries and its faded striped throws over the easy chairs. 'What about?' He gestured for her to sit down.

'Lorna's been getting worried,' she said, subsiding onto the sofa. 'I'm sorry,' she murmured, seeing the grooves already etched around his eyes and mouth deepening. 'I didn't want to mention it. Not right now.'

'The world has to keep turning,' he said, sounding resigned. 'Do you want some coffee?'

'Something cold,' she appealed, thinking that nothing seemed so cold and detached from her as he did right then. She wondered if she should have come; wondered painfully if he was annoyed with her because she had.

He returned minutes later with two tall frosted glasses of an iced citrus drink.

'So Lorna's worried?' he reminded her as she sipped the liquid gratefully. It was sharp and very refreshing. 'What about?'

'They haven't received the contract that Havens were supposed to be supplying.'

'Supposed to be?' His eyes were darkly penetrative as he set his own glass down on a side table.

'I was just worried that...'

'Yes?'

Why was he looking at her like that? Kayla wondered. As though he wanted to plunder her very soul?

'…that you might have changed your mind. About giving them that order.'

There. She had said it. So why didn't she feel any relief? And why was he looking at her with his mouth turning down in distaste, as though she was something that had just crawled out from one of the cracks in the walls outside?

'So you still think I'd do that? You are still so shot through with doubt and suspicion over what your father and your fiancé did to you that you think every man who carries a briefcase and has a secretary can't be anything but an unscrupulous bastard?'

'That's not true!'

'Isn't it?' he shot back. 'We're a type. Isn't that what you said?'

He was standing above her, hands on hips, his legs planted firmly apart. It was such a dominant pose that her gaze faltered beneath his. With heart-quickening dismay she realised she had let it fall to somewhere below his tight lean waist—which was worse.

'Well, it's true, isn't it?' she said, hurting, feeling her body's response to his hard virility even as he stood there actively judging her. 'You lied to me about everything! Every single thing! And when I didn't like it you used my friends to blackmail me into living with you until…'

'Until what?' he pressed, relentless.

'Until you'd got what you wanted.'

'And what was that?' His eyes were shielded by the thick ebony of his lashes and his question was an almost ragged demand.

'You know very well.'

'No, I don't. I'm afraid you're going to have to spell it out for me.'

'Until you'd got me to go to bed with you.' There were flags of pink across her cheekbones, lending some colour to her pale skin beneath the summer-bleached gold of her loose hair. 'Wasn't that the whole idea of having me move in with you?' she said wretchedly. 'To salvage your pride and your ego? Wasn't it enough that you made a complete fool out of me without robbing me of my dignity and my self-respect as well?'

'Is that what I did?' His eyes as they met hers held some dark, unfathomable emotion. 'I really didn't realise that in making love with me you were sacrificing all that.'

The raw note in his voice had her searching his face with painful intensity, but his features were shuttered and unreadable.

Her fingers were icy around the glass, but she couldn't seem to feel them. She couldn't feel anything except her aching love for him and the raw agony of seeing him again when he didn't share her feelings, when he had admitted to being incapable of love—virtually ridiculing it—that night he had carried her to his bed.

'I just wasn't happy being another notch on your bedpost,' she murmured, looking down at the striped fabric covering the sofa and wondering what had happened in his life to make him so hard-bitten as she plucked absently at a loose strand of the faded weave.

'Neither was I. That was why I let you go.'

'That was very magnanimous of you.' Her throat was clogged with emotion. Pray heaven that he didn't guess just how much he had hurt her!

'Just as well I did—in the circumstances,' he said. 'I wouldn't have been able to keep my hands off you if you had stayed.'

The 'circumstances' meaning the loss of her dignity and self-respect, Kayla realised painfully, wanting to tell him that making love with him had been the most intense and pleasurable experience of her life.

'Well, you can tell Lorna that she doesn't need to worry...'

Suddenly he was talking about business, dismissing what had happened between them as easily and as ruthlessly as he had dismissed her from his life. 'That contract should have been with Kendon Interiors over two weeks ago. I'll get on to Havens right away and your friends will have it within the next forty-eight hours.'

So he hadn't been withholding it, Kayla thought. She had satisfied his requirements and he was upholding his part of the bargain. She just wished it hadn't cost her so much to make it possible. But it had. And it hurt—like hell.

'What's wrong?'

Through the crushing emotion that seemed to be weighing her down she caught his hard yet strangely husky enquiry. His eyes were narrowed, probing, digging down into her soul again, and Kayla sucked in a panicky breath as he moved closer. He'd claimed her body as his own, and she would bear the brand of his consummate lovemaking for the rest of her life, but she wasn't going to let him know that he had branded her heart as well!

'I'd better go.' She leaped up, spilling some of the juice she had scarcely touched over her clothes and over the flags. 'Oh, no…'

'I'll get you a towel.' The glass was retrieved from her shaking hand.

'I can do it myself,' she told him, her voice cracking.

'Kayla!'

There was a thread of urgency in his voice but she took no heed of it as she stumbled along to the kitchen. The pain of loving him was like a knife piercing her heart.

It would be so easy to break down. To let him see how much she cared. But if she did that then she would only be inviting more humiliation—and ultimately more pain. He would use her again, solely in the name of pleasure. And she would let him, she thought wildly, knowing she had to clean herself up as quickly as she could and get as far away from this place—from him—as was humanly possible.

She'd been a fool to come, she realised, grabbing several sheets of kitchen paper from the roll that hung next to the sink and starting to dab it hastily over her wet tunic. She should have telephoned him. E-mailed. Anything but risk coming here and putting herself through this. But she'd wanted to see him. Speak to him. What kind of a first-rate fool did that make her? She was a glutton for punishment if she'd imagined that coming here—even if it was purely to offer him her sympathies over Philomena—would leave her unaffected and unscathed. And if she'd been hoping, even subconsciously, that seeing him again might change the status quo between them, then she'd forgotten—or was choosing to ignore—every lesson she'd thought she had learned. For all his good points—and there were a lot of them—he was still a ruthless businessman. A self-confessed, hard-headed realist, who believed that love and sentimentality were for fools.

Well, she'd leave him to his laptop and his papers and his... Plans?

The word died from her consciousness as she swung painfully round to face them, having tossed the damp, scrunched-up kitchen roll into the bin. The easel was angled towards the front window, which was why she hadn't seen it when she'd peered through the back shutters earlier. But the pinboard was a canvas, and what she'd thought were plans was...

A full-length painting of *her!*

He had captured her as she must have looked that day coming out of the sea, wearing only her white smock-top and bikini briefs. Her hair was blowing loose and she was looking down at something in the water, her golden lashes accentuated with a sensuality she had never attributed to them before. What she was wearing was sheer, yet her body was indistinct through the folds of virginal gossamer. It was a work of bold strokes.

Movement. But above all else of the soul. Only a man could have painted her with such intrinsic sensuality, she thought. A man who loved his subject. Who knew her inside and out...

She put her hand up as though to touch it and as quickly retracted it, her fingers curling into a tight ball which she pressed to her mouth as tears started to fall.

They had changed to racking sobs in the time it took Leonidas to cross from the doorway and reach her.

'Kayla...' The depth of her emotion tore at him and she put up no resistance as he pulled her into his arms.

She was crying for Philomena. He wasn't blind enough not to know that. She was remembering where she had come from that day and who she had been staying with...

'Oh, my darling beautiful girl, don't cry.'

He'd intended to say it in Greek, and only realised when she lifted her head and looked at him with soul-searching intensity that he had said it in English—and that it was too late.

'Why didn't you tell me?' she breathed in a shocked little whisper.

'About the painting?' His voice trembled with emotion as he used his thumb to wipe away her tears. 'Or about being in love with you?'

There. It was out now, he thought, and he would have to bear the consequences of baring his soul.

'What?' Kayla couldn't believe that she was hearing properly. 'About the painting...' She shook her head as though to clear it—uttered a little laugh through her tears. 'Both!' Was he really saying this? Hectically, her eyes searched his face.

'Why do you think I wanted you with me?' he uttered deeply, on a shuddering note, hardly daring to believe that she wasn't ridiculing him.

'To salvage your pride.' Pain lined her forehead as she remembered that last morning. 'You said so yourself.'

'Well, there was a bit of that, I'll admit.' He pulled a self-deprecating face. 'But mainly it was because I wanted to get you to trust me again. There was no other way I could think of that would break through the barriers you'd erected against me—and not just because I hadn't been straight with you in the beginning, but because you believed I was the type of man who had hurt you so badly before—the type you so clearly despised. I was hoping you would look beyond the outer shell and see that I was different from those other men you'd known. Yet I only compounded my mistakes by browbeating you into staying with me. I would never have gone back on my word over that contract. But when I realised that you really believed I was manipulative enough to be using your friends to get to you—was actually capable of destroying everything they had if you didn't do exactly what I wanted—I guess it was more than a crushing blow to my pride. I decided I didn't have anything to lose. I needed to earn your respect. That's why I wanted to take things slowly for a while and not complicate matters by taking you to bed, though it was torture having to exercise enough restraint not to do so. When we did make love and you cried I knew it was because your heart didn't want it, even though physically you couldn't resist this thing we have between us any more than I could.'

'That isn't true,' Kayla denied emphatically, knowing she had to tell him now. 'I was crying because I love you—because the whole experience for me had been so…so amazingly incredible. And because I knew—thought—you didn't feel anything for me and that sooner or later you'd want me to go. And you did,' she reminded him, with all the agony of the past few weeks rising up to torment her again. 'Why? If you feel the same way I do?'

'Because I didn't fully realise it—or want to acknowledge it—until after you'd gone,' he admitted, his chest lifting heavily, 'and I didn't want to hurt you any more than I knew I already had.'

'And all the time you've been doing this…' She pulled back from him slightly to gaze awestruck at the painting. 'Wow! Do I really look like that?'

'You'd better believe it,' he said, with a sexy sidelong grin.

'It's brilliant. You're a genius,' she praised, and he laughed. 'No, I'm serious,' she breathed, meaning it. She couldn't understand why, with so much talent, he hadn't made art his career.

He made a self-deprecating sound down his nostrils when she asked him. 'There were reasons,' he divulged almost brokenly.

'What reasons?' she pressed gently, realising that it was stirring up some deeply buried pain for him to talk about it.

'My father had other ideas for me,' he said. 'He wouldn't countenance having a son who painted for a living. He thought it less than manly. We argued about it—and never stopped arguing about it.' And now he had started pouring out his most agonising secret he couldn't stop. 'We were arguing about it in the car the night my mother died. If I hadn't been determined to oppose his will he wouldn't have kept turning round to shout at me and we would never have had the accident that killed her. I wouldn't let up when I knew I should have, and it was my mother who ultimately paid the price. After that even the thought of painting was abominable to me. How could it be anything else?' he suggested, his strong features ravaged by the pain he had carried all these years. 'Knowing that she'd died because of it. Because of *me!*'

'You didn't kill her!' Kayla exhaled, understanding now what devils had been driving him all his life to make him so hard-headed and single-mindedly determined—understanding a lot of things now. 'You were—what? Fourteen? Fifteen? Barely more than a child! Your father was the driver. He was also an adult. It was up to him to exercise restraint until he'd stopped the car.'

'My father didn't see it like that,' he relayed. Yet for the first time he found himself taking some solace from the tender arms that went around him, from the gentle yet determined reasoning in her words.

Art was feeling and feelings were weakness. His father had indoctrinated that into him. But the feelings he had for this beautiful woman—which were being unbelievably reciprocated—made him feel stronger than he had ever felt in his life.

'This house…it's yours, isn't it?' Kayla murmured, with her head against his shoulder. 'This is where you lived when you were a boy.'

Locked in his arms, she felt the briefest movement of his strong body as he nodded. 'It was the first time I'd been able to bring myself back here since my father died last year. The first time I'd been back—apart from visits to Philomena—in over fifteen years.'

His voice cracked as he mentioned the grandmother figure who had filled the void when he had been left motherless and without the nucleus of a loving family. Understanding, Kayla held him closer. Hadn't she lost a grandmother too?

'I love you,' she whispered. It was the only thing it felt right to say just then.

He smiled down at her and her heart missed a beat when she recognised the sultry, satisfied response of the man she had fallen in love with. 'I love you too—very much, *psihi mou*. We may not have got off to a very good start, but knowing you has made me see that there are more important things in life than everything I've been pursuing. Oh, money and position are wonderful to have, but they're nothing without the most precious things in life—like a caring partner and a family. Without love,' he murmured against her lips, acknowledging it indisputably now. 'Do you think you would find it too much of a punishment to marry a company man with a brief-case and a secretary—who, incidentally, is fifty-three years

old and worth her weight in gold? A man who—also incidentally—*does* own an island and builds eyesores for a living?
Though not literally. He leaves the spade and shovel work to
his minions nowadays.'

He was joking about the minions. She could hear it in his
voice. But she couldn't believe he was actually asking her to
be his wife.

'Of course if you don't want to...' He was looking so uncertain, so vulnerable, that she reached up and brought his
head down to hers.

'Leonidas Vassalio, of course I'll marry you,' she whispered smilingly, before she kissed him and felt the surge of
power that trembled through his body as he caught her to
him. 'Leon...'

That's better, his eyes said approvingly when he lifted his
head, and the gleam in their dark depths promised everything
that was joyous and exciting. 'And now...' suddenly he was
sweeping her up into his arms '...I believe we have some unfinished business upstairs.'

Much later, after he'd gone to make some coffee, Kayla was
surprised when he returned almost immediately.

'Your cell phone is bleeping,' he told her, handing over
her bag, and she was alarmed to see the display on her phone
showing half a dozen missed calls—all from Josh.

'Lorna's in hospital,' she told Leonidas when she'd finished speaking to her friend's husband. 'She was rushed in
for a Caesarean section this afternoon but everything's OK.'
She was laughing and crying as she added, 'Both mother and
daughter are doing well!'

'Thank heaven for that!' he expressed, with his hand against
his robed chest, looking as thrilled and almost as relieved as
Kayla felt. 'This means we have to get a move on if we want
to catch up with Josh and Lorna—particularly if you're going

to fill my island with dogs and horses and babies, Mrs Vassalio. It's in the Bahamas, by the way. And at this exact moment I can't do too much to fulfil your dreams with the first two things on your wish-list, but I can certainly do something right now about fulfilling the last!'

Later, lying in his arms, Kayla stirred and stretched contentedly.

He's a good man, Philomena had tried to tell her, and Kayla knew that now. She also knew that as men came—company or otherwise—they didn't come any better.

* * * * *

GREEK FOR BEGINNERS

JACKIE BRAUN

To Roma Costanzo with thanks for all of her love and support!

Jackie Braun is the author of more than two dozen romance novels and novellas. She is a three-time RITA® Award finalist, a four-time National Readers' Choice Awards finalist, the winner of a Rising Star Award in traditional romantic fiction and was nominated for Series Storyteller of the Year by RT Book Reviews in 2008. She makes her home in mid-Michigan with her husband and their two children. She enjoys gardening and gabbing and can be reached on Facebook at facebook.com/authorjackiebraun or through her website at www.jackiebraun.com

CHAPTER ONE

IF DARCIE HAYES had any lingering doubts about her decision to call off her wedding a week before the "I dos" and end her engagement to her longtime beau, they were eradicated the moment she stepped off the plane in Athens and scanned the crowd.

A driver was supposed to meet her at the airport. That was part of the nonrefundable, all-inclusive Greek tour package that her spendthrift fiancé had booked for their honeymoon. The honeymoon she had decided to take alone.

Tad got their Buffalo, New York, condominium and their antisocial cat in the breakup. She'd figured a couple of weeks away from her well-meaning friends and family in sun-drenched Greece was a fair trade since she'd never liked the condo, and the cat had never liked her. Now, she had the sinking feeling that Tad had gotten the better end of the deal.

She saw no hand-printed sign bearing her name. Nor was anyone smiling in welcome and waving to gain her attention. For a brief moment, a handsome man on a cell phone stopped talking and their gazes met.

Her best friend Becky's last text played through Darcie's head.

Meet a man. Have a fling. Get ur sexy back.

Becky had wanted to come on the trip, but she hadn't

been able to get the time off work on such short notice. That wasn't stopping her from giving Darcie all sorts of advice on how to spend her time, including having a fling. Well, if Darcie were going to cast caution to the wind, this would be exactly the sort of man she would pick to do it with. He was so gorgeous that her mouth threatened to fall open. It settled for watering, and she was forced to swallow or she would have drooled. The crowd of departing passengers surged around him then, obstructing her view. When the travelers cleared, he was gone.

After that, the only person who made eye contact with Darcie was a portly porter who approached with a trolley as she waited for her bags at the luggage carousel. It was just her luck that only one of the designer knock-offs showed up. It was the smaller of the two—the bag in which she'd packed her "second-string" outfits, the first string being the new clothes she'd bought especially for the trip. The bag sported wheels and a retractable handle, but the handle was out and dangling uselessly to the side. As for the wheels, one had been sheared off somehow.

The porter pointed to the missing wheel and busted handle, and then pointed to the trolley. Darcie nodded. Even though the bag was only one size up from a carry-on, when she'd hefted it onto the scale at the airport in Buffalo, she'd nearly given herself a hernia. She was more than happy to have someone else do the heavy lifting now.

The porter was old enough to be her father, but nothing about the smile he gave her was paternal. After loading her bag onto a cart, he winked. Then his gaze skimmed down and he said something in Greek that, even though she didn't know what it meant, had her checking the buttons on her blouse to be sure they were fastened.

"I, um, can take it from here," Darcie said, handing him

a couple euros for a tip and then making a shooing motion with her hands.

Alone again, she heaved a frustrated sigh. So much for the part of her itinerary that read, "You will be met at the airport by a member of our friendly and efficient English-speaking staff and taken directly to one of Athens's finest hotels."

But then what her near-miss of a husband considered "sparing no expense" on the trip of a lifetime and how the majority of people would define the concept were two different things entirely. Tad had never earned a penny that he hadn't pinched mercilessly afterward. Darcie was all for getting a good deal, but more often than not, you got what you paid for. She had a bad feeling this trip was going to be a case in point. The plane ride had been her first clue, wedged as she'd been for the long, transatlantic flight into a coach seat so narrow that even a runway model would have found the dimensions unforgiving.

Darcie wasn't a runway model, nor would she ever be mistaken for one, even if at five foot eleven she had the height. She also had curves, the kind for which words such as *big-boned* and, her personal favorite, *full-figured* had been strung together. She'd long ago reconciled herself to that fact that no amount of dieting was going to result in her being considered dainty. Instead, through hard work and an amount of discipline she hadn't known she'd possessed, she'd toned her body into its best shape ever for her wedding day. She'd planned to rock the church wearing a fitted white mermaid gown, but she'd never walked down the aisle.

That had been her choice, but still…

She headed for the nearest counter, putting her back into steering the trolley, which, she discovered, had an annoying tendency to veer to the right. All the way there, she prayed that one of the two uniformed men standing behind the counter would speak enough English to understand her.

"Excuse me," she began, smiling at both. *"Yia sas."* That meant "hello" and pretty much measured the extent of her Greek.

Luckily, one of the men replied in English, "Hello. How can I assist you?"

"Someone from my tour was supposed to meet me here and take me to my hotel, but I don't see anyone. I was hoping you might know where I should wait for them."

The man nodded. "What is the name of the company?"

"It's Zeus Tours." She rifled through her purse and produced a full-color brochure and a printout of her itinerary, which she handed to him.

The mouth under his thick moustache twitched with a smile and he nodded again. "Zeus Tours. *Ne.*"

"You know of them?"

"Ne," he said again. It meant "yes," but his amused expression didn't leave her feeling relieved. Next to him, the other man had started to chuckle.

Oh, this didn't bode well, but she forged ahead. "Um, so are they here?" She gestured to the busy terminal at large.

He glanced around. "I do not see Stavros."

The other man said something in Greek that had them sharing a laugh.

"Stavros." She repeated on a nod. "Am I supposed to meet this Stavros somewhere other than here?"

"Here. There." The man shrugged. "I suggest you have a seat and make yourself comfortable." He handed the papers back to her and pointed to a nearby bank of chairs. "It could be a while."

"A while?" Her stomach dropped.

"Stavros keeps his own schedule. If he owns a watch, he never consults it."

At this the man's coworker hooted with laughter.

Darcie was tired and growing irritable. She wanted a shower, a nap and something to eat, not necessarily in that order. It wouldn't hurt to throw in a drink somewhere, either. A nice glass of chilled white wine, perhaps. Or a shot of ouzo…straight from the bottle. What she didn't want to do was spend any more of her first day in Athens in the airport as the punch line for a joke. But she worked up a smile and offered her thanks.

She was attempting to wheel the trolley away when someone tapped her on the shoulder. Darcie turned to find the gorgeous man she'd spied earlier. Her stomach took another dive, but this time for reasons that had nothing to do with disappointment.

Up close, she realized that he was taller than she was. Darcie actually had to look up. Even if she'd been wearing the highest pair of heels she owned, she only would have been on eye level. Six foot three, she figured, and every last inch of him was packaged in firm muscle beneath an untucked white linen shirt and a pair of designer jeans that fit snugly across the thigh.

His skin was tanned, his jaw subtly shadowed. His hair was nearly black and fell across brows of the exact shade. The eyes below those brows were a rich chocolate-brown and smiling even though his mouth held only the faintest curve.

"Hello," he said.

Her tongue untied long enough for her to manage a basic greeting. "Hi."

"I could not help but overhear your conversation. Maybe I can be of help," he said in gorgeously accented English.

"I hope so." It came out on a sigh and Darcie came to her senses. "What I mean is, my fi— Um, friend booked an all-inclusive vacation package with Zeus Tours. I was

promised that someone would meet me at the airport, but…"
She lifted her shoulders in a shrug.

"Ah, Zeus Tours." Like the pair at the counter, the man
apparently was acquainted with the company, but he didn't
laugh. Rather, the corners of his mouth turned down in a
frown. "May I ask why you decided to book your trip with
that particular company?"

"My, um, friend found them on the internet and got a
really good deal."

It sounded like he said, "I am sure she did." He glanced
around then. "And where is your friend?"

Tad was probably with his mother, Darcie mused. It had
taken her six years to accept the fact that an engagement
ring was no match for the tight knots in Evelyn's apron
strings.

"Couldn't make it," she replied, leaving off the telltale
pronoun.

A pair of dark brows rose. "So, you came to Greece by
yourself?"

Even a man who looked like a Greek god could be a psychopathic killer. So, Darcie said carefully, "Yes, but you
know, it's a guided tour and they're expecting me."

The man glanced around and then back at her.

"Well, I'm sure someone will be here…any minute." She
pulled out the brochure again and tapped the front of it with
the tip of one finger. "I've been assured a *safe* and *super-
vised* good time over the course of the next two weeks."

This time the man's mouth joined his eyes in smiling.

"I apologize. I am making you nervous when I am only
trying to help. Here." He pulled out the cell phone she'd
seen him talking on earlier. "If you give me the number, I
will call the company for you. I know the owner. He and I
went to grade school together."

A psychopathic killer wouldn't offer to make phone calls, she reasoned. She handed him the brochure.

Darcie could hear only one side of the conversation and it was in rapid-fire Greek, but she could figure out easily enough that the handsome stranger was irritated on her behalf. Whoever was on the other end of the line was getting an earful. When the man concluded the call, he returned the phone to his back pocket.

"Well?" she asked.

"Unfortunately, your ride has been delayed. I will take you to your hotel."

"You…but…" she sputtered and glanced around, torn. She was eager to leave the airport, unpack and unwind in the comfort of her hotel room, but… "I don't even know your name."

He smiled. "I am Nick. Nick Costas. The men at the counter can vouch for me, if you would like. I fly in and out of this airport often enough. Or I can show you some identification." Without waiting for a reply, he pulled out his wallet and produced his driver's license.

"The State of New York?" She glanced up. "You're American?"

"Yes, for the past five years, but much of my family still lives in Athens. Between business and family, I am here often." He pocketed his wallet. "And you are?"

Single now.

She cleared her throat and in a demure voice managed to respond, "Darcie Hayes of Buffalo. We're practically neighbors."

It was a stretch given that his address was on Park Avenue in Manhattan and she lived upstate, several hours away. They shared a time zone but were worlds apart based on the designer watch strapped to his wrist.

Still, he was attracted to her.

She may have been long out of practice when it came to flirting, but she knew male interest when she saw it. For a woman who'd spent several years waiting to walk down the aisle while her boyfriend deferred to his mother's wishes, it was heady stuff indeed.

"It's good to meet you, Darcie Hayes of Buffalo."

He offered a hand and their palms met briefly. The simple contact managed to make her insides quake. Of course, they were shaky to begin with as a result of exhaustion and the fact that she'd bypassed the in-flight meal of mystery meat coated in unappetizing neon yellow gravy. Still, she pulled back her hand, worried she might make a fool of herself.

"It's nice to meet you, too. And I really appreciate your help." She tucked a hank of hair behind one ear. "Um, what did the tour company people say?"

"Stavros is…indisposed."

Stavros, there was that name again. Nick said he'd gone to school with the man who owned the company, but she asked hopefully, "Is this Stavros the driver?"

"The driver, the tour guide and the owner of Zeus Tours."

"Oh, boy. A real multitasker, hmm?" She blew out a breath. "When you say indisposed, what does that mean exactly? Has he fallen and broken his leg? Or contracted a nasty virus and is racked with fever?"

Nick shook his head. "Stavros is still lying in bed. He told me that he had a late night out with his friends and overindulged."

"He's h-h-hung over?" she sputtered incredulously.

"I am afraid so."

Darcie gritted her teeth. She should have known. The moment Tad bragged that he'd gotten a great deal, it should have been abundantly clear that the dream Greek honeymoon trip he'd booked was too good to be true for a reason.

"I was really hoping this Stavros had a stomach bug,"

she muttered. This surprised a laugh out of Nick. She asked him, "How familiar are you with Zeus Tours?"

Nick wasn't laughing now. "I am familiar enough to know that Stavros pours more money down his throat than he puts back into his company. He took over when his father died two years ago. In that time, he has had to let go more than half of his employees. He is not a bad man, but neither is he a good businessman."

Although she wasn't normally one to air her complaints to a stranger, weariness had her muttering, "Terrific. Just terrific. I'm here for a vacation. God knows, I'm due for one. I haven't had a day off work in two years. I've worked overtime and taken every crappy assignment I was handed without complaint so I could save up money for…for…" She waved a hand and tried to reel in her emotions. "Anyway, I was counting on the vacation described in the brochure—first-rate accommodations, air-conditioned motor coaches for sightseeing with a knowledgeable guide, authentic Greek cuisine at some of the country's best restaurants. Is this company going to be able to deliver on *any* of its promises?"

"No." He didn't hesitate at all, making that one word all the more damning.

Darcie closed her eyes briefly. "Of course not. Half of my luggage is missing. What showed up is, well, the half I wish were missing. Not that it really matters, given that my dream vacation is turning out to be a bust and I haven't even gotten out of the airport yet." She sighed. "I should have taken the condo and Rufus."

"Rufus?"

"Also know as the spawn of Satan. He's a cat," she added when Nick continued to frown. Not that her explanation made anything clear. She shook her head. "Never mind. Trust me when I say, this is the story of my life."

"Come." Nick smiled. "You can share this story of your life on the drive to your hotel."

Why not?

Darcie decided to listen to the little voice telling her that Nick Costas wasn't a threat. After all, it was the same little voice that had told her to cut all ties and run where her ex-fiancé was concerned, so she figured it knew what it was talking about. It had taken her several years to pay attention the last time. She only had two weeks in Greece. She was going to make the most of them. Starting now.

"In the mood for a good laugh, are you?" she asked wryly.

Nick smiled again. Oh, he was in the mood...for something. A diversion at the very least, and he figured he'd found one. A pretty one, too, given the woman's tumble of chestnut hair, wide-set Aegean blue eyes and a body that would have made the ancient goddesses green with envy.

He'd come to the airport that day with every intention of leaving Greece and returning to his home in Manhattan. He'd booked a flight to New York, a flight that would be boarding shortly without him. Just as well. He'd been angry with his family and their unabashed matchmaking and had allowed his emotions to cloud his judgment.

Of course, he would have to be back in Greece within a fortnight anyway. No amount of irritation would cause him to miss his brother's wedding. He would never live down the talk otherwise. And there was plenty of that already since Pieter was marrying Nick's childhood sweetheart, Selene.

Half of Athens was gossiping about it, waiting for a fight to erupt between the brothers. Nick was determined not to indulge the gawkers, as awkward and, yes, painful, as the situation was. He lamented the strain between him and Pieter. He regretted the division in his once unified family. But neither could be helped. The best he could do was to gather up his dignity and feign indifference.

"Allow me," he told Darcie and took over pushing the trolley. Five steps later, he nearly took out a bank of unoccupied chairs.

"It wants to go in circles," she warned.

She was shaking her head and smiling. He liked her smile. Her lips were inviting even without any added gloss. A lovely diversion, he thought again.

And why not? He was entitled. He had no strings to tangle him up. He hadn't had those since Selene. That was the way he preferred it, too, as he'd pointed out to his grandmother that very morning when Yiayia expressed concern about his ongoing single status. Nick had no such concerns. What he had was a plan, a meticulously crafted five-year plan to grow his auction business. After that, he might start thinking about settling down, but never again would he allow his heart to be broken. Once was enough.

"Is this part of the story of your life?" he asked Darcie, motioning to the wayward cart.

"That's right." She lowered her voice to a confidential whisper. "I probably shouldn't tell you this, but since you're being so nice, I feel I owe you the truth. I'm a magnet for bad luck."

"Really?"

"Really. Swear." She traced a cross over her very impressive chest.

Nick followed the progress of her fingertip before allowing his gaze to lift to her lips again. "Perhaps your luck is about to change."

CHAPTER TWO

WHILE SHE WAITED for Nick to retrieve his car from the long-term parking lot, Darcie called Becky. Even if she didn't think Nick was a psycho, she decided it would be wise to let someone know she had arrived safely in Athens and was now in the hands of a stranger. Calling her parents was out of the question. Ditto for her sisters. That left Becky, who answered on the fifth ring.

"Someone had better be dying," her friend muttered ominously, and Darcie realized it was the middle of the night in Buffalo.

"I'm not dying, just checking in," she said. "Sorry I woke you, Becks. I forget about the time difference."

"Darcie? Oh. Hey." She pictured Becky struggling to a sitting position on her bed and trying to force the cobwebs from her head. "Is everything okay?"

Darcie scuffed the toe of one shoe against the pavement. "Sort of."

"What does that mean?"

"Well, my flight arrived on time, but I'm missing half of my luggage. The good half."

Becky had helped her pack, so she commiserated. "That stinks. On the bright side, now you have a valid excuse to buy more clothes."

"Yeah." Like Darcie could afford to do that. She coughed

and continued. "Oh, and there's been one other small glitch. No one from the tour company was at the airport to meet me."

"What? That's ridiculous. You need to report them to the Better Business Bureau or something."

"I know. Apparently, the owner of the company is a lush." She forced out a laugh. "Figures, right? I mean, Tad got such a good deal on this vacation there was bound to be a catch."

Becky muttered something obscene about Tad. It wasn't anything Darcie hadn't heard before. Her friend had been quite vocal in her dislike of him. That had been a source of contention between the two women in the past, but no longer. She found herself wondering what Becky would make of Nick.

"I hope the rest of the trip goes smoothly," her friend said.

Unfortunately, based on what Nick had told Darcie, she had her doubts. She told Becky as much.

"What are you going to do? Can you get a refund and hook up with a different company?"

"I don't know." The fine print on the package said the price was nonrefundable, but Darcie planned to try anyway. She figured she had nothing to lose. "In the meantime, I have a ride to the first hotel on the itinerary. The tour group is supposed to stay there for a couple of nights. That should give me time to see if the company is going to be able to deliver on any of its promises and, if not, make other arrangements." At least she hoped it would.

"Good. Darcie, if you need money—"

"No. I don't. But thanks." Not only could Becky not afford it, but she'd also been generous enough already, letting Darcie crash at her apartment until she found a place of her own. That certainly beat moving back in with her parents, even temporarily. What thirty-year-old woman wanted to do that?

Darcie took a deep breath then and, keeping her tone non-chalant, said, "You're going to love this. The person who agreed to drive me is this insanely gorgeous man with an accent that is to die for."

There was a slight pause before Becky asked, "You're taking a cab, right?"

"No. Actually, I met this man in the airport and he... offered to drive. He showed me identification," she hastened to add. "His name is Nick Costas. He lives in Manhattan, but he's from Athens originally."

"Darcie, I don't know," Becky began, worry evident in her tone.

"What happened to, 'Have a fling and get ur sexy back?' Hmm?"

"Well, I didn't actually expect you to take my advice! When do you ever listen to me? I mean, if you listened to me, you never would have given Tad the time of day, much less wasted six years of your life engaged to him."

Point taken. Becky had told Darcie from the start that Tad was a first-class mama's boy and would stay that way.

"Relax. I'm not having a fling. It's only a ride to a hotel. Nothing more." Except maybe in her fantasies.

"Okay, but call me when you get there."

"I will."

"Promise me, Darcie. I'm not going to be able to go back to sleep until you do."

"I promise. I'll call."

She hung up just as Nick's car pulled to the curb. Unlike the other boxy subcompacts parked nearby, it was a sleek, low-slung convertible.

"Nice car." She tapped a finger to her lips as she studied its graceful lines. "A 1963 Porsche, right?"

He nodded slowly. "A 356 Super 90 Cabriolet, to be exact."

"Fully restored?"

"Yes, but with original parts. And I have a certificate of authenticity from the manufacturer."

"Ooh. That pushes up its value."

"It does." Nick tilted his head to the side. "How is it that you know so much about automobiles?"

Darcie chuckled at his incredulous expression. "I work for a classic car magazine. I guess I picked up a few things along the way."

"You're a writer."

She frowned. Not for lack of wanting, she thought. "No. I just check the facts of articles other people write."

"Which magazine might that be?"

"*Automobile Enthusiasts Monthly.* It's relatively small and based in Buffalo. You probably haven't heard of it." Darcie hadn't until Tad's friend had offered her the job just before her engagement.

"I have a subscription. I find it very *factual.*" He got out of the car and stood beside her. "What else can you tell me about this particular model Porsche?"

"Well, as I recall, it was very popular in America when it first came out."

"It still is among collectors."

"And you're a collector." It made sense. A man with a Park Avenue address likely would have the disposable income to indulge his whims, even ones that ran into six figures.

But Nick was shaking his head. "I collect for others. As much as I like this automobile, I will not be buying it. It will go to whoever pays the most to possess it. It is what I do for a living." He pulled out a business card, which he handed to her. It read, Costas Classic Auto Sales and Auctions.

"Impressive."

"It would appear that you and I have two interests in common."

"Two?"

"Classic cars and…" His smile could have melted a glass and made it clear what that other interest was. She smiled in return and hoped the laughter that followed came off as worldly rather than the sort fueled by giddiness and nerves.

"Let me take your bag," he said.

The Porsche had a rear engine, meaning its trunk was in the front. When Nick opened the compartment, Darcie eyed the small space.

"Gee, maybe it's just as well the airline lost one of my bags. I don't think both of them would fit in here. I guess when you own one of these babies you have to travel light to travel in style." She glanced at Nick, a question forming. "Where's your luggage?"

The left side of his mouth rose. "On a plane bound for New York." At her puzzled expression, he added, "I was planning to fly back today."

"Why did you change your mind?"

"I decided I was being rash."

"So you missed your flight and offered assistance to a perfect stranger instead," she replied dryly. Talk about rash…and flattering. Just wait until she told Becky *that*. Her friend was going to hyperventilate. As it was, Darcie's breathing was a little uneven.

"A stranded stranger," Nick corrected. His smile was full-blown this time and very effective. "One who is also very beautiful."

Her heart fluttered and she blinked. "Oh."

"You are blushing."

"I, um…" She waved a hand, not certain how to reply.

"Surely, you have been told before that you are beautiful?"

"Of course I have." She rolled her eyes. "All the time, in fact. We're talking daily. It gets old."

The truth was no, at least not in the past several years. Tad wasn't one for compliments. Even during the courtship phase of their relationship, pretty words had been few and far between. After he'd slid an engagement ring on her finger? Forget about it.

"You know how I feel about you, Darcie. That should be enough."

Maybe it should have been. But it wasn't. Every now and then, especially when she was PMSing and feeling bloated and unattractive, a compliment would have been nice.

And then there was his mother. Evil Evelyn, as Becky had dubbed her. The older woman was quick with thinly veiled digs about Darcie's appearance, including her good "birthing hips."

"You are beautiful," Nick said again. "And your blush only makes you more so."

This time, Darcie accepted the compliment with what she hoped was a gracious smile. *Beautiful.* Why not? Wasn't beauty in the eye of the beholder? And what a beholder.

Nick opened the car door for her before heading around to the driver's side. It was another small courtesy that made her feel like she'd stepped into some sort of fairy tale.

"Shall I put up the top?"

"No," she told him. "Leave it down. I can use the fresh air after all those hours in a stuffy airplane."

And, okay, in her fairy tale, a ride in a Porsche convertible only added to the romance.

He was seated behind the wheel now. "Even if it means tangled hair?" He reached over and coiled the end of one lock around his index finger. If he wound it any tighter, she would be forced to lean closer to him.

While their gazes held, she blindly plumbed the depths of her oversized purse until her fingers encountered an elastic band. Pulling it out with the same verve a magician uses to produce a white rabbit, she announced, "I believe I have a solution for that."

Nick eyed the elastic band a moment before uncoiling the lock, and she hastily tugged her hair into a ponytail.

"Very clever, but you missed some."

This time, he made contact with more than her hair. His fingertips were warm against her cheek as they corralled the wayward strands and tucked them behind her ear. The gesture might have been construed as friendly if not for the gleam in his dark eyes or the Richter-scale-worthy effect it had on her pulse.

A car horn blasted behind them. Its driver yelled something in Greek. Nick yelled something back in the same language, but his tone was more circumspect than annoyed, and his expression could only be described as pleased.

To Darcie, he said, "People are in too much of a hurry. I prefer to take things slowly. Rushing is no good."

With that, he turned the key in the car's ignition. The Porsche's powerful engine growled to life and they were off.

Nick wasn't familiar with the hotel listed on her itinerary, but he plugged the address to The Santor into his cell phone and downloaded directions as he merged into traffic.

"It should take about forty minutes to get there," he said as they left the airport behind.

Darcie settled back in her seat, determined to take in the sights along the way. Not only was this her first time in Greece, but it was also her first trip abroad. Indeed, other than a couple of weekend jaunts to Toronto with Becky, she'd never been outside the United States. Despite the passing scenery, however, she remained almost painfully aware of the man seated next to her, and her gaze kept returning to his profile. God, he was handsome and he'd made it plain that their attraction was mutual. This might not be a fling exactly, but it was awfully damned flattering to have such a good-looking man paying attention to her.

When he turned and caught her staring, she blurted out, "Were you always so buff? I mean, a car buff. Were you always a car buff?"

"Car buff?"

"Interested in cars," she clarified, relieved that her slip of the tongue hadn't made it past the language barrier.

He nodded. "My uncle raced them for a time, and the summer I turned sixteen, I traveled with him on the European Grand Prix circuit."

"That sounds exciting."

Nick smiled in agreement. "It was. Very."

"Did you ever race?"

"I considered it at one point, but no." He shrugged. "Ultimately, I was more interested in the cars—that is to say their overall design—than how fast they could travel on a closed course. So, when I was eighteen, I bought a 1957 Porsche Speedster I found advertised in the newspaper."

"Wow. Nice first car." Hers had been her grandmother's ancient sedan. It was the size of a small country and guzzled fuel like a college student guzzles coffee while studying for final exams. Darcie had happily traded up to the decade-old compact she still owned.

Nick was chuckling. "Not really. It needed a lot of work, which is why I could afford it. I spent the entire summer tracking down all of the parts to rebuild its engine." His smile was both nostalgic and proud.

"And you were hooked," she guessed.

She'd felt that way the first time she'd composed an article for her high school's newspaper. Three paragraphs on changes to the lunch menu and she'd known what she wanted to be when she grew up. Now, eight years after earning a degree in journalism, she could barely claim to be a journalist.

Nick was saying, "Hooked. Yes, I was. Especially after I decided to sell the Speedster at auction in Kalamai two summers later. Collectors came not only from all over Greece, but from other parts of Europe to bid on it. I loved the excitement. So, I used the money from the sale to buy another car, fix it up and auction it off. Later, I decided I did not want to go to the auctions, I wanted to run them. So, that is what I do."

She heard satisfaction in his tone. Pride. How long had it been since she'd felt either of those emotions when it came to her own job? How long had it been since she'd dreamed of bigger and better things for herself when it came to her career? Her life? Settling. Darcie had done so damned much of it.

"Did you come to Greece on business then?" she asked.

Nick shook his head and some of his dark hair fell across his forehead. It lent an air of recklessness to his already pulse-pounding good looks.

"Not this time. I came for a family wedding."

Wedding. Even spoken with Nick's gorgeous accent, the word brought Darcie up short, reminding her as it did of her recent close call with "I do." How different her life might be right now if a week ago she hadn't finally found the courage to act on what her heart—and, well, Becky—had been telling her for so long. Tad wasn't the right man for her.

"Yet you were going to leave today."

"I would have been back. The ceremony does not take place until the Saturday after next."

His response had her blinking in surprise. "That's more than two weeks away, and you're already here?"

"It is expected," he replied.

Darcie detected a slight edge to his tone and thought she understood its source. She knew all about family expectations. She had three sisters, two older, one younger, all of them happily married and busily procreating as if the survival of the human race depended on them. Meanwhile, Darcie had passed the big three-oh mark in the spring and the only thing that remained of her eagerly anticipated nuptials was the stack of gifts that would have to be returned when she got back.

A groan escaped. At Nick's quizzical glance, she said, "I feel your pain. My family can be, well, difficult to please at times. So, who's getting married?"

"My brother Pieter."

"I take it he lives here."

"Yes. As does my entire family."

Yet Nick made his home in a city across the Atlantic. Interesting. "No apron strings for you," she murmured.

"Apron strings?"

"Nothing. Are you and your brother close?"

"We used to be closer."

At that, his lips flattened into a grim line, leaving her with the distinct impression there was much more to the story. Still, she kept her curiosity in check and changed the subject. They engaged in polite small talk until they arrived at their destination. Even before she saw the hotel, she knew it would be a dive. The oath that slipped from Nick's lips told her as much.

Luxury accommodations? Right. The squat, two-story building looked like it should have a date with a wrecking ball, despite the sign out front printed in Greek and English that announced it was Under Renovation. It was more rickety than some of the country's ancient ruins. Glancing around, Darcie realized The Santor wasn't located in the best of neighborhoods, either. As hungry as she was, she didn't think she would be comfortable hoofing up the block to the restaurant she spied there. At the moment, two men were loitering out front, smoking cigarettes and passing a liquor bottle back and forth.

With her earlier hysteria threatening to return, she muttered, "Rufus really wasn't so bad."

Nick's brows drew together. "Your cat?"

"No longer. I was thinking good riddance after what he did to my favorite silk dress. But now…" She shrugged.

"Has anyone ever told you that the story of your life is very confusing?"

"Only all the time."

"I'll walk you in and see you settled."

No protest passed Darcie lips. Since it would have been token at best, she didn't see the point. No way did she want to go inside that death trap by herself.

"Thanks. I'd appreciate it."

Nick retrieved her sorry-looking bag and they made their way to the entrance on a makeshift walkway of cardboard that had been placed over mud puddles. On either side of the door were potted palm trees whose fronds were coated with thick, grayish construction dust.

Nick held open one of the grimy glass doors. "After you."

"Gee, thanks."

She took a halting step inside and waited for her eyes to adjust to the dim lighting. Once they did, she wished they hadn't. The lobby was filled with an assortment of power tools and building supplies, and every last inch of the place was as dust-coated as the palms outside. Her apprehension kicked into high gear as she imagined the condition the rooms would be in.

As if sensing her hesitation, Nick placed a hand on the small of her back and propelled her toward the reception desk. A woman stood behind it. Darcie pegged her to be about forty-five and a chain smoker. A lit cigarette dangled from her lips and a second one burned merrily in the ashtray on the countertop. The woman squinted at them through the haze created by both dust and smoke.

"Good afternoon." The greeting was offered in Greek as she set the cigarette in the ashtray.

"Good afternoon," Nick replied. His gaze flicked to her name badge and he added, "Pesha. How are you today?"

He said this in English, which Pesha apparently understood and could speak, because she switched to English as well.

"I am much better now." Her smile was flirtatious and made it clear why. Darcie couldn't fault the woman for that. Nick had certainly brightened her day. "How can I help you?"

"My friend has a reservation."

"Friend." Her smile widened and she exhaled. Residual wisps of smoke curled out from the woman's nostrils. Not terribly attractive, but they did distract one from the tar stains on her teeth. "What is the name?"

"Darcie Hayes," Nick said.

There was no computer to consult, only a thick, leather-bound book through which Pesha began flipping. Finally, she glanced up.

"Sorry. I have no one by that name registered here this week."

"Um, what about for a Darcie Franklin." It would have been her married name. She avoided meeting Nick's questioning gaze.

More page flipping ensued before Pesha shook her head. "*Oxi.* I cannot find that name among my guests, either."

"There must be some mistake. The tour package was booked months ago and paid in full."

"Tour package?" Pesha said slowly. "Which tour package might that be?"

"A multicity, sightseeing excursion that was booked through Zeus Tours."

"Stavros!"

The woman spat out the name with enough force to turn the two benign syllables into the vilest of curses. But she wasn't done. She continued in Greek, gesturing wildly the entire time. Darcie was left with no choice but to grit her teeth and listen. By the time Pesha switched to English again, she had worked up a good head of steam.

"That man owes me for the last three tour groups that stayed here. I have told him, no more! I have been turning his customers away all day."

She selected one of the cigarettes from the ashtray and took a long, lung-blackening drag.

"Um, when you say no more," Darcie began.

"I will not honor any more of his bookings unless he pays me in advance." Pesha stamped out the cigarette for emphasis.

"I can understand your annoyance with Stavros." Darcie was pretty annoyed with the man herself. "But I paid in full for a room at The Santor."

Sure, the accommodations were crap, but it was the principle of the matter. They were crap for which Tad's credit card already had been hit.

Pesha picked up the second cigarette and inhaled deeply before blowing out a stream of smoke that shot past Darcie's left shoulder. Even so, wisps of it lingered and stung her nose.

"No, you paid Stavros in full, but he has not paid me. He has not paid me for too long!" Pesha chopped at the air with the hand holding the cigarette, sending ashes flying. Darcie was only glad the woman wasn't clutching a sharp object. "And until he does, I will not be putting up any more of his tour customers. Now, if you wish to pay with cash, I will be happy to give you a room."

Darcie could see the woman's point. Pesha had a business to run and Stavros had stiffed her more than once. Still, it left Darcie in a bind, and if she had to shell out more money for a room, it sure as hell wasn't going to be in this fleabag establishment. She turned to Nick, who apparently read her mind.

"I will take you to another hotel. Perhaps something that is closer to shopping, restaurants and nightlife."

Darcie cleared her throat and added, "But reasonably priced. My budget is limited."

Pesha bristled as they turned to leave.

"You will not find a better bargain than The Santor," she insisted.

Since so much of Darcie's life was left to fate at the moment, it was with a sense of destiny that she replied, "I'll take my chances."

Mindful of what Darcie had said about her budget, Nick took her to one of the chain hotels in the city, even though it offered neither the charm nor the ambience of the nicer and pricier establishments he would have preferred. But it was conveniently located and tidy, with a smoke-free lobby and a concierge who appeared eager to please.

After she booked a room, they lingered near the bank of elevators. He wasn't in a hurry to leave. In fact, he almost regretted having to say goodbye. Darcie didn't seem eager to end their association, either.

"How good are the chances that Stavros will refund the money for my trip?" she asked.

"Not good. My guess is he does not have the money to refund."

She made a humming sound. "That's what I was afraid of. At this rate, I will be on a flight back to New York before the end of the week."

Her budget, Nick assumed. He meant it when he said, "That would be a shame. Greece is a beautiful country with so much to see."

It might not have any effect, but he planned to call Stavros on her behalf and apply a little pressure. Darcie Hayes and unsuspecting travelers like her shouldn't have to pay for the man's bad business decisions and personal habits.

Nick's reasons, of course, weren't all pure. His gaze took in the long line of her legs. Even in flat shoes she was a tall woman. *Statuesque* was the word that came to mind. Sexy applied, too, given her well-rounded curves and the toned backside he'd glimpsed. Why did he get the feeling she was unaware of the power of her allure? In his experience, most women who looked like she did weren't. They flaunted their looks, used them to get what they wanted. The fact that Darcie didn't made her not only refreshing, but also a puzzle.

Nick liked puzzles. They ranked right up there with games of chance when it came to guilty pleasures.

"I can't thank you enough for all you've done," she was saying.

"I have done nothing."

"I disagree. You've acted as my personal driver for the past couple of hours. I'd probably still be sitting in the airport with my busted-up luggage waiting for a ride that wasn't coming if it weren't for you."

She was all but tipping over on her nose. The signs of exhaustion were unmistakable, from the shadows under her eyes to the droop in her shoulders. He doubted that she would last an hour in her room before sleep claimed her, and knew a moment of regret that he wouldn't be there when she awoke.

"I am happy I could help. I would hate for a visitor to my homeland to go away with an unfavorable impression of Greek hospitality. Stavros Pappanolos's poor example notwithstanding, you will find that the people here are very generous and helpful."

"Oh, you've more than made up for Stavros."

She cleared her throat. There was that becoming blush again. Nick leaned forward, drawn by her reserve. Before he could kiss her, she held out a hand that poked into his solar plexus. Her cheeks flamed bright red now.

"Well, I guess this is where we say goodbye," she said.

Was it? Nick didn't think so. But she was tired and he had fences to mend with his family.

He took her hand and meant it when he said, "It has been entirely my pleasure, Darcie Hayes."

CHAPTER THREE

DARCIE WAS STILL on Nick's mind the following day as he sat in his grandmother's kitchen having a midmorning snack of freshly baked *koulourakia portokaliou*. The sweet, orange-flavored cookies were a staple in Yiayia's house, precisely because they ensured company.

His parents were there as well. George and Thea Costas lived right next door. In fact, Nick's entire extended family was clustered together in a small geographic area on the western edge of Athens. True to tradition, Pieter already owned a house just down the road. In two short weeks, he and Selene would live in it together as husband and wife.

Even the sweetness of the cookie wasn't enough to wipe out the bitter taste in Nick's mouth.

"Your tea is growing cold," Yiayia said, interrupting his thoughts. The snow-white hair coiled on her head made a striking contrast to her usual black frock. Sophia Pappas had been a widow for twenty-three years and still wore the color of mourning. She also considered it her duty as the family's matriarch to meddle as she saw fit. "And you are frowning, Nikolos. Is something wrong with my cookies?"

"Nothing is wrong with your cookies." He took another bite and smacked his lips for emphasis. "I just have a lot on my mind."

"This is a difficult time for you." His grandmother nodded sagely.

"Only because everyone insists on making it so."

"Have you given any more thought to Pieter's request?" his mother asked.

It took an effort not the crush the cookie that remained in his hand. Pieter wanted Nick to be his *koumbaro* or best man at the upcoming Greek Orthodox ceremony. As such, it would be Nick who put the crowns on Pieter and Selene's heads and switched them back and forth three times to symbolize their union.

Nick wanted no part of that. He couldn't believe his brother even had the nerve to ask.

"I have said no too many times to count, Mama."

She frowned. "I wish you would reconsider. He is your brother, Nick. Your *only* brother."

"Pieter conveniently forgot that when he started seeing Selene behind my back."

"You were gone, Nick. You went to America to start your business," Thea reminded him unnecessarily. "You told Selene you understood when she said she did not want to move to New York, too."

What Nick understood was betrayal. Despite what he'd told Selene at the time, he'd held out hope that she would change her mind. In his heart, he'd believed that the two of them would marry eventually. Until Pieter.

"I will not be his *koumbaro*. Be happy that I have agreed to attend the wedding at all."

"Be happy, be happy," Yiayia chided with a shake of her head. "You would do well to listen to your own advice, my boy. You will not find a bride of your own if you do not look."

"I can assure you, I do not lack for female companionship."

"Take care how you speak around your grandmother," George interjected gruffly.

Nick recognized the tone. It was the same one his father had used when Nick stepped over the line as a boy. He was over the line now, too. And so he apologized.

"I am merely trying to point out that if I wanted a wife I would have one."

He wouldn't call himself the black sheep of the family, but his wool was definitely dyed a different shade than his brother's, much to his mother's and Yiayia's regret. In addition to his Manhattan apartment, Nick kept a house just outside Athens near the Aegean. His whitewashed home was situated on a hillside and boasted panoramic views of a harbor that was dotted with yachts and fishing boats. His mother claimed the view soothed his restless nature. In some ways, watching all of those boats sail out into open waters only fed it.

"The women you know in Manhattan are not proper wife material," his mother said.

This was true enough, in part because at this point in his life, with a business to build and the related travel taking up so much of his time, he wasn't ready to settle down.

Still, he couldn't resist asking, "How do you know this, Mama? You have not met any of the women I have been with since Selene."

"I do not need to meet them. I am your mother. I know." Thea folded her arms.

He loved his family. He loved Greece. But ever since he'd sold that first automobile to a collector living in the United States more than a decade earlier, he'd known that he would never settle for the quiet and predictable life he would have endured living here and working with his father.

His family had never understood Nick's obsession with classic cars and his desire to see them restored, much less the pleasure he took from connecting a collector with exactly what he or she sought. They were proud of him, certainly. Through hard work, shrewd investment and a little bit of luck, Nick had managed to turn his passion into a multimillion-dollar enterprise. They just wished he'd decided to base it in Athens rather than New York.

"Besides, those women are not Greek," Yiayia said.

It boiled down to that for his grandmother. His mother, too, though she was less inclined to say so out loud. Both women wanted Nick to marry a nice Greek girl, preferably one from a family they knew, so that he would return home, buy a house nearby and settle in. It wasn't going to happen, but that didn't keep them from trying.

Sure enough, his mother was saying, "I saw Maria Karapoulos at the market yesterday. Her daughter Danika was with her. She has moved back from London. Her job there didn't work out."

"Just as well. They don't know how to make a proper cup of tea in England," Yiayia observed. Both women laughed. "How does Danika look? As pretty as ever?"

"Prettier," Thea said. "She has lost some weight, and I think she has contacts now. She wasn't wearing her glasses. She has such lovely eyes."

"And she comes from a nice family," his grandmother noted.

Nick sipped his tea and said nothing. The eyes he was thinking about were blue and belonged to Darcie.

His mother went on. "I invited her to the wedding. Her parents were already on the guest list. It seemed rude not to extend an invitation to her as well."

"Good. Good. She will have fun at the wedding," Yiayia said. "Especially if she has someone to dance with."

Even though his tea was plenty sweet, Nick added a little

more honey and tried to ignore the conversation going on around him. But he knew what was coming.

Sure enough, his grandmother added, "Nick could be her escort."

He gave his tea a vigorous stir. "No."

How many times must they go through this particular exercise before his mother and grandmother accepted that he didn't need or want their help to find a date? He'd considered asking one of the local women to come with him just to get Thea and Yiayia off his back, but that posed a problem of its own. Thanks to all of the gossip, the single women in his social circle saw Nick as a challenge or as an object of pity. He didn't want to be viewed as either.

He glanced over at his father, hoping for an ally, but George pushed his chair away from the table and rose. Motioning over his shoulder, he said, "The drain in the bathroom sink is running slow. I promised your grandmother I would take a look at it."

"I will give you a hand," Nick offered.

But George shook his head. "No. You finish your tea. I can manage on my own."

"Thank you, Papa," Nick drawled sarcastically.

His father stopped at the doorway. "You might listen to your mother, you know. I remember this Danika she speaks of. The girl comes from a good family. You could do worse."

Now there was a recommendation. The room was quiet after his father's exit. Nick was just starting to think the topic had been dropped when his mom said, "You are not going with anyone. It would be a shame for two young, single people to attend alone."

Yiayia clapped her hands together. "So it is settled. Nikolos will take her."

"No. I will not take her."

"No?"

Nick blotted his mouth with a napkin and worked to keep his tone civil. "I am not going to take Danika or any of the other women you two have suggested to the wedding. I have said no and I mean no."

"No! No! Always no!" His grandmother gestured with her arms before demanding, "Give us one good reason why not."

A curvy young woman with deep blue eyes, killer legs and a thick, wavy mane of hair came to mind and inspiration struck.

"I have a date."

Both older women blinked in surprise. His mother was the first to find her voice. "You have a date?" she asked skeptically.

"For the wedding?" Yiayia added, her tone equally dubious.

Lying did not come easily to Nick, no matter how good he considered the cause, so he answered her question with one of his own. "Is that so hard to believe? I am not repulsive, you know."

"You are as handsome as Adonis," his mother affirmed, undeterred. "But just yesterday you stormed out of here after the grocer's daughter happened by and your *yiayia* invited her in for a cup of tea."

"Happened by?" His brows rose. "She was dressed for cocktails, not tea. It was a setup. I do not appreciate your matchmaking. Nor do I need your help, as well-intentioned as it may be."

Thea sighed. Nick hoped that was a sign that the matter would be dropped, at least for now. Unfortunately, his grandmother wasn't done.

"Who is this woman you have invited to your brother's wedding? When did this happen? You have not mentioned her before."

Since nothing had actually happened yet and very well might never, Nick decided to answer Yiayia's other question first. "You do not know her. She is an American."

"American." His grandmother put a hand to her chest and frowned.

"It is not a disease, you know." He chuckled, hoping both to lighten the mood and to divert the conversation. Neither woman cracked a smile, however.

"You know her from New York?" Thea asked.

"Actually, I met Darcie in Greece." Which wasn't a lie. He saw no need to mention when or where.

"Darcie. What kind of a name is Darcie?" Yiayia's frown deepened. "It does not sound like a Greek name."

His mother had other concerns. "Does she live in Athens?"

"No. She came here on holiday."

When his conscience bucked, he rationalized that he wasn't lying to his mother and grandmother. He was merely offering a selective version of the truth.

"What does she do for a living?" Yiayia inquired.

"She works at a car magazine." Beyond that, Nick knew precious little about Darcie Hayes other than the fact that he found her very attractive. At the moment, he also found her his ticket out of a tight spot. "I tell you what. I will bring her by some time and you can ask her all of these questions yourselves."

He thought he was off the hook, or at the very least had delayed his day of reckoning. Yiayia dispelled that notion.

"Good. I will set an extra plate for supper."

"S-supper?" he sputtered. "Tonight?"

"We will eat at seven."

"Come early," his mother added with an eager smile that sent his insides churning.

What had he gotten himself into?

* * *

Darcie had forced herself to stay awake until 9:00 p.m. the previous evening. She'd called Becky as promised and explained about her changed itinerary, after which she had collapsed face-first on the bed and slept like the dead. When she awoke just before ten o'clock the following morning she had a deep crease from the sheets across her right cheek, but after nearly thirteen hours of uninterrupted slumber she felt almost human. She also was starving again.

If the tour had panned out as advertised, she already would have enjoyed a buffet breakfast with her fellow travelers and been boarding an air-conditioned motor coach headed for the Parthenon on the Acropolis. She showered and dressed, donning tan shorts and a fitted white T-shirt before lacing up a pair of sneakers. For one moment she allowed herself to picture the floral sundress and new sandals in her missing luggage. Shaking off her wistfulness, she headed for the door, eager to leave the hotel and start exploring. The day before, she'd been too exhausted to do more than walk up the block from the hotel to a small market that the concierge had recommended. She'd bought bread and fresh fruit. Today, she was in the mood for a real meal and ancient ruins.

It came as a total surprise when the first sight to greet her when she entered the lobby was Nick Costas striding purposefully through the main door. He broke into a smile that made her knees weak. It buoyed her ego that he appeared so pleased to see her.

"Darcie. Excellent. You are still here."

"Hello, Nick. Is something wrong?"

"Wrong?" He shook his head. "Not at all."

She narrowed her eyes. "Why do I sense a *but* coming?"

"Because you are too perceptive." He laughed. "You were on your way out."

"Yes. To eat."

"May I join you?"

"Okay. I should warn you that I'm not sure exactly where I'm going. I was just planning to wander around until I found a restaurant that looked appealing."

"May I make a suggestion then?"

"By all means."

"I know a wonderful spot not far from here that makes the best moussaka."

"Moussaka. My favorite," she said, although she had no idea what it was. Intrigued by both the meal and the man, Darcie agreed.

Nick took her to an out-of-the-way café that made her feel as if she had stepped back in time thanks to the building's neoclassical architecture. Conversations stopped as they wound their way to a table in the back of the small, crowded establishment. Darcie got the feeling she was the only tourist among the patrons. After giving her a cursory glance, however, the other guests returned their attention to their own tables.

A waiter appeared not long after they settled in their seats and took their order. She asked for the moussaka, in part because Nick had recommended it, and because she was unfamiliar with the other items on the menu. He ordered the same, as well as coffee for the pair of them and a bottle of sparkling water.

"I get the feeling I'm in store for an authentic Greek meal," she said once they were alone.

"You are. I hope you like it."

Her stomach was growling loud enough to be embarrassing. "I'm sure I will," she told him. "Um, what exactly is moussaka?"

His rich laughter rumbled. The sound was pleasing, especially since she didn't feel his amusement came at her expense.

"It is a dish made with eggplant. Do you like eggplant?" he asked.

"I love it. Yum."

She'd eaten it…once. It had been breaded and pan-fried, and then slathered in Evelyn's homemade tomato sauce and melted parmesan cheese. The indigestion Darcie had experienced afterward likely had been the result of Tad's mother's fault-finding throughout the meal rather than the food itself.

Nick apparently wasn't fooled. "You are an adventurous one, I see. Willing to try new things."

She liked his assessment, even if the speculative gleam in his eye gave her pause.

"I believe in being open-minded. Why not take a few chances?"

Nick smiled. "Why not indeed?"

A moment of silence passed as he studied her. She found it hard not to fidget given the intensity of his gaze. Was he picturing her naked? Darcie sucked in her stomach just to be on the safe side and found the courage to ask, "Perhaps you should tell me what's on your mind."

"A favor."

"Oh." She stopped holding in her stomach.

"You look disappointed?"

She brushed her hair back from her face. "Not at all. Ask away. Ask for anything. I owe you."

This time his laughter was low, intimate and ridiculously arousing. "That is not the sort of thing you should tell a man, *agapi mou*. If I were without scruples, you could find yourself in trouble after making a statement such as that."

Darcie was too intrigued and too attracted to Nick to be alarmed. Maybe it was the warmth that radiated from his dark eyes, or the slightly self-deprecating quirk of his sensual lips. She was sure he posed no threat to her safety. To her sanity? Well, that remained to be seen.

"But you do have scruples."

"How can you tell?"

"A man without them would not have bothered to help me yesterday without asking for anything in return."

"Yet here I am one day later, begging a favor." His lips quirked again.

"Begging is different than demanding. A man without scruples would demand, I think."

"I am glad you see it that way." His expression sobered then. "You are certainly under no obligation to agree to my proposition. I want to make that perfectly clear from the outset."

Proposition? The mere word, said as it was in that delicious accent, caused heat to curl low in Darcie's belly. Sitting with Nick inside the little café, she felt worldly, sophisticated and a lifetime removed from the awkward young woman from Buffalo who had allowed herself to be browbeaten into inertia by Tad's overbearing mother.

Darcie was pleased to find her voice was magnificently matter-of-fact when she replied, "It's clear, Nick. So, what is this proposition of yours?"

"I would like to invite you to dinner tonight."

"Dinner?" She blinked.

Maybe she'd heard him wrong. Darcie wasn't disappointed, but she was somewhat surprised. Sharing another meal seemed, well, a little mundane given his dramatic lead-in. Maybe *proposition* had a different meaning in Greece than it did back in the United States. Or maybe she'd imagined the speculative gleam in his eyes. Or maybe she was just too long out of practice with members of the opposite sex to be able to figure out their intentions beyond mere flirting.

"Dinner. Yes." He hesitated then before adding. "With my family."

Her mouth fell open at that. She knew she was gaping, yet it was a full thirty seconds before she could force her lips to close. She'd dated Tad for more than a year before he'd taken her home to meet his mother. Little had she known then that he'd been doing her a favor. Still...

"Are you going to say anything?" Nick asked at last. A grin lurked around the corners of his mouth.

"Sorry," she mumbled. "I'm just a little surprised by the invitation."

"I have no doubt of that. We have only just met, after all. And it is a big favor to ask."

The server returned with their bottle of water, a couple of glasses and two demitasse cups of coffee, forestalling her reply. Darcie took a sip of the coffee. It was stronger than she was used to, very sweet and hot enough that it burned her tongue. She barely noticed the pain. She was too preoccupied with the gorgeous man sitting across from her. Things like this didn't happen to her. There had to be a catch. Or a camera crew lurking nearby, waiting to jump out and tell her she'd been punked.

She glanced around, ruled out a hoax and asked, "Why do you want me to meet your parents?"

"Not only my parents. My grandmother will be there as well."

"Why not?" She lifted her shoulders. "The more the merrier."

"Yes." But there was nothing merry about his expression. He looked downright grim.

"So, um, why? Not that I'm not flattered by the invitation," she hastened to assure him. "But I'm curious."

"I told you that I was in Athens because my brother is to be married."

She nodded. "In two weeks."

"My mother and grandmother have had their heads together for months trying to find a date for me."

"You can't find one on your own?" Darcie winced as soon as the words were out. "What I mean is, so you are single." She winced again and picked up her coffee, braving a second burn on her tongue if it would keep her from blurting out any more embarrassing remarks.

"I'm not in a relationship at the moment." A pair of dark brows rose. "And you? I should have thought to ask if you are involved with anyone."

"Nope. No one."

And she had to admit, her emancipation—that was how she was coming to view it—felt pretty darned good right now. She was free. Free of Tad's lukewarm affection and his mother's passive-aggressive jabs. Free of her own mother's well-meaning interference and her married sisters' well-meaning advice. Free of self-doubt. Well, mostly free. Yes, Darcie was happily free to flirt, to enjoy the company of a handsome man and to accept, if she so chose, his invitation to dinner.

And she so chose.

His dark eyes warmed. "That is good. Very good."

"Oh?"

"It would not do for me to be propositioning a woman who is already spoken for."

"No worries there." Feeling emboldened, she added, "I speak for myself these days."

"Another reason to like you. Now, back to my predicament. My mother and grandmother mean well. They think I am pining."

"Pining?" She didn't like the sound of that. It implied another woman was in the picture.

He shook his head. "Perhaps lonely is a better word."

Better, but improbable. "I don't think so. You don't look lonely to me."

More to the point, men who looked *like* Nick Costas didn't tend to get lonely. They tended to have smartphones filled with the names and numbers of women who were eager to share meals and mattress space.

Nick took a sip of his coffee. "Lacking for companionship," he said at last.

Laughter bubbled out before she could stop it. "Sorry. I find that even harder to believe."

"Unfortunately, my mother and grandmother are less inclined to see the truth. So, they have been…matchmaking. I told them I have no need for their help."

"Because you can get your own dates."

"Yes, as our lunch proves. But…" The corners of his mouth turned down and he shrugged.

"How do I figure into this?"

Darcie thought she knew, and she was already flattered, but since jumping to conclusions was her specialty, she decided a little clarification wouldn't hurt. Besides, it would be really embarrassing if she was wrong.

"There is a woman who recently returned to Greece after living in London for a few years. My mother knows her mother, and has invited both of them to my brother's wedding. Now I am expected to be her escort. I told her and my grandmother that I already have a date. You."

The smile he sent Darcie could have melted a glacier. She shivered anyway and gooseflesh pricked her arms.

"Oh." Her mouth threatened to fall open again. She kept it closed by putting her elbow on the tabletop and propping her chin on her fist.

"What is this look?" he asked, his eyes narrowing as he studied her face.

She dropped the hand from her chin and busied herself

lining up the cutlery next to her plate. "I was going for non-chalant, but I suppose you could call it gobsmacked."

"Gobsmacked? I am not familiar with this term."

"Um, it means shocked."

"Because we barely know one another," he guessed.

"Sure." She moved the knife one-sixteenth of an inch to the right. "That reason will do."

"It is a lot to ask, but I was hoping you would agree." When she continued to fuss with her utensils, he reached across the table and settled his hand over hers. "I would be most grateful."

Darcie glanced up and moistened her lips. It was all Nick could do not to moan. That sexy mouth of hers was going to be his undoing. The table was narrow enough that it would take little effort to lean across it and kiss her. It was tempting. *She* was tempting.

"I don't speak Greek," Darcie said, interrupting his fantasy.

For a moment, he wasn't sure he could speak at all.

"Nick?"

He cleared his throat, bemused by the strange infatuation he felt. "That will not be a problem. Both of my parents are fluent in English, and my grandmother knows enough to get by. I can always translate if she does not understand something or if you do not."

"That's…good."

And still she hesitated. So, he decided to sweeten the deal. "Have you had any luck getting a refund on your tour?"

"No. I left a message last night and planned to call again today."

Nick had left messages as well. Stavros was either passed out cold or screening his calls. If Nick had to bet on one, he would put money on the former.

"What if I were to be your guide? In return for accompanying me to dinner, I will take you to the sites mentioned on the tour's brochure."

And why not? It would give him something to do for the next couple of weeks while he dodged his mother and grandmother's well-meaning mediation and Pieter's ongoing attempts to bury the hatchet. And he couldn't think of another woman he'd rather pass the time with than Darcie.

"That's very generous of you, but without a refund from Stavros I can't afford to stay in Greece much longer, let alone for the full two weeks."

"Leave Stavros to me."

One way or another, Nick would see to it that Darcie Hayes had her trip…and enjoyed it.

"You do realize I will be heading home the day before your brother gets married, right?"

"That is fine."

Nick did not need an actual date for Pieter's wedding. All he needed was a viable reason in the interim to avoid a setup. Once his mother and grandmother met Darcie, they would cease and desist in their matchmaking. As solutions went, it was perfect. Now if only his family would stop trying to force a reconciliation between him and Pieter.

"I don't know," Darcie began. "It sounds as if I'm getting the better end of the deal."

She only thought so because she hadn't yet met his *yiayia* or the rest of his kin, Nick thought wryly.

"Does that mean we *have* a deal?"

"I… Why not? Sure." She stuck out her hand just as she had the previous day.

Nick studied the long, unadorned fingers for a moment before giving in to his previous impulse. Bypassing her palm, he leaned over to kiss her full on the mouth. Her sweetness had him lingering and wishing for privacy. Unfortunately, there was none of that here. Sure enough, when he drew back, the restaurant erupted in applause and shouts of *"Opa!"*

Darcie's blush was becoming, if at odds with the frank interest evident in her eyes. Maybe she had gotten the better end of the deal after all. Not that Nick minded one bit.

Back at her hotel, Nick insisted on parking his car and walking her inside. Darcie thought she knew why. He wanted to kiss her again. Well, no problem. She wanted to kiss him again, too.

The lip-lock they'd shared in the restaurant had been amazing. On a scale of one to ten, Darcie would rate it a ten…thousand. That didn't even take into account the degree of difficulty involved. Nick had managed that score with a table wedged between them and a wide-eyed crowd of spectators, whose spontaneous applause afterward, by the way, had been entirely appropriate. Heck, that kiss had deserved a standing ovation. Darcie would settle for an encore.

Should she ask him to come up to her room? They would have privacy but it might seem too forward. He might think she wanted to sleep with him. Did she?

Why yes, she did. She was human and breathing and he was gorgeous and sexy beyond belief. But should she?

Probably not a good idea. She'd never been the sort of woman who slept with a man on the first date. Or the second. Or the third…

"Darcie—"

"Even the fourth would be pushing it."

Nick's brow wrinkled. "Excuse me?"

"Nothing." She waved a hand. "Just, um…here we are."

They had reached the elevator and Darcie still wasn't sure what she should do. He took the decision out of her hands by pushing the button.

"Are you coming up?" she asked casually.

"I would like to, but…" He shook his head.

"A gentleman," she mused.

It sounded like he said, "A fool."

"So, I'll see you to—"

He pulled her into his arms and kissed her with all of the passion and skill he'd shown in the restaurant, but with far less of the restraint.

"—night."

Nick's breath was sawing in and out, but he managed to mutter something in Greek that told Darcie he was every bit as turned on as she was.

Before the elevator arrived, he turned and walked away.

CHAPTER FOUR

DARCIE NEEDED AN outfit for dinner since nothing in her luggage full of second-string clothes seemed appropriate. But what did one wear to meet a man's parents when one barely knew the man?

She mulled that question as she wandered the labyrinth of streets near her hotel. Shops abounded, interspersed with cafés and taverns. The only problem was that the goods the stores sold were geared toward tourists: snow globes featuring miniature Parthenons, key chains and postcards. As for clothing, it fell into two categories: logoed T-shirts and the traditional Greek garb that she doubted anyone in Greece actually wore.

Two hours into her quest the arches of her feet were beginning to ache, but she decided to stray a little farther from the beaten path. After another half an hour, her persistence was rewarded when she arrived at the door of a small boutique that the owner of a nearby bakery had recommended. After licking the last crumbs of freshly made baklava from her fingertips, Darcie headed inside.

The boutique was small and totally kitsch-free. It also was expensive, with prices that reflected the quality of the garments on display. Darcie swallowed hard after glancing at the tag that dangled from a cap-sleeved cocktail dress made of red silk. She calculated the exchange rate in her head. It was far more than she felt comfortable spending, even though the dress was gorgeous. She moved on to another rack, but it was of no use. The garments there, while also lovely, were equally expensive. On a sigh, she turned to leave.

"May I help you find something?" a woman asked in English as she stepped out from behind the counter. She was about Darcie's age and nearly her height in a pair of killer high heels. The name tag pinned to her chest read Nerina.

Darcie shook her head. "I was just looking."

"For anything in particular?"

She started to say no only to admit, "I've been invited to dinner this evening."

The woman smiled knowingly. "With a man."

"Yes. He's taking me to meet his parents."

"Oh, this is serious. He is Greek?"

"No and yes." At the saleswoman's perplexed expression, Darcie added, "No, it's not serious. At least not how you mean. We've only just met and…it's not serious. But, yes, he is Greek. Well, I guess he's actually American now, but he's from Athens. Originally. You know, he was born here." She grimaced. "I'm probably not making any sense."

"I understand. You are nervous." Again, Nerina's knowing smile made an appearance. "Even though you have only just met, you like this man."

"I do."

It was the truth. What was not to like about a man who had been gracious and kind and treated her with respect, all while making it clear that he found her attractive and wouldn't mind seeing her naked?

Okay, so maybe Darcie had extrapolated that last part, but the kiss Nick had given her in the restaurant had made her toes want to curl. And the one in the lobby of her hotel?

She was surprised she hadn't spontaneously combusted in the elevator afterward.

"Then we must find you something perfect for this evening." Nerina turned to another rack and began flipping through the garments.

Darcie cleared her throat. "I'm afraid I'm on a limited budget. Actually, a very limited budget. I shouldn't be buying clothes at all, but the airline lost my luggage and…"

"And then you met this handsome man who has invited you to dinner to meet his parents, and you want to look stunning."

Darcie sighed. "That about sums it up." Placing a hand on her stomach to quell her nerves, she asked, "Do you take credit cards?"

Nerina nodded and then tapped her lips thoughtfully for a moment before bursting into a satisfied grin.

"I have just the dress."

Later that afternoon, freshly showered, Darcie took her time getting ready, shimmying first into a bra and panties that weren't likely to be seen, but made her feel sexy and sophisticated nonetheless. Both pieces were lacy and utterly feminine, and the only articles from her trousseau that had made it into the lucky piece of luggage that managed to arrive in Greece along with her.

Afterward, she studied herself in the mirrored door of the closet with a critical eye. Turning sideways, she sucked in her stomach until her belly was concave and the bottom of her rib cage became visible. Gee, as long as she didn't breathe, she sported measurements that the pinups girls of the 1940s would have envied. But Darcie was fond of breathing, so she let out her breath on a gusty sigh. Goodbye twenty-four-inch waist.

Still, she liked her curves and the muscle tone she'd

managed to carve into them thanks to six months' worth of grueling workouts with the personal trainer from hell. She reached into the closet for the dress she'd just purchased. She had to admit it showed off all of her assets to their greatest advantage.

Since the evening's dinner was at someone's home, Nerina had suggested a more casual wrap dress in a soft jersey fabric the color of ripe peaches. Both the color and the cut flattered Darcie. Best of all, she could pair it with flat shoes she already owned, saving her a second purchase. Nerina also had been generous on the price, declaring the garment on sale even though it was not marked as such.

"Enjoy your evening," she'd said as Darcie left the shop.

Looking at herself in the mirror now, Darcie grinned. Oh, she planned to.

Peach was his new favorite color, Nick decided, when Darcie stepped out of the elevator into the hotel lobby. As he eyed her curves, the air backed up in his lungs. The reaction wasn't entirely unpleasant, but it was unsettling and rare when it came to women. Except for this woman. Around Darcie, he couldn't seem to catch his breath at all.

From the first moment he'd spied her in the airport, he'd found himself drawn to her, interested in a way that he'd initially assumed was purely the result of sexual attraction. He'd gone on instinct when he'd approached her and offered his assistance. He'd followed his gut again when he'd come to her earlier in the day, asking a favor. Nick didn't regret his impulses, but he knew a moment of panic when she smiled at him now and his mouth went dry.

"I hope I'm dressed all right. I wasn't sure what to wear," she said.

"You look lovely." He kept his gaze locked on her face,

not trusting himself to take in those curves a second time without touching them.

"Thank you."

A pair of glossed lips parted in a smile that was nearly impossible to resist. He bit back a groan and asked, "Are you ready?"

"I am."

This time, instead of a Porsche, Nick was driving a 1965 Shelby Cobra.

"Very iconic," she murmured of the cobalt-blue car that sported twin white stripes up its hood and down its trunk. "One of the most sought-after cars as I recall from fact-checking an article about one. Is it the real deal?"

"If you are asking if it is one of the ten special racing editions, yes."

"Signed by Carroll Shelby?"

"Of course." Once again, Nick appreciated the depth of her knowledge. A woman who spoke car. He'd never met one before.

"I'm almost afraid to sit in it," she told him when he opened the door for her. "This baby goes for what? A couple hundred thousand American dollars?"

"Closer to three."

"Well, there, you've put my mind at ease," she replied dryly.

Nick chuckled. "Get in." Since the car had no roof and only a low, curving windshield, he handed her a scarf. "For your hair."

"Very thoughtful. Thank you. I feel Grace Kelly-ish. Or I would if I were a platinum blonde with classical features and a slimmer build."

"There's nothing wrong with your hair color, features or your...build."

She sent him a sideways smile. It sounded like she said, "I could get used to you."

The drive to his grandmother's house was relatively short. Still, as they cruised through the city, Nick used the time to prep Darcie on his life, starting with the basics such as his age and education.

"I have not told them very much about you."

"That's because you don't know very much about me," she pointed out.

"I am eager to remedy that." His tone hinted at something much more intimate than a family dinner. "I have told them that you are American and that we have not known one another for long. That way, they will not expect us to have all of the answers."

Besides, the sexual chemistry between the two of them was very real and would go a long way to making their relationship plausible in his family's eyes.

Darcie was nodding. "All right. So, how did we meet?"

"I think we should keep it simple and as close to truthful as possible. I do not usually lie to my family." He shifted his attention from the road to her when he added, "I do not usually lie to anyone."

"I figured that. Same goes for me." She took a deep breath. "So, we met in an airport."

"Let's make it Newark."

"I saw you across a crowded room, our eyes met and it was magic." She laughed, but something about her assessment struck Nick as disturbingly accurate.

"How about if we just say I offered to give you a ride when yours did not show?" He turned, found himself lost in the same blue eyes that had sucked him in across the airport terminal and added, "I was only too happy to come to the aid of a beautiful woman."

"The only problem with that is I do not live in New York City, but upstate in Buffalo."

"You were in New York on business then."

She nibbled her lip. "There's not much travel involved in my line of work. Not like yours. I can check facts over the phone or by computer. I've never had to hop a plane to do my job. Not that I wouldn't mind."

"On holiday then?"

"I guess that's believable."

"Have you ever been to New York?"

"Once. It was right after I graduated from high school. I went with my friend Becky and her family. We stayed at a hotel near Times Square and took in a Broadway show." Her smile was wide and nostalgic. "I loved it."

"The show or the city?"

"Both. All of that energy. I felt energized, too."

Nick heard awe in her voice and understood it. That was how he'd felt the first time he'd visited New York—absolutely blown away by the mania, yet eager to be part of it, too. Athens was hardly a small town, either in population or in feel, but no other place Nick had traveled, which he did extensively for business, compared to New York.

"You will have to visit again. I would be happy to show you around."

He meant it, he realized with a start. He could see her in his adopted city, enjoying the herb-crusted salmon at his favorite restaurant, sipping coffee at a sidewalk café near Central Park, window-shopping on Fifth Avenue. Most disturbing, Nick could picture Darcie in his apartment—his quiet and at times lonely retreat from the bustle of the city—curled up on his couch with a glass of wine in her hand, smiling at him in invitation.

She was smiling at him now when she replied, "Maybe I will."

He swallowed and forced his attention to the least erotic thing he could think of. "Tell me about your family. Do they also live in Buffalo?"

"For the most part. I have three sisters. Two older, one younger, all of them married. They're scattered in the suburbs with their husbands and kids, driving minivans and carpooling to soccer games and gymnastic classes."

"But not you."

"To my mother's everlasting regret."

"And your father? What does he think of your situation?"

"He tells me there's plenty of time to get married, have kids and buy a minivan." She frowned then. "But…"

"But?"

"He thinks I'm wasting my talent at my current job," she admitted quietly.

"Are you?"

Darcie made a sound that was halfway between a laugh and a sigh. "That's the subject for a very long conversation. Right now, I think we should stick to the basics."

She was right, of course, but Nick was too curious about her to let the matter drop. "What talent is it that your father feels you are wasting?"

"I have a degree in journalism from Buffalo State University. I enjoyed feature writing. Some of my professors told me I had a flair for it. My plan was to work at a newspaper and once I had enough decent clips—"

"Clips?"

"Copies of articles I'd written. Once I had enough of those, I was going to apply for a job at one of the large women's magazines headquartered in New York."

"So, you wanted to come to the big city?"

"I did," she admitted on a shy smile. "Once upon a time I thought I could make a name for myself in publishing."

"But?"

The smile vanished. Darcie shrugged. "Something came up and then the fact-checking job at *Automobile Enthusiasts Monthly* came along."

"Do you ever do any writing for that magazine? You certainly know enough about cars to do a credible job of it."

"The editor has let me do a couple of blurbs about upcoming car cruises, but nothing meaty or in-depth. He either tackles those himself—it's a small publication—or he farms them out to a freelancer. It doesn't hurt that the freelancer is a poker buddy." She sighed. "So, I check facts."

The more she said, the more questions Nick had. He contented himself by asking the one that cut straight to the heart of the matter.

"Do you enjoy your work, Darcie?"

"I suppose." She shrugged. "It pays the bills."

A tepid and telling answer, in Nick's opinion.

"You should do something you feel passionately about. Otherwise, what is the point?"

"I guess you would know, since you're obviously passionate about your work."

He glanced over and waited until he was sure he had her full attention. "I am passionate about much more than my work."

Nick's frank reply and the accompanying intimate smile sent a spurt of pure lust coursing through Darcie's veins. The excitement churning away inside frightened her a little. It was so foreign. It seemed forbidden. But it wasn't, she reminded herself. She was a single woman, a consenting adult. Heck, if she were being truthful, she was a parched patch of desert desperate for a good dousing of rain. Bring on the storm.

"If you continue to look at me like that, I will be tempted to forego dinner and return to your hotel instead," Nick told her. Once again, his words were blunt. His smile bordered on sinful.

She called herself a chicken, but decided to play it safe.

"Sorry, I was just thinking about…all of the changes that have occurred in my life recently. Maybe more are in order." Warming to the notion, she added, "God knows, the timing couldn't be better. I need to find a new place to live. Why not a new job, too?"

It wasn't as if anything tied her to *Automobile Enthusiasts Monthly*. The pay was mediocre, the benefits were crap. She'd only taken the position after she and Tad became serious. At the time, with some help from him, she'd convinced herself that a career in New York was a pipe dream. Settling down in Buffalo with reliable if tedious employment and a future with Tad—those were what had mattered, what she had wanted most.

"You are at a crossroads," Nick said. Up ahead, the light turned red and he slowed the Shelby to a stop.

Darcie gestured with her hand. "It's really more like this busy intersection, but with no working traffic light."

"Ah, then you need to take care in getting to the other side."

Treading carefully, that was how she'd spent the past several years. Feeling reckless now, she said, "Or I could just run like hell and hope for the best. After all, we've established that I am adventurous."

"I like your style." Nick's hand left the gearshift to caress her cheek. He was leaning toward her, eyes hooded with unmistakable intent, when a horn blasted behind them.

"The light is green," she said, suppressing a laugh.

"Yes. A green light. I believe I got that very impression."

The car shot forward. Darcie's pulse lurched as if trying to catch up. The scarf was in no danger of blowing off, but she pulled it snugger around her head, just to have something to do with her hands.

"Let's talk about you."

"All right. You know what I do for a living. You also know I have a brother who is to be married."

"A younger brother. Pieter."

"Very good. You pay close attention to details."

"It's what I do." She shrugged. "I check facts for a living, remember?"

"Or you did."

The seed, so recently planted, seemed to be taking root. But she forced herself to focus on the present. "Tell me about Pieter. How old is he? What's he like? Are you close?"

A muscle ticked in Nick's jaw, although when he spoke, his tone bordered on blasé. "He is a year my junior. As boys, we did everything together. Now…he works with our father at his shop. They are electricians by trade."

"The family business?"

Nick nodded. "My father had hoped I would follow in his footsteps as well."

"But you had other interests."

"Yes."

One syllable said without regret but full of sadness. More family expectations, Darcie decided. Hoping to lighten his mood, she shifted the subject. "Why don't you tell me about Pieter's fiancée?"

That muscle ticked in Nick's jaw again. "Selene."

The wind rushed past in the open car, but the tension grew thicker. "Um, that's a pretty name."

He snorted. "We grew up together, the three of us." Nick paused before adding, "Selene and I used to date."

Darcie blinked, too surprised to apply tact when she said, "You dated the woman your brother is marrying?"

"It would be more accurate to say that my brother is marrying a woman I dated," he replied tersely.

"Oh." More like *uh-oh*. Darcie had stepped into something unpleasant, and she had no clue how to scrape it gracefully off her shoe.

"You are wondering if I am heartbroken."

"Are you?" she asked bluntly.

"It was over a long time ago."

Nick might not be heartbroken—and the jury was still out on that as far as she was concerned—but Darcie didn't think it was as over as he claimed it to be. She heard another emotion in his tone. Anger? Betrayal? If it truly was over, he would feel nothing. She wanted to ask why he and Selene had broken up, but she sensed that topic wasn't open for discussion.

She said quietly, "It has to be awkward."

"It is."

Did this mean Nick was on the rebound, too? She wasn't sure how she felt about that or even if she had the right to feel anything. They had been driving in silence for a couple of minutes, when something occurred to her.

"Um, speaking of awkward, will Selene and Pieter be at dinner tonight?"

As it was, Darcie had enough to worry about what with convincing his parents and grandmother that she and Nick were an item without adding bad blood and an old lovers' triangle to the mix. Thankfully, Nick shook his head.

"They have other plans. Some last-minute meeting with the caterer about changes to one of the side dishes. Apparently, a cousin of the bride has a severe peanut allergy."

"Oh, thank God." Darcie closed her eyes and grimaced. "Not about the allergy. Those can be deadly. Anaphylactic shock and all. But—"

"I know exactly what you mean." His dry laughter served to put her at ease.

A few minutes later, they arrived at a two-story white stucco home surrounded by lush, terraced gardens.

"We're here."

Showtime, Darcie thought, as she removed the scarf and checked her appearance in the rearview mirror.

"You look beautiful," he assured her.

Even so, nerves fluttered in her belly. She offered up a prayer that in addition to passing parental inspection, she wouldn't humiliate herself by getting sick.

"This is my grandmother's house, but my mother and father live just there."

He pointed to the home next door that was similar in size and appearance and whose yard was equally well-landscaped. Concentrating on the details helped quell her nerves. As limited as her knowledge of plants was, she recognized geraniums spilling from the pots near the front door, as well as near the iron railing that girded a second-story terrace. And even without the assistance of a breeze, she could smell the heady scent of roses.

"Wow. Your mother and grandmother must have green thumbs. Everything looks so, well, *green*. My mom is like that. And my sisters. They can grow anything, anywhere. As near as I can tell, my thumb is black."

"Black?" He took her hands, studied the digits in question. "They look normal to me."

"It's just a saying. It means I'm a plant killer, which is why the only plant I own is a ficus whose leaves are made of plastic. There's no chance of killing that sucker."

"I see," Nick said patiently.

No, he didn't, because there was no point to this conversation, except for stalling. Darcie was babbling like an idiot, but she couldn't seem to stop herself. More words tumbled out. "Although the ficus still looks pathetic thanks to Rufus."

Nick's lips twitched. "The cat you referred to as the spawn of Satan?"

"That's the one. He used it as a scratching post."

Nick got out and came around the car to open Darcie's door. "Come." Suddenly he seemed so formidable, as though he were prepared for battle. The sudden change from playful to guarded did nothing to settle Darcie's nerves.

He led her to the door, entered without knocking. This might have been his grandmother's house, but he didn't stand on formality. She liked that. The foyer opened into a living room with a fireplace. It was a comfortable room, a place that invited one to sit and relax. Darcie wished she could, but she was wound up as tight as a spring. From the rear of the house, she could hear voices, although she couldn't make out anything that was being said since it was in Greek. She heard Nick's name mentioned and then she thought she heard her own. When she glanced at him, his expression was apologetic.

"They say they are eager to meet you."

Darcie doubted his translation was complete or completely accurate.

He took her hand. "This way."

The mingled scents of spices and roasting meat wafting from the kitchen should have had her mouth watering, but it was dry as sawdust. She stopped walking.

"I need another minute," she whispered and sucked in a deep breath.

"You are nervous. I understand."

Did he? It wasn't only her part in the deception that had her worried, but what his family would think of her. Her old insecurities bubbled up before she could stop them. What if they found her as lacking as Evelyn had?

"You will be fine."

"Fine," she repeated, feeling anything but.

"It is only one meal."

Yes, but it felt like her last supper.

"Darcie." Nick framed her face with his hands. His palms were warm, the pads of his thumbs slightly calloused as they brushed over her cheeks. "You…"

Whatever else he said, and she thought it might have been in Greek, was lost to the rushing in her ears. Besides, words, no matter what the language, were superfluous. He was going to kiss her again. That much came through loud and clear. And she wanted him to. So much so that she didn't bother to wait for him to lean in and claim her mouth. She clasped the back of his neck and closed the gap between them herself.

She'd always been a fan of fireworks, though it had been a very long time since she'd experienced any. This kind lit her up inside until she was sure her skin glowed from the heat. Someone moaned. She was pretty sure the sound came from her. Regardless, Nick took the opportunity to change the angle of their mouths. His hands no longer framed her face. His fingers splayed over the small of her back, exerting subtle pressure that brought her flush against his hard chest.

A woman's voice cut through the haze of hormones.

"This must be Darcie."

They sprung apart. Fireworks fizzled until they were but pesky smoke. Way to make a first impression, Darcie thought, giving herself a mental slap. Nick, meanwhile, offered the sort of charmingly sheepish smile that probably had helped him out of plenty of scrapes as a boy.

"Mama. My apologies. I seem to have gotten carried away."

"Yes. That much I could see for myself," she replied dryly.

But she was smiling. And so was the older woman standing just behind her in the doorway.

In heavily accented English, Nick's *yiayia* said, "Manners, Nikolos, manners. Introduce us."

He rubbed his hands together. "Of course. Darcie Hayes, this is my grandmother, Sophia Pappas, and my mother, Thea Costas."

Hands were shaken, greetings exchanged. Darcie knew she was being sized up. Funny, but some of her earlier nervousness had evaporated. Nick's mother and grandmother were curious about her, that much was very clear. But she sensed no antipathy, no animosity. She felt welcome if not accepted. And that was before his grandmother slid one of her boney arms around Darcie's waist and propelled her toward the kitchen.

"Come. I will pour the wine. You will tell us about yourself. Start with your ancestors. Might there be a chance some of your people came from Greece?"

CHAPTER FIVE

NICK'S FATHER ARRIVED just before the meal was served. By then, Darcie's nerves had calmed substantially. It helped that while seated in the kitchen watching Thea and Sophia finish the preparations she'd polished off a glass of a lovely dry red wine.

She refused a refill when Nick would have poured her one. It wouldn't do to get snockered. But she told them, "This was very good."

"It is bottled by Nick's uncle, my brother, and his sons," Thea said proudly. "They have a small vineyard in Thrace."

"Nick is the only one of his generation to leave Greece to work," Sophia lamented. "We keep hoping he will return for good one day."

"Yiayia," he said.

"What? I only say what is true. That is what we all hope will happen. Is it not, Thea?"

His mother flushed and was saved from answering by Nick's father, who said as he entered the kitchen, "He is here now. Let us enjoy our time together."

The older man wasn't as tall as Nick, but his shoulders were just as broad. Age had added more girth to his waist, deep lines to the corners of his eyes and gray hair to his temples. But he remained a handsome man. This is how Nick would look in thirty years' time, Darcie thought. Warmth spread through her. She chalked it up to the wine.

"This is my father, George Costas," Nick said.

"Darcie Hayes." When she would have shaken his hand, George kissed both of her cheeks.

"She is prettier than Danika." He winked at Nick.

"Danika?" Darcie mouthed.

"I will explain later," Nick mumbled.

"Stop flirting, *Baba*, and go wash up," Thea said with an exaggerated shake of her head. "Dinner is ready."

They ate *alfresco*, seated around a table under a pergola in Yiayia's backyard. Vine-covered trellises lined the pergola's sides, offering shade from the late day sun. The center of the table was heaped with enough food to feed twice as many people.

Darcie smoothed a napkin over her lap. "Everything looks wonderful, Mrs. Costas and Mrs. Pappas."

"Call me Yiayia. Everyone does."

"And you may call me Thea," Nick's mother said, passing Darcie a platter of sliced lamb. "You are not a vegetarian, I hope. A lot of young people are nowadays."

"No." Even if Darcie had been, the delicious-smelling meat would have tempted her to take a bite.

"That is good," Yiayia said. "Nick likes red meat."

"True." Thea nodded. "But he will fly home for dinner on a Palm Sunday if I promise to make *bakaliaros tiganitos*."

At Darcie's perplexed expression, he explained, "It is a salt-cured cod that my mother then batters and deep fries. It is very tasty, but it is the dipping sauce she makes to go with it that has me booking my flight."

"Here, we are so close to the ocean that the fish is fresh and plentiful," Yiayia said.

"Manhattan is next to the Atlantic," he pointed out patiently and Darcie got the feeling this was a long-standing argument.

"It is settled," George offered. "Water and fish are everywhere."

But Yiayia wasn't done. "Do they even know how to make *bakaliaros tiganitos* in America?"

"I will look on the menu at the next Greek restaurant I visit."

Sophia shrugged. "It does not matter. They will not cook it as well as your mama does. I taught her, just as my mother taught me. Just as your mother will teach your future wife." She glanced slyly at Darcie.

George apparently didn't get the memo about playing it coy. "Maybe you could teach Darcie, Thea."

Everyone at the table turned and gaped at him. Nick was the first to recover. There was a gleam in his eye when he said, "I do like Mama's *bakaliaros tiganitos.*"

"Nick likes *all* of his mama's cooking," George said with a hearty laugh. "He gets that from me."

"If he is not careful, he will get this, too." Thea patted her husband's stomach. More laughter followed, chasing away a bit of the strain.

"If you would like, I could share some of my recipes with you," Thea said to Darcie, "including the one for *bakaliaros tiganitos.* It is not so hard to make, but you must soak the fish overnight or it will be too salty."

"Thank you. I would like that."

"Are you a good cook?" Sophia asked.

"Um, I…" Darcie had mastered the art of microwaving in college, and she knew how to whip up staples such as grilled cheese and spaghetti, as long as the sauce for the latter came from a jar. But her culinary skills didn't go much beyond that since, at Evelyn's insistence, Darcie and Tad had eaten most of their meals at his mother's. In Darcie's new home, wherever that might be, she was going to take the time to learn. "I plan to be."

Yiayia's eyes narrowed. Clearly, that answer hadn't won Darcie any points.

"Do you cook for Nick?"

Before she could formulate a response, he explained, "We eat out whenever Darcie comes to town."

"And where does she sleep when she comes to town?" Yiayia asked pointedly.

Darcie felt her face flame, but Nick took the question in stride. "She sleeps in a bed," he replied without specifying whose. Since his grin left little doubt, she kicked him under the table.

Earlier, in the kitchen, they had discussed how Darcie and Nick met. Now, the topic turned to what she did for a living, what her family was like and the names of her siblings, brothers-in-law, nephews and nieces. Yiayia, of course, snuck in a question about how many children Darcie wanted. By the time coffee and dessert were served, Yiayia had determined two things. One, Darcie was too thin and, two, she must have some Greek in her, if only because she liked the strong coffee.

"I like the cake, too," Darcie noted after taking a bite. It was topped with powdered sugar and lightly toasted almonds. "It's delicious. What's it called?"

"Revani," Yiayia said.

"Revani," Darcie repeated. Or so she thought. But Yiayia was shaking her head.

"No, no, no. Re-vah-*nee*."

"Emphasis on the last syllable," Nick supplied.

Darcie tried the word again, this time earning his grandmother's nod of approval.

"I make this special for Nick. I will be sure to give you the recipe so you can make it, too."

Darcie sent him a smile and asked, "Is this another favorite of yours?"

But it wasn't Nick who answered.

"My brother is fond of all sweet things."

Pieter stood just outside the door that led from the house. At least, Darcie assumed the man was Pieter. The family resemblance was there in the shape of his eyes and the athletic build. And if he was Pieter, that would make the woman standing beside him Selene.

OMG!

Darcie set down her fork and blotted her mouth on the napkin. Then she sat up straighter in her chair and sucked in her stomach. Selene was slender and petite. Darcie felt like an Amazon in comparison. And the other woman was drop-dead gorgeous with high cheekbones, delicately arched brows and sleek black hair. In short, she was Aphrodite incarnate. A glance at Nick confirmed what Darcie already knew: if he was over what had happened, he was doing a poor job showing it. His eyes had turned as hard as stone.

"Pieter! Selene!" Thea smiled nervously. "We did not think you would be here."

"We finished our appointment with the caterer early and thought we would stop by for cake."

"How did you know about the cake?" Nick asked.

"Yiayia called earlier and mentioned it."

All eyes cut to Yiayia.

"I am an old woman," she muttered with the wave of an arthritic hand. "I cannot remember what I say, who I say it to."

Half of Pieter's mouth rose in a resigned smile. "The only reason you are here is because you did not think that we would be. I guess I was foolish to hope."

Nick said nothing, but that muscle started to tick in his jaw again.

"It does not matter. I am glad to see you, Nick. We both are." Pieter curved his arm around Selene's shoulders and she offered a tentative smile.

The tension built along with the silence. Darcie was the one who breached it.

"Pieter and Selene. Nick has told me so much about you both. It's so nice to finally meet you."

"And you are?" Pieter asked.

"Darcie Hayes. Nick's…Nick's girlfriend."

She'd already stepped in this mess with one foot. Why not both?

"You played your part well this evening," Nick told Darcie once the two of them were in the Shelby and heading back to her hotel.

At times he had forgotten their bargain and actually enjoyed himself. That was until Pieter and Selene's arrival. Seeing them together never put Nick in a good mood. This evening it had been tolerable. He had Darcie to thank for that.

"You weren't half-bad yourself," she told him. "If your car auction business doesn't pan out you might consider a career on Broadway."

She smiled, but her tone didn't match the lighthearted comment.

"Is something wrong, Darcie?"

She fussed with the scarf's knot under her chin. "Your family is really nice, Nick. I enjoyed meeting them all."

"And they enjoyed meeting you," he replied warily.

"I don't like lying to them, Nick. Even if most of our lies were ones of omission."

He nodded. "Most of them."

The one that stood out had come from Darcie at the end of dinner: *I'm Nick's girlfriend.*

Upon hearing that, Pieter's expression had reflected not only surprise, but also happiness and hope. More than anything else from the evening, it was the hope that bothered Nick's conscience.

"Sophia is something else." Darcie chuckled. "But she only has your best interests at heart. All of them do."

Nick saw his brother's hopeful expression again only to banish it. "If that is so, they should be satisfied now. You made quite an impression on them."

"I suppose." She cleared her throat. Her tone was tentative when she said, "Your brother seems nice. Selene, too."

Nick made a noncommittal sound and concentrated on driving, hoping Darcie would drop the subject.

She didn't.

"They both seemed genuinely happy for you...us...well, you know what I mean."

"Guilty consciences looking for absolution," he muttered. But was that the cause? He decided to change the subject. "Are you really going to try the recipes my mother and grandmother gave you? Or did you just say that to humor them?"

"Oh, no. I meant it. I'm not sure where I am going to get salt-cured cod, but everything else looks pretty manageable."

"They love to fiddle in the kitchen. I think they should have their own television program."

"*Cooking with Thea and Sophia,*" Darcie offered. They both laughed. "I would watch it. I really do want to learn. I know the basics, but for the past six years, we pretty much ate all of our dinners at Evelyn's house."

"Evelyn?"

"Tad's mother," Darcie said quietly.

Nick glanced sideways. Darcie was staring at her hands,

which were now folded in her lap. "What is a Tad? Or should I ask who?"

She ran a tongue over her teeth. "He's my former fiancé."

Nick nearly blew through a red light. He brought the Shelby to a stop to the protest of skidding tires. Giving Darcie his full attention now, he asked, "How recently former?"

She wrinkled her nose. "Pretty recent. We were supposed to get married last Saturday, but I called it off the week before."

The breath left Nick's lungs in a gust as he added two and two together and came up with four. "He is the reason you are now looking for a new place to live."

"Yes. Tad got the cat and the condo in our breakup. I got...Greece."

Nick's eyebrows shot up in surprise. "So this trip was to be your..."

"Honeymoon," she finished for him. Her smile was tight, her laughter apologetic as he absorbed a second bombshell that he hadn't seen coming.

He should say something, he thought, although "sorry" didn't feel right, even if what she had just shared must have been painful. Endings always were. Briefly, he considered telling her about Selene and Pieter. She probably would welcome a little quid pro quo under the circumstances. But the words stuck in his throat. They drove the rest of the way in silence.

"Stop here," she said when they reached her hotel. "There's no need to park and walk me inside."

He wanted to disagree. But the evening was over and it was time to say good-night. It was just as well. His emotions were all over the place. He didn't care for the confusion. One thing he knew for sure, however, was that his interest in Darcie had not diminished one iota.

"What time shall we meet tomorrow?" At her puzzled

expression he reminded her, "I said I would act as your tour guide. I intend to live up to my end of the bargain."

"Oh. I'll leave the time up to you."

"I am an early riser, but how about nine o'clock?"

"All right. We can meet in the lobby again, if that works for you."

He nodded. "Where would you like to go?"

"The Parthenon."

Nick smiled. "Then the Parthenon it is." When she reached for the door handle, he said, "Aren't you forgetting something?"

She glanced around, her expression uncertain. "What?"

"A kiss good-night." Unable to resist, he leaned over the gearshift and captured her mouth. As the kiss deepened, he regretted the car's bucket seats. "Sleep well, Darcie," Nick said, pulling back.

"Right. As if…" she muttered, getting out.

The phone in Darcie's hotel room trilled at an ungodly hour. She pushed the pillow off her face and, eyes still closed, felt around on the nightstand until she found the receiver.

"'Lo," she mumbled.

"Are you alone?" It was Becky.

Darcie rubbed her eyes. "Yes, I'm alone. Why wouldn't I be alone?"

"You were supposed to call after your date with Mr. Tall, Greek and Gorgeous," her friend reminded her. "When you didn't, well, I thought…"

No need for Becky to fill in the blank. Darcie's imagination had been busy doing that very thing for most of the night.

"Nick dropped me off at the hotel just after ten. I fell asleep soon after. Alone. Sorry I didn't call. I was just too tired. Jet lag and all." It was a handy excuse, but not the whole truth. The whole truth was Darcie hadn't wanted to examine more closely the evening, its ending or the insane attraction she felt for the man in question.

But Becky wasn't giving her an out this time. "So, how was it?"

"Nice. I had a good time."

"Nice? A good time? Sheesh, Darcie. I called for details. Not the abridged version you save for your mother."

Darcie chuckled at that. "My mother is never going to hear any version, abridged or otherwise, where Nick is concerned. I think she still may be holding out hope that Tad and I will get back together and there will be no need to deal with the stack of gifts she promised she would help me return."

"Speaking of Tad, I ran in to him at our favorite coffee shop."

"Tad doesn't like coffee." He complained the beverage stained his teeth.

"I know. Even stranger, he made a point of coming over and saying hello to me."

That was surprising. Tad and Becky didn't like one another, but over the years, they had brokered a truce of sorts—a truce Darcie would have assumed null and void now that the wedding had been called off.

"He asked if I'd heard from you."

"He did not."

"Swear. He wanted to know how you were doing."

"What did you say?"

"I told him we'd talked and that you were having a fabulous time with a hot Greek man."

"You did not!" Darcie exclaimed.

"Okay, those weren't my exact words. But I did tell him that his bargain trip had turned out to be a bust and that you'd been stranded at the airport until a nice man came to your aid. Tad said he'd been trying to reach you on your cell. For that matter, I have, too."

Darcie glanced toward her discarded purse on the chair in the corner. "I silenced the ringer before dinner with Nick's family last night. I haven't turned it back on. Did Tad say why he was calling?"

"No. He looked, well, like he was kind of lost without you."

"Tad?" Darcie couldn't help but be surprised. "I didn't think he would notice my absence. He still has his mother, after all." She shook her head. "That was mean. I don't want him to be unhappy."

"That's because you're a nice person, Darcie. Too nice. Tad took advantage of that. So, are you going to call him? I don't think you should."

"I won't. At least not until I return home." When her friend started to object, Darcie pointed out, "We have to talk, if only so he knows where to forward my mail. Besides, I'm the one who called off the wedding, Becks. That makes Tad the injured party."

A snort came over the line. "Do yourself a favor, and don't feel too sorry for him. Remember, he's the reason you found yourself stranded in Greece."

"Yes, but that's turning out okay." A grin spread over Darcie's face.

"I knew it! Tell me everything about last night. And remember, no skimping when it comes to details."

She still wound up giving Becky an abridged version of events, leaving out completely the arrival of Pieter and Selene at the end of dinner, and the awkward tension that had followed. Darcie didn't want to more closely examine the feelings Nick stirred in her. It was easier just to leave it at mutual attraction. The timing for anything else was completely wrong—apparently for both of them.

As their conversation wound up, Becky said, "Have fun exploring the Parthenon. Hey, take a picture of Nick with your phone and send it to me. I want to see your hot man for myself."

After they said goodbye, Darcie had less than an hour to get ready. The elevator doors slid open at the lobby with five minutes to spare. When she stepped out, the hot man in question was standing to one side of the reception desk. His mouth curved into an appreciative smile that turned her insides to mush. With one look, he made her feel beautiful, desirable and once again ready to toss caution to the wind. That was enough, she decided.

"Kalimera su," she said when she reached him.

His brows rose.

"One of the few Greek phrases I know. Did I say it right?"

"You did. Good morning to you, too." He kissed her cheeks, lingering long enough to make the greeting less platonic. "You look lovely, by the way."

"You do, too. Not lovely, but…" Good enough to gobble up in a T-shirt that fit snugly across his chest. She coughed and forced her gaze back to his. "Um, ready to take in the sights?"

By way of an answer, he took her hand.

Growing up in Athens, Nick had been to the Parthenon dozens of times. He experienced it anew seeing it through Darcie's eyes. She was in total awe.

"It's hard to believe something built more than four hundred years before the birth of Christ is still standing."

"Not all of it is," Nick pointed out.

"But enough of it remains to hint at its former grandeur," she argued. "Those columns are massive. Haven't you ever wondered how the ancient Greeks managed to get them up without modern tools and machinery?"

He grinned. "I am now."

"I'm serious, Nick."

"So I see."

"There's very little in the United States that dates back more than a couple hundred years. Yet here stands a temple, a stunning example of Doric-style architecture, I might add, that was designed by Phidias to honor Athena, the patron goddess of your city, and constructed more than two thousand years ago."

"Your knowledge of the Parthenon is impressive," he said.

"I read about it." She started to laugh. "Over there."

Nick turned to find a large sign listing the same facts Darcie had just spouted. He started to laugh, too, and then pulled her into his arms. He didn't let her go. Both of them sobered.

"I like your sense of humor," he said.

"It's one of my better attributes."

"I can think of other attributes that I prefer even more." He slid his hands down her back and, even though he wanted to place them elsewhere, he forced them to stop at her waist. They were in public, after all, and surrounded by camera-toting tourists.

"You must mean my eyes." She batted the lids. The eyes in question were laughing at him. "I've been told they're a pretty color."

"You are enjoying this," he accused.

"Enjoying what?" she asked a little too innocently. "I don't know what you mean."

"I do like your eyes," he agreed. "But they aren't what kept me awake last night." As intended, his bald assertion wiped the smile from Darcie's face. Then he asked, "How did you sleep? Did you toss and turn?"

"I...I..." She swallowed.

"That is what I thought."

Those blue eyes narrowed. "That's not fair."

"Why?"

"I did toss and turn, but I'm still suffering from jet lag."

"You are full of excuses."

"It's true."

"All right. I have a cure for that." His voice was low and for the briefest moment his hips bumped against hers as he spoke. "Would you like to know what it is?"

"Right now? Right here?" She gave a panicked glance around.

Nick brushed the hair back from her cheek and leaned closer. His lips purposely grazed her ear when he whispered, "Warm milk."

"Warm—" Darcie dissolved in a fit of laughter that drew curious stares from passersby. When she composed herself, she accused, "You set me up."

"I cannot be responsible for the thoughts you entertain." His voice dropped an octave. "Although I would not mind hearing what they are."

She put a hand on his chest and playfully pushed him backward half a step. "Oh, no. I'm not walking into a trap a second time."

Just that quickly, he erased the distance she'd created, and pulled her close. "Now I *really* want to hear those thoughts. Over dinner, perhaps? Say yes."

"Well, when you put it that way. Yes."

CHAPTER SIX

NICK CHANGED HIS mind several times before settling on a restaurant. Even then he wasn't sure he'd made the right choice. He had no doubt Darcie would enjoy the food and the ambience. They were what made it so difficult to get a table at Moscophilero...unless one had a long history with the owner, as Nick did. But the restaurant's location gave him pause. It was in Piraeus and, as such, much closer to his house above the harbor than anything in Athens would be. Within fifteen minutes of his paying the check, he and Darcie could be ensconced in his living room sipping a nightcap. As for what they could be doing within an hour, that gave him pause.

Where was this heading? Where did he want it to head? Such questions had never arisen with the other women he'd dated, but Darcie was...special. In addition to turning him on to an extent he'd never experienced, she also brought out his protective instincts. Add in her recently ended engagement and Nick didn't want to rush her. But he did want her. So, he needed to be sure they were both after the same thing: a mutually satisfying, albeit short-term, sexual relationship. Recriminations afterward wouldn't do.

Ultimately, he decided to tell her their destination and see if she would prefer to stay in Athens proper.

"I wouldn't mind seeing the seaside," she told him when they met in the hotel lobby.

Her assent did little to quell his nerves. But when they stepped outside, her laughter did.

"Nick Costas, man of many cars. I never know what you'll be driving next." Her lips curved.

Earlier, when he'd taken Darcie to the Parthenon, he'd been driving an Aston Martin coupe. He liked to get behind the wheel of the automobiles he would be auctioning, especially those he purchased himself and for whom he had no specific collector in mind, to get a feel for how they handled. In this case, however, the cherry-red Jaguar roadster would never see the auction block. It belonged to him and had for the past few years. He kept it at his house in Greece for personal use. In New York, his vehicle of choice was a 1966 Corvette Sting Ray.

"You will get a prize if you know the year this car was manufactured," he said.

"Hmm. Let's see. Streamlined body and covered headlights." She pursed her lips and glanced inside. "Sunken floor pans. Four-speed manual gearbox." Straightening, she said, "I'm going to say it was built in nineteen sixty…five."

"You are close. Sixty-six."

She wrinkled her nose. "What would my prize have been?"

She had to ask. His body tightened, but he managed a casual shrug. "I was going to let you drive it."

"Then it's just as well I got the answer wrong," she told him on a laugh. "The steering wheel is on the wrong side of the car."

"For the United States," he agreed.

"That increases the value, of course, a fact of which I am sure you are aware."

He nodded, pleased by her astuteness and an idea nig-

gled. He pushed it to the back burner. "Fewer than a thousand of the right-hand drive models were produced in 1966."

The restaurant was busy when they arrived. They were
shown to their table in a prime location at the window that
offered an unparalleled view of the harbor. The day was
winding down, the sun starting to set. Boats, both commercial and pleasure craft, were heading in for the night.

"I could sit here all day," she murmured. "What is it about
water that is so…compelling?"

Nick lifted his shoulders. He couldn't put it into words,
but he understood what she meant. The view drew him. It
always had. It was one of the things he missed when he was
in Manhattan, and one of the reasons he knew he would
never sell his home here, even though he did not spend very
much time in it.

A black-vested waiter came by and took their beverage
order. Darcie opted for a glass of white wine. Nick ordered
the same. A moment later, the man was back with their
drinks and a complimentary platter of olives, cheese and
dense bread.

"Khristos sends his regards," the waiter said.

"Khristos?" Darcie asked once they were alone.

"The owner. He and I are old friends."

She lifted her glass of wine. "To old friends then."

Nick raised his glass as well, but he had a different toast
in mind. "And to new friendships."

She smiled in agreement and clinked her glass against
his.

"You know, even though I have only known you a short
time, I do consider you a friend, Nick."

In the time it took her to say so, the word lost all of its
appeal. "Merely a friend?"

"A very handsome one." She arched her brows. "Better?"

"A little. My ego thanks you."

Darcie selected an olive from the platter and popped it into her mouth. His started to water, only to go dry when she turned the question back around on him.

"What do you consider me? If your answer is a nuisance, feel free to make up something else. My ego will be every bit as appreciative as yours was."

Nick chuckled. "I suppose I should confess that initially I considered you a delightful distraction."

"That was when you offered me a ride from the airport." She nodded, selected another olive. Before popping it into her mouth she added, "Then you saw me as your ticket out of a tight spot with your mother and grandmother."

"A lovely ticket."

She batted her eyelashes comically and murmured her thanks. "And now, after spending the better part of the day touring ancient ruins with me, are we pals?"

Another time, Nick would have laughed. But he weighed her words carefully and then weighed his own. "Not by my definition, but English is my second language. The fact is, Darcie, friendship seems a rather bland term for us. Do you not agree?"

"What other term do you have in mind?"

"That is my dilemma. I have no other term." He sipped his wine. "I was hoping you might."

"Well, if we're being honest, I don't think platonic applies to our situation."

He agreed, of course, but was curious to hear Darcie's reasons. "Go on."

A couple blotches of color worked their way up from her neck until they flamed on her cheeks. "Speaking only for myself, I like kissing you. I'm pretty sure people who are merely friends don't kiss—" she cleared her throat "—like that." She cleared her throat again. "Or enjoy it quite so much."

"We are attracted to one another," Nick agreed. "And I, too, like kissing you."

"My friend Becky would say that what you and I have going qualifies as a fling. Well, a baby fling, really, since we're not..."

Sleeping together went unspoken, but Darcie may as well have screamed it. Nick heard the words loud and clear and finished her thought with a silent *yet*.

He hid his grin behind the rim of his glass and sipped his wine. He liked Darcie's friend's assessment. After all, in addition to sex, *fling* implied impermanence. It bolstered his assumption that Darcie, who had so recently freed herself from her own betrothal, wasn't looking for true love and a lasting commitment any more than he was. She was after excitement, a little fun.

Still, he needed to be positive.

"And, if instead of this baby fling, we were to have a very adult one, what then?"

She moistened her lips. "I'm not sure I understand your question."

"What would you expect?"

The waiter picked that inopportune moment to return and take their dinner orders. Nick clenched his teeth and waited to hear Darcie's response.

"This is all very hypothetical," she began once they were alone again. "I'm not really the sort of woman who goes around having flings, especially of the adult variety."

"I never assumed otherwise," he hastened to assure her. "In fact, you might say that is the reason I am seeking clarity on the matter."

Her expression turned thoughtful. "First and foremost, I would expect the truth. I won't tolerate lies."

Her response surprised him a little. Even though it was none of his business, he asked, "Did your fiancé lie to you?"

"I'm sure he would say no." She pursed her lips, as if considering. "I think Tad lied to himself much more than he lied to me. He said I was the one he wanted to spend the rest of his life with, but, in the end, it wasn't going to be just the two of us."

Nick's brows shot up at that, but he kept his voice neutral when he asked, "What do you mean?"

"I wouldn't have been marrying just him. I would have been marrying his mother, too." The shiver that accompanied her words appeared involuntary rather than manufactured for effect.

"I gather that his mother did not like you."

"I wasn't good enough for her son. Tad's quite the catch. A *doctor*, you know." She emphasized the word in a way that Nick imagined other people had in speaking to Darcie. "But that doesn't change the fact that he's a world-class mama's boy."

"Obviously, I do not know Tad or his mother, but my guess is that no one would have been good enough for her son, even a woman as wonderful as you."

"Thanks." Darcie smiled. "And I know what you mean."

Did she? If so, Nick thought that might have been a recent development. Her uncertainty would explain why Darcie had been flustered by a simple compliment when he first met her.

She was saying, "Evelyn's fault-finding might not have been such a big issue if we hadn't spent so much time with her. Dinner practically every evening, church on Sundays. The last straw was when Tad started talking about adding another master suite on to her house instead of continuing to look for a house of our own after we got married."

"Pieter and Selene will live down the street from my parents, who, as you know, live next door to my grandmother."

"Next door and down the street are not the same as under

one roof with shared main living spaces. I always felt on guard around Evelyn. I couldn't slouch without hearing her comment on my poor posture."

"Tad allowed this?"

"He has a blind spot a mile wide where his mother is concerned."

"Then he got what he deserved," Nick said. "He lost you, but gets to keep his mother."

Her lips twitched. "And don't forget Rufus. He's keeping the cat, too."

"Good riddance, spawn of Satan."

Darcie laughed.

They were both quiet for a moment. Then Nick said, "I am sorry that things didn't work out."

Sympathy was expected, though Nick actually felt no such thing. If Darcie were now a married woman, they never would have met, and he still would be dodging his family's matchmaking attempts. His relief was selfish, his reasons rooted in his current situation, he assured himself. They had nothing to do with that tug of attraction and something less definable that he felt when he was with Darcie.

"Well, I'm not sorry. I mean, I'm sorry that I let things go on for so long and that Becky wound up shelling out good money for a tangerine gown that she isn't going to be able to wear anyplace except maybe a costume party." Darcie shook her head on a laugh. "God, I must sound so cold."

"Not at all. More like honest," Nick said.

He appreciated honesty. And he appreciated her situation. A woman who had recently ended her engagement would not be looking for another relationship so soon. But...

"Getting back to our possible fling, in addition to honesty, what else would you expect?"

"I don't know. This is an awkward conversation."

"It is all hypothetical, remember?"

"Hypothetical or not, it's still awkward. As worldly and sophisticated as I'd like you to think I am, I'm…just not." She shrugged.

When she said things like that, his protective instincts kicked into high gear. For all of her bravado and flippant comments, she was vulnerable and uncertain. She could be hurt. Hell, she already had been by a man who claimed to love her, but had allowed his own mother to belittle her.

Darcie shifted in her seat. "Maybe you should tell me what you would expect."

"Fair enough." He picked up his glass and took a drink, allowing the crisp white wine to bathe his tongue as he searched for the right words. "I would expect to have more dinners such as this one. I enjoy our conversations."

"And?"

"Well, like you, I would expect honesty."

"Of course." She nodded. "And?"

"Whatever were to happen naturally between us, it would be mutually agreed upon and enjoyed."

"A very diplomatic answer," she said.

"Something for both of us to think about."

Their entrées arrived then and the conversation turned to benign topics. Nick was eyeing the dessert menu, if only to prolong their evening, when Darcie said, "That was almost as good as the dinner your mom and grandmother made."

"I will be sure to pass along your compliment. You have room for dessert tonight, yes?"

She grinned. "I'm on vacation. I get to indulge." When he lifted a brow, she clarified, "In sweets."

They ordered coffee and two pieces of chocolate cake layered with a decadent mousse filling. The cake was delicious, but what made his mouth water was watching Darcie savor each bite.

He set his fork aside and, after taking a sip of coffee,

asked her, "Have you decided where I will be taking you tomorrow?"

"I was thinking the Temple of Zeus and Hadrian's Arch. That is if you have the time."

"I will *make* the time."

Darcie had blown her diet big-time with that delicious dessert, so it was a good thing the scrumptious man she'd spent the evening with came calorie-free. Still, if one of them had to go straight to her hips, she would rather it be Nick.

"You are smiling," the man in question noted as they returned to the hotel. "Care to share your thoughts?"

"No." She pressed her lips together tightly afterward to keep from smiling again.

"Ah." He nodded.

"*Ah* what?"

"There is no need for you to say anything now. I know." He glanced over, winked. The accompanying smile was smug.

"What is it that you think you know?"

"You want to invite me in for a drink."

"I want to—"

He cut her off with a *tsking* sound. "But I must refuse."

The hotel was just ahead. Its sign lit up like a beacon.

"You're saying no?" Forget that Darcie hadn't asked or, for that matter, having a drink with him wasn't what had caused her to smile in the first place.

"I was, but all right. One drink. Since you insist."

Nick winked again and turned the car to the right. Just that quickly, he was pulling into the valet parking lane at the front entrance.

"You're something else," she murmured with a shake of her head.

"I will take that as a compliment."

Inside the hotel, he steered her to the lounge. At her questioning glance, he said, "I will not claim to be a saint. A drink in your room poses too much temptation. And we have not yet defined our expectations of our hypothetical fling. Let us move slowly."

"Take our time."

"Drive ourselves insane," it sounded like he said.

So they had a drink in the lounge. Afterward, Nick not only walked her to the elevator, but he also insisted on accompanying her all the way to her room.

"I am not coming in," he assured her when the doors of the elevator slid open on her floor.

"Testing your restraint?" she teased.

He snorted, and it was her restraint that was on the line when he told her, "I want to picture where you will be sleeping tonight."

She opened the door and switched on the light. The room was small with just enough space to accommodate a double bed, dresser, writing desk and television. Housekeeping had been by, so the duvet was turned down, the pillows freshly plumped. A foil-wrapped square of chocolate sat in the center of the one closest to the door.

It wasn't the treat that had her mouth watering.

Darcie's gaze cut to Nick. He was studying her as well, his expression seductive. She had to remind herself that it wouldn't be wise to hop into bed with a man she barely knew, even if what little she did know about him she found very appealing.

"I must go." His tone was brusque.

"Yes."

He gave her a quick kiss on the forehead, pushed her inside and shut the door himself.

"Engage the security chain," she heard him order from the hallway.

With their talk about flings and expectations swirling in her head, it was well after two before Darcie finally fell asleep.

The next day, as promised, she and Nick visited the Temple of Zeus and then Hadrian's Arch. It was a small consolation that he appeared as ill-rested as she was. She had her guidebook out and was reading about how the arch, which was built in 131 AD, had marked the boundary between ancient Athens and the new Roman city of Hadrian, when her cell phone rang.

Thinking it might be Tad, she considered ignoring it, but when she saw that it was Stavros, she flashed Nick an apologetic smile.

"I need to take this."

"I will be just there." He pointed to a nearby street vendor's cart and headed off. Darcie unabashedly enjoyed the view as he walked away. She was smiling when she answered. By the time the call ended five minutes later, however, she was fuming and feeling dejected. It didn't come as a surprise that Stavros would not refund her money. Still, she'd hoped.... She went to join Nick.

"I took a chance that you would like chocolate." He handed her an ice cream cone.

"Gee, big risk," she teased. "Where's yours?"

"Ice cream will melt quickly in this heat. I thought we could share." With that, he ran his tongue over the top scoop, all while keeping his gaze on her.

When Nick said things like that, when he looked at Darcie the way he was looking at her right now... She'd never felt like this. Ever. So wound up. So wanted. Wouldn't it just figure that she would be leaving soon?

"It is your turn now." Nick nodded to the ice cream.

Unfortunately, when she went to lick the ice cream, the

top scoop fell off the cone. It plopped on the pavement between their feet.

"The story of my life," she muttered, closing her eyes. She wanted to scream, cry. She settled for sighing.

"It is only ice cream. There is no need to be so upset."

She opened her eyes. "It's not just the ice cream."

His expression sobered. "The phone call, has something happened? Your family?"

"All fine as far as I know. That was Stavros. He finally got around to returning my call."

"And?"

"Well, he was very apologetic when I asked for a refund, but…" Her shoulders lifted. "He did offer to personally drive me to several of the locations on my itinerary, but I declined. He didn't exactly sound sober."

Nick threw the empty ice cream cone into a nearby waste container and plucked his cell phone from his back pocket. "I will call him. I will make him see reason."

"Thank you, but no." She placed a hand over his. "You've already left messages on my behalf. Besides, you said it yourself that first day. He doesn't have the money to refund."

"What will you do now?"

"I can't stay the full two weeks." Even if she wanted to—and oh, yeah, she really wanted to—she couldn't afford it. As it was, her three nights in Athens were going to set her back half a week's pay.

"How long?"

"Another couple of days." And even that was going to stretch her financial limit. It would be worth eating mac and cheese for a month, though, if it meant spending more time with Nick.

"But you cannot leave so soon. You have barely seen any of the sights. You have barely been outside of Athens."

"Believe me, I wish I could afford to continue my vacation, but I can't."

"If you had a place to stay, one that would cost you nothing, would you postpone your return to the States?" he asked slowly.

"What do you mean *if* I had a place to stay that would not cost me anything?"

"I know of such a place, a house that is not far from where we had dinner last night."

"A house?" He had to be joking. A house near the harbor that would not cost her a dime? Her tone light, she asked, "Does it boast the same spectacular view as the restaurant?"

"The view is even better."

"You're serious."

"I am. Do you want to see it?"

"I…"

He took her hand and started toward where he had parked the car. "I will take that as a yes."

Darcie expected the house to be nice. Nick didn't strike her as the sort of man who would recommend anything even remotely substandard. Nor had he exaggerated about the view. The house was farther up the hillside than the restaurant and its windows were placed to make the most of the stunning scenery.

The foyer opened into what she assumed was the main living space. It was spacious, well-appointed.

"Is this really a rental property?"

He didn't answer. Instead, he pointed toward an arched doorway across the room.

"The kitchen is through here," he said.

The home's kitchen was bigger than the one Darcie had glimpsed at Nick's grandmother's house. Even though it was equipped with state-of-the-art appliances, it appeared less used. The stainless steel pots and pans that dangled from the rack over the butcher-block island showed little sign of wear, and there was not so much as a grease splatter on the tiles on the wall behind the cook top. That seemed odd and she said as much to Nick.

He shrugged. "Some people prefer to eat out."

They returned to the living room. She glanced around again. The furnishings were modern and leaned toward masculine with their no-frill lines and muted colors. The massive plasma-screen television would appeal to a man, too. And all of the magazines spread out over the coffee table were geared toward sports and the automobile enthusiast.

"The bedrooms are upstairs," Nick said.

He was three treads up when Darcie's words stopped him. "That's all right. I think I've seen enough."

He turned on a frown. "It is not to your liking."

"Oh, I like it. How can I not? This home is gorgeous." She folded her arms. "It's also no rental. It's yours, Nick."

At least he didn't insult her intelligence by trying to deny it. "I am so rarely here that I could rent it out. In fact, my accountant has suggested I do just that."

Oh, she didn't doubt that. The location was prime, the view stunning, its amenities and furnishings were top-of-the-line. He could lease it by the week or even by the month. It would fetch an outrageous sum.

"You could, but you don't. You're making an exception for me. And my stay would be complimentary."

He dipped his chin. "Yes."

"But there's a price, right?"

She wanted to be irate, maybe even insulted. She was having a hard time getting past flattered and turned on. And that was before he smiled. Heat shimmied up her spine like a brush fire out of control.

"I assure you, it is not what you are thinking."

Arms still crossed, for self-preservation more so than out of pique, she asked, "And what is it that I'm thinking, Nick?"

"That I am trying to take advantage of both you and your current situation."

"Are you?"

"As tempting as I find that, I am a man with scruples, remember? You said so yourself."

"So, what you are saying then, is that if I agree to stay here you would be sleeping on the couch."

His laughter was sharp. "I have scruples, Darcie. But I will not claim to be a saint. If I were to spend the night under the same roof as you, sleeping on the couch would not be an option for either of us."

A disturbingly erotic image of the pair of them—sweaty, sated and tangled up in bedsheets—swirled through her mind. She swallowed hard and managed to say, "Then what do you have in mind?"

He took a step toward her, and even though he was still more than arm's length away, her body began to hum like the plucked strings of a harp.

"I will stay with my family. My mother will be glad for the intrusion. She complains that she does not see me enough when I am in Athens." He took another step forward. "You would have this entire place to yourself. How does that sound?"

Lonely. "Lovely."

"Is that yes, then?"

Darcie gave herself a mental shake. "Nick, your offer is very generous, a little too generous for me to accept."

"I am only repaying your kindness. You did me a favor," he persisted.

"Repayment wasn't necessary. I enjoyed dinner with your family. Besides, you have taken me sightseeing and out to dinner last night. You have more than repaid any debt you feel you owe me."

"Perhaps you will consider staying here in lieu of payment for a job?"

That caught her interest. "What sort of job?"

"You are a trained journalist, yes?"

"I'm a fact-checker."

"You *were* a fact-checker. Regardless, you are a journalist and, most importantly, you know an astonishing amount about vintage automobiles."

"I do," she agreed, still unable to figure out where this was heading.

"In exchange for writing background information for my auction catalog, a service for which I currently pay someone in New York, you can stay in my home for the remainder of your vacation and I will continue to act as your tour guide. We may not be able to hit all of the sites on your original itinerary, but we should be able to manage many of them."

Darcie ran her tongue around her teeth. What he was proposing sounded reasonable. It sounded fair. And, God knew, she didn't want to cut her trip short and fly home to the mess that awaited her. There was so much more she wanted to see and experience in Greece.

And then there was Nick…

"Um, the person who usually does this sort of thing for you, will they be out of work if I agree?"

Nick shook his head. "I have no one on my payroll, if that is what you mean. I contract with a couple of freelance writers in Manhattan whenever the need arises. In this case, I simply would be contracting with you instead."

"And my payment would be free lodgings here."

"And sightseeing. You will have a car at your disposal, should you need one. And I am happy to accompany you."

The smile that spread across his face caused heat to curl

in her belly. As much as she wanted to agree right then and there, Darcie hesitated. "That seems like such an imposition. I can't help but feel like I'm getting the better end of the deal."

"Hmm," Nick murmured thoughtfully as he closed the distance between them. His hands found Darcie's waist and he said, "Then perhaps I should apply conditions."

"Oh? What might those be?" she asked, and gave herself a mental high five for not hyperventilating on the spot. Indeed, for someone who had already confessed to being unsophisticated when it came to matters such as this, Darcie thought she sounded downright blasé.

"You will have to accompany me on my business trips. I have four lined up between now and the day you are to return home." He leaned in after saying so. She felt his lips brush the curve of her neck. "We can combine my business with your pleasure."

"I—I suppose I could fit those into my schedule." She tipped her head to the side, giving him greater access to her neck. While he took advantage of that, she closed her eyes and murmured, "Anything else?"

"You will help me research the vehicles in question. I usually do this on my own, but I would appreciate your insight." His breath tickled her ear.

"Mmm. 'Kay. I have no problem with that."

"No?" He kissed her cheek.

"None whatsoever."

"Good."

"It is good." Bordering on incredible, she decided, as his hands moved up her sides and his thumbs brushed the underside of her breasts.

"So, that is yes?" His voice was low, strained. "You will stay?"

Darcie wrapped her arms around his neck and kissed him. "I'll stay, Nick."

CHAPTER SEVEN

"WE HAD BETTER GO."

Nick made that pronouncement with no small amount of regret. But if he and Darcie stayed in his home much longer, the sparks he was experiencing were bound to ignite into an all-out blaze. And he had just convinced her that he was not, in fact, offering her a place to stay in exchange for a bed-mate. He still had no doubt that Darcie and he would move beyond the hypothetical when it came to having a fling, but he'd meant what he said last night—he wanted both of them going into it with open eyes and clear expectations.

That and he couldn't explain exactly why, but he didn't want the flash and burn of spontaneous sex. With Darcie, when it happened, he wanted to take his time. He wanted to make it last, make it count. Something told him she deserved that. So, he collected his keys from the kitchen counter and steered her out the door as quickly as possible. She didn't object.

On the drive back to her hotel, he said, "I will be by to-morrow morning at nine to collect you. We can move your belongings to the house and then spend the afternoon wandering near the seaside, if you would like."

"That sounds fine, but what about work? Do you have a car you need to go see or one that you want me to start re-searching online?"

Nick shook his head. "I think tomorrow will be a day off for both of us. Work can start the following day."

"Oh, my God! You're moving in with Nick!"

Becky didn't sound as scandalized as she did jealous. And no wonder. After Darcie had sent her friend a photograph she'd snapped of Nick at the Parthenon, Becky had emailed back that she would be on the next flight to Athens if Nick had a friend she could meet who was even half as good-looking.

No friend. Only a brother and he's getting married, Darcie had emailed back. She'd left out all of the nuances to that particular story, not sure what to make of them herself.

Now, she told Becky, "I'm not moving in with Nick. I'm moving into his house."

"You say potato…. Is there really a distinction?"

Darcie couldn't help but laugh. Nor could she help but be grateful that she'd called Becky before calling her family. She could only imagine what her parents were going to make of the latest twist in her trip itinerary. They hadn't exactly been thrilled about her going on her honeymoon solo. Even though she was a grown woman, she knew they worried. She'd promised to check in a few times during her trip. Her conversation with Becky qualified as a test run, so Darcie strove to clear up any misconceptions. She needed to have her story down pat before relaying it to her mom and dad.

"There's a big distinction. Nick will not be there. He is going to stay with his parents."

She went on to explain the rest of the arrangement to Becky—the work she would be doing for Nick in exchange for the free lodgings. By the time she finished, it sounded like a perfectly platonic business deal, especially since she didn't mention the skill with which Nick kissed or the way she responded to those kisses. No sense pouring kerosene on a fire that was already burning cheerfully all on its own.

"So, it's a business arrangement," Becky said slowly.

"Exactly. Who knows? Nick says he uses freelancers to put together his auction booklets. Maybe I'll be able to snag some of that work when I get home, too. It's not exactly full-length feature writing, but it's a start. I can get my feet wet, begin collecting clips."

"You want to write again?"

Darcie had never stopped *wanting* to write, but as a practical matter, while working full-time as a fact-checker, she hadn't had the wherewithal to seek out freelance opportunities. Besides, Tad had not been encouraging. A journalism career, especially one that eventually might take her to New York, wasn't in the cards for his future wife.

"My life is in chaos anyway. Why not try new things? You know, take some chances."

"Oh, you won't get any argument from me. I always felt you gave up on your dream job much too easily. That's another reason I never liked Tad. He wasn't supportive when it came to your goals. It was all about him. His happiness. His career. His mother," she added drolly. "I'm glad to see your backbone returning."

"Greece has been good for me," Darcie replied. "A new start."

"Yes, and a hot man who treats you like a goddess doesn't hurt, either."

They both laughed, but Darcie knew there was some truth to her friend's words. In the short time she'd known Nick, she had started to feel more confident, more desirable, more in control of her future. Maybe those changes would have occurred regardless once she'd called off her engagement. Still, she credited Nick for accelerating the process.

But did that mean she could handle a no-emotional-strings-attached fling with him? Darcie didn't know. Sure, she flirted a good game, but she'd also confessed her unworldliness to Nick. She was pretty sure that was what had him holding back.

After Darcie hung up, she called her mom and dad.

Neither of her parents had a problem with her new living arrangements, especially since Darcie left off the part that Nick owned the house where she would be staying. In fact, she left out a lot of details where Nick was concerned, only mentioning that he'd offered her a freelance opportunity.

Like Becky, her father was thrilled that Darcie was returning to writing.

"That's the best news I've had in a long, long time," he told her. The pride she heard in his voice made her eyes sting. He'd never stopped believing in her.

"Thanks, Dad." Since her mother was on the extension, Darcie asked, "And you, Mom? What do you think?"

"I'm happy if you're happy." But her voice didn't hold pride as much as trepidation.

"But?"

"I don't know." Then, apropos of nothing, she said, "Tad stopped by today. He dropped off some wedding gifts from our side of the family that had been mailed to the condo."

Not sure what else to say, Darcie replied, "That was nice of him."

"He also brought a box of miscellaneous things you left behind when you moved out."

"Oh." Again, she was at a loss for words.

"I know you often felt second in line to his mother, but by calling off the wedding, well, I think you've made your point. I think things would be different now if you got back together. He…he really loves you."

Darcie swallowed, wishing it were as simple as that.

Wishing she could want the same suburban life her married sisters had so happily embraced.

"But I don't love him, Mom. Not the way I should if I am going to spend the rest of my life as his wife."

"He said he's been trying to reach you but that you haven't returned any of his calls."

Four on her cell. All of which Darcie had let go to voice mail. "I know. And I will."

"When?"

"When I get back."

"Honey—"

"Mom, please. It's over. You need to accept that and so does Tad. He and I, well, we want different things in life."

"What is it that you want, Darcie?" Her mother's tone had turned impatient. "What is it you *think* you're looking for?"

It was her father who answered. "Stop badgering the girl. She simply wants more than what Tad can offer."

Darcie closed her eyes. Bless her dad. He got it. He understood. Her mother, meanwhile, remained perplexed.

"Are you sure it's not just a case of cold feet?" she asked. "A lot of brides get them. It's natural."

"I'm positive, Mom."

And Darcie was, especially when she thought about Nick and all of the heat the man could generate inside of her with a single, simple smile.

The move to Nick's house the next morning was accomplished easily. Darcie had only the one, forlorn-looking bag after all. She'd still heard nothing from the airline about her missing piece of luggage. With her luck, it would show up in Greece about the time she was to return home. Whatever. She was making do and, now that she didn't have to worry about paying for lodgings, she'd decided she was entitled to make a few more wardrobe purchases. Already Nick had mentioned having dinner again. She couldn't very well keep wearing the same dress. And she was starting to feel a little too touristy outfitted in T-shirts, shorts and sneakers. She might as well hang a camera around her neck and strap on a fanny pack to complete the cliché.

Once they arrived at Nick's house, she stood in the driveway and breathed in the sea-scented air, looking forward to the stroll through town that he promised her. The day was warm, but the breeze kept the temperature from being unpleasant.

That was until they went inside and Nick offered a tempting smile and said, "We never got to the bedrooms yesterday."

They hadn't gotten to a lot of things while in his house the day before, Darcie thought, not sure whether it was relief she felt or something more damning.

Even so, she smiled in return and made a sweeping motion with one hand. "Lead the way."

Three bedrooms opened up off the hallway at the top of the stairs. Each had its own bath. Two of the rooms, including the master, faced the harbor and sported private balconies. The master was large enough to accommodate a small sitting area in addition to a king-sized bed. The chairs were upholstered in a luscious aquamarine, which, when combined with the deep blue duvet cover, mimicked the colors of the harbor. The art on the walls featured nautical themes, although the works themselves were more abstract in nature. Darcie was no connoisseur, but the pictures appeared to be signed originals or numbered prints, all of which were expertly matted and framed.

Nick came up behind her as she gazed out at the harbor. She swore she could feel the heat from his body warming her back even though he stood a respectable distance away.

"This is a very, um, restful view," she said.

"You would think so." Dry humor tinged his voice. "Right now, I am feeling very restless, especially when I think of you sleeping in my bed."

"About that." She cleared her throat and turned. "I think I will take one of your guestrooms."

"Are you sure? I spared no expense on that mattress. I think you would be more comfortable in here."

She didn't agree. Indeed, she had a feeling that she would toss and turn all night on the mattress in question, tortured by detailed fantasies and the lingering scent of his cologne. She wasn't quite ready to slip into Nick's bed—alone or otherwise.

Darcie chose the guestroom next door. It offered the same stunning view as the master and could hardly be considered small, even if it only had one chair rather than an actual sitting area. If she wanted to sit at all up here, she would do it on the balcony in one of the cushioned chaises.

It only took her a few minutes to unpack her clothes and toiletries, and then she met Nick downstairs, where he showed her around his home office. Like the rest of the house, the furnishings were modern with clean lines. The wooden desk was stained a deep brown. The bookshelves just behind it were glass and metal. Every electronic gadget one could wish for—tablet, laptop, digital printer and copier—would be at her disposal.

He showed her how to log on to the internet using his laptop, as well as how to access her own email account. With a few clicks of the mouse, he also brought up a raft of research sites that he used to locate collectible cars and determine their value. Given her current job, she was familiar with several of them. Then he opened a file on the laptop and pulled up a catalog from a previous auction at his warehouse just outside Manhattan. It had been created using software Darcie knew well. In addition to color photographs of the automobiles and the prices they were likely to bring at auction, the catalog included several paragraphs describing the vehicles.

Nick tapped his index finger against the screen. "This is the sort of thing I will need you to write for me. Facts tend to be bland. Bland does not generate interest, let alone bids. People need to be persuaded to part with their money, especially in such vast sums. The catalogs are sent out in advance and help generate not only interest, but excitement."

She grinned. She knew where he was heading. "Trust me. The facts won't be bland or boring when I get done with them. I'll make those cars sound so sexy and irresistible that even you will be tempted to bid on them when they come up for auction."

"That is exactly what I was hoping to hear."

Darcie's gaze fell on a framed picture of a younger Nick standing with another man in front of a race car. His uncle, she surmised, recalling their conversation from the day they met. This was the man who had kick-started Nick's passion for cars and, ultimately, set into motion his career.

"Does your uncle still race?"

"No. He is retired. But racing is in his blood. He sponsors other drivers now." Nick pointed to the photograph. "He still owns that car. He won a Grand Prix with it. He retired not long afterward and the car retired with him. He said he couldn't part with it."

"Is it difficult?" she asked.

"Is what difficult?"

"Parting with the cars that you like?" She sent him a grin. "It's obvious that you have a weakness for a finely engineered automobile."

"I do, but they are not my only weakness." His gaze was on her mouth.

"Nick," she said pointedly.

"What were we talking about again?" he asked.

"Cars. Selling them. Even the ones you would like to keep for yourself."

"Ah. Yes. I remember now." He shook his head and shrugged. "I enjoy the automobiles while they are in my possession. That is enough." His gaze was on her mouth again. "I do not need to own something to enjoy it. Not everything is meant to last."

His words, the intensity of his gaze, caused a shiver to run up her spine. A vacation fling was the perfect example. Meant to be enjoyed. Meant to end. Darcie found the thought unsettling, but she shouldn't have. If it was permanence she sought, she should have stayed with Tad. He was the man who'd offered for her hand. No, Darcie had other ambitions, newly revived ones that were just begging to be explored, exploited. Nick was giving her that chance. Anything else that transpired between them came without strings.

"Well, it had better be enough, because you'll never see them again once I give them a write-up."

He stroked the hair back from her face. Where a moment ago his expression had been intense, it was thoughtful now. "I heard it said once that writers are artists who paint pictures with words. So, you are an artist, Darcie Hayes."

How long had it been since she'd seen herself that way? Since she'd last dared to see herself that way? Confidence—new and heady—swelled inside her.

"Thank you."

"I do not want your gratitude."

"But you have it," she argued. He couldn't possibly know what he'd done by giving her this opportunity. To lighten the moment, however, she rubbed her hands together and said, "I can't wait to get started."

"So eager." He took her hands in his. "But tomorrow

will be soon enough. Today we will enjoy ourselves. Are you hungry?"

"Starving. I skipped breakfast," she admitted.

"That is no good. You should never deny yourself."

The man had a point, Darcie thought. She had denied herself a lot the past several years—not food, but other things that, in some ways, were every bit as vital to her well-being. He still had her hands in his. He turned one over, brought it to his mouth for a kiss. A moan escaped. Who knew the palm was an erogenous zone?

Nick leaned toward her, their mouths met. Not far away was a bedroom, one with a mattress for whose quality he had already vouched. She edged back on a sigh.

"Lunch?"

He rested his forehead against hers. "I thought we had just established that you should not deny yourself."

"You're tempting me."

"I should hope so." His laughter was gruff as he stepped back. "But you are not ready and I promised that whatever happened between us would occur naturally and be mutually agreeable. The timing is not right. You need more romance, I think."

She swallowed, liking the sound of that. "So, lunch?"

He swept a hand toward the door. "After you."

They ate near the harbor, in a small bistro that Nick frequented when he was in town. The owner was a big man with craggy features and a booming laugh. He knew Nick by sight if not by name, so he smiled in welcome when they entered.

Lunch was a busy time, but since it was later in the afternoon, the crowd already had thinned. They took a table near the back of the small restaurant.

"Do you know everyone in Greece?" Darcie asked once they were seated.

"No, but I make it a point to get to know the people I like." He reached for her hand. "Take you, for example. I find myself wanting to know everything there is to know."

He said it lightly, but he meant it. He hadn't felt this interested in anything besides automobiles in a very long time. But there was no denying he was curious about Darcie, not to mention intensely curious about the man to whom she so recently had been engaged.

"You want to hear the story of my life?" she asked on a laugh.

"Yes. I believe you promised to tell it to me that first day."

"You already know I'm a magnet for disaster and cursed with bad luck. The rest, I'm afraid, is rather boring."

"I will be the judge."

"All right. But you go first." When he blinked in surprise, she added, "It goes both ways, you know. I have a lot of questions I wouldn't mind having answered, too."

"So, we should satisfy each other's curiosity. Is that what you are saying?"

"It's only fair."

"Ask then."

Nick knew Darcie had chickened out when she inquired, "What's your favorite color?"

"Red. My turn." And he went for the jugular. "How long did you know your former fiancé?"

"Too long."

"That is not an answer," he chastised.

"Get comfortable then," she teased. "And, don't worry. I'll wake you up if you fall asleep."

The server came for their order. When they were alone again, Nick motioned with his hand. "Go on. I am wide-awake and promise to stay that way. For the record, I am always interested in what you have to say."

Darcie swallowed. While it was a bit disconcerting to have Nick's full attention focused on her, she liked that about him. He didn't just pretend to listen to her. He really did, making it impossible to hide behind her usual flippant replies and offhand remarks. Who knew, maybe telling him about Tad would be cathartic rather than merely embarrassing. Maybe it would make it clear not only to Nick, but also to herself that the past was behind her and it was time to grab the present by the horns.

"Well, I met Tad during my senior year of college. I had a really bad throat infection and went to the clinic on campus to get it checked out. He was a first-year intern and working that afternoon."

"He was your doctor? Kinky." Nick arched his eyebrows.

"No! Well, I guess technically he was for that one visit, but I kept my clothes on. Remember, tonsils." She pointed to her throat. "They're up here."

"I am well-versed in a woman's anatomy."

"I'm sure you are." She cleared her throat. "Anyway, the two of us got to chatting. My tonsils were enlarged, something that happened quite often. He thought they might need to come out."

"You talked about enlarged tonsils and somehow still wound up going on a date?"

Darcie pulled a face. "It must have seemed romantic at the time."

"If you say so. Go on."

"There's not much more to tell. Tad and I started dating and then, six years ago, he proposed."

Nick's eyes widened at that. "The two of you were engaged for six years? Did you live together the entire time?"

"No. I moved in once he agreed to a wedding date. That

was two years ago. Tad didn't want to get married until he was done with his residency and ready to start a practice of his own. Evelyn thought it would be too distracting."

"His mother."

Darcie frowned. "I tried to be understanding. She's a widow and Tad is her only child. He's all the family she has. But the closer our wedding came, the clingier and more demanding of Tad's time she became."

"What did your family think of him?"

"Ah-ah-ah. It's my turn to ask a question."

He bowed his head.

"Do you…like scary movies?"

Nick stashed his grin. She'd chickened out again. "No. What did your family think of Tad?"

She exhaled, clearly irritated. "My sisters liked him. I think they liked the idea of me being engaged and heading toward the altar even more than they liked Tad. My mom is still hoping this is just a case of cold feet. Tad was very sweet to her, always full of compliments."

"And your father?"

She rubbed her chin. "Dad never really said anything one way or another while Tad and I were engaged, but I get the feeling he isn't all that upset I called it off, even if he's on the hook for a lot of nonrefundable deposits now."

"Let me guess, you gave up pursuing your career around the time you and Tad got engaged? Your father did not like Tad because he wanted you to follow your dream, and he knew you would give up on it forever if you married someone like Tad. You had taken a job checking facts rather than writing pieces whose facts other people would check for you."

It made sense to him now how she wound up in a career for which she had no passion.

"That about sums it up," she said.

"And so you ended things."

"One week before 'I do.'" Both her tone and her expression were grim. "Not exactly my classiest moment."

"Better one week before than one week after."

"I guess that's one way to look at it." The server returned with their drinks. "My turn again."

"All right."

He figured she would wimp out again. So, he nearly spit out the mouthful of sparkling water when she said, "What are your feelings for Selene?"

"I have no feelings for her. She is marrying my brother. End of story."

"Okay." Darcie accepted the cryptic answer with a nod. Then she hit him with both barrels by asking, "What are your feelings for your brother?"

"I miss him," Nick replied honestly, surprising himself.

CHAPTER EIGHT

NICK WOKE IN his boyhood bedroom to the smell of fresh bread—the crusty variety that his mother and grandmother routinely made in an outdoor wood-burning oven that straddled the property line between their two houses. The scent wafted through the open window, drawing him upright.

He'd spent the past four nights under his parents' roof after spending his days with Darcie. As promised, they divided their time between sightseeing and work. He was enjoying both and he thought she was, too.

Already, she'd presented him with research on three vehicles, including estimated values for the vehicles based on what similar models had brought at recent auctions. She was thorough, conscientious and professional, and damn if he didn't find that all very sexy.

He wanted her. Had since that first glance in the airport. But he was treading carefully for reasons that he couldn't quite explain, since nothing about their relationship called for permanence. Darcie was newly single, finding her way, spreading her wings. He admired her for that. She wouldn't be looking to settle down so soon again. Especially with a man who lived so far away. Besides, Nick had no personal capital to invest in a relationship. He hadn't since Selene.

So why was he finding the idea of sleeping with Darcie and then saying goodbye less appealing by the day?

They were taking things slowly, more slowly than he'd ever moved with a woman. Nick supposed Darcie's candor where her ex-fiancé was concerned was among the reasons he was treading with care. She had been marginalized, made to feel unimportant by the man who was supposed to love her. Recalling the conversation at the restaurant, Nick could admit she had been painfully honest about her past relationship, whereas he had not divulged much at all when it came to Selene. The only secret he'd shared was that he missed his brother.

Admittedly, the revelation had come as a surprise to Nick. But it still didn't come close to all of the soul-baring Darcie had done, and he regretted that.

Meanwhile, he and Darcie continued to play it safe, flirting with abandon, even as they tiptoed around the land mines of their pasts. Safe. Sure. As long as he didn't recall how heated their flirtation turned at times.

On a groan, he got up and took a shower—the cold variety—before wandering to the kitchen. He came up short when he saw Pieter seated at the table. Nick had managed to avoid him since that evening at Yiayia's.

"What are you doing here?"

"Do I need a reason to visit our parents?" Pieter shot back. "Besides, the better question is what are you doing sleeping here when you have a bed elsewhere?"

"It's occupied at the moment."

Pieter smiled. "Precisely my point."

"Is there more coffee?"

Nick motioned to the *briki*. His mother had been brewing coffee in the traditional, long-handled pot for more than three decades. He had a *briki* at his house, too. The copper pot was as bright and shiny as the day it was made since it never saw any use. The same could be said for his electric coffeemaker—both the one here and the one back in New

York. What did it say about him, Nick wondered, that he owned a house and an apartment, but neither felt like home?

In answer to his question, Pieter got up and poured the last of the coffee into a demitasse cup and handed it to Nick.

"Thank you," he said stiffly. Although he was tempted to leave, he took the chair opposite his brother.

"It looks like you had a rough night." Pieter didn't bother to hide his grin.

Until just a few years ago, such good-natured teasing between the brothers had been common. Nick didn't want to miss it. He didn't want to miss Pieter. But, just as he'd admitted to Darcie, he did. He sipped the coffee. It was strong and very sweet. That was how their mother always made it, but it did little to improve his sour mood.

Head bent over his cup, he grumbled, "I don't remember that mattress being quite so lumpy."

The mattress wasn't why he'd slept so poorly, though, and they both knew it.

"I never realized how chivalrous you were. Yiayia even commented on it."

Nick grunted and took another sip of coffee.

"She is sure this is a sign."

"Yiayia and her signs," Nick mumbled. "Everything is a sign to her."

"But is she right in this case?" Pieter set his cup back on its saucer. He was no longer grinning when he asked, "Have you found someone…special?"

Nick stared into his coffee. "Darcie is special."

"Is it serious?"

"It is…complicated," Nick replied truthfully, uncomfortably.

The evasive answer had his brother nodding. "Love is always complicated."

"And you would know!" Nick challenged.

Pieter didn't take the bait. Instead, he replied, "I am happy for you. All of us are. Mama and Yiayia can talk of nothing else."

That should have pleased Nick. It was why he had introduced Darcie to them, after all. With his supposed girlfriend as the topic of their conversations until the wedding, he would no longer have to worry about them trying to set him up. But he felt uneasy.

"What are they saying about Darcie?" he asked.

"It's not so much what they are saying about her, although obviously they like her. It's more the effect Darcie has had on you. You seem like your old self again. Mama and Yiayia are happy you have found someone. As am I."

Emotions crowded in. Nick pushed away all but anger. Arching an eyebrow, he said sarcastically, "So we can be one big happy family again? Do you really think that possible, Pieter?"

His brother swallowed. "It is what I hope, what I want."

"And you get whatever you want. Or you take it, as the case may be."

Pieter looked gut-punched. "You are not being fair."

"Fairness, brother? Really?" His voice rose. Nick rose along with it. Palms planted on the tabletop, he demanded, "You want to talk about fairness?"

Pieter was on his feet as well. "You made your choices, Nick. You are the one who decided to leave Greece, to set up a business in New York, far away from family. Far away from Selene."

"And you were here to offer comfort and company," he added caustically.

But Pieter didn't back down. "You chased *your* dream without bothering to ask her what she wanted. You just expected that she would drop everything, leave everyone behind and follow you."

Nick's conscience stung. Was that what he'd done? Darcie
came to mind. She'd sacrificed her dream of feature writing for her fiancé, settling for a fact-checking job at a small
trade publication instead. Ultimately, what she'd given up
had only fed her dissatisfaction and resentment. Had Nick
done the same thing to Selene? If she had followed him to
New York, would their relationship have survived?

Because he did not care for the face staring back at him
from the mirror in his mind, his tone was harsh when he
told his brother, "That is not what I expected, dammit!"

"Then what?" Pieter challenged. "What did you expect?"

Darcie, Selene—both women were forgotten now. Nick
saw only Pieter, his brother and, at one time, his very best
friend.

"I did not expect you to betray me!" He pounded his
fist on the tabletop with enough force to rattle their coffee cups. There it was, the crux of the matter. The one big
stumbling block Nick could not surmount, regardless of the
number of times he'd tried. "While I was gone, I asked you
to look after Selene for me. I knew she would be lonely. I
did not think—"

Pieter's fists were clenched at his sides. "How many
times must I tell you that is not how it happened? Selene
and I did not betray you!"

The brothers glared at one another across the table.

"I do not care about Selene." And it was true, Nick realized. His feelings for his childhood sweetheart were over.
"But you! My own brother. I *trusted* you."

"I did nothing to betray you or your trust. God knows!
I fought the attraction I felt for her, and I felt it since we
were all teenagers. Do you know what it was like to have
her choose you?"

Nick blinked. He hadn't known. Had not even suspected.
Would he have cared if he had? His anger now, however,

was greater than any concern he felt for Pieter's feelings in the past. "So, you got even? Is that it?"

"No." The fight had gone out of his brother. Pieter slumped down in his seat. His voice was quiet, but his words were no less potent when he said, "I love her, I have always loved her, but I never imagined…I never dared to hope… You have to believe me that it was long after the two of you had parted ways that anything developed between us. Even so, we both tried to deny it." Pieter shoved a hand through his hair, his eyes bright with pain, frustration and resignation when he added, "Some things cannot be denied."

The door opened and their mother rushed into the kitchen from the yard. Her face was flushed, her expression one of worry.

"What on earth has happened? Your raised voices can be heard all the way to the coast!"

"Nothing happened," Nick told her, feeling more shaken than he wanted to admit. He crossed to the sink and tossed the remainder of his coffee down the drain.

As he stalked from the room, he heard Pieter say wearily, "He cannot forgive me."

Darcie was at the computer in Nick's home office working on some research when she heard a car pull up the driveway. Her mouth curved into a smile as she recognized the purr of the Jag's powerful motor. Then she glanced at the clock, puzzled. He was almost two hours early for their drive to Trikala. They had an afternoon meeting with a potential buyer for the Porsche he'd been driving the day they met.

Was that really only a week ago? It was hard to believe given all that had occurred since then. Indeed, over the past two weeks Darcie's entire life had been turned upside down. She'd gone from being an uncertain and disenchanted bride-to-be to a single woman who was determined to hammer out a new future for herself. And having a fine time doing it, thanks to Nick.

Her heart skipped a beat when she heard the door open. She turned, intending to tease him about being so eager, but her own smile died upon seeing his dire expression.

"Are you ready to leave?" he asked.

"I, um…" She glanced back at the computer, where she had several files open. "Can you give me another fifteen minutes? I just need to check a couple more things and print this out."

He nodded. "I will be on the terrace."

When she finished, she joined him there. He was so preoccupied that he didn't even hear her approach. When she laid a hand on his shoulder, he turned abruptly, almost as if he expected to find someone else standing there.

"Nick, is everything all right?"

"Yes. Of course." But his eyes remained dark and fathomless and at odds with the smile that turned up the corners of his mouth. "I am looking forward to our trip."

After Trikala, they were going to continue on to Meteora, where they would stay the night in a hotel. Even though Darcie had not asked him to, Nick had booked separate rooms for them, and of course he had insisted on paying for both. First thing in the morning, the plan was to tour a couple of Meteora's remaining six Greek Orthodox monasteries that were built atop rocky sandstone towers. Then the two of them would head back to Athens.

She had been looking forward to the trip as well. But now…?

"What's wrong?" She laid a hand on his arm. "And please don't tell me 'nothing.' I want to help."

"I thank you for your concern. But you cannot help me."

"Nick," she pleaded.

"I had an argument with my brother this morning." He

waved one hand in dismissal. Even so, Darcie's stomach took a tumble.

"Selene?" she suggested.

Nick's gaze returned to the sea. In profile, Darcie watched his jaw clench. "It is an old wound, but it has not healed properly." He sighed wearily then. "I do not know if it ever will."

"Sometimes talking to a neutral third party helps. I've been told I'm a good listener." When he turned, she offered an encouraging smile. Even so, it was a full minute before Nick said anything.

"I have been so angry. And I have felt entitled to that anger."

"But now?"

He swallowed and shoved a hand through his hair, leaving it as messy as his emotions. The expletive that followed—and she didn't doubt it was an expletive—was spoken in Greek.

"Why don't you tell me what happened between you and Selene?" Maybe by taking a step back in time, he would be able to move forward.

"Selene and I had been seeing one another for a couple of years when I went to New York for the first time. I had saved up some money, and my uncle had a contact in the United States. I planned to attend a few auctions, gain some understanding of the business and return to Athens to build my company here."

"But you stayed."

"Not at first, but eventually. The market for classic automobiles is so much larger in America. It made sense!" He was less emphatic when he added, "Selene did not see it that way."

"Were the two of you engaged at the time?"

He shook his head. "I never proposed, but I thought we had an understanding."

"And moving to another country, was that part of the understanding?"

He frowned. "She did not want to leave Athens."

"Of course not. Everything familiar to her is here," Darcie said. "It was a lot to ask."

"I know." He pinched his eyes closed. "We argued about it more than once, each trying to sway the other. I tried to find a solution. The best I could manage was a compromise. I came back to Greece as often as I could." He lifted his shoulders in a shrug.

"Did she ever come to New York?"

"Once. It was right after I took an apartment there. As much as I love Manhattan, that is how much she hated it. Still, I told myself that eventually…" His words trailed off and he shook his head.

"How long have Pieter and Selene been together?"

"Officially, they have been engaged for the past year. They dated for a year before that. Unofficially? I do not want to know, although they have both assured me repeatedly that I was long out of the picture when they started seeing one another."

"You don't believe them?"

"I am not sure what I believe." He sighed heavily.

Darcie glanced out at the harbor. The water was calm now, as was Nick, but when storms blew in, she imagined that the surface would turn choppy and become dotted with whitecaps that could wrest a small boat from its moorings and swamp it. That must have been how Nick had felt when he'd returned to Athens to find his brother courting Selene.

"You feel betrayed."

"Pieter and I are—were—more than brothers. There is barely a year between our births. We did everything together. We were always the best of friends. There was no one I trusted more."

"That must make this situation all the more difficult," she said softly and rested a hand on his arm. "You lost your best friend and…and the woman you loved."

"Did I?" Nick uttered the question softly. His dark eyes were full of pain when he added, "Did I truly love her? Did Tad love you? Is that how love works?"

Darcie frowned. "I'm afraid I don't understand what you mean."

"Real love would not take more than it gave. It would not be selfish," Nick said. Darcie thought of the Bible verse from First Corinthians that she'd asked one of her brothers-in-law to read at her wedding. *Love is patient. Love is kind… it is not self-seeking….* She always felt it underscored love's many good qualities.

"But Tad was selfish with you. From what you have told me, he put himself, his needs and his wants first. And I was that way with Selene. I knew from the beginning that she did not want to move to America. I knew that she wanted a life here, a life like the one she now will have with Pieter."

"Are you sorry?" Darcie swallowed.

"I hurt her. Yes, for that I am very sorry."

But that wasn't what Darcie meant, so she tried again. "Knowing everything that you know, do you…do you wish you had made a different set of choices?"

"I cannot rewrite history."

"Tad wants to." She hadn't meant to say that.

"What do you mean?"

"Nothing."

"Darcie," he pleaded.

"He's left several messages on my cell." She shrugged.

"And?"

"There is no *and*. I'm just saying that even if we cannot

rewrite history that doesn't mean we don't have regrets. So, do you?" She returned to her original question, afraid of what the answer might be.

"No."

But his expression remained so pained that she wondered. Could he still love Selene? The possibility left her uncomfortable, but why? She had no claim on Nick. No right to expect exclusivity when it came to his affection. They hadn't slept together, even if Darcie could admit that was the direction they were heading, albeit at a slow and measured pace. And when they did, she knew it would be casual. Mind-blowing, but casual. So why did it matter?

Because Darcie feared she was trading one emotionally unavailable man for another.

CHAPTER NINE

NICK SWAPPED HIS Jag for the 1963 Porsche 356 that was parked in the garage and they were on their way. If all went as planned in Trikala, his client would buy the Porsche and they would drive away in a 1956 Austin-Healey roadster that, depending on its condition, would knock off most of the Porsche's asking price. The Austin-Healey, meanwhile, would be featured in Nick's next auction.

It took them just over three hours to make the trip to Trikala. Nick remained preoccupied and introspective the entire way, even though Darcie tried to draw him out in conversation. It was a relief when they finally arrived at their destination, but they were more than two hours early for their meeting.

"We can take a walk through Trikala's scenic old town, if you would like?" Nick said.

Since it would kill some time and might just help shake him from his mood, she readily agreed.

Fifteen minutes into their stroll, she was fanning herself. The heat was stifling and the light breeze's effect on it negligible. They stopped at a café and he bought her *Kliafa*, a refreshing orange drink that was perfect given the day's heat.

After taking a sip, she gravitated to the window of a nearby shop. She couldn't help herself. Shoes were on display and all but calling her name.

"Would you like to go inside?" Nick asked. He was smiling, the first real smile she'd seen all day.

"You don't know what you're saying," she warned with mock sternness.

"Pardon?"

"No man in his right mind encourages a woman to shop."

He took her drink and sipped it straight from the straw. All the while his gaze was on her. "I have a condition."

The simple statement managed to raise gooseflesh on her skin despite the day's heat.

"And that is?"

"Everything that you try on you must model for me."

She glanced back at the shoes. "I'm game."

It was an easy enough deal to keep in a shoe store, but then Nick steered her into a shop two doors down.

"Remember our deal," he said, pointing to a display of lingerie.

"I am *not* trying that on," she said resolutely of the bustier. "But I will try on these." She selected a pair of stone-colored capri pants from one of the racks. "And this."

Nick fingered the soft fabric of the turquoise tunic-style blouse in her hands. "The color will complement your complexion and bring out your eyes."

Darcie tried not to glance at the price tag, which she knew would not complement her bank account. For kicks, she added to the growing selection a white halter dress that made her think of Marilyn Monroe.

"I would really like to see you in this."

Clipped to the hanger he held was a tiny bikini that would leave even more of Darcie exposed than the lingerie.

"Right." She snorted indelicately. "I haven't worn a two-piece swimsuit since I was six years old."

He thrust the hanger into her hands. "Then I would say you are overdue."

"Nick."

"Ah, ah, ah. We had a deal." He nudged her toward the changing room in the back of the store. "Keep in mind that on many European beaches it is perfectly acceptable to go topless."

Laughing, she ducked into the small room. She lined up the hangers, leaving the bikini for last and far from certain she would honor their bargain. The first thing she stepped out in was the white halter dress.

"Ta-da!" In her bare feet, she executed a twirl for him and then posed with one hand on her hip. With the other she primped her hair. "I'm channeling Marilyn Monroe."

"Very sexy. Perhaps the store has an air-conditioning duct you can stand over top of. I would not mind seeing a little more of your legs."

Darcie hiked up the hem of the dress's skirt by a couple of inches to accommodate his wish, but he wasn't satisfied.

"Make no mistake, you have very nice knees. However, I was thinking about your thighs." His smile held a dare.

She glanced around. The shop was busy, but the dressing rooms were at the back. A couple of sale racks helped to shield her from view.

She inched up the dress more slowly this time.

"I will tell you when to stop," Nick said quietly.

"I bet."

The hem was not quite to the middle of her thigh when Nick uttered a gruff, "Enough!"

"You don't want to see any more?"

"Not out in public."

Darcie didn't smile, but she wanted to. The same went for pumping her fists in the air. Eat your heart out, Marilyn, she thought, feeling every bit as desired as the famous sex symbol.

Nick stood. "I'm going to buy another *Kliafa*."

"Right now? I was going to model the bikini next," she teased ruthlessly.

After muttering something she couldn't quite catch, he said, "I will wait for you outside."

So it was that Nick never got the chance to see Darcie wearing a clingy wine-colored dress that an ambitious saleswoman slipped into the changing room along with some sexy satin undergarments that the young woman claimed were essential to ensuring the dress's proper fit.

Darcie had to admit, they definitely smoothed out certain areas while lifting others, which was why she purchased them. As for the bikini, she wasn't sure why she bought it. She didn't need it. Wasn't sure she had the guts to wear it out in public. But she looked good in it. Damned good. A little voice that sounded suspiciously like her friend Becky told her she should buy it.

At the cash register, she wound up charging enough to her credit card to leave her feeling guilty and a little giddy.

"You are flushed," Nick noted as they made their way to the restaurant.

"Yes, well, spending more than I earn in a week has been known to have that effect on me." She chuckled weakly.

Despite their shopping trip, the man they were to meet had not yet arrived when they reached the restaurant. Nick requested a table in a shady part of the patio that offered a lovely view of the Litheos River.

"While we're waiting, why don't you tell me a little about Ari Galanos," Darcie said.

"Ah, Ari." Nick chuckled fondly. "I should warn you, he will flirt shamelessly with you. The man goes through cars almost as quickly as he goes through wives."

"Thanks for the warning." The waiter came by for their beverage order.

"A glass of wine?" Nick asked.

"Why not? I'm not driving."

"You could, you know. If you wished."

"No, no." She shook her head. "With or without a glass of wine, that wouldn't be a good idea."

"The roads can be a little treacherous if one is not familiar with them," he agreed.

"Yes, not to mention the fact that it's been a decade since I last drove a manual transmission." She tilted her head to one side and asked, "Are you familiar with the expression, 'If you can't find 'em, grind 'em'?"

"I am not."

"Well, suffice it to say, that was my motto whenever I was trying to shift from one gear to the next."

"Ah." He grimaced as understanding dawned. And they both wound up chuckling.

"This is nice," Darcie said on a sigh a few minutes later, as she sipped her wine and gazed at the river. "I feel very relaxed."

"That is the point of a vacation, yes? To relax, rejuvenate one's spirit."

She nodded. But they both knew this wasn't a normal vacation for Darcie. The trip had been booked as her honeymoon. After calling off her wedding, she had intended to use it as a getaway, a timeout from her post-breakup reality. Now, it was turning into a job opportunity and so much more.

"Thank you."

"For what?" he asked, surprised.

"For helping me get my life back in order."

"Your gratitude is not necessary. You have done that all on your own."

But she persisted. "No, you had a hand in it, Nick. If not for you, I would be on a plane headed home right now, and going back to a job that I'd talked myself into believing was good enough since it pays the bills."

He reached across the table for her hand, giving it a squeeze. "You sell yourself short, Darcie. You would have reached for your dream again, with or without my help. I gave you a gentle push in the right direction. That is all."

Her smile told Nick she didn't quite believe him. Her gratitude made him uncomfortable. Another man might have used it, exploited it even, to maneuver her into his bed. Nick was too scrupulous for that. He wanted Darcie there, and the waiting was taking its toll, but he did not want her to say yes because she felt she owed him something. He meant it when he told her she would have sought out her dream again on her own, even without his prodding. If her passion for writing was anything like his passion for cars, it wouldn't be denied.

Ari arrived as they were finishing their wine. He ordered a second round of drinks, although this time Nick switched to sparkling water. Not only would he be driving later, but he also preferred to keep a clear head in business. Ari was shrewd and he was used to getting his way.

As predicted, the older man's eyes lit with appreciation when Nick introduced him to Darcie.

Still holding her hand, he said in Greek, "Nick did not mention hiring an assistant. Or is your relationship more personal in nature?"

Smiling, Darcie glanced helplessly at Nick.

"Darcie does not speak Greek," he said. "She is an American."

"I apologize," Ari replied in heavily accented English. "I was asking about your relationship with Nick."

"My re—"

"Darcie is a writer," Nick explained. "I have hired her to prepare feature articles on some of the automobiles that will appear in my next auction brochure. Already she has done some research on your Austin-Healey."

Ari didn't appear convinced. His tone was just shy of condescending when he asked, "What have you managed to learn about my automobile, my dear?"

"Let's see, I know the 1956 model is worth more than other 100M Roadsters." She ran a fingertip around the top of her wineglass as she spoke. "That was the only year they manufactured the performance-enhanced model, which tops out at a speed of one hundred and fifteen miles per hour. The car was marketed to customers who wanted to compete or who just plain liked to go fast, which is why it has a tighter front suspension, added louvers to keep the hood in place at high speeds and a fold-down windshield."

Ari's bushy brows shot up. "Beautiful *and* smart. I apologize."

"Darcie is not to be underestimated," Nick agreed with no small amount of pride. And he knew a moment of panic as he wondered if he had underestimated the impact she was having on his life.

Earlier, she had thanked him for helping her to get her life back in order. For helping her find passion again where it long had been missing. It dawned on Nick that she had returned the favor. He always had enjoyed business. It was his personal life that had been lacking. Oh, he'd dated plenty of women, one or two of them for several months before breaking off the relationship and moving on.

None of those women had affected him the way Darcie was. None had made him envision a future with a family that he'd taken for granted when he was a young man.

The drive from Trikala to their hotel in Meteora would have taken less than half an hour, but Nick wanted to put his newly acquired Austin-Healey through its paces.

"Satisfied with the car?" Darcie asked when traffic finally forced him to slow down.

"I am, yes. Ari has taken good care of her. She runs like a dream." He rubbed the leather seat. "And other than this one small tear in the upholstery, her body is in mint condition, as well."

"Why do men refer to cars with female pronouns? I've never understood that."

"It seems more natural to be riding in a female than a male." Nick grinned. "Maybe it is simply the way we are wired."

"So, you're saying it's in your genes?" Darcie rolled her eyes. "Please."

His grin turned wicked. "A different kind of jeans then."

Darcie crossed her arms over her chest and rolled her eyes a second time, but she looked more amused than exasperated. He wasn't sure how she'd managed it, but over the course of the day, she'd drawn him out of his foul mood. Indeed, Nick was actually enjoying himself, whereas he often found buying trips tedious.

He reached for her hand, forcing her to unfold her arms, and then gave her fingers an affectionate squeeze. He was still holding her hand when they reached their destination.

The hotel where Nick had booked their rooms was nicer than anything Darcie would have chosen had she been picking up the tab herself. It went without saying that it was nicer than anything Stavros would have provided as part of the all-inclusive tour.

Their rooms were on the third floor, which like all of the floors, was open to the atrium on the main level. They made plans to meet for a late dinner, which would give them both a chance to unpack and unwind.

"Wear the white dress to dinner," he suggested as he handed her a key card.

"I didn't buy the white dress."

"What is in there then?" He pointed to two bags she carried that were printed with the shop's logo.

She smiled benignly. "I guess you'll just have to wait and see."

When Darcie said it, she was referring to the sexy wine-colored dress. But that changed when she slipped into her room and realized that it joined with Nick's via an interior door. Because she could quite vividly picture him on the other side of it, undressing, she decided to go for a swim. The hotel had a nice pool in a courtyard outdoors. A quick dip and a little lounging on one of the chaises might be the perfect distraction.

She eyed the tank-style one-piece in a bland shade of blue that she'd brought with her from Athens before deciding to slip into the red bikini. She wouldn't wear it downstairs. Probably. But...

She had just finished tying the top's knot behind her neck when a tapping sounded on the interior door. She grabbed her robe, hastily pulled it on before going to answer it. Her mouth went dry at the sight that greeted her. Nick's shirt was open, the buckle of his belt hung to one side of his unbuttoned trousers. The man was built like a god, with ripped abs and the kind of chest that it seemed a sin to cover with a shirt. This was why she'd decided to go for a swim. This was exactly how she'd pictured him looking.

"I interrupted you," she said.

"I believe I am the one who knocked." He sounded amused, but his expression was intense, aroused.

"R-right. I knew that."

"Is this what you plan to wear to dinner?"

She shook her head and managed to drag some air into

her lungs. She had one hand on the doorjamb and plunked the other one on her hip. "Terry cloth is a little too casual, I think."

"You will not hear me complain."

She laughed softly.

"But I am disappointed."

"Oh?"

"I see red." He reached out and plucked at the bow that peeked from the collar of the robe. "You promised to model *everything* for me."

"I offered. You left."

"Because we were in public," he reminded her. "Will you keep your promise now?"

She swallowed. Nodded. And nearly forgot how to breathe when he loosened the robe's belt.

"Do you like it?" she found the courage to ask.

"Take off the robe."

She did as instructed. The robe slipped from her shoulders and pooled at her feet.

"Well?" She tilted her head to one side and managed a smile.

Nick, however, did not smile. Nor did he say anything. He acted, swiftly and decisively. One minute Darcie was on her side of the door, posing provocatively in the itty-bitty red two-piece. The next she was in his room, pinned between his hard body and the wall while his mouth devoured hers.

"I'm taking this to mean you like what you see," she told him on a breathy laugh when the kiss finally ended.

"I do indeed."

"I was thinking about going swimming. You know, in the hotel pool. Um, that's why I'm wearing my bathing suit."

"Is that why?" he asked. He had maneuvered her away from the wall and was now slowly walking her backward toward the bed.

"Why else?" she asked innocently, even as the edge of the mattress pressed into the back of her thighs.

"I think you put on your bikini to torture me." He stepped back far enough so that he could do a slow inspection of her body. A groan of approval vibrated from his throat.

"I didn't know you were going to knock on my door," she pointed out. "So, that's merely a bonus."

Darcie was amazed at her boldness. Not only did she feel comfortable standing nearly naked before him, but she also felt sexy and confident. She planted her hands on her hips and turned slowly side to side before presenting him with her back and glancing flirtatiously over one shoulder.

"So, you like my suit, hmm?"

His gaze skimmed down a second time and he let out a low whistle. "The suit, what little of it there is, is nice. I like the way you look in it, Darcie. You are beautiful."

Better yet, she felt that way. Smiling in earnest, she asked, "So, are we going?"

"Wh-where?" he stammered.

In addition to looking turned on, Nick looked off balance. Darcie's confidence shot up another notch.

"Swimming." She grinned. "You remembered to pack a pair of trunks, right?"

"I did."

"Good. Put them on."

She slipped around him and started for the door, but only managed two steps before his hands clamped on her waist and she was hauled back against his rock-hard chest, abs and…

In the mirror that hung on the opposite wall, their gazes met. Neither one of them was smiling now. The time for humor and teasing had passed. Nick brushed her hair aside and nuzzled her neck a moment, then his hand came up, his fingers fiddled at the nape of her neck. The knot in the bikini's halter went slack.

"It appears that your top has come loose," he murmured huskily.

He gathered both sides in his hands, holding them at her collarbone. If he were to let go…

"So I see, although I believe it had a little help."

"I can retie it," he offered.

She met his gaze without blinking. She thought she might have stopped breathing, too. "Have you got any other suggestions?"

His hands moved lower, slowly exposing more of her skin inch by inch. They both watched his progress in the mirror.

"I can stop. I *should* stop." His eyes pinched closed a moment and he uttered an oath before pulling the straps taut and retying them. At her questioning gaze in the mirror, he said, "My grandmother thinks I am chivalrous. This is a moment that calls for such old-fashioned thinking."

"It is?"

He turned her to face him, framed her face with his hands. "I want you, Darcie. But I…we…" He pulled his hands away and started stalking around the room. The rest of his explanation was in Greek. Oddly enough, she thought she understood what he meant.

"I only have another week left in Greece."

"Yes. But it is more than that."

A lump formed in her throat. It was?

"Remember when we spoke of your life being at a crossroads?" he asked.

"I said it was more like a busy intersection without a working traffic light."

"In other words, dangerous. Which is why we are going slowly."

There was slow and there was snail-like. "I thought you

saw me as adventurous for wanting to rush across and hope for the best."

"I have changed my mind."

"Worried I could get hurt?" she asked with a tilt of her head.

He didn't answer her question, at least not directly. Instead he said, "The stakes have gotten higher. For both of us. Do you understand?"

Her heart gave an unsteady thump. She knew she had been developing strong feelings for Nick. Real feelings. Feelings that could make walking away from a casual fling in a week very difficult. But until now she hadn't thought Nick might feel the same way. Or that having those feelings might be a problem for him. She knew Nick didn't do more than casual, not since Selene. Darcie sighed. "I think so. Now what?"

He expelled a gusty breath and asked, "Do you still want to go for a swim?"

"Sure. You?"

"Yes." He kissed her cheek before adding, "If I am lucky, the pool will be very, very cold."

Nick got his wish. The water was chilly, especially compared to the hot afternoon air. He and Darcie had the pool to themselves and they stayed in it for nearly an hour. Even so, it wasn't long enough to counteract the effect simply being near her was having on him.

It wasn't only lust he felt when it came to Darcie, which was why he begrudgingly had retied her bikini top and hustled her out of his hotel room. Other emotions were involved that made the prospect of a mere holiday fling less and less appealing.

He liked her. He respected her intelligence, her drive, her resilience. The last thing he wanted was to be responsible for her returning home filled with regrets. That was where chivalry had come in. But self-preservation, he could admit, played a role, too.

So much had happened between the pair of them in such a short time. The feelings Darcie inspired were not unwelcome, but they were unexpected. He'd meant it when he said the stakes had gotten higher for both of them.

Now what?

The question Darcie had asked earlier haunted him. He had no clear answer.

CHAPTER TEN

DARCIE YAWNED AND stretched as she lay on the bed in Nick's guestroom. The sun had crested the horizon a few minutes earlier, but she had been awake for more than an hour listening to the distant sound of fishing boats heading out of the harbor.

Since her and Nick's return from Meteora, time had passed much too quickly for her liking. She blamed it on their busy schedule, which was a combination of business and pleasure. Lots and lots of pleasure, even if it stopped just short of actual sex. In addition to doing research on the internet and writing articles for the auction brochure, she and Nick had met with a deep-pocketed repeat client who was eager to add a 1950s-era, American-made muscle car to his already expansive collection of automobiles, and a new client looking to score his first vintage Porsche.

They also had managed a couple more sightseeing day trips on Greece's mainland, and they'd spent one glorious afternoon lazing on a beach on the island of Andros. She'd worn the bikini again. And she'd known from Nick's expression that he loved seeing her in it, whatever the cost to him personally.

Darcie was having the time of her life. It didn't matter what she and Nick did. She enjoyed being with him and talking to him, whether about the automobiles she was re-searching or movies they'd seen or current happenings in the world. It amazed her, really, how much they had in common for two people who had grown up in different cultures on different sides of the world.

As for their relationship, she wasn't quite sure how to categorize it. *Fling* didn't fit since the word implied sex. She and Nick hadn't had sex, although she swore that every moment she spent in his company qualified as foreplay. She enjoyed kissing him, the exquisite torture of feeling his mouth and hands on her skin. But she wanted more.

On a frustrated sigh, she rolled to her side and hugged a pillow to her chest. She'd never met another man who made her feel more desirable or quite so aware of her femininity. Yet since Meteora and their brush with physical intimacy in his hotel room, Nick had shown the kind of restraint possessed by the monks who lived in the terra-cotta-tile-roofed monasteries they'd toured the following day. No matter how far things progressed between them physically, he always stopped just short of taking her to bed. Now their time together in Greece was almost over.

Part of Darcie acknowledged that maybe it was just as well they hadn't had sex. Physical intimacy would complicate things, at least on her end. As she'd told Nick, she wasn't the sort of woman to fall in bed with a man simply to scratch an itch.

But another part of her ached to be with him in every sense of the word, no matter how short their time together.

She wasn't on the rebound, as her family might assume. Nor was she confused or vulnerable over her breakup with Tad. Indeed, Darcie had never felt clearer on her reasons for ending her engagement, despite her ex's continuing messages, the most recent of which had been surprisingly conciliatory in tone. Tad wanted her back. He wanted to work things out. But Darcie knew no matter how much he was willing to change, she already had changed more.

There was no going back, even if in a matter of days, she would be flying home to Buffalo. She wouldn't be returning to her old life. The old Darcie was gone. The new Darcie wasn't going to settle and make do. That almost made up for the fact that her idyllic vacation with Nick was coming to an end.

Would they see each other again? That was the million-dollar question, and it weighed heavily on her mind.

Not long after she returned to the United States, he would as well. From what she knew of his schedule, he would leave Greece the day after Pieter's wedding. But even without an ocean to separate them, she and Nick would hardly be neighbors. Besides, he had made no mention of getting together once they were both back in America.

Sure, at one point early in their acquaintance he had offered to show Darcie the sights should she ever find herself in the Big Apple again, but the offer had been more polite than anything else, and he hadn't made a similar one since then, much less issued a formal invitation.

In fact, the more involved they had become the less was said about what the future held for the two of them. Personally, at least. Nick made it plain how pleased he was with the features she'd written for his upcoming auction brochure.

"Use my name as a reference if you think it will help," he'd told her.

He'd also given her the contact information for the editor of an online car collectors' blog that sometimes used freelance writers. Why not? she thought. Clips were clips and the more experience under her belt the better.

Overall, Darcie was pretty satisfied with the work she'd done while in Greece. It wasn't going to win her any Pulitzers, but it was a start, a first step in a new and exciting journey.

She had one last feature to write for Nick for an upcoming auction brochure. The car was a 1914 Packard 4-48. The owner lived in New Jersey and was selling it to finance his daughter's college tuition. Nick had inspected the Packard prior to his trip to Greece and estimated it could bring in up to half a million dollars. He agreed with Darcie that, with the right buyer, the sixty-horsepower touring phaeton might bring in even more since many of its parts were original. That was what made her articles every bit as important as the photographs included in the brochures that would be sent out in advance of the auction.

Darcie tossed the pillow aside and rose. She might as well start to work on it. She was nearly finished with the article and was making a second pot of coffee when the doorbell rang. Nick's appearance was unexpected, even though they had plans for later in the day.

When she opened the door, his gaze swept down to her toes before returning to her face.

"You are dressed."

"And you were hoping otherwise."

He didn't bother to hide his smile. "I was. It's why I didn't call first."

"Sorry to disappoint you then."

"Did I say I was disappointed?" He yanked her into his arms for a hard, fast kiss. While she was still recovering from it, he said, "I have a favor to ask."

"After kissing me like that you can ask me anything."

He made a humming sound and she swore his pupils dilated. "Anything?"

Darcie was playing with fire, but she no longer cared. She wanted to feel not just the heat, but the burn. "Anything."

The devil was in his eyes when he asked, "My grand-mother has invited us for coffee. Do you want to go?"

The mention of his *yiayia* threatened to put a damper on seduction. She thumped his chest with the back of her hand. "*That's* the question you come up with? Seriously?"

His lips quirked. "Not the only one, but I would like to know your answer." Darcie was wearing the turquoise tunic she'd purchased in Trikala. It had a peasant-style neckline that closed with a ribbon tie. Nick fiddled with the ends of the ribbon as he added, "First."

Her brows shot up. First sounded promising.

Still, she asked, "Will the rest of your family be there? I want to know exactly how large of an audience to expect for this command performance."

He shook his head. "My mother is with Selene and her mother—some last-minute wedding preparations. My fa-ther and Pieter are working today. It will just be Yiayia."

"All right," she said slowly.

"We will not stay long," he promised. "Afterward, I thought we could ride the cable car to the top of Lycabet-tus. The view from the hilltop is even better than that from the Acropolis."

It would be the last touristy thing Darcie did in Greece, but that wasn't why she frowned. "Nick, about spending more time with your grandmother, I really like her, which makes me feel—"

He stopped her with another kiss. This one was slower, deeper, sweeter. By the time he finished, they were fully inside his house with the door closed behind him and the foyer wall against Darcie's back.

"If it helps, I am as uncomfortable as you are with the charade, but it is not all an act now." He tipped her chin up. "Is it?"

"It was never *all* an act."

"Exactly. We might not have met when and where we said we did, but I have not lied to them about my feelings. I have always been attracted to you physically, but it is more than that now. Yes?"

"For both of us," she agreed.

"Which brings me to my other question," he said softly.

Darcie could barely breathe, but she managed to say, "And that is?"

Nick tugged on the tunic's ribbon until it gave way. The neckline gaped open, offering a tantalizing glimpse of cleavage.

"May I please make love to you?"

A chorus of *Hallelujah!* rang in her head, but she couldn't keep from asking, "Right now?"

He flicked open the button on her capris. "Right now. I can wait no longer."

They arrived at his grandmother's house two hours later. Darcie was still tingling all over from the best orgasm she'd ever experienced. At one point she hadn't known whether to laugh out loud or start to cry. She'd done neither, thank goodness. Nor had she burst into song, though the lyrics to U2's "Beautiful Day" had been on the tip of her tongue.

As Nick shifted the car into Park, she checked her reflection in her compact mirror for the third time.

"You look the same as you did five minutes ago. In other words, perfect," he assured her, leaning over to give her a kiss.

"I feel…conspicuous," Darcie replied. "Like your grandmother is going to take one look at me and *know* what we were doing less than an hour ago."

"There is no need to worry. She might suspect, but she will not *know*." Nick winked.

"Gee, thanks. That puts my mind at ease."

* * *

"Something about you is different," Yiayia said to Darcie the moment she and Nick walked through the door.

Darcie felt her face flame scarlet and she shot Nick a panicked look.

He put his arm around her shoulders and said mildly, "Greece agrees with her."

Yiayia's expression was shrewd. "Something agrees with her." Then she motioned with her hand. "Come. We will eat outside. The day is too nice to sit in the kitchen."

They followed her through the house and out to the veranda. Darcie took a seat in the shade of the pergola. The midday air was heavy with the scent of roses.

"I made *koulourakia portokaliou* just this morning. I have the recipe for you." She sent Darcie a wink.

"Thank you," Darcie said.

"Are you excited for the wedding?" Yiayia asked as she poured the tea. "Selene and Pieter's wedding, that is."

The older woman's smile turned wily.

"Weddings are exciting," Darcie evaded. She nibbled a cookie.

"What color is the dress you will wear?"

"My dress. Oh, um…" She glanced at Nick for help.

"Darcie wants it to be a surprise."

Yiayia frowned at that, but couldn't resist offering a little unsolicited advice.

"You should wear a bright color. Do not be afraid to stand out. When I was a young woman, I favored red. I was wearing red the night Nicolas's grandfather saw me at a dance. He said the color caught his attention even before I did. For every anniversary my Alexandros gave me red roses." She sighed.

"How long were you married?" Darcie asked.

"Thirty-seven years. It has been twenty-three years since

I lost him. But it feels like yesterday that I was a young woman planning my own wedding." She patted Darcie's hand. "Time passes too quickly. Now my grandchildren are falling in love and getting married."

Falling in love…was that what was happening to Darcie? The assessment felt alarmingly right. Her gaze connected with Nick's. His expression was one she could not read.

"What about you, Yiayia?" he asked then. "What color will you wear to the wedding?"

Now a smile lurked around the corners of his mouth. Darcie knew it was because his grandmother always wore black.

Yiayia pointed a finger at him and smiled. "It is to be a surprise."

They all laughed.

Then Yiayia asked, "Have you ever been to a Greek wedding?"

Finally, a question Darcie could answer with complete honesty. "No. Never."

"Ah, then you are in for a treat. It is too bad you will not see Selene ride the donkey to church, but there will be video to watch later."

"A donkey?" Darcie tried to picture the lovely young woman she'd met perched atop an animal in her wedding day finery. The image simply wouldn't come.

"It is a tradition that represents the bride leaving home," Nick explained. "Her family and friends will walk with her."

"It sounds like fun."

"You wait until you have your turn on the donkey. You will not think so," Yiayia warned. "The donkey I rode, he wanted to run. My father had to hold the rein tight to make him go slow. My mother said it was because the animal knew how eager I was to get to the church."

Once again, they all laughed. The good humor didn't last

long. It vanished as soon as the older woman asked Darcie, "Has Nikolos told you about the *koumbaro*?"

"Yiayia." His voice was uncharacteristically sharp.

But his grandmother was undeterred. She briefly explained it to Darcie, including the custom with the switching of the crowns.

"It sounds lovely," Darcie replied, unsure what else to say. Meanwhile, Nick's expression had grown pinched. If Sophia noticed, she chose to ignore it.

"It also is a special honor that Pieter has asked of Nikolos, but he refuses."

"Yiayia," he said again. This time, his tone was not sharp, but sad, pained.

"After we met you, Darcie, and we saw with our own eyes how you and Nikolos are together, we all hoped…" Yiayia's shoulders rose in a shrug as her voice trailed off.

"I will not do it. I cannot," Nick said. "I would feel… foolish. I feel foolish as it is given all of the talk surrounding Pieter, Selene and me."

"Pride, Nikolos? That is what keeps you from saying yes? Even now that you have found love again yourself, you will not relent? You choose to keep your pride and begrudge Pieter and Selene their happiness?"

"Yiayia—"

But she wasn't through. "Have you no forgiveness in your heart for your only brother?"

"I…" He frowned, unable to finish.

The tension that followed was so thick a machete would have had a hard time hacking through it. It was just as well that Darcie and Nick left soon afterward. The tea and cookies had begun to churn in her stomach.

She said nothing on the drive to where they would catch the cable car to Lycabettus, and during their tour of St. George's Chapel she kept the conversation focused on archi-

tecture and history. At that point, it was really more mono-
logue than conversation. Nick contributed very little. Even
when they stopped at a tavern for a cold drink before heading back down the hillside, he remained unnaturally quiet
and circumspect. It was like the drive to Trikala, only worse.

Obviously, he was troubled by what his grandmother
had said. Was it merely Nick's pride that was injured? Did
he still feel so betrayed by his brother that he was unwill-
ing to act as his *koumbaro*? Or did Nick continue to harbor
tender feelings for Selene?

They were in the cable car, descending from the hilltop,
when he surprised her by bringing her hand to his mouth
and planting a kiss on the back of it.

"What was that for?"

"An apology. I have not been very good company today."

"You have a lot on your mind."

"Yes." He nodded, then added, "Thank you, Darcie."

She blinked at that. "For what?"

"For not pushing me on this matter the way my family is."

She managed a smile. Those questions she had would go
unasked and unanswered.

For the second morning in a row, a knock sounded at the
door as Darcie was making a pot of coffee. Nick. Her heart
picked up speed and her body temperature shot up by several degrees as she recalled the tenderness with which he'd
made love to her the night before. Where that first coupling
during the day had been frenzied and rushed, Nick had been
exquisitely slow and thorough the second time.

As for those questions that had troubled Darcie earlier
in the day, they were forgotten. Surely, the man who made
such sweet love to her could not still love someone else.

She was smiling as she opened the door, a comment

about being insatiable ready on her lips. But it wasn't Nick who stood on the stoop. It was Selene.

"Forgive me for being so rude and not calling first," the other woman said in halting English. She smiled nervously as she clutched her handbag to her chest. "I hope I did not catch you at a bad time."

"No. Not at all," Darcie replied, trying not to feel self-conscious in a pair of jersey cotton shorts and a tank top that doubled as her sleepwear.

Thank goodness she had at least dragged a brush through her hair and rubbed the sleep from her eyes. Meanwhile, Selene looked picture-perfect in a cotton skirt and sleeveless blouse. Even in a pair of high heels, she barely came to Darcie's shoulder. The old Darcie would have slouched. This Darcie squared her shoulders and settled her hands on her "good birthing hips."

"May I come in?" Selene asked.

"Of course." Darcie stepped aside. It seemed odd to be welcoming Nick's former girlfriend and soon-to-be sister-in-law into his house, but neither woman commented on it. "I just poured myself coffee. Would you like some?"

"Please."

They made their way to the kitchen, where Darcie got a cup down from one of the cupboards.

"I don't know how to use a *briki.* I hope this is okay," she said, pouring from the carafe of the automatic coffeemaker.

"This is fine. Thank you." After stirring in an obscene amount of sugar, Selene took a delicate sip. To her credit, her grimace was barely detectable.

Darcie sipped her own coffee. Silence ensued as the women eyed one another.

"So…" Darcie expelled a breath.

"This is very…"

"Awkward."

"Yes. You must be wondering why I am here."

"Um, a little," Darcie admitted. She didn't ask if Selene had ever been in Nick's home before. Quite honestly, she didn't want to know.

"As you must be aware, there is a...strain between Pieter and Nick. It goes back years to when...when Pieter and I began to date."

"Because you used to date Nick," Darcie added, figuring it best not to tiptoe around the big white elephant sitting in the center of the room.

Selene closed her eyes briefly, nodded. She looked miserable. Ridiculously put-together and gorgeous, but miserable all the same.

"Pieter is...I do not know the English word to describe it." Selene set her coffee down on the counter and paced to the window. "He loves his brother very much."

"I'm not trying to be rude, but *you* loved Nick at one time, too."

"I did or at least I thought so. Nick and I, we were so young when we began seeing each other. I was a teenager, barely one year out of school. I thought I knew my heart, but my feelings for him changed as time passed."

Darcie was in no position to cast stones. After all, she'd thought she'd loved Tad. She'd accepted his proposal of marriage and then had spent six years making wedding plans, a couple of those years living under the same roof. She'd been a lot older than Selene at the time, too.

"You didn't want to relocate to another country."

Selene shook her head. "I love it here. Greece is...home."

"It must have been difficult when you realized how you felt about Pieter."

Selene nibbled her lower lip. "It happened...slowly. At least for me. Pieter and I have known each other for so long. We started as friends. After Nick moved to New York and we broke up, Pieter would call. Checking up on me, he said." Her expression turned soft and her smile was nostalgic. "We started meeting at a café in town after work for coffee. Then it became drinks at a tavern in the evening. At first, we talked about Nick. How much we both missed him. Then we just talked. About everything."

"And you realized how much you had in common," Darcie said, her thoughts turning to Nick.

"Yes. We liked the same things. We *wanted* the same things in life."

"You were falling in love." Darcie wanted to ignore the voice whispering that she was in the same predicament. Could this really be the Big L?

"The first time Pieter kissed me, I had never felt that way before. Then he told me he loved me and confessed that he had been in love with me for a very long time. We both cried, because by now I was in love, too. But..." Selene pinched her eyes shut. When she opened them, they were bright with unshed tears. "I never meant to come between brothers."

Darcie didn't doubt the other woman's sincerity. Selene's pain was nearly palpable. Still, she felt the need to point out, "All the same, Nick felt betrayed. He trusted Pieter."

"Pieter never betrayed Nick's trust. Nick and I were no longer a couple. Even though we had done nothing wrong, we both felt guilty at first. We even stopped seeing each other for several weeks, but..." She lifted her shoulders. "Eventually, we could not deny what was in our hearts."

"I'm happy for you." How could Darcie be otherwise? "But I'm not sure I understand what this has to do with me."

"Pieter's mother and grandmother have tried to bridge the gap between the brothers."

"By trying to set Nick up on dates," Darcie mused. "He told me."

"They did not know about you at the time," Selene hastened to add.

"I know." How could they?

"They want him to be happy. That is what we all have wanted for him. And now he is. He has found love again."

Selene smiled. Darcie nearly choked. She rested a hand on her chest. Her heart beat unsteadily beneath it.

"About that, I don't know that I can claim the credit." Could she?

"I do not understand what you mean."

"Nick and I haven't been seeing each other for very long." As in less than two weeks. And even though they'd made love, neither of them had attached a label to their feelings.

"The length of time does not matter. He *is* happy. Anyone who knows him can see that."

Okay, Darcie would give her that. And she had to admit, she was pretty darned happy, herself. But… "It's not like you and Pieter."

And it wasn't. Not by a long shot since they would be saying goodbye soon, and their future, assuming they even had one, was far from determined.

Selene was nodding. "I understand. Pieter and I denied we were in love at first, too."

"Oh, hey. Look, I'm not denying anything. It's just that… and Nick and I aren't…he hasn't said…" She swallowed.

Selene's smile was serene. "He loves you, even if he has not said so. Yiayia is right about the two of you."

Darcie squinted at Selene through one eye. She was going to regret it, but she had to know. "What is Yiayia saying?"

"She has seen the way Nick looks at you. The way you look at each other. She says it is a good sign."

Even as Darcie's heart kicked out a few extra beats, she was protesting, "But I'm not Greek!"

"And *still* Yiayia likes you!" Selene chuckled softly before sobering. "Our wedding is in just two days. The only gift Pieter and I want, the only one that truly matters, is Nick's blessing."

Uh-oh. "I don't know what you expect me to do, Selene."

The young woman reached across the table and took Darcie's hand in both of hers. "If you could just talk to him. Please."

"It's not my place." And hadn't Nick already thanked her for staying out of it and not pushing? But Selene looked so heartbroken, Darcie found herself softening. "What would I say to him? What could I possibly say that Pieter and the rest of the family haven't already?"

"I do not know," Selene admitted on a ragged sigh. She let go of Darcie's hand and rose. "I am sorry to have bothered you."

"It was no bother. Really."

They were at the door when Selene said, "At least Nick will be at the wedding. For a while that seemed doubtful. Even with you at his side, I know this will not be pleasant for him."

Darcie swallowed. She wouldn't be there. He would be on his own.

Selene was saying, "Perhaps I am being selfish in wanting more for Pieter's sake."

Her words struck a chord in Darcie. *For Pieter's sake.* Not her own.

"Love isn't selfish," Darcie murmured when the door had closed.

Nick had told her that very thing after his argument with Pieter. At the time, he'd seemed to be examining his old reasons behind the brothers' feud. She had an idea.

Darcie hadn't pushed, but she cared about Nick too much not to offer a little nudge.

CHAPTER ELEVEN

SOMETHING WAS ON Darcie's mind, but Nick couldn't figure out what. Women were rarely a mystery to him. But then, Darcie had been from the very beginning. Not mysterious in the way some of the women he'd dated back in New York tried to be. Darcie wasn't one to play games. For her, seduction wasn't an art that she practiced. She came by it naturally.

Nick would be lying if he said he hadn't enjoyed the little pieces of herself she'd revealed in their short time together. Or if he said he wasn't looking forward to seeing, learning more. All of which made her looming departure from Greece more disconcerting. Their time together had been amazing and sweet, and was proving all too brief. Already he was trying to think of ways to prolong it. But to what end? The answer he kept coming up with left him staggered.

Was he falling in love?

For her last night in Athens, Nick had made reservations for dinner at one his favorite restaurants, determined to show her a wonderful time and, as a side bonus, to keep his own mind off the fact that his brother's rehearsal dinner was that same evening. Nick had no official role in the wedding, but he'd still been invited. Both he and Darcie had.

"That sounds nice," Darcie said when he had called to confirm their plans. Then she'd thrown him completely when she added, "But you need to cancel the reservation. I've decided I'm going to make dinner for you here."

"You are? And what will be for dessert?" he'd asked.

"I think you know."

She'd sounded a little breathless. And Nick had been torturing himself ever since with fantasies of her prancing about his kitchen, wearing a little white apron and nothing else.

When he arrived at the house just after five o'clock, however, the kitchen was missing both a cook and a meal. Darcie was on the terrace, reclining on one of the chaise lounges with a glass of chilled wine in her hand. Her eyes were closed, her face tilted toward the sun. She was wearing a tank top and shorts that ended high on her thighs and her tanned legs looked ridiculously long. Her feet were bare. Her toenails painted a festive shade of tangerine.

"I thought you were making dinner?"

"That was just part of my ploy to lure you here."

He leaned over and captured her smiling lips for a long, thorough kiss. "Should I be worried for my safety?" he asked as he straightened.

In answer, she set aside her wine, grabbed his tie and tugged him back for a second kiss.

His breathing ragged, he said, "Perhaps we should take this inside and skip ahead to that dessert you promised."

"Sorry." She sounded seriously contrite. "I'm afraid there's no time. You'll be late."

"For?"

"Dinner."

He couldn't think straight with his hormones staging a riot. A common occurrence around Darcie. "I canceled our reservations, remember?"

She inhaled deeply before letting out her breath. "I'm not

talking about the restaurant. I'm talking about Pieter and Selene's rehearsal dinner."

He snagged the wine she'd set down and took a sip, stalking to the terrace's rail. "I am not going."

Darcie stood and joined him at the railing. "I want you to reconsider. In fact, I am asking you to."

"Why?"

"Because if you don't go, Nick, you're going to regret it. Just as you will regret not playing a meaningful role in their wedding."

"It is not as simple as that!" he shouted.

But Darcie was undeterred. "I'm not saying everything will magically be all better. But it's a start. This rift between you and your brother, it will never truly begin to mend otherwise."

"And to think I thanked you for not interfering," he said dryly as his temper began to simmer. He shoved a hand through his hair. "I know you mean well, but this is not your business, Darcie. You are a tourist here on holiday. This is my life!"

She didn't back down, even if just for a moment she looked as if she'd been slapped. "I may only be a tourist, Nick, but your family thinks otherwise, which is why Selene came to see me."

Nick didn't bother to mask his surprise. "Selene was here? What did she want from you?"

"From me? Nothing." Darcie waited a beat. "What she wants is something only you can give. She wants you and Pieter to be brothers again. In short, what she wants, Nick, is your blessing on their marriage. Not for her sake, mind you. For Pieter's. Love isn't selfish, remember?"

Nick swallowed. He recognized the lump lodged in his throat as guilt, and that was before Darcie said, "Selene asked if I would talk to you. She thought you might listen to me since we're supposedly a couple. You know what?" Darcie poked a finger in his chest. "I got the feeling that she would have gotten down on her knees and begged if she felt it necessary. It is that important to her. To both of them."

Nick closed his eyes as emotions tumbled fast and furiously inside him. His anger of a moment ago had drained away. As for the betrayal he'd felt for so long, that was gone, too. It had been ebbing for a while now, he knew, the last remnants disappearing as he'd gotten to know Darcie. The emotion that remained was undiluted shame. He hung his head as it crashed over him like a rogue wave.

"I'm sorry." Darcie's hand was on his back, her touch tentative. Where a moment ago her tone had been confrontational, it was apologetic now as she said, "I don't mean to cause you more pain, and I know I have no business whatsoever interfering in your personal life, but I said what I said because I care about you. Deeply. I want you to be happy. And, frankly, Nick, in addition to having regrets, you'll never truly move on with your own life until you let go of the past." Her voice hitched when she added, "And you haven't done that."

He turned. "You think I still love Selene?"

"No. Well, maybe I've sort of wondered," she admitted softly. She made her tone light when she added, "I know you're insanely attracted to me and all, but—"

Was that all it was? He didn't think so, but what he really needed Darcie to know right now was the absolute truth. "I do not love Selene."

"Oh. Good. That's *really* good." A smile fluttered briefly on her lips before she added, "But you've held so tightly to the past, Nick, that you're robbing yourself of a future with your brother and the family you clearly adore."

She understood him so well, better than any woman ever had. His conscience flared as he thought of how only a moment earlier he'd called her a tourist just passing through. He owed her an apology, but he didn't trust his voice enough to speak. Darcie apparently took his silence to mean something else and continued.

"You've helped me start over these past couple of weeks. I only wanted to return the favor. For what it's worth, I believe Selene when she says that she and Pieter did everything they could to deny their feelings for one another."

"I know."

"Did you also know that when they realized they were in love they even stopped seeing each other for a while?"

"No." The news didn't sit well with Nick's conscience now that he no longer saw himself in the role of the injured party. He said softly, "I think I always knew Pieter had not set out to betray me."

Just as he knew he had been selfish in his expectations of Selene. Nick had disregarded her feelings to follow his dream. Then, even after they had parted ways, he'd somehow still expected her to change her mind, to—what? Pine for him? Because it would have soothed his pride. He didn't care for what that said about his character.

He turned, caught Darcie's hand in his. His smile reflected the remorse he was feeling.

"My grandmother was right. I have let my pride get in the way of what truly matters. And you are right as well, Darcie. I already have regrets where my brother is concerned. I do not want to have more."

She squinted at him. "So, you're not angry with me for butting in?"

"No. I am angry with myself for many things, including what I said to you just now. A tourist just passing through." He winced as he repeated it. "It was insulting to you and an outright lie. You are so much more than that to me, Darcie. Can you forgive me?"

She kissed him in answer. Afterward, she asked, "Does this mean you are going to the rehearsal dinner?"

"No. It means *we* are going." When she opened her mouth to protest, he said, "Do not even think about backing out. I want you with me. I…*need* you there."

She smiled. "I'm so happy you will give them your blessing. It is the only gift she said they want."

Nick had already swallowed his pride, now he searched his heart and reached a decision.

"I will give them my blessing, but I can think of an even more meaningful gift to offer."

The rehearsal dinner wasn't at a restaurant. Rather, it was at the Costas home. More specifically, in his parents' yard, which had been decorated with white streamers and flowers to fit the occasion.

Even though the actual wedding party was quite small, Nick's mother and grandmother had been cooking for the past two days in preparation of the feast. In addition to his parents and grandmother, the bride-and-groom-to-be, and Selene's parents, of course, only a few friends and close relatives would be in attendance. The size of the audience would make it easier to humble himself, Nick decided.

The house smelled of lamb and simmering vegetables when he and Darcie arrived. She'd been quiet on the drive over, but she'd rested her hand over his on the gearshift and had never let go. Nick appreciated her support. He appreciated *her*. If not for her interference… No, it went further than that. If not for her appearance in his life, what he was about to do would not be occurring. Nick would have jetted back to New York and remained locked in his bitter disillusionment, isolated from his family, angry with the brother who had always been his best friend.

Love is not selfish.

Now, as they walked through the door that opened into the yard, he held her hand tightly, not only because he needed her support, but because he also didn't want to let her go. Ever.

God help him. Nick fully understood his brother's predicament now. Love happened. Even when one didn't go looking for it. Even when the timing was all wrong. It was terrifying and wonderful all at the same time. And denying it served no purpose.

His mother and grandmother were in the kitchen, arguing over the doneness of the roast.

"Nick!" Thea cried out when he and Darcie entered the room.

"Mama." He kissed her cheek, wiped the tears that had started to leak from the corners of her eyes.

"Please tell me you and Darcie will be staying," she whispered hoarsely, hopefully.

"If it is not too much trouble."

She huffed out a breath that served as her answer. "I will set the extra plates on the table."

While Thea bustled to the cupboard and got to work, Yiayia stood rooted in place, her hands clasped in front of her as if praying. She nodded, opened her mouth but said nothing. It was the first time Nick could recall his grandmother being speechless. He kissed her cheek as well.

"I know," he said softly. "I know."

"Do you want me to send Pieter inside so you can speak to him in private?" his mother asked.

It was tempting, but too easy. "No. I will go to him." Taking a deep breath, he extended a hand to Darcie. "Will you come with me?"

"You don't need to ask."

Conversations dried up midsentence when he and Darcie stepped out into the yard. Selene's parents, who he had not seen in years, looked horrified at first, as if they feared Nick was there to make a scene.

"Nick!" Selene called. Then her hand shot to her mouth, as if she wasn't sure she should draw attention to his arrival.

Nick's gaze cut to his brother, who was standing beside her. Pieter's eyes grew wide in surprise. Afterward, he neither smiled nor frowned. His expression remained wary, although Nick told himself he saw hope flicker in his brother's eyes as he closed the distance that separated them.

"Hello, Pieter. I hope I am not too late."

"Dinner has not yet started."

"That is not what I mean," Nick said quietly. "I hope I am not too late to repair the damage my stubbornness has done."

The stiffness left Pieter's shoulders. His mouth curved in a smile. "You know better than to ask."

In an instant, he had made his way around the table and was embracing Nick.

"Thank you," Pieter whispered.

"One more thing," Nick said afterward. "If you still want me to act as your *koumbaro*, I would be honored."

"There is only one thing to say to that," Pieter replied before shouting, *"Opa!"*

"I am sorry, Pieter." Nick transferred his gaze to Selene then. Long ago, he'd thought he would spend the rest of his life with her. Even after their breakup, after he'd understood how ill-suited they were, he'd refused to accept how perfectly suited she was to Pieter. When he started to apologize, however, she stopped him with a shake of her head.

"The past is the past, Nick."

For once, they were all in agreement.

"Pieter and Selene are so happy," Darcie commented as Nick drove her back to his house later that evening.

She got misty-eyed just thinking about how the brothers had embraced and the joy on Thea and George's faces after Nick agreed to act as Pieter's *koumbaro* at the service. She wished she would be there to see it.

As if he could read her mind, Nick said, "I know you are scheduled to fly back to the States, but I would like for you to attend the wedding with me."

It's what his family was expecting. What they had been expecting since the first time they met Darcie. Only she and Nick had known that her flight was scheduled to depart before the nuptials ever occurred and that he had intended to attend on his own.

"My family will be disappointed if you are not there to share in the celebration. They credit you for making me come to my senses, you know." He cast a smile in her direction, and then sobered. "I do, as well."

Something about his expression was different. Darcie couldn't quite put a finger on it. "I think you would have eventually."

"Perhaps. But not in time for their wedding. Not in time to ease their hearts with my blessing or to act as my brother's best man. So, will you come with me, Darcie?"

"I want to, Nick," she said slowly.

He studied her a moment. "Saying that you want to is not the same as saying you will. Please say yes."

Darcie took a deep breath and gave herself over to fate. "Yes."

"You're staying in Greece?"

"Sheesh, Becks, you make it sound like I'm moving here for good," Darcie replied on a laugh. "It's only for an extra couple of days. You and I will still meet for coffee and gossip when I get back. It will just have to wait until Tuesday now."

Darcie had already called her father with similar news since he had volunteered to pick her up at the airport. He'd taken the change to her itinerary in stride, probably because Darcie had left him with the impression it was the result of the airline overbooking her return flight. She felt a little guilty about that, but figured the white lie was better than having him worry.

Becky, however, wasn't buying it.

"What's really going on? And, no, I will not wait until Tuesday for an explanation. I want to know right now."

"Okay." Darcie sighed. "You know how I mentioned before that Nick and his brother were estranged, and the rift between them was a source of friction for the entire family?"

"Uh-huh. You said that was why his mother and grandmother kept trying to set him up on dates," Becky said.

"Right. So, he was pretending to be dating me so they would cease and desist."

"Uh-huh. His family wanted Nick to find happiness himself so he would— Oh, my God!"

An ocean away, Darcie could see her friend jumping to conclusions. "Becky, no. It's not—"

But her friend was shouting excitedly, "He's in love with you! That gorgeous Greek man is in love with you!"

"No." Despite the denial, Darcie's heart took off at a gallop. She swallowed and forced it to slow down. "He hasn't said anything about love. He's patched things up with his brother, and now he's asked me to stay and attend the wedding. It's his way of saying thanks, I think. Because…I don't know…I helped him put aside his lingering feelings of betrayal and move on."

"And how do you suppose you managed to do that?" Becky asked, her voice laced with triumph. "The man has moved on…to you! Are you in love with him?"

"I just broke off my engagement." Darcie's protest sounded weak even to her own ears.

"The timing sucks, I'll give you that. But your breakup with Tad was a long time coming, and we both know it."

"Nick and I hardly know one another," Darcie said, well aware that the explanation carried little weight. True in terms of time, they had only just met. In other ways…it was as if she had known him forever. He understood her so well.

"My mom and dad met on a blind date, eloped a month later and have been going strong for thirty-five years."

"Becks—"

"You knew Tad for years, Darcie. *Years!* And you still weren't sure in the end. Doesn't that tell you something? When it's right, it's right. And you just know it. The amount of time doesn't matter."

"I've got to go."

"Darcie—"

"See you Tuesday," she said and quickly disconnected.

She didn't want to talk about it. She didn't want to *think* about it. What Becky suggested was preposterous, outrageous and very, very probable, at least on Darcie's end. As for Nick…well that was a whole other matter.

Rain was forecast for Pieter and Selene's big day. The sky was thick with fat dark clouds when Darcie and Nick entered the church, but nothing could dampen the excitement of the guests assembled in the church's pews. When the bride started up the aisle, all eyes were on her, and even the insistent tapping of rain against the stained-glass windows was ignored. Selene made a gorgeous bride. And she was so obviously in love.

Darcie had never attended a Greek wedding, but in many ways it was not so different from the American ones she had attended, even if she didn't understand much of what was being said. Love and commitment, such things were universal. At Nick's family's insistence, she was seated in the front row, wedged between his mother and grandmother. Even before the ceremony started, Sophia had stuffed a lace-edged hankie into her hand.

"You will need this," the older woman predicted.

Thea had nodded, dabbing her eyes.

Nick, of course, was on the altar with the bride and groom during the exchange of vows. He looked as handsome as ever in formal attire, his dark hair tamed for the event. As the *koumbaro*, he placed the crowns on their heads at the appointed time, and then switched them back and forth three times to symbolize their union.

Darcie might not have understood the words being spoken but the emotions translated perfectly. She found herself sniffling and dabbing at her eyes right along with Thea and Sophia, grateful for the hankie.

"Thank you," Nick's mother whispered to Darcie as the bride and groom shared their first kiss as husband and wife. "You have given me back my sons."

"I…oh. Actually, Nick—"

"Nick is so happy." Thea smiled. "Maybe soon Pieter will be switching the crowns on your heads."

Darcie's eyes filled and the tears spilled over. As Thea squeezed her hand, Yiayia wiped them away with a knowing smile.

By the end of the ceremony, the storm had passed. As they left the church for the reception hall, patches of blue were visible in the sky. It was fitting given all that had happened.

Darcie had never enjoyed herself at a wedding reception more, especially when the dancing began. Nick and his family showed her some of the basic steps to traditional Greek dances.

"I'm afraid I have two left feet," she told him after one dance, during which she had stepped on his toes at least half a dozen times.

Now they were seated at a table, enjoying a glass of wine. Darcie had sworn off the ouzo after the first toast. The inside of her throat still felt as if it were on fire from the strong spirit.

"You were doing well for just learning. It takes time."

Time that she didn't have. "I can't believe I'll be going home soon."

"Let's not speak of that now." The band began to play a new song. The melody was familiar, if old. Darcie placed it by the time Nat King Cole started to sing "Unforgettable." Nick stood, held out his hand. "I requested this one especially for you."

"Am I unforgettable?" Darcie found the courage to ask.

"What do you think?"

Gazing into his dark eyes, she chickened out. "I think I have had the best vacation ever, and I'm going to be really sorry to see it end."

On the dance floor, Nick gathered her closer and rested his cheek against hers. It was just as well that he could no longer see her face, because despite Darcie's best efforts, her eyes began to tear.

CHAPTER TWELVE

"Is this goodbye or is it 'see you later'?" Darcie asked Nick as they sipped coffee in a crowded Newark airport café.

The question had been weighing heavily on both their minds, but Darcie apparently was the only one brave enough to give it voice. Another time her newfound courage might have made her smile. After all, mere weeks ago, she had been a go-along-to-get-along girl. Right now, her transformation took a backseat to heartache.

Her connecting flight to Buffalo wouldn't board for another hour yet. She'd insisted he didn't need to wait with her, but Nick was just as insistent that he would—prolonging the inevitable.

Neither of them had slept on the long flight from Athens. They'd spent the time talking, each sharing details of their lives from the mundane to the profound. Even so, they had scrupulously avoided making any reference to their relationship and the future.

Until now.

"Is there a difference?" he asked.

"You know there is." She gathered up the empty sugar packets and crushed them into a ball. Her gaze was fixed on her fist when she continued. "I'm only asking because if this is the last time I'm likely to see you, I'm going to want to make my kiss count."

"They have *all* counted," he assured her.

"True. Some more than others," she added thinking about their lovemaking.

Back at his home after the wedding, Nick had undressed Darcie slowly, hands caressing her skin as if memorizing her body's every dip and curve. The exquisite tenderness of his touch, the soft cadence of his voice as he spoke in his native tongue, both had been in stark contrast to his fierce expression and ultimate possession.

Afterward, he'd gathered her close.

"Tonight, I will stay," he'd told her. "I want to watch you wake."

True to his word, when Darcie opened her eyes early the next day, Nick had still been beside her and already awake. Indeed, given the shadows under his eyes, she'd wondered if he'd slept at all.

"Just as I suspected," he'd said quietly.

"What?"

"You are even more beautiful in the morning."

So, now, she had to know. "Will we see each other again, Nick? Whatever the answer is, I promise I can handle it. I'm not fragile."

No, Darcie wasn't fragile, but that didn't mean she couldn't be hurt or manipulated. She had been in the past. Nick was determined to do neither. Unfortunately, he found himself in a predicament. The past two weeks had been amazing, so much so that he didn't want them to end. They made for a great beginning. But...

It would be much easier if they lived in the same city. Then they could fully explore their feelings and decide over time where they were heading. But Darcie lived on the other side of the state, which was better than being on the other side of the ocean, but still not close enough for a relationship to develop naturally. As it was, what had occurred between them in Greece had been shaped by outside forces, not the least of which were her broken engagement and his strained family ties.

Now that they were returning to their everyday lives, what would happen? In the light of a new day, would she look back on her time in Greece and see it as a romantic holiday dalliance and nothing more? That was how it had started. That was all it was supposed to be.

Nick didn't wonder how he would feel once he was back in his old routine. He knew. He loved Darcie.

So, he said, "I want to see you again."

"You don't sound happy about that."

"I am being cautious, I suppose. For both of our sakes."

"Are you worried that I'll suddenly realize I still love Tad or that I want to go back to my old job as a fact-checker?" she asked.

"No, but you have choices to make, Darcie. And I don't want to put any added pressure on you."

"I think I've already made those choices."

Nick nodded, somewhat mollified, but he still felt the need to point out, "Darcie, your life is in a state of upheaval. It has been since we met. In a way, you are starting over. I was selfish once. I expected someone else to bend her life to suit my needs. I don't want to do that again. You have so much to sort out right now."

"I need a new address and to revamp my resumé. The rest…" She shrugged. "It will sort out itself."

"Your plane leaves in less than an hour for Buffalo. That is where you live. I am in Manhattan."

"And if I lived in Manhattan, too?"

His heart took off like a shot at the idea. That was Darcie's dream, he knew. To move to New York City and work as a serious journalist. Even as he wanted to offer to help her pack her bags and move that very day, he also knew she needed money to do so, and she wouldn't accept his financial assistance. He'd had a hard enough time convincing her to accept it in Greece, and even then she had insisted on a *quid pro quo* arrangement. But without a reliable source of income, she wouldn't be able to swing New York's high cost of living.

"I want you in New York. Make no mistake about that." He swallowed hard then as he pushed what he wanted behind what would be best for Darcie. "But the city is very expensive, and I am trying to be realistic. Also, your entire family is in Buffalo. When everything is said and done, you may...you may decide that is where you want to stay. I would understand."

It would kill him, but he would understand.

Darcie's smile was reassuring. "I'm not Selene, Nick. I'm not going to change my mind. I *will* come to New York." The smile disappeared then. "But it's going to take a little while, before I have established myself as a writer and can afford to move."

"A little while," he repeated.

They both fell silent.

"And in the meantime?" she asked.

"It is a short flight. I can be in Buffalo every weekend."

"That's a lot of frequent flyer miles," Darcie murmured.

"It won't be forever. Eventually, we will be together in the same city." Even as Nick said it old memories swirled like vultures. He did his best to ignore them, but some of his concern must have shown on his face.

"You're wondering if while we are apart I will reach the conclusion that what happened in Greece was simply meant to stay there," she said softly.

He didn't care for Darcie's assessment, but he couldn't argue its accuracy. "I would understand."

"Because I'm supposedly vulnerable and confused and

we only just met?" She arched an eyebrow. "Oh, please. I spent years with Tad and I never felt for him what I'm starting to feel for you, Nick."

He knew what he was starting to feel, too, but, as much as Nick wanted to give voice to the words, he was afraid. "Absence does not always make the heart grow fonder. Sometimes...feelings change."

Her eyes were bright, but she nodded. "And you think mine will."

"No!" God help him, he hoped not.

"All right. Let's put it to the test."

"What do you mean?"

"We won't see each other until I can afford to move to New York," she said baldly.

Her suggestion caught him off guard. "How long will that be?"

"I don't know," Darcie admitted on a frown.

"Six months," he declared. "That is all the time I will give you." It might take longer than that for her to build her resumé, but half a year was all the time Nick was willing to be apart.

She nodded. Exhaled. "And during that time, we won't see one another."

"No." He swallowed before adding, "Nor will we speak to one another on the telephone."

She nibbled her lower lip. "I assume texting and emails will be out of the question then, too, huh?"

He chuckled in spite of himself. Mirth didn't last long before he sobered. "We will have no contact at all. If I am in contact with you, I will want to *be* with you. My resolve will weaken."

"And that would be bad?"

"Not bad, but...selfish." It kept coming back to that.

"You need time, Darcie. You may not think so, but I want you to have it."

And he wanted her to be sure of her feelings for both of their sakes.

She exhaled slowly and nodded. "Okay. No contact at all. And then what?"

"If after six months we both still feel the same way we will meet."

"Where?" She chuckled as she added, "On the observation deck of the Empire State Building?"

"If that is where you wish."

"That was a joke, Nick. Sorry. Obviously you've never seen *An Affair to Remember* or *Sleepless in Seattle*."

She quickly explained how the couples in both movies had made plans to meet at the New York landmark.

"I like the idea of a neutral site so there is no pressure, but too many other variables appear left to chance," he said. "I do not want to leave anything to chance where you are concerned."

She smiled. "Then where?"

An idea came to him. "Are you familiar with Tidwell's?"

"The big auction house in Brooklyn that is your main competitor?"

He nodded. "The first Saturday of each month, it auctions classic automobiles. We can meet there in January."

"The start of a new year." She smiled. "I like it. Very symbolic."

If all went as he hoped, it would be the start of much more than a new year. He jotted down the pertinent information on a paper cocktail napkin and handed it to her.

"Remember, we will not be in touch between now and then, so do not lose this."

The smile she gave him now was wobbly. "I've already got it committed to memory."

"If...if you do not come—"

"I'll be there. I'll wear red in honor of your grandmother. If you change your—"

Nick stopped her from finishing the thought with a kiss. Then, with time ticking down until her flight boarded, he walked with her as far as the airport allowed.

"This is not goodbye, so there is no need to make it count," he reminded her as he drew her into his arms.

"That's right. It's see you later. Or, more accurately, see you in six months."

Still, the kiss counted. When it came to Darcie, everything did.

CHAPTER THIRTEEN

DARCIE HAD BEEN back in Buffalo a full week when she saw Tad. She had called him upon her return to the States and left a brief message to let him know she was home safe and sound, and appreciated the concern he'd expressed in his many voice mails. She'd tried to make it clear in her tone that she didn't want to rehash the past, but he showed up at her parents' house one evening anyway.

Becky had been nice enough to let her move in after the breakup, but Darcie couldn't keep imposing on her friend, nor could she afford to pay half the rent if she wanted to save up for New York, which meant she'd moved back in with her parents.

"Tad, it's so good to see you. Isn't it good to see him, Darcie?" Her mother beamed a smile in her direction as they stood in the foyer.

"Come on, hon. Let's leave them alone," her father said. He sent Darcie a wink of encouragement as he led her mother to the kitchen.

"I probably should have called first," Tad said. He smiled weakly. "I guess I didn't want to take the chance that you would tell me not to come. I think we need to talk."

"I think we've said all there is to say."

His expression made it clear he didn't agree.

"I ran in to Becky while you were in Greece. She told me

you'd met someone. A smooth-talking local who was squiring you about Athens because of a little misunderstanding with the tour company."

A little misunderstanding?

"Tad, the company you booked our honeymoon trip with was all but bankrupt. If not for Nick I would have been stranded at the airport and then booking a return flight to Buffalo within two days."

"I'm sorry about that. I'm sorry about a lot of things, Darcie." He reached for her hand. Because it would have been rude to tug it away, she let him hold it while he went on. "When you didn't answer any of the messages I became worried that something had happened to you."

How sweet, she was thinking, until he added, "Or that you'd done something stupid."

"Stupid?"

"You haven't been acting like yourself, Darcie. Your mother mentioned that you're thinking of quitting your job. You love that job."

"I've *tolerated* that job," she corrected. How could he still not understand that? "I've always wanted to be a serious journalist and live in the city."

"I thought you outgrew that dream."

"No."

Tad went on as if she hadn't spoken. "When your mother told me that you'd postponed your return from Greece, I almost booked a flight to Athens."

That came as a surprise. Tad had never been the sort to do anything spontaneous. "Why would you do that?"

"To save you from doing something rash. Given your fragile state of mind and what Becky had said about your tour guide…"

She did tug her hand away now and then crossed her arms over her chest. "My fragile state of mind?"

"You weren't thinking clearly. I hoped by giving you time, you would come to your senses and then we could sit down and have a rational discussion about our future."

She shook her head. Her smile was sad, even if she knew she had made the right decision. "We had plenty of time to talk, Tad. We were engaged for six years. I thought I wanted to be your wife, but—"

"I know you were upset about moving in with my mother. You've made your point. I'm willing to compromise. We can buy our own house. We won't build the addition onto Mother's. She understands." Of course he would have run it by Evelyn first to gain her approval. "Besides, she's only sixty-six and in good health yet. We can revisit our living arrangements in a few years."

"No!" Darcie screamed before moderating her tone. "Look, Tad, I don't want to hurt you, but we aren't getting back together."

The Taylor Swift song played in her head and she nearly added a few *evers* just for emphasis.

"It's the man you met in Greece. He turned you against me," Tad muttered sourly.

Of this much Darcie was certain. "Nick doesn't have anything to do with our breakup. I made that decision before he and I met."

"You're stressed out, confused," Tad insisted. "You don't know what you want. You don't know what you're saying."

"But I do know, Tad. I can't marry you. I'm sorry. I don't love you."

She loved Nick.

Nick's apartment was quieter than he recalled it being, and some of the delight he found in Manhattan definitely was missing. He went about the business of living and working, but the days ticked by slowly and it was a constant struggle not to pick up the phone and call Darcie. He wanted to talk to her or even just hear her voice saying his name.

The brochure she'd helped him with went to the printer. He popped a few copies of it in the mail to her when he got them. That was business and as a contract employee she was entitled to them. As much as he wanted to, he didn't include a personal note, only his business card paper-clipped to the first page of one of the copies. In addition to no phone calls, they were to have no correspondence of any kind. He cursed himself a fool for coming up with the idea.

How was she? What was she doing? Such questions haunted him. Most of all, he tortured himself wondering: would she change her mind? Come January, would she be at the auction house? Six months was starting to feel like a life sentence.

Darcie felt the same way, but she was using the time wisely. Since her return to Buffalo, she'd nailed down several more freelance jobs. The articles she'd written for Nick's auction brochure helped open some doors. Others she unlocked with sheer persistence. Interestingly enough, it was her work as a fact-checker at the trade publication that proved to be the deal sealer when it came to finding full-time employment in New York.

The week before Thanksgiving she interviewed with three magazines in the city, coming into town early on a Friday morning. She'd been tempted to seek out Nick after the interviews were over. His business card was in her purse. But they had a deal. She flew back to Buffalo the following morning, watching the city grow smaller from the plane's tiny window.

Regardless of what happened with Nick, she would be back. Two of the magazines had offered her a job on the spot. Darcie had already called to accept one of them. The pay was low, and she wouldn't be doing as much writing as she'd hoped. At least not at first. But the potential was there in the future not only for assignments, but also for a monthly column in the print magazine as well as in the online version.

In the meantime, she would be living her dream.

Nerves fluttered like a dozen butterflies in her stomach the morning of the auction in January. If all went as she hoped that day, Darcie would be with Nick, and they would be kicking off a new chapter as a couple. In anticipation of that, she made sure to put on her sexiest underwear.

And if he wasn't there?

She pushed the thought away and finished dressing. When she was done, she eyed her reflection in the full-length mirror that was attached to the back of the bathroom door in her tiny Brooklyn efficiency. She had purchased a new dress for the occasion. Red, as she'd promised him. It scooped low in the front and fitted snugly across her hips. When she'd tried it on at the store, she'd snapped a picture with her cell phone and sent it to Becky for confirmation.

Her friend had texted back: Va-va-va-voom.

It was a bit much for a daytime auction, but Darcie didn't care. She wanted to make a statement. And, truth be told, she couldn't wait for Nick to slip it off and then work his way through her sexy undergarments.

The day was cold and it had snowed the night before, leaving the sidewalks covered in slush. After she got out of the cab, she sloshed her way to the auction house's main door in a pair of impractical high heels. Her toes were frozen by the time she got inside the large, cavernous building. She was early by an hour, but the place was already crowded with would-be buyers, car enthusiasts and others who just enjoyed the spectacle. Even though she didn't plan to make any purchases, she had to sign in and received a numbered paddle. Then she made a loop of the main room, hoping to spot Nick. With just minutes to spare before the first automobile went on the block, she hadn't had any luck.

What if he had changed his mind?

She hadn't wanted to consider the possibility, but now, with her nerves working overtime, she could think of little else. Before they'd said goodbye at the airport, he'd seemed so concerned that Darcie would be the one to have second thoughts, given all of the upheaval in her life, but what if he had? What if after six months apart, he'd decided he didn't want to pursue a relationship with her after all?

"Ladies and gentlemen, we'd like to get started. If you could please take your seats," a man's voice said over the public address system.

Darcie found an open spot in the middle of a row halfway up the main aisle.

The first automobile up for bid was an Austin-Healey similar in age to the one Ari had traded to Nick as part of the Porsche deal in Trikala. It needed some body work and the upholstery on the driver's side was in poor condition. It came as no surprise when it went for a song to a man with a handlebar mustache seated three rows behind her.

"Come on now, ladies and gentlemen. You can do better than that," the auctioneer teased the crowd. "These cars are classics. Even the ones that need work are diamonds in the rough."

By the time the fourth automobile came up for bid the crowd was primed. Paddles were shooting into the air all around her, but Darcie had stopped paying attention. She was too busy glancing about for Nick and trying to keep her hopes from deflating.

Maybe she had misunderstood their conversation in the airport. For the third time since arriving at the auction, she looked at the cocktail napkin she'd saved from six months earlier and read the information. There was no mistake. This was the right place. The right time. But where was Nick? Even as she tried to deny it, the answer she kept coming up with was that he'd changed his mind.

Finally, the last vehicle listed in the program came onto the block. It was a 1962 Maserati Spyder. The cherry-red convertible was in mint condition. The auctioneer opened the bidding at seventy-five thousand. It quickly shot up to twice that and kept climbing even as Darcie's spirits started to free-fall.

"I have one-ninety, one-ninety, can I get two? Can I get two?" The auctioneer's chant was rapid-fire. The two in this case referred to two hundred thousand dollars.

The auctioneer got his wish and then some. The vehicle ultimately sold for a quarter of a million dollars. And that was it. The auction was over. Nick wasn't there.

Darcie could barely swallow around the lump in her throat. Her eyes were stinging, her nose starting to run. In a few minutes, she was going to look every bit as wretched as she felt. She wanted to be anywhere but where she was. Unfortunately, leaving wasn't going to be accomplished quickly given the crowd. She rose along with the other people packed in the auditorium. The first tear was sliding down her cheek when the auctioneer's voice boomed over the loudspeaker again.

"Hold on, folks. Hold on. Take your seats again, please. We have one last item up for bid today. It's not listed in your programs. It's something very special."

A murmur of surprise went up from the crowd as people returned to their seats. Darcie swiped at her damp cheeks. Unless she wanted to draw attention to herself by stepping over the half-dozen spectators in her row that were between her and the aisle, she had no choice but to take hers as well.

Once the audience had quieted down, the auctioneer continued. "This item is a little unusual. It's going to require a special buyer, which is why the seller has set a reserve."

Darcie was hunting through her purse for a tissue and only half listening, but she knew that meant the seller had requested a minimum bid be met in order for the sale to go through. Such a strategy could prove risky, but it also ensured that an item of great worth didn't wind up selling way under value simply because the right buyers weren't in attendance.

Must be some car, she thought, momentarily halting her quest for a tissue to glance at the stage. She didn't see an automobile. Instead, she saw Nick saunter out.

The women in the crowd went wild, cheering and clapping and whistling shrilly. Darcie would have joined them had she been capable of making noise. But at that moment, even breathing was proving difficult.

He was here!

And looking gorgeous in a classically cut tuxedo with a snowy white shirt and black bow tie. His dark hair was neatly combed. Just wait till she got him alone. She was going to run her fingers through it, leaving it mussed and sexy.

"I've got a platinum credit card!" a curvy blonde near the front hollered. "Whatever the reserve is, I'm sure I can meet it."

Other women began shouting out dollar amounts then, even though the auctioneer had yet to start the bidding.

"Ladies, ladies. Quiet down. As I said, this is a special auction item. Nick Costas is offering a personal tour of Manhattan and dinner at his favorite Greek restaurant to the woman who meets his reserve."

"What's the amount?" someone called out.

"Nick and I have known one another for a long time.

We're competitors in business, but friends, too. Still, he hasn't told me. All he has said is that he will let me know when or if the terms of the sale have been met."

When the audience began grumbling, the auctioneer silenced them. "It gets more bizarre, folks. Nick will pick up the tab for the winning bid and give the amount to the charity of the winner's choice."

"So, there's no risk?" a woman asked.

"Only to your hearts. So, ladies, get ready to raise those paddles. Bidding starts at one thousand dollars."

It escalated quickly from there, hitting ten thousand before Darcie could process what was happening. He was selling himself, but not to the highest bidder. That was where the reserve came in. Nick was waiting for her. If she loved him, he was, quite literally, hers for the taking.

Darcie set her paddle on her seat. She didn't need it. She had a better idea.

"Excuse me," she said to the gentleman seated to her left. She had to repeat the process five more times before she made it to the aisle and was heading toward the stage. She no longer cared about making a spectacle of herself.

Nick spotted her when she was halfway there. His mouth curved into a grin that set her heart bumping irregularly.

"I believe the reserve has been met," he told the auctioneer. His gaze never wavered from hers.

She climbed the steps and met him center stage. The huge crowd fell silent. For Darcie, at that moment, they simply didn't exist.

"I was getting a little worried that you weren't here," she admitted, wrapping her arms around his neck.

His hands found her waist. "I apologize for that. I wanted to make a statement."

"You certainly did. I was going for that with this dress, by the way."

"So I see. I can't wait to take it off you. Six months is very long."

"Felt like a lifetime," she agreed. "But I've kept busy."

"Writing?" he asked.

"And plenty of it. Did I mention I moved here to take a job at a magazine? I just started last week."

His smile was wide and tinged with pride. "I knew you could do it."

"Kiss him already!" the woman who'd offered her credit card at the beginning of the auction shouted.

Darcie grinned. "How do you feel about public displays of affection?"

In answer, Nick lowered his mouth to hers.

"I love you, Darcie Hayes," he whispered afterward.

"I love you, too."

EPILOGUE

BECKY FUSSED WITH the satin folds of Darcie's wedding gown as they stood at the back of the church. Although the denomination wasn't Greek Orthodox, much to Yiayia's dismay, Darcie had insisted that some of the elements of a traditional Greek ceremony be incorporated into their wedding.

One year to the day after they'd met in the Athens airport, Nick had gotten down on one knee and proposed. Now, Darcie was minutes away from becoming his wife.

The music began. Her sisters, wearing dresses the same shade of blue as the Aegean, started up the aisle one at a time. As Darcie's maid of honor, Becky went last. Then it was just Darcie and her father standing at the back of the church, a white runner strewn with rose petals the only thing between her and Nick.

"Slow down," her father whispered, as they began to walk as the wedding march began. "Make him wait a little longer."

It might have been good advice if Darcie had not been so eager herself. She already felt as if she'd waited a lifetime for this moment, even if by many standards her romance with Nick had been a whirlwind.

Finally at the altar, she smiled at Nick, took his hands. Vows were spoken. Rings were exchanged. A unity candle was lit. Then Pieter, grinning broadly, placed crowns on their heads and switched them three times.

"You may kiss your bride," the priest said.

Nick's eyes were bright. His expression mirrored the sheer joy Darcie felt.

"At last," he murmured just before their mouths met.

* * * * *

MY SEXY GREEK SUMMER

MARIE DONOVAN

To my grandmother and my grandfather

Marie Donovan is a Chicago-area native, who got her fill of tragedies and unhappy endings by majoring in opera/vocal performance and Spanish literature. As an antidote to all that gloom, she read romance novels voraciously throughout college and graduate school. Donovan graduated magna cum laude with two bachelor's degrees from a Midwestern liberal arts university and speaks six languages. She worked for a large suburban public library for ten years as both a cataloguer and a bilingual Spanish story-time presenter. She enjoys reading, gardening and yoga.

1

"LOOK AT HOW BEAUTIFUL this place is, Cara! I can't believe you didn't want to come."

Cara Sokol elbowed her friend in the ribs from where they were leaning on the ferry railing. Emma Taylor's cheerful voice had carried to the clumps of locals. The ones who understood English looked at Cara with marked unfriendliness.

Welcome to Greece. As if Cara needed another reason for the Greek populace to hate her. "Aphrodisias is as beautiful as its namesake," she told Emma loudly.

At her compliment to their admittedly lovely island, the scowlers turned to gaze at the landmass they were approaching. Cara poked her friend in the ribs again. "Emma, enough about my not wanting to come to Greece. I never said it wasn't a beautiful country."

"Sorry, Cara." Emma swiped a hunk of straight blond hair out of her face.

Cara had expected the wild sea winds on the ferry ride and had pulled her curly red hair back into a braid. She couldn't get a comb through her hair on a good day, and the June Aegean trade winds would snarl her hair into a copper-wire scouring pad. "That's okay. I know you're excited about our trip."

"Well, who wouldn't be?" Emma gestured broadly at

the vista in front of them. "Greece—the cradle of mathematics, the birthplace of Euclid, Pythagoras, Archimedes—did you know that before Archimedes died at the siege of Syracuse, he requested his favorite mathematical proof be carved on his tomb?"

"Wow." Cara would be hard-pressed to think of an appropriate proof for her own tomb. Maybe a big, fat zero with a slash through it, but she didn't even know the fancy math name for it. She shook off her Greek-induced grumpiness and instead stared ahead. Emma was still talking about Greek mathematicians, understandably since she was a Ph.D. student in math at the University of Michigan in Ann Arbor, where they were neighbors in the same apartment building. Emma looked like a cuddly blond cheerleader but had the brain of a supercharged computer.

While Emma subsided into silence with a happy sigh, Cara fell into the rhythm of the Greek speakers, their rapid-fire consonants and vowels sorting out into words as her ears adjusted to the language. The older men were complaining about ever-volatile Greek politics and the crooks mismanaging things in Athens, the women were discussing children and clothes, and the two young men closest to Cara and Emma were commenting on the girls passing by.

Cara hid a smile as the guys wondered if she and Emma dyed their hair and discussed their hip size in favorable terms. Chauvinistic Greek men might be, but at least they liked girls with some meat on their bones.

She straightened from the railing and let her gaze travel casually over the two young men. She knew better than to wink at them, since she didn't want them following her around Aphrodisias like eager puppy dogs. They met her gaze and grinned, obviously enjoying the idea of putting one over on the foreign girl. *Sorry, dudes, I've been there and done that.* She'd like to meet the Greek guy who could put one over on her now.

Despite her previous travels in Greece, Cara had never been to Aphrodisias, part of the Cyclades group of islands. The island was straight out of Greek legend, craggy hills where undoubtedly shepherds still tended their flocks, blindingly white cubic houses dotting the town and a wide crescent of sandy beach pouring out into the ocean.

Emma followed her gaze. "Oh my gosh, look at that beach! As soon as we get settled, I am going to practically live there."

"Athena says that beach is where the goddess Aphrodite first came ashore. That's why the island is named after her."

"Amazing." Emma's eyes gleamed with anticipation. "A whole island named after the Greek goddess of love? I can hardly wait to find out what kind of men must live here."

Cara could. She had things to do other than cruise around Aphrodisias for Greek men. Visit Athena, for one. She sighed quietly but Emma heard her anyway.

"Oh, hey, here I am blabbing about guys like we're on spring break in Florida and you must be worrying about your friend. What did her daughter-in-law tell you when you called from Athens?"

Cara shrugged. "Oh, Demetria says Athena is still having complications since they brought her home from the hospital. It wasn't so much the broken hip, but the pulmonary embolism she got after the surgery. They're having trouble making sure she doesn't get another clot. Athena refuses to go back to the hospital, so they're limited in what they can do for her."

Emma patted her back. "Nasty stuff. But I'm sure she'll

recover quickly now that she's home." Emma stared out at the island. "There's something about this place…but I don't know what."

Cara stared at Aphrodisias. The island was something, all right. Home to the only person in the world who could get her to return to Greece.

"IS SHE HERE? Is she here?" Athena Kefalas pulled herself to her feet using the aluminum-frame walker her doctor insisted on. Walkers were for old ladies, bah! And Athena Kefalas was not an old lady at seventy. Hadn't her own dear mother lived to ninety-five and just passed away last year, God rest her soul, *O Theos na tin anapafsi*. She shook out her long black skirt and clumped over to the kitchen, where Demetria was hanging up the phone.

Her daughter-in-law pursed her lips and blinked a couple times, no doubt to get some patience with her mother-in-law. As far as Athena was concerned, she was a model mother-in-law compared to her own Giorgy's mother. Now *she* had been a mother-in-law straight from the Evil One himself. *She* had also lived to a ripe old age, probably because the *daimones* were afraid to have her in Hell. They had eventually relented, though, and no doubt welcomed her as one of their own.

Ah, but perhaps Athena *was* getting old, reminiscing about long ago and not focusing on the present. And more importantly, the future. "Demetria, did Karoleena arrive?"

"Yes, Mother, she and her friend arrived at the villa you arranged for them and will come to see you this afternoon. But remember, Karoleena wants us to call her Cara, her American name."

"Of course, of course." Athena nibbled at a dish of

pickled olives on the sturdy kitchen table. "And when *Cara* and her friend come, they must think I am still sick."

Demetria snorted. "You may need that walker for a couple more weeks, but you look as healthy as a lamb in springtime."

"Hmm." Athena frowned. "I need to be pale and sickly. Demetria, bring me the flour."

"Flour? Why? Are we baking *kourabiethes* for Cara?"

Athena paused for a second. Karoleena did love the sugared almond cookies, but no time for baking now. "To powder my face, of course. If Karoleena knows I am well, she will leave quickly and she *needs* to be here on Aphrodisias."

Demetria didn't bother to ask why again but brought the flour.

Athena looked up from where she was patting the white powder into her overly healthy-looking cheeks. "Thank you, Demetria. You are a good daughter."

"Now, Mother, you only say that when you want me to do something."

"Actually, if you could loan me your gray eye makeup to put circles under my eyes…"

Demetria blew out a breath strong enough to rival the ocean breeze but left to fetch the eye shadow.

Athena stared out the kitchen window overlooking the beach from where the Goddess of Love had appeared. So little love in this world anymore. But Athena had always known best, especially since her own dear mother had named her after the Goddess of Wisdom. She would do anything to help Karoleena, her poor girl who was so unhappy. And if Athena needed to wear enough flour on her face to make *kourabiethes* for the whole island, then by Aphrodite, she would!

CARA FINISHED UNPACKING her clothes into the dresser and took a deep breath. Athena, or probably Demetria, had chosen well in their vacation villa. The apartment was large and airy with whitewashed walls and pale gray marble floor tiles throughout. The furniture was solid dark walnut and would take a team of strapping Greek youths to move.

She walked into the big living room with a long, burnt-orange, L-shaped sectional couch and stared at the large weaving hanging on the wall. She'd seen Athena's work often enough to know it was either hers or someone whom she'd taught. It had the look of an ancient Greek textile with its black figures on a red background, but the subject matter was typical of Athena—Artemis, the goddess of the hunt chasing down some man who had offended her. There was even a tiny arrow sticking out of the offender's butt.

Cara giggled, her first laugh since landing in Athens. Emma, coming out of her own room, saw her smiling at the weaving. "Now that's more like it. Isn't this place great? That breeze blowing through the windows—and look, a balcony." Emma hurried to the French doors and threw them open. "The flowers are amazing, and the sea beyond."

Cara followed her onto the balcony. It held a small tiled table and two chairs overlooking bright blue–painted window boxes. Masses of bougainvillea trailed from the boxes down the side of the building, their ruffled fuchsia flowers soft and delicate against the spiky dark green leaves. Prim pink geraniums stood upright as if to reprimand their lazy sisters for falling over. She inhaled a deep breath of their sweet fragrance mixed with the salty air. The startlingly blue Aegean glittered in front of them.

"I'm getting my camera." Emma rushed back to her

room and returned with her small digital camera. "Say cheese, Cara."

Something loosened in her stomach. This was what she loved about Greece—the open sea; the flowers; the crisp, pure air, where the sun shone differently than it did anywhere else. Cara grinned at the camera and Emma took her picture.

"Now take mine." They switched places and then Emma took several more photos of the harbor view.

Cara wandered back into the villa's kitchen to pull two mineral waters from the small fridge. "Here, be sure to drink something. We haven't had much chance since we got into Athens, and the long plane ride dries you out."

"Thanks. Cheers." Emma clinked her bottle against Cara's. "Or should I say *'Opa!'* and fling my bottle against the wall?"

"I don't think the maid would like that. But if you want, we can find a tourist restaurant where they fling plates and dance around like Anthony Quinn in *Zorba the Greek.*"

"And of course that's a terrible stereotype since Greeks don't like to dance?" Emma lifted a blond eyebrow.

Cara grinned. "Of course they do." She drank her *metaleekó neró* and stared at the ocean. She loved the sea— ironic, since she now lived in Michigan, a thousand miles from the nearest salt water. She spotted a sail on the horizon and her heart quickened. "Look, Emma, a sailboat."

"That's right, you used to crew on sailboats before you moved to Michigan. Getting paid to sail the ocean blue must have been a great gig."

"I did travel all over—California, Mexico, the Caribbean, even once around Corfu—that's one of the western Greek islands more influenced by Italy." She changed the subject hurriedly. "Anyway, we should go sailing if we have time. Maybe Athena has a cousin who can take us out on the water."

"Great! Speaking of Athena, isn't she expecting us now?" Emma checked her leather-banded watch.

Cara laughed. "You may as well take that thing off. Greek time doesn't work the same as American time. Athena is expecting us sometime this afternoon. And if we don't show up until evening, she'll just feed us then."

Emma set down her empty bottle. "Greek time or no, I want to go explore the town. Ready?"

Cara nodded and followed, grabbing her wide-brimmed hat and sunglasses. She locked the villa and they descended the narrow stone stairs down to street level. "Athena's house is only supposed to be a half mile away. If we get lost, everyone knows where she lives."

It was a slow half mile, with Emma stopping frequently to admire the cobalt-blue front doors and shutters and masses of pink and purple flowers. When they emerged into the sun from the shadowed back streets, Cara popped her hat and sunglasses on.

Emma glanced over at her. "You're not going to get any color at all if you keep bundling up." She tipped her face up to the blazing afternoon sun and chuckled happily.

"And *you* are going to spend your vacation crying on the couch from sun poisoning. This isn't Michigan, you know. The sun is much stronger and you get a triple dose when it bounces off the water and sand."

"I don't suppose there's any way we can pass for locals anyway, is there?" Emma sent her a teasing glance.

"Not many redheaded Greek women out there." Cara smiled at her friend. She could have been the county fair Corn Queen for her Midwestern looks, a far cry from the supertanned blond beach bunny often spotted at topless beaches around the country.

Emma said theatrically, "Alas, alas, I'll just have to be the legendary American co-ed on summer vacation." She looked around in delight. They were now in the center of town and passing quaint tavernas and sidewalk cafés. "But I thought there'd be more people around. You did say summers were crowded in the Cyclades."

Cara studied the scene, spotting cameras and white limbs sticking out from shorts and tank tops. "The locals are probably home napping. They often have a siesta time, especially in the summer. Everybody else is a tourist."

"Including us." Emma laughed. "But we have to hit the club tonight. On a Friday night it should be pretty lively, right?"

"Definitely." Seemed as if they were in for a girls' night out. Emma wasn't used to Greek guys and didn't speak more than five words of the language. Cara snickered to herself. Too bad Cara didn't have the long black clothes and black beady glare typical of an old widowed aunt protecting her naive charge from the big, bad men of the world.

"Doesn't that sound fun, Cara?"

Actually, it did. Cara had loved going out on the town, particularly to a raucous Greek nightspot. "Sure, but don't forget we're still getting over jet lag."

"Yes, Mother. Wait, how do you say that in Greek?"

"Ne, meetéra."

Emma repeated it with an accent awful enough to make Cara groan. "Let's practice your Greek after lunch."

Emma waved her hand. "No thanks, I'll practice on one of those Greek men tonight."

"And they'll be happy to let you." Cara turned a corner and checked her directions. "Here we are." Suddenly sick with anxiety, she pressed her hand against her stomach.

She'd never been good around illness, and Athena was one of her best friends.

"Easy, Cara." Emma must have picked up on her panic. "Take a couple deep breaths and we'll see how she is." Emma reached around her and knocked on the door. "I wonder why all the doors and window shutters are painted blue."

"To keep out the Evil Eye," Cara replied automatically, clicking back into tour guide mode. "It all dates to ancient times…." She continued talking until Demetria threw open the door and beckoned them into the narrow stone-tiled foyer.

"Karoleena, is that really you?" She pulled Cara to her bosom, kissing her heartily on each cheek. "Your hair, it's so red and—how you say?—fluffy?"

"Emma, this is Demetria, Athena's daughter-in-law," Cara called to her friend as Demetria fussed over her.

"Oh, look at you! So round and healthy!" Demetria eyed Cara's breasts and hips, which had expanded a bit since they last met. "You're eating now!"

Time to change the subject. "Demetria, this is my friend Emma Taylor. She was kind enough to come to Aphrodisias with me."

"Emma!" Demetria fell on a startled Emma with the same fervor with which she'd greeted Cara. After kissing Emma on the cheeks, she pulled back. "Another lovely girl! And so fair!" She pinched Emma's cheek. "The boys here will love you! If only my son Spiro wasn't away for the summer. A pretty blond American—he'll be heart-broken he missed you."

"Demetria…" an old voice quavered from a room beyond.

"Is that Athena?" Cara tried to control her nervousness, meanwhile, Demetria's cheerful expression had turned grim.

"Yes. We're coming," she called. "Mother has been anxious to see you." She ushered them into a sitting room where Athena lay on a couch, swathed in blankets.

Cara bit back a gasp. Her old friend looked terrible, pale and shadowed. "Oh, Athena, how are you?" She reached for Athena's hand, and Athena grasped hers with surprising strength.

"Better, now that you are here."

Cara looked over her shoulder at Demetria for confirmation. Demetria nodded. "It's a miracle how much better she is."

Athena let out a little moan and Cara spun back to her. "I'm glad to see you again," she said soothingly. "And Aphrodisias is even more beautiful than you described."

Athena nodded. "My birthplace, the place I knew I would return to in my old age. The place to fulfill my dream of a museum of Greek island weaving and other women's arts."

"When you feel better, you can work on your project."

Athena's black eyes went wide. "I was just about to purchase the perfect property when I fell and broke my hip. I was at the market and stepped on an olive. An olive, I tell you! I have been walking on my own two feet for over sixty-five years and a miserable olive trips me." She lapsed into Greek and muttered several imprecations against that hapless squished fruit.

Emma looked blankly at Cara and Cara shrugged. Those weren't words Emma needed to practice for polite conversation. "Emma, come meet my friend Athena."

Cara made the introductions and Emma shook Athena's hand gently. "Thank you for inviting me to come with Cara. I have nothing but the highest respect for the Greek land and its wonderful history of mathematics."

Athena nodded regally, accepting all honors to Euclid, Pythagorus & Co. as her due. "Would you like to see Demetria's lovely garden? The flowers are beautiful, thanks to a wet spring."

Emma agreed and followed Demetria toward the end of the house, leaving Cara and Athena together.

Athena continued in Greek. "Karoleena, your friend speaks Greek?"

"*Oxi.*" Cara shook her head.

"Good. How does she think you and I know each other?"

"I told her I was working on a cruise ship through the islands and let her assume we met that way."

"And that is all she knows?" Gone was the sick old lady, and in her place was the woman spearheading a new museum.

"Yes, Athena." Cara checked Emma's whereabouts, her voice faded as she went into the courtyard garden.

"Fine. I will keep your privacy, if that is what you wish."

"*Efkhareestó,* Athena."

"You're welcome, *chriso mou.*" Athena smiled up at her with such sweetness that Cara bent down and hugged her gently. *Chriso mou*—my golden one. It had been so long since she'd heard those words. Athena patted her on the back.

"I'm glad you're feeling better."

Athena heaved a sigh. "Yet not well enough to continue my project, which is why I need you."

Cara sat up on the edge of the couch. "Me? What do I know about building a museum?"

Her friend waved a negligent hand. "You will be my eyes and ears. Just some minor details to finish, and if the men do not know you understand Greek, so much the better."

"Athena…" Cara stood. "I only came to Aphrodisias because you were so sick and I wanted to make sure you were getting better. I wasn't planning to stay."

"Do you have a job in America you need to return to?" Athena raised an eyebrow.

Cara paced across the room. Stay in Greece? "No, but I'm taking classes at the university."

"During the summer?"

"Well, kind of." Athena gave her one of those baleful black stares older Greek women had perfected. "Well, they start in September, which is technically summer, at least until the twenty-first." Cara never could lie to Athena.

"September? *Pfft*. It's only June. And your friend Emma can stay, as well, unless she has a job."

"No, she can work on her studies from here." Cara looked out the window facing the courtyard. Emma was having a ball, sniffing the flowers and laughing at whatever Demetria was telling her. "Summer in Greece?" she murmured.

"It will do you good. Put some color in your cheeks and take that frown off your face."

Cara made an effort to smile. Poor her. A summer on an idyllic Greek island with nothing to do but help an old, ailing friend. Boo hoo.

"Ah, that's better." Athena struggled to her elbows and smiled up at her. "Now come here for a kiss and have Demetria make us some coffee."

Cara kissed Athena on both cheeks as she was bid and then sneezed. Something dusty was tickling her nose.

"Yia sou," Athena blessed her.

"Thanks." Cara sniffled and sought out Emma and Demetria in the garden.

Emma predictably squealed in glee at the idea of a Greek summer but then got a worried look on her face. "Be sure to tell me how much I owe you for rent and groceries, that kind of thing."

Cara exchanged glances with Demetria. "Don't worry about the money. We'll get a deal since it's a long-term rental."

"Great!" Emma hugged her and pulled away. "Cara, you have some white stuff in your hair." Emma brushed it out.

"Probably some dust or sand. So you girls are staying for the summer!" Demetria hugged them and pinched their cheeks again.

"Anything to help Athena."

Demetria led them into the kitchen and began measuring cold water into the small metal coffeepot. "With you here, I think my mother-in-law will recover faster than you expect."

2

"Is that true, Cara, what Athena said about Aphrodisias?"

Cara blinked as Emma's voice penetrated the late-afternoon haze as they stretched out on beach towels on the warm, sun-drenched sand. "Hmmm?" She took off her floppy sun hat and raised her head from where she'd been cradling it on her forearms.

Emma had been lying on her back in a tiny lavender-purple bikini but she'd propped herself up on her elbows. "You know, about the island being a magnet for lovers?"

Cara gestured to the surrounding beach. "It's a popular vacation spot. People either bring their lovers or find a new one here." She and Emma were practically the only non-romantic couple there. Pretty girls were snuggling with men, from potential male underwear models to men who should have had their banana-hammock swimsuits confiscated by Greek border security before they even entered the country.

Cara winced at one particularly gray and hairy dude in a neon-orange bikini bottom, the color of a traffic hazard cone. *Warning, warning, hazardous materials, stay away…*

Emma continued, "Athena said there was more to it than just fun and sun. She said the old ways still hold sway here."

"I suppose that's fair to say of many of the islands. Like

you asked me before, the blue paint on doors and roofs is to block the Evil Eye, and some of the old gods were folded into Christian customs. That's probably what Athena meant."

"Maybe. But while you were in the kitchen with Demetria making coffee, she said that those who have been unlucky in love would always find love on Aphrodisias."

"What?" Cara rolled onto her side and sat up. "What does that mean?"

Emma shrugged. "Something about Aphrodite taking pity on losers in the game of love."

Great. Not only was Cara a loser pitied by her friend Athena, but also pitied by an ancient Greek goddess. "Are you looking to get lucky in love here?" Cara sure wasn't.

"Love?" Emma pursed her lips thoughtfully. "I think I'd settle for sex at this point."

Cara gaped at her usually staid friend, who waggled a finger at her. "Don't look at me like that. I just wrapped up one set of my Ph.D. exams and haven't even been on a date for months. The only men I've had any contact with are my happily married academic advisor and a couple fellow students who either want to rip off my work or discuss the Freudenthal suspension theorem in loving detail. So I deserve a little personal time with a man who has more to offer than his perspective on advanced mathematics."

"If that's what you want, you won't have any trouble. Like Demetria said, Greek guys love blond Americans." Several of the men on the beach, accompanied or not, had noticed Emma reclining on her towel, her bikini a perfect foil for her creamy skin.

"Thanks for the vote of confidence, but what about you, Cara? Not that you're unlucky in love—who hasn't been?"

Cara muffled an ironic snort. Calling her unlucky in love was like calling the *Titanic* unlucky in seaworthiness.

Emma lifted her sunglasses and looked around. "But Aphrodisias certainly has a nice crop of men. If you don't find one you like, wait for the next ferry to bring another. And when he leaves, look for a different one. We have the whole summer."

Cara was momentarily speechless at her friend's logical approach, and couldn't help but tease her. "And if we don't find suitable men here," Cara went on, "we could always hop the ferry over to Naxos or Paros and search there. Or would leaving the island negate the Aphrodite Effect?"

Emma scoffed. "You're still not getting into this place, are you?"

Cara shifted and rested her head on her arms so Emma couldn't see her expression. "It's lovely, and I don't mean to rain on your vacation."

"So don't. You've needed to unwind ever since we've met, and this is your chance. Come fall, it's back to the salt mines."

Cara couldn't disagree. She was signed up for a full course load, leaving no time for even thoughts of hot beaches and hotter men. "We'll see about the men." Maybe a nice, calm Brit or German would pass through to do a spot of bird-watching or nature photography. She could dip her toe in the water with a guy named Graham or Klaus.

"Although if you're going to be lucky at love, you'll need a hotter swimsuit than that." Emma made a disparaging gesture at Cara's white terry cloth cover-up and perfectly serviceable black one-piece suit. "Put a skirt on that thing and you'd look like my grandma going to her water aerobics class."

Cara groaned. "Nice, very nice."

Emma stretched her arms over her head. "I think I've had enough sun for the first day. Like you said, I don't want to spend the summer crying on the couch from sun poisoning."

"Maybe you wouldn't have that problem with a swimsuit like mine." Cara couldn't resist the gibe.

"Smart off all you want, but we're going to the swimsuit shop on our way back to the villa." Emma sat up and reached for her shorts and sandals. "My treat."

"You don't need to pay for a swimsuit for me." Emma was a typical cash-strapped grad student.

Emma stood and brushed the sand off her limbs. "Consider it a thanks for this incredible summer vacation." She offered a hand up to Cara. "I insist."

Cara started to protest, but changed her mind. Emma had her pride, and Cara understood pride. After all, how much could a bikini cost?

"ONE HUNDRED twenty-five euros? Are you nuts?" Cara yanked at the spaghetti straps of the turquoise string bikini. On reflection, she shouldn't have been surprised. Any swimsuit store located half a block from a tourist beach was not going to be a bargain hunter's paradise.

Emma lightly slapped her hands away from the neck ties. "Come on, Cara, this suit looks amazing on you. The color makes your eyes as blue as the ocean—"

"And my skin as pale as the sand," Cara interjected.

"So you aren't tanned to the consistency of saddle leather. I'm telling you, this is the suit for you and I won't take no for an answer."

"But—"

"The proper response is 'thank you.'"

"Thank you, Emma."

Emma pulled her into a hug. "No, thank *you.* I'm going to look at that hot-pink bikini while you change." She left Cara in the small curtained changing room.

Cara studied her reflection. She couldn't remember the last time she'd examined herself closely in the mirror. Once upon a time, she had done practically everything but measure herself with calipers to see how fat she'd been. Which was to say, not fat at all.

And she still wasn't fat, despite how her former self would have fainted with horror to know how much weight Cara had gained over the past couple years.

Cara shook her head, glad to be past that craziness. Instead, she looked healthy. She pivoted to see her back in the mirror. Her butt looked full but not jiggly under the thin stretch material, and she even had a couple dimples at the base of her spine. She turned to see the front view and cupped her breasts to make sure the two triangles of fabric would be sufficient. Not that that really mattered since no one batted an eye at topless sunbathing. As she adjusted her breasts, her nipples tightened and poked against the fabric. She impulsively brushed one with her thumb and shuddered in pleasure. The suit was too tight, she should have realized. It rubbed all sorts of sensitive areas, her breasts, nipples, especially the strip between her legs.

"Cara? Are you ready?" Emma called. Cara started; she'd been about to slip her hand inside her suit bottom.

"Just a minute." She hurriedly changed back into her heavy black swimsuit and white terry cloth cover-up. They felt like a muumuu in comparison to the sexy blue bikini. She burst out of the curtained cubicle, suit in hand. "I'll take it."

"I'm paying, remember?" Emma plucked it away and set it on the counter in front of the young, dark-haired girl.

Cara turned to the salesclerk. "Do you have it in any other colors?"

Emma raised her eyebrows. "I told you it was a great suit."

The clerk ambled over to the racks and selected three suits—one black, one yellow, and the last a melon-orange. Emma shook her head at the yellow. "You'll look like your liver's acting up with that color. How about the black?"

"I like the melon color." Cara held it up in front of her.

"You look very nice in that color—most ladies not so much," the clerk offered.

"She's right, Cara. It's great with your hair and the gold trim on the cups and beads on the ties really make it shine."

Cara took the black one from the clerk, as well. "The blue, the black and the orange." She reached over to another rack. "And both of these crocheted cover-ups. I think the white one will look nice with the turquoise and the black with the black bikini, of course. And those three pairs of matching thong sandals in American size nine." The woman scurried around, gathering up Cara's selections. "Emma, what are you getting?"

Emma's eyes had widened. "Cara, are you sure you should get all this? We'll be here for longer than we planned moneywise."

Cara stopped for a second. "Really, Emma, don't worry about it. I built some shopping into my budget. You know how frugally I live."

Emma laughed and visibly relaxed. "Frugally is right. Some might even call it cheaply. But shopping spree or no, the blue suit's still on my bill."

"Agreed." But Cara noticed how Emma returned the hot-pink bikini that she'd been admiring to the rack.

Emma paid for the blue suit with a wad of euros and took the parcel. Cara caught the clerk's eye and gestured for her to pull that hot-pink suit back out. The woman nodded. "Emma, why don't you walk down to that café we passed and grab a sidewalk table for us? We should have an afternoon snack since dinner doesn't start until about nine or ten o'clock."

"You have a good idea," the clerk chimed in. "The outdoor tables are always busy and they have excellent pastries, as well."

"Sure!" Emma scooted out of the shop. She'd been eager to try different Greek desserts. Once she was gone, Cara quickly selected a matching cover-up and sandals for the hot-pink bikini. The total came to over six hundred euros, which Cara put on her platinum credit card without a second thought.

As the clerk was wrapping her purchases, a jewelry display under the glass countertop caught Cara's eye. Definitely beach jewelry—various ankle bracelets, toe rings and belly button rings. She stopped and touched her own navel. Her piercing was still open, although she almost never wore anything but a plain tiny silver ring.

"Would the lady like to see the jewelry? We have a gold-and-pink ankle bracelet that would look lovely with your friend's suit," the clerk offered.

Cara cursorily eyed the bracelet. "Fine, add the matching toe ring, as well." But she couldn't take her eyes off the belly button rings. "What about the light blue stone?" It was large and the same color as the afternoon Aegean sky.

"Very high quality. In Greek is *akouamarina*—water of the sea. In English, nearly the same."

"Aquamarine." A stone named after seawater was a perfect choice for an island summer. Almost…destiny? Cara dismissed the echo of Athena's words. "I'll take it, as well."

The clerk did a little half leap of joy but managed to restrain herself enough to tally up the second bill. Cara figured it was fitting to return some of her dough to the Greek economy, back from whence it came.

"You come back again, okay? You ask for me. My name is Niki, and I take good care of you."

"Thank you." Cara was royally ushered to the exit, where Niki held the door for her. The late-afternoon sun blasted her in the face, so she popped her hat and sunglasses back on.

The café Emma was waiting at was only about two or three blocks down the main road from the shop. Cara strolled down the sidewalk and walked in front of a narrow alleyway.

A screech of brakes made her stop dead in her tracks as a Vespa-type motor scooter skidded to a halt a foot from her legs. The sunglasses-wearing driver gave an angry shout in Greek that questioned her brains and skills of observance.

Cara fought the urge to tell him where to get off, using several pungent Greek verbs, and instead pulled her sunglasses off, giving the young, curly-haired guy her best freezing glare. "Why don't you look where you're going, you bonehead? Pulling out of an alley where you can't see who might be walking in front of you—where'd you learn how to drive—Apollonias?" She figured that might twist the knife a bit. Apollonias was the nearest island and Aphrodisias's fiercest rival for soccer matches and tourist dollars. She didn't know if he'd understand much of her English tirade, but it felt good to get it off her chest. When in Greece, do as the Greeks, and they hadn't been the silent, stoic type for several thousand years.

The guy's jaw dropped, and instead of continuing their insult-fest, he began to laugh. "Woo, watch out for those

American girls—they'll straighten you out anytime." He repeated his comment in Greek for the interested passersby, who all laughed.

Cara fought a smile, but the corners of her mouth must have given her away, because Vespa-Boy turned his charm in her direction. "And they don't hold grudges, either, do they? Come for coffee with me, beautiful blue-eyed girl. Everyone knows Americans are so friendly." He spoke English well, the hint of a Greek accent lending a sexy touch.

"I'm not *that* friendly," she retorted, ignoring the curl of awareness running down her spine. "Try running over an Italian girl—they go for that sort of thing."

He laughed again and adjusted his stance to balance the scooter. She couldn't help notice how his strong thighs straddled the narrow seat, the denim pulling across his zipper. "But will she be as clever as you?"

Cara gave him a pull-the-other-leg look. "A guy like you doesn't do cleverness."

He leaned close to her, close enough for her to see the black stubble along his hard jaw and smell the tang of sun and sweat. "You'd be surprised what I do. And who I do it with."

Wow. Suddenly her staid one-piece suit was rubbing the same places as the racy turquoise bikini had. She licked her suddenly dry lips, her face reflected in the lenses of his sunglasses. Vespa-Boy's nostrils flared, picking up on her unexpected response.

He started to say something, but another scooter came up the alley behind him and the driver shouted for him to get out of the way. "I'll see you around, clever American." He made it a promise and zoomed past her.

Cara exhaled noisily and walked toward the café, mentally scolding herself. She was here to help Athena and take a break after her first year of college, not boink the first guy who had floated her boat in years.

Emma caught sight of her and waved from the café. Cara made her way through the maze of tables and set down her packages. "Good, you went ahead and ordered." An assortment of desserts crowded the small table.

"I just pointed at a bunch of items on the menu and told the waiter to bring coffee, too. You'll have to tell me what these all are."

Glad for the distraction, Cara fell into tourist guide mode. "That custard with phyllo dough is *galaktobouriko,* the almond nut cake is *amygdalopita,* various cookies and the ubiquitous baklava." She leaned over the table. "Purists insist baklava has Turkish roots, but the last person who claimed that out loud was run out of Greece."

Emma laughed, drawing the admiration of the young waiter who'd just arrived with their coffee. He bowed. "Enjoy your sweets. I am at your disposal." He tossed a meaningful look at Emma, who just smiled.

"A possibility," she said, once he'd departed.

"A possibility for what?" Cara made a face. "He's probably seventeen years old."

"True," Emma agreed. "I don't want to find out the hard way the Greek penalties for fooling around with minors."

"Believe me, you won't have any trouble finding men who are old enough to stay up past curfew." Cara shoved the passing thought of reckless motorscooter drivers out of her mind and remembered her plan for finding an even-tempered Northern European type to test the waters with. No drama kings for her.

She spotted a possibility of her own and leaned over the table to Emma. "Emma, do you see that blond guy a few tables away?"

Emma casually turned as if she were watching people passing by and turned back. "That guy? The one wearing the hemp-looking Peruvian hoodie and sandals?"

"Emma, it is perfectly acceptable for European men to wear sandals."

"With woolen hiking socks?" Emma didn't wait for a response, mostly because there wasn't one Cara could think of. She gestured broadly. "All these Greek guys dying to meet American women and you're looking at some yahoo who probably has five pairs of lederhosen and yodels on the weekend?"

"Maybe Greek men aren't all they're cracked up to be."

"And maybe we should conduct a scientific sampling of the population to prove or disprove your hypothesis."

Cara lifted her hands in surrender. "Fine, sample away."

"I intend to." Emma broke off a chunk of nut cake and passed it to her. "Eat up. We're going out tonight, and you need your strength."

Cara accepted the cake and washed it down with her superstrong coffee. She flagged down the teenage waiter for another pot. She'd need the caffeine to keep up with Emma.

CARA HAD JUST FINISHED her shower and was toweling her hair dry in the bathroom when Emma knocked on the door. "Your cell phone's ringing."

"Oh, could you get it out of my purse and see who's calling?" Only a handful of people had her number and they wouldn't call just to chitchat. She hoped it wasn't her brother, Rick, calling with bad news about their grandmother, who was elderly and a bit senile.

Cara grabbed her terry cloth robe and wrapped herself in it, following Emma into the living room.

Emma handed her the phone. "It's a credit card company."

She sat down on the sectional couch and answered, "Hello?" After answering a multitude of security questions, she assured them she was indeed on a Greek island and likely to make even more purchases with her card. "What's my credit limit?"

She listened to the six-figure amount without blinking. "That should be fine." She had more than enough in her money market accounts to cover her purchases, short of buying the entire island.

Emma was watching her closely throughout her phone conversation. Cara hung up and wasn't surprised when Emma burst into questions. "Did you go over your card limit with all those suits? Do you need me to loan you some money?"

"No, no, I'm good, really—"

Emma paced back and forth over the marble floor. "Oh my gosh, Cara, I don't want you to go broke on this trip. I know we're both strapped for cash, and this trip out here must be costing you a fortune. Oh, I am so thoughtless. I have my teaching fellowship and living stipend, and you don't have any scholarships at the university."

"Emma, Emma, wait." Cara held up her hands and her friend finally stopped. "Come sit with me, Emma. It's okay."

Emma plopped down on the couch next to her. Cara thought for a second, considering the best way to alleviate her friend's worries. "Before I started college, I was married for a few years."

Whatever her friend was expecting, it obviously wasn't a confession of matrimony. "Cara, you were married? You never mentioned that before."

"It turned out not to be a good fit." That was the understatement of the century. "My husband was a bit older than I was and pretty set in his ways. I was young and naive and didn't realize he and I were looking for different things from life." Con had wanted a baby-maker, and she had wanted a faithful husband.

"Oh, wow." Emma's brown eyes widened. "Married. I just can't imagine it. Where did you live?"

"We had a condo in Chicago." Her brother had lived there for a brief time and then put it on the market for her when he moved out and got married. That alone had brought her a significant dollar amount. "When my marriage ended, I got a pretty good financial settlement, enough to send me back to school and allow for occasional trips."

"Your ex, do you see him anymore?"

"No, never." Cara heaved a sigh despite herself.

Emma must have picked up on her melancholy mood, because Cara found herself enveloped in a bear hug. "Thanks for telling me, Cara. I won't worry about you moneywise anymore."

Cara realized her lip was trembling. Aside from a couple people sworn to secrecy, she hadn't told anyone that her supposedly fairy-tale marriage was straight out of the legends of the Greek Furies. "Believe me, money is not a problem." She forced her expression into a determinedly cheerful one.

"Let's list what you *do* need. Fabulous summer in Greece—check. Hot bikinis and great beach to wear them on—check. Sexy Greek boy toy to give the beach and bikinis a workout—nope, you need to add him to your list."

"Back to the men again." But Cara giggled, encouraging Emma to continue.

"Back to the men, front to the men, sideways to the men—any way you like to the men. Now go get dressed. Like that weaving of Artemis above the couch, we're man-hunting tonight."

3

"THIS ONE." CARA STOPPED in front of a taverna around the corner from the main drag.

Emma looked at the unprepossessing building. "Are you sure?"

"Absolutely. You wanted authentic Greek island culture, this is it. No neon signs, no two-for-one drink specials or limbo contests." She hooked her arm through Emma's and drew her inside.

Once the cloud of cigarette smoke around her face disappeared, Cara saw several small tables and booths set around a dance floor. Piped-in Greek pop music came over the speakers. Cara pointed out a hand-lettered sign. "Looks like the live music starts in a half hour. Let's get a drink and grab a table before they fill up."

"Great." Now that they had a plan, Emma made her way to the bar and ordered a white wine for herself and red for Cara. Cara waved to her from the corner booth she'd claimed.

"Now what?" Emma asked after a few sips.

Cara shrugged. "Toss your hair, cast a few meaningful looks around the room. I suppose you could lick your lips seductively, but that might be a bit obvious." Just as she had licked her lips for Vespa-Boy.

"Not that. Besides, I think my outfit takes care of the obvious part." Cara had to agree. Emma wore a low-cut white halter top with a matching miniskirt and backless white shoes with a kitten heel. "Not to belabor the point, Cara, but maybe you should go to another of these boutiques for a more fun dress."

"You think this dress isn't fun?" Cara put on a hurt look, but burst into laughter at Emma's worried face. "Okay, okay, maybe this isn't the fanciest dress ever." That was an understatement. Her dress was a sleeveless black tunic with no discernible waistline, and she wore the same plain sandals she'd worn to the beach.

"There have to be some clothing boutiques around here. You need something that doesn't come from the sackcloth-and-ashes store. It's not like you're one of these Greek widows." Emma checked around the taverna and sipped her wine.

Cara blinked a couple times and looked down at her dress. Sew some sleeves on it, and she *would* look like an elderly widow. Many of them wore black for the rest of their lives after their husbands died. Athena did most of the time, and Athena's mother had worn nothing but black, if Cara remembered correctly. But they were decades older than she was—Athena in her seventies and her mother had pushed one hundred.

Although Cara felt ancient sometimes, she was only twenty-eight. Too young to dress in widow's clothing. "Emma?"

"Hmmm?" Her friend pulled her attention away from where the band was setting up.

"Do I wear a lot of black?"

"Aside from that dress and your one-piece swimsuit?"

Cara'd forgotten about her old-lady suit, but that was proving Emma's point. "I mean in general. Like back home in Michigan."

Emma furrowed her brow. "Come to think of it, you do. It's nice black clothing, like your cashmere turtleneck you loaned me and that really warm, long, wool skirt, but yeah, lots of your wardrobe is black."

"I had no idea." Cara mentally sorted through her closet at home. Aside from some warm-weather T-shirts and shorts, she did have a ton of black clothes.

"You look great in black, Cara," her friend reassured her. "It's a very cosmopolitan look, almost European."

Oh, boy. She'd been dressing in widow's weeds, to coin a British phrase from one of her literature classes. Mourning her marriage? Atoning for its painful ending? She knew Con wouldn't have wasted any time on regrets or recriminations, especially since he had considered everything to be all her fault.

Suddenly, her shapeless clothing offended her. Why should Con have any more say in what she wore? "Emma, this dress sucks."

Emma choked on her wine, sputtering a couple drops on her sleek white outfit. Cara passed her a cocktail napkin. "Oh my gosh, Cara," she said after regaining her ability to talk. "You shouldn't startle me like that. Good thing I'm not drinking red wine."

"But you agree."

"Well…not in so many words, but yes, it could do with a good bonfire."

Cara laughed. "How about my old black one-piece swimsuit?"

"That, too. But it has so much padding and synthetic stretch fabric I think we might get arrested for air pollution if we did try to burn it." Emma drummed her fingers on the table. "How about we throw it all away and start fresh? Not to be indelicate, but your lingerie could use some spiffing up, as well."

"It's a plan." She'd stop in the swimsuit boutique tomorrow and ask that clerk Niki about the best places to shop. She drained her wineglass and set it down. "You want another glass of wine, Emma?"

"That would be great."

Cara's trip to and from the bar took a bit longer than before. The place was starting to fill up with mostly locals as far as she could tell. Cara knew she stood out as an obvious foreigner, but no one paid her much attention aside from a few stares from the men. They'd need X-ray vision tonight to guess what her body looked like.

Cara turned the corner and stopped. Their cozy booth had just become a bit cozier. Emma was sitting between two Greek guys, her blond hair in stark contrast with their black. Unsure if her friend had invited them to sit or if they needed running off, Cara approached cautiously.

Emma spotted her. "There you are! Come meet Nick." She gestured to the man practically sitting in her lap, a guy with short black hair and dark brown eyes. "And this is his friend…" She was having trouble with the second guy's name, so he supplied it.

"Yannis." He turned to look at Cara. Despite his lack of sunglasses, the poor lighting and the fact that he wasn't straddling a scooter in tight jeans, Cara recognized him right away. Vespa-Boy. And he had the bluest, bluest eyes she'd ever seen. Wow. Good thing he'd kept his sunglasses on while they argued that afternoon, or else she might have licked more than just her lips.

"Yannis! I knew it was something like that. What is that in English?" Emma giggled. Cara reluctantly set her white wine down in front of her. Emma didn't have much alcohol tolerance.

"John," Cara and Yannis answered simultaneously and looked at each other.

He smiled slowly. "You speak Greek?"

"Not really," Cara fibbed. Fortunately Nick was doing his best to charm Emma so she wasn't paying attention.

"A clever American girl like you should be able to pick up Greek during your stay. I'll teach you some if you sit with me." Yannis gestured to the small slice of booth next to him. She'd practically have to sit in the guy's lap to avoid falling on the floor, which was probably the whole idea. And a bad idea. Right? A very bad idea.

"I'm afraid I need more room than that."

He looked disappointed but gave her more space. She sat cautiously and sipped her wine, unsure of what to do next.

Yannis had no uncertainties. "You never did tell me your name."

She swallowed her wine. "Cara."

"Cara? Just Cara?"

"Cara Sokol."

"And I am Yannis Petrides. Born on Aphrodisias, grew up here—I even learned how to drive here. *Not* on Apollonias." He lifted one black eyebrow in amusement.

Cara burst into laughter, remembering her insult regarding his driving skills.

"Ah, much better, Cara Sokol. I am sorry I almost ran you down today. All I can say is that your beauty stunned me so much I forgot how to stop my scooter."

She laughed even harder. "Oh, come on. In that outfit I could have been your grandma."

"My grandmother doesn't have eyes blue as the sea or hair as red as the sun when it drops into the ocean." He didn't touch her with anything but his words and his gaze, but that was more than enough.

Again at a loss, Cara glanced away. Really, she needed to get a grip. She was no blushing virgin ready to fall at the feet of a smooth-talking Greek charmer. And please, just because his blue eyes sparkled in his handsome bronzed face was no reason to go all stupid over the man. He was probably a total dud in bed.

After all, who wanted to sleep with a guy whose shoulders were wide from some kind of manual labor, whose hard thigh had pressed on hers, whose strong forearms would be more than able to hold his weight as he moved on top of her…. She drank more wine. "Oh, my, looks like I drank it all. I'll just go get a refill." She needed to catch her breath and stood, but he came out of the booth right after her.

He plucked her empty glass from her hand, his firm, callused fingers brushing hers. His white, straight teeth flashed in the dim light, his lips perfectly curved around them. "And what kind of Aphrodisian would I be if I let a lovely visitor get her own wine?"

For a split second, Cara thought he had said *aphrodisiac*. Oh, yes, Yannis Petrides was a potent aphrodisiac for her, judging from how her breathing had sped up and her nipples had tightened under the baggy black linen dress. She tossed a look Emma's way, but she was engrossed in dark-eyed Nick.

Yannis seemed to pick up on her nervousness. "Will you still be here when I come back with your wine, Cara?" he asked quietly. "Or will you run like a frightened maiden from the pursuits of the Old Ones?"

He meant like the girls who tried to escape the amorous attentions of Apollo and Zeus in Greek mythology. Cara tipped her chin up at him. "Why? Are you going to turn me into a tree if I don't return your attentions?"

He grinned again. "Ah, very good. You do know our stories."

"Since I didn't see Apollo's sun-chariot parked outside the taverna, I think I'm safe. And I don't run." At least not anymore.

"Good. Although if you spend much time here, you'll find Greek men enjoy the chase."

"But do you know what to do once you've caught your prey?" she retorted, annoyed yet aroused at the idea of him chasing her.

Yannis gave her a long sweeping look from her feet to her rapidly heating face. "I can't say for other men, but yes, *I* definitely do."

YANNIS BLEW OUT a long breath as he stood at the bar waiting for Cara's red wine. He'd planned to go out for a few drinks with his old friend Niko Theodoridis, listen to some live music, and maybe talk about the latest football matches. But he'd never expected to meet the girl he'd almost run down earlier. He felt a bit guilty, speeding down a narrow alley and then shouting at her for not paying attention. She hadn't understood his Greek, but had sure understood his message, giving it back to him in full measure.

He grinned. When he'd seen her beautiful blue eyes and the fiery red hair poking out from her ugly beach hat, she could have called him the son of a motherless goat and he would have just stood there and nodded.

Why was redheaded Cara here and not at an obnoxious tourist bar? Niko had tried to convince him to go to one of them since Niko had a thing for blondes, but Yannis had not wanted the lights and noise tonight.

Not to say he hadn't planned to find Cara. He had seen her shopping bag from the store where his cousin Niki worked and would have asked Niki about her tomorrow.

"Yannis!" Niko thumped him on the shoulder and ordered two white wines, what the blond girl had been drinking. While the bartender poured, Niko leaned his back on the bar and rested his elbows on top. "You're a great friend, man." His grin spread from ear to ear.

"What for?"

"For picking such a great place tonight."

They'd both been there dozens of times. "Glad I could find you your blond girl." Not really. Niko put too much store in looks. "It's been, what? A couple weeks since the last?"

"Yeah, Monika went back to Sweden in May. I've been lonely ever since."

Yannis shrugged. Niko liked the tourist girls because one, they left for home before things got awkward; two, they weren't related to him as half the girls on Aphrodisias were; and three, his mother was certainly not going to pressure him to marry some foreigner from Scandinavia, Great Britain, or God forbid, America.

The bartender passed them the wineglasses, and the men paid. Niko took a sip from his white and grimaced. "Give me a beer anytime."

"So get a beer." That actually sounded good to Yannis, so he ordered one.

Niko shook his head. "No, the girls like it if you drink the same thing they are. Makes you look more compatible."

"Whatever." Yannis reached into his pocket to pay for his beer, but Niko tossed some euros on the bar.

"This one's on me—as a thanks for distracting that redhead so I can get a little alone time with Emma."

"What?" Yannis set his bottle down on the bar with a decided thunk. "You think I'm talking with her as a favor to you?"

"Why else? It's not like you can see her body under that awful dress, and her hair's so red and pulled into that braid thingie." Niko made a face.

Well, if Niko couldn't see anything but blatant charms, Yannis wasn't about to point out the generous curves of Cara's breasts and hips that even that dress couldn't hide. And as for her hair...it *was* the color of the sun as it set over the western coast. Loose, it would drape over her pale shoulders like the painting of Aphrodite rising from the sea that he'd seen on a trip to Florence.

Yannis picked up his beer and Cara's wine. "Let's get back to the ladies, shall we? They might think we've ditched them and left."

Niko's look of alarm was almost amusing enough to distract him from his lustful thoughts of Cara. Almost, but not quite.

"Wow, CARA, you really picked a great place tonight." Emma had stars in her eyes. "This Nick guy is so-o-o-o cute."

"Great." This was not what Cara had planned. None of it. Vespa-Boy had a name—Yannis Petrides.

Cara listened halfheartedly while Emma chattered about Nick's manly charms. "Don't you think that sounds fun, Cara?"

"What?" Cara dragged her thoughts away from Yannis and focused on her friend.

"Double-dating. Maybe if tonight goes well, we can go out with Nick and his friend again. Nick seems fun, and Ya—Ya—"

"Yannis," Cara supplied.

"Whatever his name is, he sure seems into you." Emma giggled. "With him around, you can forget about that hippie hiker you were eyeing earlier."

Cara fought the urge to tell her that Greek men wore sandals, too, and usually despite extremely hairy feet, as well. "I just don't want to get involved with a Greek guy, Emma. They have the home field advantage, and they don't go home at the end of the week. I'd rather not spend the rest of the summer ducking down alleys to avoid running into the guy again. Too awkward."

Emma waved a hand negligently. "Who cares? Move on to the next guy."

Cara shook her head. Emma just didn't understand how a small Greek island worked. "All these guys grew up together and half of them are related to each other. It would be like dumping a guy and then dating his brother or cousin."

"*I'm* the one going home at the end of the summer, so who cares what the guys think? Besides, if Nick turns out to be as hot as I think he is, I won't need to look any further."

"As long as you have a plan," Cara commented drily.

"You should seriously consider following the same plan. What happens on Aphrodisias stays on Aphrodisias. Oh, look, here they come."

Cara hadn't needed Emma to tell *her* that. Her guy-dar had gone off as soon as Yannis was within ten feet of her.

He slid in the booth next to her. "Your wine, *despinis,*" he announced with the suavity of an experienced waiter. Across the table, Nick delivered a white wine to Emma.

Cute. He'd called her miss. "Thank you." Cara took several sips while she thought of something to say. "This wine isn't what I had before."

"You like it? It's one of the island's vintages. The bartender usually saves it for the locals."

Cara could already feel its headier buzz rushing through her veins and wondered if he was trying to get her tipsy. "I guess it's okay." She felt as if she'd kicked a puppy when Yannis's face fell. "Well, you must not like it, since you're drinking a beer."

"I like it fine. My grandfather makes it from his vineyard." His sentences were short and clipped.

"Oh." Well, that certainly was an uncomfortable exchange. She toyed with the stem of her wineglass and looked anywhere but at Yannis.

Her gaze fell on Emma. Her alcohol intolerance was kicking in, and she gave a big yawn before snuggling on Nick's shoulder.

Cara needed to draw this evening to a close. "Emma, time to go." Her friend blinked a couple times and then shut her eyes.

"What?" Nick protested. "We just got here. The dancing hasn't even started." He wrapped an arm around Emma's shoulders.

"We also just got here from overseas. Emma's barely conscious thanks to the booze and jet lag." Cara tugged her friend out from under his overfriendly embrace. "Besides, Greek men can dance with each other. You two should go for a spin."

Nick gave her a blank look, but Yannis snorted and replied to his friend in Greek, "Look, Niko, they obviously don't want to hang around with us."

"But the blonde does—"

"Her friend's right. She's almost passed out. What fun is that?"

Cara broke in then, "Excuse me, please, Yannis." She

scooted into him, and her hip pressed along his. The long muscles of his thigh flexed at the contact, and she felt an answering pull. "Yannis?"

He shook his head and stood, letting her slide free. Emma fussed a bit, but straggled after her.

"You sure you can get her back to your hotel?" Yannis asked. "We can walk with you." Nick was pouting into his wineglass and didn't bother seconding Yannis's offer.

"No, thanks. We're not far." Cara tugged Emma's elbow.

"Nick, we're at the Aphrodite Bay Villas, Apartment Three," Emma announced loudly, unfortunately not drunk enough to forget their hotel information. "Call me."

Nick raised his head and a grin erased his sulky expression. "How do you Americans say it? Oh, yes. Count on it."

Probably too far into the busy season to find another hotel. Oh, well, Emma was a big girl, and hell-bent on getting her Greek groove on. In the meantime, Cara would try for a handsome tourist who'd be off to another island once the ferry arrived.

"Good night, then." Yannis gave her a curt nod and sat next to Nick. He reached for her wine and raised it mockingly. *"Yia sou."* He toasted her and drained the glass dry. "Ah, delicious. I'll have to tell my *pappous* what a good job he did on this vintage. There's a good reason we save it for ourselves and don't waste it on tourists."

She spun on her heel but forgot she was still holding onto Emma, who teetered dangerously on her flimsy shoes. Emma threw her arms around Cara's shoulders for balance and Cara staggered a bit under the weight. "Come on, Em, straighten up," she muttered, peeling Emma off her.

"Eh, it's okay here for women to dance together, too, but most of them wait for the music," Yannis called.

Cara tossed him a nasty glance and stalked off. The

dignity of their exit was ruined, however, by Emma blowing a kiss to the men and giggling again.

Cara finally got them out the door into the warm Grecian night and steered Emma uphill to their villa.

"Cara, the blue-eyed guy likes you! Could be something special."

Cara groaned. Since meeting Yannis Petrides for the very first time less than eight hours ago, he had almost run her down, she had chewed him out on the street, he had tried to get her tipsy and she had insulted his beloved grandfather's wine. *Special* wasn't the word that came to mind, but the other words that did would shock even a drunken Emma.

4

"SO HOW WAS YOUR EVENING OUT with Niko Theodoridis?" Yannis's aunt Eleni poured him a cup of coffee and set plates of hard-boiled eggs, olives and thick slices of homemade bread on the table in front of him.

"Eh, all right. I had some of *Pappous*'s wine at the taverna."

"Must not have been too much, or else you wouldn't have found your way home. Your uncle uses that wine to clean tarnished brass sometimes. It works like a charm."

It sure hadn't charmed a certain Cara Sokol. Ah, well. The ferry that brought her would take her away soon enough.

"Eat, eat!" his aunt urged. "A big handsome boy like yourself needs good food, especially to work construction for your slave driver uncle."

Yannis helped himself to the eggs and olives and drizzled local wild honey on the bread. He smiled up at *Theia* Eleni after a couple mouthfuls. "It's as delicious as you are beautiful."

She beamed down at him and patted her carefully combed and sprayed black hair. He'd seen her only once with her face bare and her hair limp and wet around her shoulders and had for a split second wondered if his uncle had sneaked a girlfriend into the house. "Oh, you! Your mother warned me you were a charmer. Like I told you before, my friend Georgia has a daughter who would be perfect for you. Just let me know if you want to meet her. Such a nice girl and a good cook." His aunt pinched his cheek and bustled back to the stove.

Yannis winced. Most of his aunt's friends were on the lookout for a husband for their girls, but he wasn't interested in girls in their late teens who only giggled when he tried to talk about more than the weather.

His uncle Gus came into the kitchen, still buckling his belt. Uncle Gus was wearing one of his dressier shirts today, a button-down white linen with embroidered panels down the chest over black dress pants. He must not be planning to visit a job site today. He sat and gestured to the empty table in front of him. "Coffee." Yannis's aunt quickly filled his cup and set down an ashtray, as well.

Yannis took a deep breath of the last clear air of the morning. Sure enough, his uncle lit a cigarette to smoke while drinking his coffee. Having grown up in Greece, Yannis was used to cigarette smoke, but didn't care for it at meals, where it seemed to change the flavor of his food.

He popped a couple more olives into his mouth and pushed the bowl toward Uncle Gus who raised a work-roughened hand in refusal.

"None for me. Time to go to work, anyway." He stubbed out his cigarette and stood. Yannis followed, his aunt fluttering after them with a couple bundles of pastries for their *kolatsio,* or midmorning snack. Yannis's uncle more than made up for missing breakfast then.

"Have a good day! I'm making lamb for dinner tonight." Aunt Eleni waved goodbye and then went back into the house, presumably to do whatever Greek women did all day at home.

"Lamb, eh?" Uncle Gus grinned at him as they hopped in his white compact car and backed out of the driveway. "And not even your name day for another couple weeks."

Yannis grinned. His name day was June 24, the birthday feast, or Nativity, of Agios Ioannis Prodomos, St. John the Baptist. Yannis's own birthday was in September, but name day feasts were celebrated more than birthdays, especially on an island where at least a quarter of the men were named some version of Ioannis.

"Ah, well, your aunt loves to have somebody else around to cook for since the girls are off in Athens." He lit another cigarette. "Up to no good there, I'm sure. But they won those islander scholarships to university and were on the next ferry out."

Yannis rolled down his window to let the ocean breeze blow through the car and privately thought his two cousins Marina and Petra had done well to get their education. Aside from tourism, fishing and small-scale farming, Aphrodisias didn't have many career opportunities. "Athens isn't as pretty as here. I'm sure they miss the island."

Uncle Gus grunted. "Probably marry boys from the mainland and only come back once a year."

Yannis nodded. That was a real possibility. Marina and Petra were related to half the guys on Aphrodisias and knew the other half too well to ever want to marry them. His uncle finished his cigarette and stubbed it out in the car's full ashtray. The island was too dry during the summer to flick butts out the window. Nobody wanted a brushfire, especially his uncle, who was in the middle of several building projects. "What's the plan for today, Uncle Gus?"

"You go over to the villa site and make sure those lazy bastards who call themselves finish carpenters are doing the door and window moldings correctly. The buyers are Germans and they'll come in with magnifying glasses and rulers to make sure everything's square." Uncle Gus would take foreigners' money for building houses, but that didn't mean he approved of them moving to Aphrodisias.

"Sure thing, Uncle."

"After our *kolatsio,* get them working again and then come back to the office. I want you to sit in on a meeting with some Belgian property investors. They're brand-new to the island and I don't want them to sign a contract with my competitors."

That would explain his uncle's dressier clothes. Yannis looked down at his own light blue T-shirt, well-worn jeans and steel-toed brown construction boots. "Should I change before the meeting?"

Uncle Gus made a dismissive gesture. "No. Let them see we are real working men who are not afraid to get dirty."

Yannis wasn't sure he wanted to be the poster boy for dirty working men, but he wasn't the boss. "What property is this about?"

His uncle pulled into a small parking spot in the alley behind his office and got out of the car. Yannis grabbed his tool belt out of the trunk. "One we don't have yet. *Kyria* Nomikou was about to sell it to Athena Kefalas for some weaving museum, but *Kyria* Nomikou just died a couple days ago, before any papers were signed. Her nephew from Athens is asking around to see if he can get a better price— maybe he can, if these Belgians are interested in building their villa condominiums there. If we can help arrange the real estate, they are interested in contracting us for the build." His uncle tipped him a wink as he unlocked the office door. "Now take a truck to the site, but—" he held up a hand "—park behind the trees where they can't see you and sneak up on them."

Yannis laughed. Sneaking up on men while he wore heavy boots and a bulky, noisy tool belt would be quite a feat. "Just how lazy are these carpenters?"

"Eh, they're from Apollonias. They think they're the sun god himself and the world revolves around them." His uncle tossed him one of the pastry bundles. "Bribe them with your aunt's baking if you have to. Those German buyers are coming next week and I need them to release the rest of the construction money—they won't, not unless everything is perfect. And don't forget to come back for the meeting."

"Okay, Uncle." Yannis stowed his gear in the battered Aphrodisias Builders pickup truck and hopped behind the wheel. The engine roared to life with a cloud of black exhaust. He pulled away and shook his head. So much for sneaking up on the lazy Apollonian carpenters—they'd hear and smell the truck a mile away.

"Wake up, sleepyhead, it's shopping time!"

Cara cracked open an eyelid and squinted up at the giant lemon sitting on her bed. She peeled open the other eye and realized it was Emma wearing a yellow T-shirt and matching shorts, her blond hair fluffed around her face. "Why am I feeling the wine and you aren't? You were a riot to get home last night."

"First, I seem to remember you made me drink a lot of water and take some aspirin before I fell asleep. Second, white wine makes you less hungover than red."

Cara grunted. She'd had several disturbing dreams featuring Yannis Petrides that had left her tossing and achy with need. Probably jet lag thrown in on top of it, too. "What time is it?"

Emma checked Cara's bedside clock-radio. "Ten o'clock."

"Good. Just in time for *kolatsio*." Cara sat up in bed, the sheet falling away from the oversize T-shirt she customarily wore to bed.

Emma grimaced. "What's with the big duck on that shirt?"

"It's comfortable." The caption below read, I'm on the Verge of a Quack-up, which had appealed to Cara's dark sense of humor a couple years back.

"Maybe we can give it to the housekeeper for her cleaning supplies. Don't be surprised if it mysteriously disappears. Even that hempy hippie you were eyeing yesterday would turn up his nose at it."

"But I sleep well when I wear it."

"Who said anything about sleep?" Emma winked at her and stood up. "I'll run to the bakery downstairs and get some breakfast. What sounds good?"

"Oh, get me a *bougatsa*—that's a baked phyllo pastry with sweet cheese if they have any fresh ones. Otherwise, whatever looks good."

"It *all* looks good to me. How do you want your coffee?"

"Black. I don't need the sugar and cream calories," she replied automatically.

Emma laughed. "Cara, you dingbat. You want me to get you a cheese-stuffed pie-thingie and you're worried about a packet of sugar and a drop of cream?"

Cara took a deep breath. Emma was right. As long as Cara walked or swam every day and didn't eat only *bougatsa,* she would be fine. "Okay, cream and sugar both." She liked her coffee a bit lighter and sweeter thanks to the strong brewing customs.

"That's more like it. And don't worry, I have no intention of letting you sit on your heinie on the beach all day. Have I mentioned we're going shopping?"

"Only about ten times," Cara replied drily. "Now be off with you and don't come back without my food."

"Yes, ma'am!" Emma saluted briskly and hurried out the door.

Cara hopped out of bed and looked down at her night-shirt. "No more quack-ups—or crack-ups, either." She stripped off the shirt and dropped it into the wastebasket.

By the time she'd finished her shower and wrestled her hair into submission, Emma was setting up breakfast on the terrace table.

"These cheese pastries are fresh out of the oven." Emma slid them onto bright blue-and-yellow plates from the villa kitchen and poured coffee from the foam containers into matching mugs. "Sit, sit."

Cara relaxed into one of the small wrought-iron chairs and dropped a napkin into her lap before slicing the pastry into flaky, gooey triangles. She forked one corner into her mouth and closed her eyes in ecstasy. "Oh, yum."

Emma sat down across from her and did the same. "Yum is right. Almost as delicious as that Nick guy from last night. I wonder if we'll run into him again?"

"Probably, since you gave him the address of our villa."

Emma hooted. "Did I? I don't remember that part, but I do remember his friend wasn't exactly hard on the eyes, either, judging from how you were looking at him."

Cara almost choked on her coffee. "How I was looking at him?"

"Yep, like he was the male equivalent of this pastry thingie." Emma wiggled her eyebrows and licked some cream filling off her fork.

"I have no idea what you're talking about." Cara tried

hiding her face behind the coffee cup, but Emma's laugh told her she'd been unsuccessful.

"Hey, no need to blush. I'm glad you've found a guy that piques your interest. There sure wasn't anybody back in Michigan, was there?"

"No, not at all." Cara had been asked out a few times, but had always declined due to her lack of interest. But being on Aphrodisias seemed to have flipped on some long-dormant libido switch.

But just because Yannis had featured prominently in her dreams last night didn't mean he was automatically her first choice for Chief Libido Fixer. After all, Cara was on an island. Surely, there were other fish in the sea.

"AND THEN SHE SAID, 'That's no goat, that's my mother!'" Uncle Gus delivered his punch line triumphantly as the Belgian real estate investors roared with laughter.

Yannis laughed along with them even though he'd heard it a million times.

His uncle caught his eye. "Eh, Yannis, fetch some of that red your *pappous* makes." He turned back to the Belgians. "My father-in-law makes this wonderful wine by hand up in the mountains. Stomps his own grapes and everything. Famous all over the island."

Famous for polishing tarnished metal and pissing off American girls. They were entertaining their foreign guests in the taverna around the corner from his uncle's office, the same taverna where he and Niko had run into the American girls last night.

Yannis leaned on the bar and placed his order for two bottles of red. Red wine for the redhead. Boy, had he read her wrong. Sure, she had a tart mouth on her, but he thought he could sweeten her up. A little local color, some homegrown spirits, but no luck. Maybe next time he'd try for a girl whom he hadn't almost run down in the street. Showed a lack of finesse, a modern version of clubbing her over the head and dragging her off to his cave.

But what a fun time they could have had together in a cave, her pale body shining up from a bed of furs, her red hair glowing in the light from a small fire, her full lips calling his name as he moved inside her... Yannis sighed and discreetly adjusted his tightening jeans.

The taverna owner, an old family friend, returned with the uncorked bottles. "Tell your grandfather I need another case. His stuff is a hit this summer."

"I'll be sure to let him know."

"And tell your uncle to have those foreigners sign his papers before they pass out."

Yannis grinned and thanked the bartender, his construction boots squeaking on the stone floor as he joined his uncle and their guests. If this deal went through, Yannis would be too busy to worry about what one prickly redhead thought of him anyway.

"WHEN ON EARTH did you get your belly button pierced?" Emma stared at Cara's navel in fascination as Cara took off her new beach cover-up and settled onto her beach towel. "I only left you for a few minutes to get breakfast."

"Silly." Cara laughed and applied sunblock with a heavy hand, careful to get the parts that her new turquoise bikini left bare. "I've had this for years. You've just never seen my stomach before."

"And that is a beautiful stone. Aquamarine?"

Cara nodded. "I thought it was appropriate for our island adventure. Oh, I almost forgot. I have a little something for you."

Emma frowned. "You already got me this fancy pink bikini when I was the one supposed to be treating you. It better be something cheap like a souvenir refrigerator magnet saying Welcome to Aphrodisias."

"Sorry. Although I suppose you could hang them on your fridge if you want." Cara reached into her tote bag and pulled out the box holding the ankle bracelet and toe ring she'd bought at the swim boutique yesterday.

Emma opened the box and squealed. "Oh my gosh, Cara! They're beautiful. I've never seen pink crystals like this."

Cara just smiled. They were actually pink topazes, but she didn't want to shock Emma's thrifty Midwestern side. "Try them on."

"If you insist." Emma giggled and clipped the bracelet on her ankle and slid the toe ring on the opposite foot.

"Whoo, sexy." Cara gave a wolf whistle as Emma admired the jewelry.

"Thank you so much, Cara." Emma smiled down at her feet, but turned a serious face to Cara. "Are you sure—" she dropped her voice to a whisper "—are you *absolutely* sure this present and this whole trip is not going to cause a money problem for you? I would just *die* if this was your tuition money you're spending on us."

Cara patted her shoulder. "Please don't worry. Athena got us a good deal on the villa and like I told you, I have money of my own." Actually it used to be Con's money, but he wasn't around to complain how she spent it.

"Okay." Emma's sunny expression returned. "But our evening out tonight is my treat."

"Oh, are we going out tonight?" Cara pulled her beach hat low over her eyes and lay back on the towel, the sun warming and relaxing her.

"Our first Friday night on vacation? Of course. I thought

we could go for dinner and dancing, and you can wear one of your new outfits. Maybe that jade-colored dress."

"Whatever you want." Cara yawned. Maybe she could catch a nap, hopefully one without dreams of that blue-eyed Yannis.

5

"YOU SET ME UP, EMMA!" Cara stopped dead in her tracks as she spotted the table her friend was aiming for.

Emma hooked her arm through Cara's elbow and tugged her through the dark, romantic restaurant toward where Nick Theodoridis waved to them, his buddy Yannis seated next to him. "Come on, Cara. Who else do we know on this island?"

"Athena, Demetria—"

"Who are very nice ladies, but not what I had in mind for a fun evening out. Now smile at the men."

Cara managed a small lip curl. Her only consolation was that Yannis seemed as surprised as she was.

"Ladies!" Nick called. Yannis stood as they approached the table, Nick hastily following his example.

Emma greeted the men and let Nick kiss her on the cheek. Cara stuck out her hand when he tried the same with her. He was Emma's problem.

Now for *her* problem, dressed in a silky-looking dark blue button-up shirt and black dress pants. "Hello, Yannis."

He didn't try to kiss her, only engulfed her hand with his. "Cara." Her name, combined with the warm, hard strength of his fingers made her a bit fuzzy, as if she'd been drinking his grandpa's homemade red. "Shall we sit?" he asked. "Emma told Niko to order for you ladies, so dinner should be here in a few minutes."

Realizing she still held his hand, she let go. "Oh. Sure." She found herself staring at his chest, a slender chain and small gold religious medal resting right below the warm hollow of his throat.

Emma was already absorbed in Nick, her blond head almost touching his dark one.

Cara sat, suddenly uncomfortable in her new clothes. She was wearing the jade dress she'd bought just that morning. The halter top left bare a revealing amount of her cleavage and shoulders. She wished she'd worn a wrap to the restaurant despite the warm room. She sneaked a glance sideways at Yannis, but he was staring ahead with an expression she couldn't read.

YANNIS HOPED the lovely Cara couldn't tell what was going through his mind. Probably not, since she'd be up and running away again if she knew a lightning bolt the size of Zeus had zapped him as soon as he saw her again.

He'd known she was hiding decent looks under her baggy outfit last night, but *gamoto!* He'd had no real idea. This dress was sleeveless, too, but other than that, they might as well have come from different planets. *This* dress had absolutely no back, which was sexy enough by itself, but then the top wrapped around the nape of her neck and squeezed her breasts together in the middle of her neckline.

Her breasts were full and pale, like the moon that shone over the sea, lightly sprinkled with golden freckles. He wanted to connect them with his tongue and then lick a line to her nipples.

He cleared his throat and she jumped. She was as on edge as he was. For the same reason? He couldn't tell. Across from them, the blonde giggled again, and this time she was drinking mineral water. Nick might get his wish tonight. Yannis wouldn't. But that was no excuse to be rude. "So, what do think of our island?"

She turned her face up to his and he swallowed hard. She'd left her hair long and loose and one red curl had trickled onto her breasts. He wanted to reach over to stroke her with it, but figured she'd slap him, and deservedly so.

"Aphrodisias is very nice," she replied politely. "The beach is nice, the views are nice and the sea is…"

"Nice?" he supplied, gratified at the hastily tamped-down flare of anger in her eyes.

"Something like that." She shifted away from him and sipped her mineral water.

He suppressed a sigh. "Where do you live in the States?" He picked up his wineglass, figuring he'd need a belt to get through this long evening.

"Michigan. A town called Ann Arbor."

The red burned its way down his windpipe. He choked for a minute while she thumped him on the back. "Ann Arbor? Isn't there a big university there?"

"University of Michigan. I go to school there." She furrowed her brows. "Have you ever been there?"

He could honestly say no and shook his head. Ohio State University, where he was finishing his master's degree in architecture, was several hours away from Ann Arbor and University of Michigan's fiercest sports rival. Not that he had any time for that. Grad school was brutal, and he was determined to do well.

Not that he'd tell her anything about his schooling. She didn't seem interested at all. Probably thought of him as some hearty Greek peasant, strong but stupid. "Is your friend a student, too?"

"Emma is one of the most brilliant young mathematicians in the country."

"Which country?" He couldn't help himself. Americans were fiercely territorial about having the best, being the best.

"Any country. She has one more year until she earns her doctorate in math and already has several top job offers— Cal Tech, Jet Propulsion Labs, even MIT wants her." She leaned in close, her blue eyes snapping. "Nothing or nobody should distract her from her degree. We are here for a relaxing summer, but that's it."

"You're here for the whole summer?" He didn't know whether to groan or cheer.

"The whole summer." Funny, she didn't look pleased at the idea.

"Won't you get bored?" He spoke without thinking. Just because he needed to be active didn't mean she was the same.

"Don't worry about me—I have plenty to do. Shopping, swimming, sunbathing."

Typical tourist stuff. But for a whole summer? "Sounds fun."

She widened her eyes in alarm. "I'm not fishing for you to take me around or anything." She gestured to Niko, who was whispering to her friend. "Whatever they get up to is their business."

"Oh. Sure." Why was he disappointed? He had plenty on his plate, especially now that the new investors had signed on the dotted line for the condo villas during their slightly drunken meeting. He had to help get that real estate deal for the actual property so he could tweak the designs.

The rest of dinner was a long, drawn-out affair. Niko couldn't stop hand-feeding the giggling blonde and Cara picked at her lemon chicken until he snapped.

"What's the matter? Don't you like Greek food?"

She looked at him, her big eyes even wider. "What?"

"Your dinner." He gestured at her barely touched plate. "You won't enjoy your summer on Aphrodisias if you don't eat."

"Oh." She stared down at the uneaten remains. "I think it's the cigarette smoke. People don't smoke nearly this much at home and it's giving me a headache."

Yannis nodded. Americans often complained about the smoky atmosphere. "You need to go back to your hotel?"

"Well…" Her gaze drifted over to Niko and her friend. "I don't want to ruin Emma's evening. She works very hard and this is her first vacation in years."

"Niko will look after her."

A spark of her previous spirit resurfaced. "I'm sure he will. But yes, I need some fresh air." She dropped her napkin on the table and slid out of the booth. "Emma, honey, the cigarettes are getting to me. I'm going to call it a night."

Emma dragged her attention away from Niko and focused on her friend. "Cara, you hardly ate anything. Are you feeling okay?"

"Fine, fine." She shrugged. "I thought I'd just walk back to our villa and see Aphrodisias at night."

Emma bit her lip and looked at Niko. "Is that safe?"

"Perfectly safe, *chriso mou*. That means 'my golden one,'" he added meaningfully.

"Oh, Nick," she sighed, her fingertips fluttering at his chest. He captured her hand and brought it to his lips to kiss.

Yannis rolled his eyes and saw Cara doing an eye roll to match. At least they agreed on something.

Then Niko gave him a pleading look. Yannis gave him a narrow stare back, but gave in and stood. "I'd be happy to take Cara back to your place if that would make you feel better."

"Not necessary," Cara clipped out. "No one's going to bother me."

Yannis wasn't so sure, judging from the interested looks she was getting just in the restaurant. And the way back to her villa passed by several raucous tourist bars.

"You know, Nick, we can always get together some other time," Emma offered, pulling her hand from his friend's grip.

Cara must have seen the other couple's disappointment, since she visibly softened. "Okay, Yannis, I'll take you up on your offer. Emma, you stay and enjoy yourself."

Niko quickly masked his triumph. "Cara, nice to see you again, and I hope you feel better soon. Emma, have you ever seen the sea by moonlight?"

Yannis took this as his cue to hustle Cara out the door before she could wreck Niko's grand plan. Cara walked in front of him, showing the long slender curve of her spine. He caught up to her near the bar where a group of people blocked her and put his hand on her back.

She stopped, startled. "Yannis?"

He fought down his reaction to her silky-smooth skin and instead steered her through the crowd. Once they were clear, though, he wasn't in any hurry to remove his hand.

They emerged into the warm night air and Cara took several deep breaths, forcing Yannis to drop his hand.

"Better?" he inquired.

"Much." She laughed, walking away and giving him a nice eyeful of how her hips swayed under the tight green skirt. "Can you believe I used to be a smoker?"

He followed her before she could catch him staring. "Really?" She didn't seem like the type.

"For four or five years. And now I can't stand to be around it for very long. When I first quit, I would purposely stand close to people smoking so I could breathe in some fumes. Secondhand smoke was better than nothing. Are you a smoker?"

"No, I never started. I must be the only Greek man on the island who doesn't smoke."

"I thought so—you smell really good."

"I do?"

"Well, not like stale smoke," she backpedaled, picking up her pace.

He sighed inwardly. Not willing to give an inch. They were almost back to her villa anyway. Cara suddenly slowed at the entrance to a discotheque, Greek pop music pulsing through the air.

"You like to dance?" he asked.

"Sometimes." She was tapping her toes, though, their red-painted nails peeking out through her sexy high-heeled shoes.

"Come on." He caught her elbow and guided her into the dark club, ignoring her protests. Time for him to be a stereotypical overbearing Greek male. "You want to dance, let's dance."

She was yelling at him and gesturing ferociously, almost like a native Greek. Fortunately, he couldn't hear her over the music and just shook his head and pointed at his ears.

She glared at him for a minute, but the heavy beat of the music was getting to her. He started moving his shoulders and she joined him, gradually relaxing enough to swing her hips in time to the beat. "That's it," he shouted. "You're a great dancer."

She relented and gave him a slight smile, raising her arms as she twirled in a tight circle on the crowded dance floor, colored lights flashing around them. Her breasts shifted under her thin halter, and he could swear he saw the edge of her puckered areola, waiting for *him,* Yannis Petrides, to free it from her dress and lavish attention on it. He hardened immediately as her dress gaped enough for him to see the beautiful slope of her breast, as well.

Gamoto! It was difficult to keep dancing in his aroused state. Cara did some shimmy-type moves and had turned her back to him when some drunk guy staggered by and knocked Yannis into her. He automatically wrapped his arm around her waist to keep her from falling. By some awkward coincidence, his cock rubbed her as she squirmed against him and then nestled him right between her curvy cheeks.

She froze as if in shock. He was about to apologize and explain, but groaned instead as she slowly began grinding her hips into him, her breath coming faster. His hand crept up from her waist, her heavy breast resting on his fingers. Only a few more inches to slip inside her top. It was dark there, and everybody was caressing each other in lustful abandon.

Then the music changed to Giorgios Mazonakis singing "Summer in Greece," a pop hit from a couple years ago that described foreign girls getting drunk on the beach and appreciating the sensual skills Greek men had to offer them.

She faced him, her breasts rubbing his chest. He smiled in satisfaction, and her easy expression stiffened. What now? Was it that stupid song? She jumped away from him and stalked out of the club. He considered not following her for a second.

Who was *she* to lead Yannis Petrides around like a pet goat on a string? He had no responsibility for her. He wasn't her brother, cousin, boyfriend *or* lover. Although the last…

"Gamoto!" He muttered a Greek curse and went after her. He'd promised to see her home, happily or not. And once she was there, she could stay there for the rest of the summer for all he cared.

WHY DID YANNIS have to give her that smile in the club? Just shy of a smirk, it told her, *I win and you lose.* And Cara was not about to lose anything else to a man. She'd lost enough.

She heard him following her, his breath loud and angry in the quiet streets nearing the villa. She reached the wrought-iron gate at the foot of the staircase leading up to her place and turned. His face was shadowed, but she could feel the tension radiating off him.

"Thanks for bringing me home, Yannis." Her tone meant the exact opposite.

"My pleasure, Cara." His tone was a match.

She unlocked the gate and passed through, acutely aware of his stare as she climbed the stairs. She rounded the corner onto the landing and his steps sounded, growing fainter and fainter.

But a noise was growing louder and louder as she approached the door to their villa. A kind of moaning, groaning sound.

Cara's shoulders slumped. She recognized that sound. Sure, it had been longer than she wanted to admit, but she knew the sounds of sex when she heard them.

Oh, crap. Emma and Nick must have rushed back to the villa as soon as Cara and Yannis left, passing them during their side trip into the nightclub.

Cara touched the doorknob, which turned under her grasp. Maybe Emma had managed to lure Nick as far as the bedroom, and Cara could steal some blankets and sleep on Athena's couch.

She peeked into the apartment and fought back her own groan. Apparently Nick's charm was such that they hadn't made it any farther than the rug in front of the couch. Fortunately Cara only saw Emma's legs wrapped around Nick's calves, but she had a full-on view of naked Nick's backside in all its hairy, thrusting glory.

Cara cringed and closed the door as carefully as avoiding a trip wire. So much for taking blankets—she'd use Athena's bath towels for bedding before interrupting *that* scene. She went back down the stairs and took the street that would eventually lead her back to Athena's.

"Hey, what are you doing?" a male voice called.

She jerked to a halt and cautiously looked around. Damn it, the stupid street was as dark as Hades, to coin a Greek simile. "Go away and leave me alone!" she yelled in Greek.

"Cara, it's me." A big figure appeared out of the shadows and she stifled a scream. "It's Yannis."

"Oh. Yannis."

"Sorry I startled you. You have a good Greek accent, though. Did you learn that brush-off from a phrase book?"

"Something like that." She blew out a long breath.

"Why are you wandering around out here anyway? I walked you home so you'd be safe at night."

"I'm not under house arrest, you know."

He raised his hands in mock self-defense. "Fine, do what you want. Wander around the island on a Friday night full of drunken tourists who will only see your beautiful red hair and tight dress and won't bother to listen to your Greek phrase book protests." He turned back to his Vespa, which was tucked into a corner along the sidewalk.

"Look, you're right." She hated to admit it. "I need to sleep at my friend's house tonight. *My* place is, um, occupied."

"Occupied? But your blond friend is with Niko." He trailed off into a big grin.

"Yes, yes, Emma and Niko are *together* at my place." She hoped the dim light hid the heat creeping up her cheeks.

"They must have practically run back to beat us there." He shook his head. "Not very considerate. And don't you have separate bedrooms anyway?"

"They weren't *in* her room." Geez, did she have to spell it out for him? "They were apparently overcome with passion and made it as far as the rug in front of the couch. The only thing I saw before I quietly backed away was your buddy's hairy ass!"

Yannis doubled over laughing and stayed that way for a couple minutes. "You poor girl. I'm not surprised. Niko needs to shave three times a day to keep from looking like a gorilla."

"Maybe he should shave his ass," she replied sourly.

That really sent Yannis over the edge. "Oh, Cara, I won't be able to look Niko in the face without laughing."

"What about me? I may have to pull an Oedipus and put my eyes out at the horror." She shook her head. "I hope I can sleep tonight."

"Where *are* you sleeping tonight? You have a friend on the island?" He sounded puzzled.

Cara knew she needed to be more forthcoming, especially if she wanted him to walk her to Athena's house. "I know Athena Kefalas from when I crewed charter boats on Corfu."

"Athena? She's my mother's second cousin. I know where she lives. Do you want a ride to her place?"

"Sure, that would be great." If she could get on the Vespa in her dress.

"Come on." He rolled the scooter onto the street and straddled the seat. She hesitated and then hitched her skirt up, hopping on. She grabbed the edge of the seat for balance.

He cast an amused look back at her. "Are you going to ride with me or run along behind?"

"Ha-ha." She scooted closer to him, the insides of her bare knees gripping his thighs. How long had it been since she'd gripped a man's thighs with hers? Before things had started going south in her marriage, which would be about five years ago. And her husband's thighs had never felt like this, hot and hard with muscle.

"And you have to put your arms around me so we don't tip going around corners."

She hesitated for a second. Of course Greek men didn't put their arms around each other when sharing a scooter, but she wasn't sure she had enough upper-body muscle anymore to hold on to the seat, and she already knew Yannis was a fast driver.

"Niko and your friend are probably finished if you'd rather go back."

"Oh, yuck!" Cara slapped her arms around his waist and felt his laughter. She pinched his very tight abs and he jumped. "That's for bringing up your hairy friend again."

"You sure you're not Greek? You have a well-developed sense of revenge."

"I wish," she muttered.

Yannis started the scooter with a roar and U-turned onto the narrow road. "Hold on, Cara," he called.

She did, and with pleasure. The night wind rushed by them, the smell of the ocean combining with the earthy night-blooming flowers. All they needed was fire to complete the four classical Greek elements.

He turned onto the old stone coastline road overlooking the beach. Out from the shadow of the overhanging houses, Cara tipped her head up to the sky.

There was the fire, the stars that had looked down on Aphrodisias since time began, the stars that had been named and turned into legend by Yannis's ancestors, but never tamed.

Untamed like Yannis. Under his urbane clothes, he was earth with a core of fire, his body radiating heat out to her hands through his silky shirt.

Silk or synthetic blend? She stifled a slightly hysterical giggle at her mind's attempt to bring her body back under control.

But it was a futile attempt, considering how his very presence was softening her like the afternoon sun on the beach. She brushed her hand over his stomach and moved closer, her legs gliding along him.

The scooter jerked slightly, as if he'd tightened his grip on the handlebars.

And he smelled so good, like Greek bay leaves with a hint of lemon. She inhaled again, hungrily but quietly. The machine's vibrations were softening her, too, sending jolts between her thighs as they bounced along the uneven pavement. Her nipples hardened against his back, their sensitive tips aching for his touch.

Soon they would leave the coastline and move inland to Athena's house and her time with Yannis would be over. She'd made it plenty clear to him earlier in the evening that she was just tolerating him for Emma's sake, but the truth was, Cara couldn't handle a man like him.

Coward. Where was the eighteen-year-old girl who'd left home after a lifetime of her parents' squabbles? Where was the twenty-one-year-old woman who had crewed one hundred thousand nautical miles over two oceans and five seas?

Lost. As lost as Odysseus wandering the Aegean for ten years. And it had been exactly ten years since she graduated high school and left home. Funny, she had seen herself more like Odysseus's long-suffering wife, Penelope, weaving, wringing her hands and waiting for her husband to stop lolling around with seductive nymphs and haul his butt back home.

Constantine Constantinos, her very own Greek husband, had never come home from the nymphs, and Cara had done her share of hand-wringing and waiting, choosing to leave the weaving to Athena.

Maybe it was time to take a page out of Homer and indulge in her own lolling. Yannis Petrides was as endlessly seductive as anything from Greek legend.

6

"YANNIS?"

He jolted the scooter again as her breath tickled the back of his neck. She was lucky she hadn't sent him swerving off the road every time she pressed her breasts against him or brushed her cool hands over his belly, mere inches above where he really wanted her to touch him. He'd never had an erection riding along on his scooter before and it wasn't a comfortable sensation.

"What is it?"

"Why don't we stop along at the beach for a minute? I haven't seen the ocean at night, and there's a full moon."

"Are you sure? It's getting late." Yannis desperately thought of things to calm down his arousal. Disgusting things, like slimy piles of seaweed, washed-up octopi, red-headed half-naked mermaids…no, not that last one.

"Yannis, take me to the beach."

He didn't hear much past her first three words. *Yannis, take me.* But he pulled off into one of the parking lots that dotted the shore and cut the engine. "Well, we're here," he said cheerfully, as if he weren't trying desperately not to embarrass himself.

Cara put her hands on his hips and boosted herself off the scooter, surveying the black expanse of water dotted with moonlight. Figured, it was a clear night, perfect for romance.

Yannis guessed he had himself back under control and stood. Then Cara bent over to remove her sexy black sandals, and his control went under. The perfect halves of her bottom outlined in her tight skirt, the slit in the middle hiking up to where he could see what seemed like a meter of pale thigh.

"Oh!" She lost her balance and started to tip forward onto the pavement. He moved quickly and hooked an arm around her waist, dragging her bottom flush up against his crotch again. His erection went from zero to sixty at her closeness.

She gave a little gasp and looked over her shoulder at him, her full lips slightly parted.

"You okay?" It was the only thing he could think of to say. He gently eased her away from him and she nodded. He shoved his hands in his pockets and fervently wished that flat-front, tight-cut pants were not the fashion.

Cara slung her shoes in the small basket behind the seat. "Want to walk?" She was already stepping onto the rocky path leading down to the water, making little exclamations of pain until she rapidly passed onto the sand. "Ooh, the sand's cool."

Maybe he should pack some into his pants. He took a deep breath.

"Yannis, take your shoes off, too."

He conceded and set his Italian leather slip-ons and thin socks next to the back tire. His feet were tougher than hers and the rocks didn't bother him. "Where to?"

She was already pattering away. "The water." She stopped at the water's edge and fearlessly waded in up to her knees. When a larger wave started to crest, she pulled up her skirt even farther. She saw him waiting in the sand. "Come in with me, Yannis. It's lovely and warm."

Not as lovely as she was, her skin silvered by the moonlight. "I can't. I'm not wearing a short dress like you."

She giggled. "And for that, I'm glad."

He couldn't help laughing, as well. This side of Cara was one he'd never seen, happy and playful. "Yeah, lucky for you."

"If you don't want to get seawater on your pants, you could just take them off," she suggested teasingly.

"Oh, yeah? And, what, wander around on the beach in my underwear?" Not that his swimsuit wasn't about the same coverage as his briefs, but psychologically it was very different.

"I will if you will."

Her suggestion zapped him like Cupid's arrow. Her gaze met his, slightly nervous but steady. "And where are we supposed to leave our clothing while we play in the water?"

"Up there." She pointed behind to a spot along the boulders framing the beach. "A cabana—looks like it's empty." She hiked up to the building and once again, he followed.

The empty cabana was a small wooden shack set back among the boulders, providing some privacy for its occupants. The doors were padlocked shut, but he noticed a narrow patio, some beach chairs and a chaise longue. "Are you sure?" He was asking her more than just about a moonlight swim.

"Positive. And I'll go first to prove it." She unfastened the bow behind her neck. The green fabric dropped to her waist, baring her breasts.

Yannis gaped at her. She had a belly button ring—a big round stone that glittered like the waves under the moon. "You have a ring there. I never expected you to have *that*."

She grinned at him. "Why? You thought I was too stuffy to get my navel pierced?"

"Maybe."

"I was a wild girl in my youth."

He laughed. She talked as if she were ancient, instead of a ripe, sexy woman in her prime. "Wild enough to swim naked?"

"Sometimes."

"Still wild enough to swim naked with me?"

"What do you think?" She crossed her forearms under her breasts, offering them up to him.

As he stared, her nipples tightened even further, and he didn't think it was from the cool breeze. "I think yes." As if of its own accord, his hand lifted and hovered above her right breast.

She caught his wrist and pulled his hand to her. They gasped simultaneously. Her breast filled his palm, full and heavy like an apple ripe for the picking. He instinctively thumbed her nipple, making her shudder.

Encouraged, he cupped her other breast, teasing and plucking at the hard berries of her nipples. She tipped back her head. "Oh, Yannis."

He'd never felt skin so soft, so smooth before and closed his eyes in sheer sensual pleasure. Then suddenly, his hands were empty.

Cara had stepped back from him and dropped the rest of her dress to the sand. She spun on her heel and ran toward the water wearing only a tiny pair of black panties. "Last one in is a rotten egg!" she cheerfully called over her shoulder.

She'd literally pulled heaven from his grasp and now she called him a rotten egg? Yannis stripped down to his briefs and charged after her. No matter. A true man of Aphrodisias could pleasure a woman just as easily in the water.

CARA HOPED the crash of the waves masked the beating of her heart. She'd been so, so close to dragging Yannis down on the beach furniture and having her way with him, but panic had made her pull away.

Her feet splashed in the warm surf and she dived into the breaking waves as soon as she was deep enough. So much for her hair. She had bigger concerns. Where was Yannis? She scanned the water. Had she lured him to his doom? What if he'd gotten a cramp from diving in? Or gotten stung by a jellyfish? Sure, they were rare, but you never could tell what the ocean current would bring.

"Yannis?" she called out, stifling a squawk as his head broke the water next to her.

"Miss me?" His hair was black and glossy against his scalp, droplets of water beading on his full upper lip.

"Were you gone?" she retorted automatically.

He gave her what could only be described as a smirk. "You've been waiting for me." He pulled her to him, his hot skin sliding over hers, her nipples catching on the mat of black hair furring his chest.

She swallowed hard. She hadn't realized it until now, but she *had* been waiting for someone to break through her shell of indifference and bring her back to life. Snow White in her glass coffin, Sleeping Beauty in her tower of thorns, and most fitting considering the surroundings, the statue of Galatea brought to life by Aphrodite herself for sake of a love-struck Pygmalion.

No more waiting for someone to rescue her. That *someone* was *her*. Cara Lillian Sokol Constantinos would break through her own self-imposed prison and come back to life.

She laughed giddily, the rusty sound echoing over the water.

"What?" Yannis tightened his grip on her as if afraid she'd run from him again.

"This." She twined her legs around his and grabbed his ears to pull her mouth to his. He eagerly met her kiss, their wet lips softening and sliding on each other, nipping and teasing gently and then more frantically. She wrapped her arms around his broad shoulders, enjoying how easily he supported them both in the water. He still wore his bikini briefs but they couldn't hide the erection pressing on her thigh.

His tongue dived inside her mouth, exploring every corner of that moist cavern and stroking along her own tongue. He tasted of that potent red wine, but of something more, too, something uniquely his own flavor.

She dipped her tongue into his mouth, but he closed his teeth to her when she would continue. She pulled back. "What? Greek men are too macho to get a woman's tongue in their mouth?"

"Believe me, I can't speak for other Greek men, but I'm, uh, pretty ticklish." He gave her a sheepish glance.

"Ticklish? All over?" She stroked down along the hard curve of his back and grabbed two handfuls of firm ass through his briefs. "Here?"

He groaned and thrust his hips into hers. "No, not there."

She slipped her hands under his waistband and touched his bare buttocks, cupping and pinching him. "How about now?"

"Oxi." He shook his head. She smiled as he unknowingly slipped into Greek.

"And here?" She slid her fingers around to the bulge in front, clasping his thick erection and heavy sac.

He was past words now, English or Greek, only gasping as she fondled him. Like most European men, Yannis was uncircumcised, his foreskin and tip obviously extremely sensitive. She played with him, stroking his silky hot skin as his balls tightened under her touch. Slippery fluid leaked from him, mixing with the gentle seawater.

"Stop," he gritted out, clasping her wrist painfully. "Stop now." He was almost panting with the effort to rein himself in.

She let go, not wanting to accidentally hurt him. "Didn't you like that?"

"Too much." He wasn't joking, his face tight and almost pained. "Damned if I'll lose control without pleasing you first."

He reached under the water and actually tore her bikini panties off her, breaking the strings over her hips. The savage act made her gasp. He tossed the black silk away in the water where it quickly sank.

She floated totally naked, the water rushing over the heated skin between her thighs.

"Now." He dragged her to him again. "Wrap your legs around me, and when I make you come the first time, don't scream too loudly. Sound carries over water, and unless you want an audience...?" He lifted a brow, and Cara realized he didn't care if the whole island watched them. She'd let the tiger out of the cage, and it wasn't interested in returning anytime soon. She shook her head. No audience for her.

She wrapped her legs around his waist as he commanded, her pussy resting against his belly, his erection still rock-hard on her bottom.

His fingers dived and unerringly found her clit. She tossed back her head and moaned.

"There. So hot, so wet." He stroked her swollen button leisurely. "Tell me, Cara, *mou,* when I put my mouth here later, will you prove to be a natural redhead?"

She smacked his shoulder, and he laughed. "No matter, you have a redhead's temper. Are you a woman who will scratch my back or bite me when I am pumping between your thighs?"

"Who says you'll find out?" she said with as much bravado as she could muster with his hand pinching her aching clit.

"I do." His fingers sped up. "I knew as soon as you showed me your beautiful tits in the moonlight. You'll let me do whatever I want to you, and then beg me for more."

Cara's protest broke off into a squeal as Yannis bent and captured a nipple in his mouth. His clever mouth teased and sucked her breast into an aching peak as his fingers moved over her clit. She rocked frantically on his belly, his cock rubbing her sensitive inner folds.

Yannis let go of her nipple and she choked back a sob.

"That's not enough, is it, baby?" She shook her head, and he worked his hand between their bodies. "Move back for a second."

She eased away and was amply rewarded by a callused finger slipping in and out of her. "More, more," she begged.

"This?" He added another finger and did a little scissoring motion deep inside her that stretched her wide, wider than she'd been for a long time. But still not as wide as his cock would stretch her. She felt his fingers play in her juices, stroking the walls of her passage.

His thumb brushed her clit over and over and he dipped his glossy head to her breasts, caressing his smooth-shaven cheek over each mound. "So soft, so pretty," he murmured, his Greek accent becoming thicker. His cock, still imprisoned in his briefs, bobbed between her buttocks. She wished she could just free him and take him into her body, but obviously had no handy condoms stashed anywhere.

Yannis found a sensitive spot with his fingertips and pressed. Cara yelped. Was that her G-spot? She'd thought that was as mythological as the Minotaur.

Obviously encouraged by her response, he worked it until she was panting and writhing, her hips creating their own tide as they rode up and down his hand.

He captured a nipple in his mouth and sucked hard, his blue gaze silvery in the moonlight. She slipped her fingers through his hair and held him there, his lips and tongue sending currents of lust down to where his fingers pleasured her.

She knew she couldn't last much longer; it had been so long since she'd felt even close to this level of desire. "Yannis!" She was startled to hear the neediness in her voice echo over the water, but was powerless to resist him.

He abandoned her breast and captured her mouth just as her orgasm washed over her with the force of a tidal wave, sweeping her away until she thought she might drown from its power. She screamed his name into the wet cavern of his mouth, begging him to let her go, to make the sensual torment cease.

He was merciless, though, trapping her with a net woven of her own pleasure, making her ride the climactic wave once or maybe even twice more before he stopped.

She released his shoulders and floated in the water, boneless as a jellyfish. Still holding her lower body firmly against him, Yannis withdrew his fingers from her. Instead of washing them off in the ocean, however, he lifted them to his lips and tasted them. "Delicious. Salty and sexy, like the sea."

Cara could only stare at his obvious enjoyment of her. He took her silence for acquiescence and tugged her toward shore.

She finally found her voice. "I guess it's your turn now."

"Who said you don't get another?" He found his footing on the hard-packed sand and swung her naked into his arms, her panties probably washed up on Crete by now. She looped her arms around his neck and looked around anxiously to make sure they were still the only beachgoers.

"Yannis, put me down. I'm too heavy for you." She didn't want to get sand in her more delicate parts when he dropped her.

"You think I am so weak?" He carried her easily uphill on the soft sand toward the cabana.

A rush of excitement ran through her despite her protests as she saw how dark and powerful his hands were on her pale skin. The breeze tightened her nipples, and he slid his hand around to cup her breast again, brushing its sensitive tip. His other hand squeezed her thigh, promising additional delights.

She loosened her grip and combed her fingers through the black mat on his chest, toying with his golden chain and medal before exploring further. His pecs were like rock, capped with tight little peaks that hardened under her leisurely touch.

He groaned deep in his throat. "Cara, you redheaded witch." They had reached the cabana and he set her not-so-steadily on her feet.

She laughed with delight and ran her hands down his abs to his poor, overworked briefs. Despite his halfhearted protests, she stripped them down to his ankles, returning to kneel in front of him. Freed from constriction, he was even thicker and longer than she'd realized, his dark shaft jutting out proudly from a nest of thick black curls that cradled a heavy sac. The head was eggplant-purple and beads of his desire shone in the moonlight.

Yannis was a man on the brink, and Cara was going to push him over it.

"Cara, wait." He stopped her just as she was about to take him in her mouth. "I have something in my wallet. Let me come inside you."

Cara hesitated. To fully let him inside her body? She'd not done that with anyone since Con, and those occasions with him had been memorable only in their mediocrity.

Yannis stood silently, not coaxing or pressuring her, but definitely tempting her. If he was so skilled with his fingers, how much pleasure could he bring her moving inside her, thrusting, pushing, teasing… She stood so abruptly her head spun.

"Yes." That was the only word she spoke, but it unleashed a hurricane. With one smooth move, Yannis set her on the reclining chaise, grabbed his wallet and pulled out a packet.

He set it at the foot of the chaise and lay on his side next to her. "Yes." He echoed her and then dipped his head to hers. Like the Greek pirate he resembled, he plundered her mouth, nipping and sucking her lips until they were sensitive and puffy.

She squirmed under him as he dragged his fingers up her thigh and found her red curls. Without the seawater to wash her juices away, she could feel her moisture slick up his fingertips again as he played with her folds, teasing them apart before landing on her clit. She arched off the chaise. "Oh, Yannis, *now.*"

His laughter was quick and joyful as he protected himself and moved between her thighs. "Now."

She let out a scream as he sank into her with one stroke. Her legs quivered as she hooked them around his waist, not wanting to ever release him. He closed his magnificent eyes and gasped out her name. "Cara, I could *live* inside you."

She closed her own eyes at his heartfelt compliment. Then he began to move, and that was the biggest compliment of all. He was too far gone to hold back and tease her as he had in the water, slamming in and out instead. It was wild and savage with the moon silvering his curls and the waves crashing on the beach in time to her heart.

Cara dug her heels into his ass, her fingernails sinking into his shoulders. His gold medal swayed with his efforts, brushing her face as he moved above her. His cock dipped and plunged, stretching her wider than she'd ever been. Surely, she couldn't come again, not with just his thrusting.

But to her surprise, desire washed over her again. He angled up so the base of his cock bumped her clit. He throbbed and pulsed inside her, grunting as he moved in and out.

Cara slipped her finger between them, desperate to enhance his touch. Her fingernail scraped his cock, and he groaned again. A few quick strokes over her clit and she was as wound as he was.

The knot of tension tightened unbearably and then Cara flew apart underneath him, writhing and twisting as her world narrowed to his body on top of hers and his shaft inside her.

His face pulled into a grimace and he let himself go with a bellow, slamming her deep into the cushion. Cara muffled her scream in his shoulder, clutching and grabbing at him like a wild animal.

He collapsed onto her, his breath hot and fast on her neck. His medal dug into her skin, but it was just proof of his passion for her.

After a few minutes, he stirred and shifted out of her onto his side. His expression was languid and sleepy but sharpened as he looked down at her. "My medal marked your fair skin." He traced a small circle on her chest. "I should have been more gentle, but…" He shook his head. "I didn't mean to be so rough."

Cara's eyes widened as she saw several purple marks on Yannis's chest. "Me, either." She gingerly touched one and he looked down in surprise.

"Cara, you bit me." He noticed the other bruises. "Several times."

Her face heated, and she was glad for the shadows. "Sorry."

He laughed heartily and then winced. "Oh, my back." He sat up and rotated his shoulders to face her. "Tell me, did you scratch me, too?"

She gulped. Yannis looked as if he'd been in a fight with a cougar—and lost. "There are some red lines, yes." Her face had to be as red as his scratches. "They should fade by Monday, and if not…" She gave a casual shrug. "Something for you and the guys at work to joke about when you take off your shirt." She laughed brightly.

He didn't laugh in return. "The guys at work, as you call them, won't be laughing over this because it's none of their damn business. I'll leave my shirt on until they heal. How does the phrase go? I don't kiss and tell. Or tell about anything else."

"Oh," Cara whispered. She seemed to have stumbled on a genuine gentleman. She smiled up at him but broke into a yawn.

"Rest here for a second. I'll get cleaned up and then take you to Athena's house." He pulled a beach blanket over her and went around the corner. The tension that had bugged her since coming to Aphrodisias was finally gone, thanks to her amazing encounter with Yannis. She yawned and closed her eyes to rest for a minute until Yannis came back. Maybe there was something to this whole goddess of love thing….

"HEY, YOU BUMS, get out of here!"

Yannis bolted upright from the chaise, where a very naked Cara curled around him. Her blue eyes opened wide and she dived back under the beach blanket with a squeak.

"Yannis? What are *you* doing here?" His cousin Vasilios regarded him openmouthed. Yannis grabbed for his pants and bit back a curse. He hadn't planned on sleeping in the cabana, but when he'd come back for Cara she'd looked so peaceful he joined her rather than waking her and driving her to Athena's place.

"Vasos, sorry, is this part of your hotel? I didn't know." Yannis hastily buckled his belt and moved in front of the lump under the blankets that was Cara.

"It's okay." Vasos was too distracted now to chew him out, craning his neck to see first off, who the girl under the blanket was and secondly, if she was naked.

"Come with me, Vasos." Yannis caught his cousin by the elbow and steered him around the corner out of sight of Cara, hoping she would take the hint and dress.

"Yanni, who is that?" Vasos asked.

"Nobody you know." Vasos pouted. "Oh, okay, a tourist girl I met." If he didn't give Vasos some information, his cousin's speculations would be worse.

"Figures. You get all the luck."

"Don't give me that bullshit, Vasos, you've gotten more than your share of invitations up to rooms once your shift is finished."

His cousin preened. "Yeah, did I ever tell you about that Spanish girl who was all over me in April?"

"No." Then Yannis had to listen to his cousin's exploits while Cara was hopefully dressing. His cousin had just launched into the part where the girl had danced the flamenco naked for him when Yannis elbowed him.

Cara had found a scarf to cover her wild red hair and large sunglasses to hide her eyes. A lady of mystery, she was wearing the backless gown without a stitch under it, Yannis knew, and in the bright morning sunlight she looked naughty and sexy, a bad girl who'd stayed out all night having sex on the beach.

Vasos gave a low whistle and Yannis elbowed him harder this time. His cousin rubbed the sore spot but cheerfully asked, "Aren't you going to introduce me to your friend, Yannis?"

"No. And keep quiet about this, or else your mother will find out about the naked Spanish dancing girl."

"No fair." Vasos frowned while Yannis offered Cara his arm to help her up the path to where his scooter was luckily still parked.

Yannis turned back to his cousin. *"Efkhareestó, ksathelfos."*

Vasos smiled. "Yeah, you're welcome, cousin. But next time, find a room." He turned away and started dragging the beach furniture out onto the sand.

Cara still hadn't said a word since they woke. "Are you all right, Cara? I'm so sorry I fell asleep. I didn't plan to keep you out all night."

"It's okay." Her voice was morning-rough and sexy. Maybe from screaming his name several times? "I hope Emma's not too worried."

Niko had probably kept Emma too busy to worry, but

Yannis just nodded. Uncle Gus and Aunt Eleni wouldn't say anything to him. After all, he was a grown man and given way more leeway than Uncle Gus's daughters, who would have been locked in their rooms if they'd stayed out all night with a man. Which was probably why they were in Athens and not on Aphrodisias.

Cara made a sound of distress and stopped walking. "What is it?"

She lifted her foot and wiggled it. "Just a sharp rock."

"Let me check if it broke the skin." He dropped to his knees before her and rested her foot on his knee. He brushed away the sand and checked her skin, but it appeared okay aside from a small red mark. "You might have a little bruise, but no bleeding."

"Thank you, Yannis." She unconsciously flexed her toes on his thigh, making him want to suck on their shiny red tips. He cupped her ankle and stroked her calf up to the hollow behind her knee. Her breath caught, her full lips slightly parted. They were bare and pink and just as sexy as when she'd worn the glossy red lipstick last night. If he ran his hand up just a bit farther, he'd caress her bare bottom.

"Yannis." Her urgent voice snapped him out of where he'd actually begun to stroke the back of her thigh. "Stand up, or else your cousin is going to think you're proposing to me."

He stood so fast, she almost lost her balance. He steadied her and then swung her into his arms with a muttered Greek curse. He carried her up the rocky path and set her next to the scooter. She brushed off her feet and slipped them into the sandals. He slipped on his own shoes, not bothering with his socks.

He hopped on the seat. "Ready?" She settled behind

him and wrapped her arms around his waist. His arousal came roaring back, but too late to do anything about it. He gunned the engine and zoomed away, teeth gritted at the press of her practically naked breasts. Unfair. He was back to where he was yesterday, and his sexy night with Cara had just whetted his appetite for more.

7

"MORE COFFEE, CARA? Cara? Do you want more coffee?" Athena tapped her spoon against the copper coffeepot and Cara jumped.

"What?" She jerked up from where she'd been doodling patterns with her fork in the leftover almond cake crumbs and saw Athena pointing at the long-handled coffeepot. "Oh, no, thank you." She'd been mentally reliving her time on the beach with Yannis and just reached the part where he easily carried her up the sandy slope to the cabana. She checked herself quickly. Athena would doubtless notice her woolgathering.

Athena just smiled at her. "It was good of you to spend the morning with me while Demetria is out. She doesn't like to leave me alone, but she always runs errands on Monday."

"I don't mind visiting at all, and you're looking much better. Not so pale."

Athena clattered the dishes in the sink. "You think so?"

"Oh, yes. When Emma and I first came over, you were white, almost like a ghost."

"Mmm."

Cara stood and carried her plate and cup to the sink. "What would you like to do this morning? We can go for lunch at the café around the corner if you want to get out of the house."

"Yes, that would be nice." Athena washed the dishes in a twinkling of an eye, brushing aside Cara's attempts to help. She was just drying her hands when the old black phone in the front hallway rang.

Cara let Athena answer it while she wiped down the already-gleaming stove and countertop. Her friend's voice rose in bursts of frustration interspersed with silence. Whoever had called was obviously irritating Athena.

"And that is all you have to say to me? I may be an old woman but I am not senile!" The phone slammed in the cradle and Cara rinsed the dishcloth and hung it to dry. Athena stomped back into the kitchen, her black eyes snapping.

"Are you okay, Athena?"

"No, I am not. Some thief is trying to wreck my museum project. We are going out." Athena gripped Cara's elbow with surprising strength and steered her toward the front door.

"Wait, don't you need your walker?"

Athena never broke stride. "That thing makes me look old and weak. You will be my support today."

Cara settled Athena into the front seat of Demetria's blue compact car and started the engine. "Where to?"

"Left here and then the road leading out of town. We are going to visit one of the hill bandits."

"Hill bandits? Didn't they all give up, oh, about a hundred years ago?"

Athena gave her a baleful glance. "Their descendants merely found similar occupations, occupations where they can steal and rob without fear of arrest. When you come to the corner, turn right."

Cara steered along a narrow road through groves of olive trees, their pale green leaves silvered with dust. The road opened to a clearing where construction workers busily put the finishing touches on an ostentatious villa. "Is this where the hill bandit lives?"

"The hill bandit built this overdone heap. And sold it to a bunch of *xenoi*. Park here next to the trailer."

Cara pulled over and stopped, circling around to help Athena out of the low seat. Once standing, Athena moved with surprising agility around the construction supplies and over the uneven ground. She established herself square in the middle of the front veranda, cupped her hands in front of her mouth and shouted in Greek, "Gus Galanopoulos, you old thief, come out and face me like a man!"

Geez, Athena was a master of insults—combining blows to this guy's age, honesty, as well as his manhood in one sentence.

The leaded glass front door slammed open and a man with graying curls strode out wearing a paint-stained, white T-shirt and a tool belt riding low under his straining belly. He tossed his cigarette butt to the ground. "Athena Kefalas, no one comes to my job site and calls me names. Get out of here before you fall and break your other hip."

Cara frowned at him, then remembered that, per Athena's instructions, she wasn't supposed to understand Greek. Still, she could always say she disapproved of this Gus guy's tone.

"You! You must have fallen and broken your head if you think I'll let you get away with stealing that land for my museum."

Oh. Cara nodded to herself. Gus was probably trying to get the museum property for one of his villas he sold to *xenoi*, or foreigners. But Cara had thought the land, at least, was a done deal.

Gus and Athena exchanged a few more insults before Gus bellowed, "Yannis! Yannis! Get down here!"

Yannis? No, the odds were it was a different guy. Half the men on the island were named some version of Ioannis, or John, the other half Nick.

"What, Uncle Gus?" a voice shouted back. It *was* the same Yannis. With odds like that, she should have played the lottery. He came around the side of the house, his sweaty muscular chest outlined in his tight, white T-shirt, his leather tool belt framing his zipper as if to emphasize the mighty nice tool inside. Oh, boy. Cara wanted to strip him naked, except for his belt and work boots, and have her way with him on a stack of drywall.

He spotted her, too, coming to her side. "Cara? What are you doing here?" He had to raise his voice to be heard over the shouting. Although to be honest, Greeks usually talked like that anyway.

"Athena asked me to drive her here. Sorry, I didn't know she'd come to brawl with Gus here. Is he your boss?"

"Yeah, my boss and my uncle."

Gus stopped yelling long enough to tug Yannis away from Cara to stand next to him. As though it was boys against girls. "Yannis, do you see what happens when old crones interfere in men's work?"

Athena narrowed her eyes. "Men's work, hah! A real man would not dishonor the wishes of the dead. *Kyria* Nomikou meant to sell me that land for a museum to honor our ancestors."

"Well, now she's *with* her ancestors, and her grandson wants to sell the land to *me*."

"Such disrespect!" Athena advanced on Gus, her gnarled forefinger pointing menacingly at his nose. In her long, black dress and with her wild, dark eyes, she looked like a witch about to curse him. "You bring shame to our island."

Gus involuntarily took a step back, his hands twitching

in the sign to repel the Evil Eye that a lot of Greeks believed in. And Athena was looking mighty evil at this point.

Cara shot Yannis a glance. He seemed more amused than frightened, but then he probably didn't know Athena as well as she did.

"*Kyria* Kefalas." Gus held up his hands in reconciliation. "There is no shame in building houses and making jobs for our young people here on Aphrodisias. If all our children leave to find work, our island will slowly wither away."

"My museum will give them jobs, too, and not ones that dry up once the houses are finished. And who can afford these homes anyway?" She gestured at the immense villa with contempt. "Foreigners, who were happy to invade us and starve us when you and I were young. *Xenoi,* who come for the summer and leave them empty for the rest of the year. Empty houses on an empty island. Is that what you want?"

"Where is your grandson Spiro? Where are my daughters? They are all in Athens. Will they ever move back home?" Gus threw up his arms. "Who knows? But right now there is nothing here for my daughters unless they want to be shop clerks or hotel maids. And they do not. Does Spiro want to be a bartender or a tour boat captain?"

Athena shook her head. "No, but Gus, this is not the way—"

"Eh! Do not talk to me of empty islands, then. I *will* buy that land, and I *will* build those villas. And if I have to sell them to the man in the moon, I will." He turned on his heel and left.

Athena pursed her lips and headed back to the car. Cara started to follow her to make sure she wouldn't trip, but Yannis caught Cara's elbow, stroking the tender skin in the crook of her arm. "Cara."

"Yannis." Her whisper came out huskier than she planned.

"God, you smell great." He tipped his head down and inhaled deeply. "What is that, peaches?"

"Yeah, but you smell great, too."

He laughed. "Oh, yeah, construction work in the summer makes me smell like a flower."

He did smell wonderful, like sun and warm leather, sweat and sexy man. "Cara, I think my uncle and Athena are fighting over some property, but I don't want it to interfere with us."

"Me, either." She couldn't stop staring at his lips.

"I had a great time Friday night, and I want to see you again." Both of them were breathing faster, and she knew exactly how he wanted to see her. Naked and underneath him.

"What time do you finish today?"

"Three, but I might have to come back in the evening, depending on what the crew gets done."

"I'll meet you here at three, then we can go for a drive in the country." She was getting him naked as soon as possible.

"But Cara, I really should go home and shower first, and then we can…" His protest died as she ran her tongue around her lips suggestively. "Three o'clock."

"Don't be late." She swung her hips as she walked away. He was silent for a second and then started shouting orders to the crew to work faster.

She tamped down her grin as she reached the car, where Athena was waiting for her.

"So, Karoleena, you've met Yannis Petridis before? His mother is my second cousin."

"Yeah, his friend Niko is spending time with Emma." She gave a casual shrug. "We met that way."

Athena sat silently for a couple minutes as they drove back into town. "Karoleena, I have another favor to ask you. Spend time with Yannis. As much as you can."

"What?" Cara stared at her friend for a second and then had to swerve to avoid a stray goat.

"Yannis works for his uncle. He may tell you things about this project we are fighting over. And you can make up things to tell him. We can confuse Gus—not a difficult thing to do," she muttered.

"I don't know…" Cara didn't want to seem eager to help Athena's machinations. Heaven only knew where *that* would lead them.

"Please, *chriso mou*, it would help the weaving and women's art museum. There is nothing here on Aphrodisias to celebrate our mothers' achievements."

"Not my mother. Her only achievement was to make our lives miserable." She bit her lip, but the bitterness had burst from her before she could stifle it. She focused out the windshield and steered toward town.

"Karoleena." Athena's voice was gentle. "Karoleena, from what you have told me, your mother was a very insecure woman, and your father did nothing to help her feel better."

Huh. That was an understatement. From what she could remember and then later piece together, her father had had a string of bimbos on the side for many years.

"And I have always considered you to be a Greek woman."

"Why? Because I was once married to a Greek man?"

"No. You have the soul of a Greek woman. Strong yet caring. Proud yet humble. Fiery yet sweet."

Cara shook her head. "You're giving me too much credit. I'm not any of those."

"Bah!" Athena threw up her hands. She was the only person Cara knew who could get away with saying "bah." Athena continued, "I see it in you. I could see it in you when Constantinos brought you home, and I see it still."

The dusty road blurred into mud as her eyes filled. She hurriedly pulled over to stop. "Oh, Athena, I was so weak. You don't know…" She let out a sob.

Athena pulled her into her arms, tugging Cara's head to rest on her pillowy bosom. "You think I didn't know? I, Athena Kefalas, knew everything."

"Everything?" She couldn't have.

"Everything, darling. Why do you think I made you fattening milk shakes all the time? Why do you think I always told you long, boring stories right after breakfast and lunch? You were such a polite girl to listen to me when all you wanted to do was run to the bathroom and get rid of all my good cooking. I knew it all."

"I had bulimia." It was a relief to admit it.

"Yes." Athena's chin bobbed against her curls. "Oxhunger—a word I wish we Greeks had never had to invent. I told Constantinos you needed help, that you were desperately unhappy, but—"

"All he could see was that I was thin and pretty and looked good in my party dresses."

"Blind, stupid man, concerned only with himself!" Athena spit out. "His father was my cousin, but that did not make me blind to his faults after being his housekeeper for fifteen years. He did not see your hair I pulled from the drain, your bones sticking through your skin."

She took Cara's shoulders and pushed her away, her black eyes piercing Cara. "Constantinos failed you. *I* failed you." She overrode Cara's protests. "No! It has worn heavy on my heart since you left Greece. Seeing you so healthy and well has lightened my spirits." She yanked Cara close again and kissed her on each cheek, wiping away her tears. "Now if only I could see you happy."

"I am happy," Cara protested.

"No. You are not miserable. That is not the same thing." Athena smiled. "But you *will* be happy. I promise."

CARA FINISHED winding her hair into long ringlets and stood back to survey the results in her bathroom mirror. Her white, sleeveless, linen blouse ended right above the waistband of her pale peach shorts.

Her cheeks were flushed and pink, and she had the same kind of giddy relief that had once come with her eating disorder, but without the accompanying shame.

She had admitted all of it to Athena, and Athena hadn't judged her harshly. In fact, Athena had known it already and had worried over her. Just like a mother. The sly old lady. Cara laughed out loud.

Geez, all of Athena's excruciatingly long stories about her children, grandchildren, cousins, Greek mythology, even the in-depth descriptions of how to string looms for different tapestries had been an attempt to get Cara even a bit of nutrition from her meals.

Athena was a plotter, like her mythological namesake. Was she encouraging Cara to see Yannis for cloak-and-dagger reasons, or was her matchmaking radar picking up some interesting signals?

Cara decided she didn't care and slicked some coppery gloss over her lips. She tied a peach silk scarf over her hair for the drive and grabbed her sunglasses.

When she exited the bathroom, she found Emma in the kitchen pouring some fizzy lemonade into a blue wine-glass.

"Hey, Cara, how was your day with Athena?" She began slicing some ripe melon and arranging the pieces on a blue-and-yellow stoneware plate sitting on the countertop.

Cara smiled. How to describe the day's ups and downs? She settled for the simple. "We took a drive, saw Yannis, and I'm going to meet him in a few minutes."

Emma looked sidelong at her and grinned. "And you said you didn't like him. Shows what the romantic air on this island can do for you." She opened a carryout container and set a few slices of baklava and *galaktobouriko* in the middle of the melon slices. The pastries were oozing honey and nuts.

"Fancy," Cara commented. "Do you have a guest coming over?" If it was Niko again, she'd be sure to listen carefully at the door before entering.

"Nope." Emma rinsed off her hands and dried them on a towel. "All for me. I'm just as special as any guest."

Cara stopped. She'd never thought of it that way. Until she'd come to Aphrodisias, food was a necessary evil to be battled for sustenance. But to make it beautiful for herself? She'd never cared enough to try.

"Here." Emma pushed the plate toward her. "A small snack before you go. Who knows when you two will come up for air?" She laughed, and Cara joined in before hesitating over the food.

"Come on," Emma coaxed. "The old lady at the market said it was the freshest melon in Greece, and the bakery clerk said the honey for the pastries was gathered by genuine vestal virgins."

"What? There's no such thing anymore...." Cara stopped when Emma broke into laughter. "Ha-ha."

"Gotcha. Lucky for the bees, there's a shortage of

lifelong virgins around. But that doesn't mean the desserts aren't fabulous," Emma said.

Cara took a deep breath. The presentation was lovely, and at least the fruit was healthy. "Sure." She took a bite of the orange melon, its juices light and sweet in her mouth. "Yum."

Emma took a forkful of the custard pastry. "And a bit of *galaktobouriko*. You said that was your favorite."

"Okay." Cara ate the creamy filling and crunchy phyllo dough topping. It was delicious, but it didn't make her want to eat a whole pan to cover up whatever else was bothering her. "Thanks, Emma. That was great."

"Isn't it?" Emma began eating her snack with enjoyment. "Sometimes, even a taste is enough."

Cara nodded. "There was a time for me when that wasn't the case." Athena knew, why not Emma?

Emma sipped her lemonade. "No?"

"I had a problem with knowing when to stop eating, and then I felt bad, so I'd get rid of the food, um, the wrong way."

"Yeah." Her friend nodded. "I had a roommate in undergrad who did the same thing. It took us a while to figure out what she was up to, but when we did, we dragged her to campus health services. Unfortunately, they have a lot of experience with this. Are you okay now?"

Emma's matter-of-fact response silenced Cara for a minute while she blinked back tears. "Yes, I'm getting there. I haven't purged in a couple years."

"Good." Emma set down her lemonade and hugged her. "So this goes double for you." She gestured to the pretty dishes and artfully arranged food. "Make it nice for yourself. Food isn't your enemy anymore. You deserve to enjoy it. After all, it's giving you the energy to romp around with Adonis."

Cara gave her a mock frown. "Yannis."

"Right, right. You know my Greek is terrible." Emma winked and nibbled at the baklava. "Now go have fun."

FUN WAS CERTAINLY on Cara's mind as she pulled next to where Yannis was parked at his job site. She cut the engine and listened to the Greek birds singing in the trees until they were drowned out by angry bellowing.

A man was giving the crew hell, calling them the laziest SOBs on the island and questioning if they planned to finish sometime before New Year's Day. It sounded like Yannis.

The workers obviously didn't appreciate it, yelling in response. Finally Yannis shouted for them all to go home since they weren't bothering to work anyway.

Cara watched in amusement as the crew members tossed their tools in the pickups and crammed into the cabs. A couple grinned at her and one even whistled as they left. She ignored them, only having eyes for the rumpled, sweaty, sexy man coming toward her.

She climbed out of the car. "Hey, Yannis." She wanted to lean casually on the hood, but knew better in the afternoon heat.

"Cara." He stopped short when he saw her, his face ruddy from either heat or anger, plaster dust frosting his hair. She could guess what he'd look like when he was older, and he'd still be extremely sexy. "You're here."

"I told you I'd be here at three, but I didn't think you'd fire your crew just to get them out of the way."

He laughed, his tension dissipating. "Eh, they'll be back tomorrow. Tonight they'll just sit around complaining about me while they drink beer and watch football matches on satellite. No big deal."

"So they left you here all alone and unprotected?" She

ran her hand over his chest, the thin T-shirt molding to every muscle. "Strange women might come by and take advantage of you."

He groaned and caught her wrist as she found his nipple under the worn cotton. "Cara, I really should go home and clean up. It will only take me a few minutes."

She gestured to the water cooler in the bed of his truck. "Do you have water in there?"

"Yeah, some."

"You can wash the worst of the dirt off with that."

He threw up his hands. "I give up. Where *do* you want to go with me looking like this?"

"Somewhere alone."

His eyes widened. That obviously hadn't been the answer he expected. "Uh…"

"You've lived all your life on this island. Surely you know somewhere private, some place where no one ever goes."

He slowly nodded. "My grandfather's vineyard up in the hills. He's visiting his sister over on Naxos for the week."

"I assume this is your truck. Let's take it. I don't know if Athena's car can make it." Cara decided to confess her friend's schemes. She and Yannis could have at least that much honesty between them. "She was more than happy to loan it to me since she wants me to pump you."

He grinned, and Cara started to blush at the connotation. "For information, I mean. She wants to know what your uncle is up to."

"So I have to choose between being pumped and being loyal to my family?" He shook his head in mock dismay. "No choice any man should have to make."

"Oh, you!" She balled her fist and thunked him in the chest.

He grabbed her hand and kissed her wrist, his hot lips sliding over her tender skin. "You smell wonderful again—this time, like ripe, sweet melon."

"I ate some before I came here." Her hand fluttered open and he nuzzled her fingertips.

"Such pretty hands, so pale and delicate. I can practically see the blood running through your veins." He laced his fingers through hers, his rough palm against hers. "Much too fine to press on mine."

"That's not true. You work for a living, and you should be proud of that. Do you think women want a soft-handed man?" When she had been crewing sailboat charters, her hands had been as tough as his.

"I don't care what other women want. I only care what you want." He slowly drew her closer until mere inches separated their bodies. "What do you want, *latria mou?*"

He had called her his darling. How sweet. She went up on tiptoes and kissed him. It was what their first kiss should have been, tender and sweet, only their lips and hands touching. The birds had started to sing again, and Cara felt almost dizzy with their sound and the fecund smell of the trees and wildflowers.

He made no effort to deepen the kiss, only brushing his mouth over hers despite the desire radiating off him. It was absolutely the most romantic kiss she'd ever had, and she almost cried out in disappointment when he lifted his face from hers.

"Come to the vineyard with me before I lose control and take you here on your car. We'd rather not get painful metal burns in sensitive body parts."

Cara giggled at his welcome humor. Humor, she could handle. Desire, or even blinding lust, she could handle. Tenderness, she wasn't so sure. She let go of his hand and took some blankets from her car. Yannis set them in the pickup bed and helped her into the front seat.

Yannis vaulted into the driver's seat.

"Do you like surprises?"

"The truth?" He gave her another quick smile as he navigated a rough road leading uphill. "Not usually. I know what I want to do and how to do it. But you, I don't know what to expect. In the nightclub Saturday, you looked at me like you hated me, and half an hour later, we're naked in the ocean."

"You surprised me, too." She defended herself. "I thought you would be…" How did she describe a male bimbo without being deathly insulting? "Not quite so generous with your, um, togetherness skills."

He laughed heartily. "Thought I'd be, how do you say, a loser in bed?"

"Well…" She stared out the windshield, willing her blush to subside.

"Cara, I am a builder. I can make wonderful things, but only with good-quality materials. And you, *chriso mou,* are excellent material." He stroked her knee with his free hand, gliding up her thigh. "Your skin is smooth Greek marble, your eyes and hair the finest tints." He slid his hand between her legs. "And here—" he rubbed the center seam of her shorts "—the fountain of inspiration that quenches my thirst."

Cara gripped his wrist as he traced the peach fabric. "Yannis…"

"Uh-uh." He removed his hand and put it back on the steering wheel. "This time, we take our time. And today, we have all the time in the world."

8

"HERE WE ARE." YANNIS parked under a grove of olive trees
next to the vineyard and helped Cara down from the truck.

Cara surveyed the neat rows of vines stretched up the
rocky hill, the leaves dusty from the typically dry summer
weather. It was silent except for birdsong and the occasional buzz of an insect. No one was within miles, as far
as she could tell. "What a lovely place, so peaceful."

He smiled over at her from where he unloaded the
blankets. "That's because it's not harvest time. Get my
grandfather out here bossing his crew and you'd wish
yourself anywhere else."

"Sounds as if you've been on his crew a few times."

"More than a few." He knelt and spread the blankets
under an ancient olive tree.

Cara rubbed the gnarled trunk and gazed up into the
silvery green leaves, its slightly bitter scent reminding her
that not everything beautiful could be sweet.

A gentle touch on her shoulder brought her out of her
introspection. She turned to see Yannis staring at the tree,
as well. "My *pappous*—grandfather, that is—says the tree
is almost two thousand years old."

"No, really?" Cara peered at the sturdy trunk. "I didn't
know they could grow so old."

Yannis nodded. "One of the university agriculture professors came to the island several summers ago and studied them. This is the oldest of all."

Two thousand years old. Standing silent and still in an olive grove bordering a vineyard, bearing fruit year after year. How many people had rested under its canopy, laughing, weeping, making love? It was beyond Cara's grasp. Sometimes she couldn't bear to contemplate the past several years or consider what the future might bring.

"So quiet, Cara *mou?*"

She quickly pasted a bright look on her face and turned to him. "Just admiring the tree."

"Yes." He clasped her shoulders in his hands and kissed her forehead, somehow knowing her solemn mood. "Something so old, so valuable. It can make thoughtful people melancholy when they contemplate what times the tree has passed through."

"The tree endured more than we'll ever see."

He shrugged. "Maybe, maybe not. The tree cannot laugh, the tree cannot cry, the tree cannot love someone or lose them."

Or lose people they didn't love, but had once upon a time. What was worse? The anguish of lost love or continued guilt? She didn't know.

But Con was gone, and she was here, and with someone else, who seemed very nice, nicer than she deserved. She stopped herself. Emma was right, and so was that counselor she'd seen. She did deserve better.

And Yannis was her "better."

Yannis wondered what else had put the serious look on her face. Surely it had to be more than an old olive tree? But she smiled at him with some effort that gradually lightened. "You must be uncomfortable after a hot day at work. Give me the water, Yannis."

He handed her a jug that had been sitting in the back of the pickup most of the day. "I have bottled water that probably tastes better."

"We're not drinking this, Yannis. I'm going to clean you up. Take off your shirt."

Her wet hands rubbing over him? He almost pulled off an ear taking off his T-shirt. He subtly flexed his chest and arms as her blue eyes grew smoky with desire. "Oh, Yannis." She circled him slowly, her finger brushing through his chest hair and toying with his medal. "You're even more sexy in the sunlight." She traced one of the healing marks on his back. "I'm sorry about your back."

"I'm not. It'll be one of my best memories."

"Good." She stood in front of him again and lifted the jug. "Bend over so I can clean you up."

He did, and she poured the cool water over his back and into his short, sweaty hair. She must have set the jug down since she began massaging the water into his hot skin. He sputtered as some ran into his face, and stood up and wiped it away.

"Oh, dear." She frowned. "The water seems to be running down below your waist. That can't be comfortable." She fumbled at his jeans and he quickly unfastened them. He reached down to undo his leather work boots, but she stopped him. "I, uh, want you to leave your boots and jeans on." Color blossomed in her cheeks. "I thought you looked really sexy at work that way."

"Okay." He couldn't help the smile that spread over his face. So Cara had a construction worker fantasy. "I'd wear my tool belt, but it might get in the way."

"I know." She looked disappointed.

"But I'd be happy to let you work with my tool."

Her red brows drew together in puzzlement. "I've never

built anything before…." Her face cleared as he roared with laughter. She scoffed, "You and your jokes. We'll see who's laughing in a minute."

"Nobody," he countered. "Laughing is not the noise I had in mind." He shoved down his pants and briefs. "Come to me, pretty Cara. Let this hard, sweaty construction worker build something good for you." He reached for her, but she ducked away and he couldn't chase her with his jeans at his ankles.

Cara was staring at his erection. "I just realized this was the first time we've seen each other naked in the daytime. You're beautiful."

His cock bobbed up even higher at her rapt admiration but to his annoyance, he felt a blush creep up his face. "Beautiful is for women. Women like you." He made another grab for her, but she easily evaded him.

"You'll hurt yourself if you fall now. And I don't want anything to happen to your lovely tool."

"I'll put it away and drive you back to your car unless I see you naked in the next sixty seconds." They both knew it was an empty threat, but she started unbuttoning her blouse.

The upper curves of her breasts appeared first, then the full mounds encased in ivory lace. She shrugged the blouse off and dropped it to the blanket.

She turned her back to him and unfastened the bra closure, the bra falling from her shoulders. Her back was great, soft and smooth, but he still couldn't see her breasts.

He craned his head, but then she was unfastening her shorts and her ass came into view. *Gamoto!* She was wearing a matching thong and the ivory lace made her appear naked from the back. Her skin was smooth as the beach and her hair red as the sunset. She gave a wiggle and dropped her shorts to the blanket.

He couldn't stand it anymore. Hiking up his jeans just enough not to trip, he moved behind her. She squealed in surprise as he cupped both breasts with one hand and dragged her against him. His cock pressed into the perfect flesh of her ass, the thong a laughable barrier. Speaking of barriers…he reached into his wallet and pulled out the brand-new condom he'd stashed there after the beach.

He quickly rolled it on while he played with her nipples. Damn, she felt great, warm and round and soft with tips tightening under his fingers, but he still hadn't seen her naked in the daylight.

She then made low moaning noises and rotated her butt back into his erection. Encouraged, he dipped his other hand down the front of her thong and stroked the little button there as he licked and sucked her neck. He told her in very explicit and graphic Greek exactly what he was going to do to her and how much she'd like it, knowing she'd be shocked if she understood him. But something of his message must have gotten across because she clutched his arm and came under his fingers, her juices creamy-wet and hot. He held her steady until she stopped pulsing.

He switched to English to make sure she was ready. "Take me into your pussy now, Cara."

His cock twitched at her sexy groan, her face still flushed from her orgasm. "Yannis, I'm going to fall."

"Grab the tree for balance." She clutched the gnarled trunk of the olive tree and braced herself. He hooked her thong to the side and nudged her thighs apart with his knee. "Open for me."

She immediately tipped her ass up to him. He eased between her folds and sank into her warm, welcoming passage. "Oh, Cara." He wanted to cry, scream, explode at the perfection.

"Yes, Yannis." She held perfectly still for a minute, her flesh pulsing around him. Then she began to rock her hips, his cock slipping out until he couldn't stand it and rammed back inside her.

"Don't tease me, Cara. I need you too badly." His admission shocked him, but he was too far gone to censor himself. He'd been thinking of her since their night on the beach, and he'd been semiaroused since she'd promised to meet him at the job site. And now here he was, taking her against an olive tree like an oversexed, half animal, half man satyr. Legends told that they had uncontrollable, permanent erections, and since meeting Cara, he could sympathize.

"I need you, too." Her knuckles were white against the tree trunk. "Move inside me. Take me hard."

The aroma of the olives and grapes, the light buzzing of the bees, while his dark, swollen erection plunged into Cara's perfect pale body was too much for him. She was his wood nymph, his obsession. He succumbed to the drunken lust pounding through him and slammed in and out of her, his rough hands fondling her delicate breasts as they swayed in time with his thrusts.

He pinched her nipples hard and was rewarded by a fresh gush of her juices to slick his way. He changed his angle to rub deep inside her and she moaned, her pussy beginning to clench around him.

Nuzzling her damp red curls out of the way, he licked her neck, tasting her sweat and inhaling the scent that was only hers. "That's it, baby." He realized he was speaking in Greek, but couldn't help himself. "So pretty, so soft, so hot." He encouraged her with words and actions as she writhed in front of him. "Come for me, sweet Cara. Let my cock give you pleasure."

Quivers built inside her, cupping and squeezing him until his balls tightened and threatened to spill over. He bit her earlobe and clamped his fingers over the swollen peaks of her breasts.

She screamed his name, startling the birds from the trees, and bucked wildly. He grabbed her around the hips and pounded into her, burying himself to the hilt. She was so tight and wet…he fought off his orgasm for a few seconds to give her more pleasure, but then a red wave rose before his eyes and he exploded blindly, bellowing with just as much force as his seed erupting from him.

He couldn't tell where his flesh ended and hers began as they were locked together in a wild, savage climax. Aeons passed, and then they were both trembling. It was almost too hard to stand. He eased from her and quickly disposed of the condom in a trash bag before taking her hands. "Come, lie down."

He helped her sit on the blankets and feasted his eyes. Cara was perfect. Her full breasts were tipped with hard peaks still rosy-pink from his touch. Her belly was firm but curvy, the bright blue jewel winking sexily up at him, leading down to a damp red nest.

She followed his gaze. "Yes, I am a natural redhead," she said drily.

"I wasn't thinking that." He finally unlaced his boots and kicked off the rest of his clothing. He sat next to her and brushed aside a red curl before pressing a kiss to her shoulder.

"No? Then what were you thinking?" She ran her finger down his chest, stopping just below his belly button.

He swallowed hard. "I was thinking you look wonderful, and I want to toss you down on the blanket and start all over again, this time with some finesse."

She slowly lay back on her elbows and stretched her arms over her head, pulling her breasts up high and firm. "Sometimes, finesse is overrated."

He was glad she thought so, since he hadn't shown any so far the two times he'd made love to her. Stretching out next to her, he propped himself on his elbow and looked down at her. "Stay with me this afternoon. I can't get enough of you." It was true. He'd dreamed of her the past few nights and woken up with his dick so hard he could drive nails with it.

He'd never been so obsessed with a woman before and didn't know if she felt the same. He didn't know how long she'd be in Aphrodisias, or even how long she would want him for a lover. Uncertainty was not a familiar or welcome feeling for a man who designed his life with the same care he designed his buildings.

CARA STARED UP at Yannis, who was wearing a frown. "Yannis?" Her finger traced the furrow between his eyebrows. "Something bothering you?"

He shrugged. "Just wondering how much time we have."

"Athena's not expecting her car back for a while. I told her and Emma we were going out for the evening. Why? Do you have to be back for something?"

"No." He flopped onto his back and stared up at the sky. "Men don't answer to anyone but themselves."

"Is that so?" Cara sat up and stroked the hard muscles in his chest, enjoying how the black hair curled around her fingers, his gold medal glittering up at her.

"Yes." His breathing sped up, though, especially when she found his coppery nipples. She knelt next to him and licked one. He groaned and threaded his hands through her hair. She sucked his nipple until it peaked in her mouth and then moved to his other one. Instead of sucking it, she bit it, making him flinch.

"And what do these men do when they have no one to answer to? No one to…relieve…their loneliness?" Cara slid her hand down his belly and cupped his penis. He was already half-hard and quickly filled under her gentle touch. "Do they do this?" She stroked him slowly. "Have you done this, Yannis?"

"What?" His blue eyes were dazed.

She stopped caressing him for a second. "Have you touched yourself when the need becomes too great?"

He nodded slowly, his hips jerking.

"When was the last time you couldn't stand to go another minute without it?"

"Yesterday. And the day before." He swallowed hard as she discovered a silvery bead on his tip and she massaged it into the skin there.

"Yesterday and the day before?" They'd just had sex Saturday night. Her insides quivered. A man who wanted sex every day was a new and delicious creature to savor. "What made you need it so bad?"

"You." His gaze cleared. "I dreamed you were fucking me and woke up about to come. I used my hand and wished it was you."

Wow. "I suppose your hand is better than nothing." She licked a trail down his stomach and stuck her tongue in his belly button. "But not as good as this."

She lifted her mouth and planted it firmly around his cock. He let out a cry of half pleasure, half pain. He was salty and slick, his foreskin slipping back and forth over the taut head as she moved him deeper into her throat.

He burst into frantic Greek, his fingers tightening

almost painfully in her hair. "Slow down, slow down." She did as he asked, wanting to pace herself. Then he lifted her off him. She let go, not wanting to hurt him. "Come here." His big hands manhandled her thighs apart until she knelt facing away from him.

She wasn't sure what he had in mind until he slid under her and parted her folds. Her squawk of surprise quickly turned into a moan as he sucked her clit for the first time. She wavered between embarrassment and lust at the realization she was sitting on his face and he was enjoying it, as well, judging from his deep purple erection and his hums of satisfaction.

He gently pushed on her back until she leaned forward over his body and braced her hands on either side of his hips. His cock beckoned her as it had before, much bigger than any other she'd seen. He glistened in the sunlight, thick and turgid, with heavy distended veins feeding his desire.

Cara dropped her head and panted as Yannis gave several long licks, spearing his tongue deep inside her. She couldn't keep away from him for one more second and sucked his cock into her mouth. His muffled cry encouraged her as she bobbed up and down his shaft.

He was so hot and hard and wet. No wonder she'd been filled to the bursting point. All of him, inside her on the beach, against the tree…her thighs quivered as he enthusiastically tongued her clit. She was about to come again— she couldn't believe it, but there…oh, there it was. Rays of the sun burst orange against her closed eyes as his heat rolled up from his tongue and throughout her whole body. She trembled on top of him, crying out against his cock. She felt him shake and knew he was going to lose control, as well. She sucked him hard. His moan vibrated her pussy and he exploded up into her mouth, flooding her with his warm, salty essence. He pulsed between her lips for several long seconds and then gave a shuddering sigh.

Somehow, she didn't know how, she climbed off him and collapsed next to him. He stroked her hair. "*Fos ton mation mou,*" he murmured.

"What?" She hadn't heard him.

"Light of my eyes, Cara *mou.*"

"Oh, Yannis." She closed her eyes, and he tugged her so her head rested on his shoulder. She'd never been anyone's light of anything before, but lying in a sunny Greek olive grove with a kind, sexy man, it seemed perfectly right.

9

"THIS IS THE PLACE. The land where I am to build my museum—if those *men* don't interfere with my plans." Athena scowled at the scrubby vista in front of them, her arms folded over the ample bodice of her black dress.

Cara nodded. It looked like the rest of rural Aphrodisias, yellowed grass and gnarled old trees, like the vineyard where she and Yannis had made love only a few days ago. Like the vineyard, no buildings dotted the land, and a mostly dried-up stream drizzled through one side of the property. Hardly turf to go to war over, but Athena and Gus had staked their positions. "Athena, I don't see why I can't just go to *Kyria* Nomikou's heirs and make them a better offer. I have the money to do it, you know that."

"No! Absolutely not." Athena held up her hand in denial. "I would never take your money for my own gain."

"You could pay me back—" Cara was once again silenced by an imperious hand.

"I thank you, but no. I have my own money for this, and I will make it work. You are a young woman and need to pay for your education."

"Athena…" Cara rolled her eyes. She had enough money to pay for the education of every single kid on Aphrodisias plus all of their kids and grandkids. And in a weird twist of fate, her anonymous scholarship fund was currently paying for Yannis's cousins to study in Athens.

But Athena had narrowed her eyes and was staring over the land, her gaze mapping every contour and valley. "*Kyria* Nomikou was the oldest woman on the island and the property had been in her family since anyone could remember—hundreds of years."

"Sure." Until foreigners had become interested in buying property on Aphrodisias, islanders had rarely sold land, keeping it for their sons and grandsons. Foreigners—now Cara was starting to think like an Aphrodisian, regarding outsiders with suspicion.

"But I seem to recall a curious thing—this land was only passed down to the oldest daughter—not to the sons."

Cara raised an eyebrow. That was certainly unusual in the traditionally patriarchal Greek society. "Was that even legal back then?"

Athena shrugged. "We Aphrodisians are the ones who say what is legal on our island. Now if only my dear mother were still alive. She and *Kyria* Nomikou were great friends and that is partly why *Kyria* Nomikou agreed to sell the land to me."

"If she'd kept the property so long, why would she sell it to you?"

"Ah…" Athena tapped her chin. "She had no daughters and no granddaughters—only boys to inherit. She said it was important to keep the property for the honor of women, like it had been in the old days."

Cara frowned. "The old days? How old?"

"Maybe even back to the times of the ancients. The old lady used to brag about how her family was descended from the priestesses of Aphrodite, but half the men on the island used to claim they were descended from Zeus or some such nonsense." The old lady cackled. "I saw enough of their so-called lightning bolts to know *that* was a lie."

Cara covered her eyes. Another appalling image that needed burning from her brain. "Oh, Athena," she whimpered in protest.

"Eh, don't be so missish. We're neither of us virgins anymore, and you should be glad of it, considering how that Yannis Petrides looks at you."

"Really?" Cara peeped out from her fingers. "How does he look at me?"

Athena smirked. "Like you're a platter of pastries and he's been herding goats up in the hills for months."

Cara couldn't help but giggle as her stomach growled. Food, food and more food. Athena had served her some *kourabiethes* with their midmorning coffee.

Athena overheard that noise. "So come on! The sooner you help me think of something, the sooner I can cook you a nice lunch," she wheedled. "And you can get back to your young man."

"He won't be happy if his uncle's plans fall through," Cara warned her.

"Don't worry about your Yannis. You have been truthful with him about helping me build our museum."

"It's practically the only thing I've been truthful with him about," Cara retorted.

"That is your choice, although I think you'd be surprised at his response if you did tell him about your life with Constantinos. Yannis is not such an old-fashioned man to disdain a previously married woman."

"He's old-fashioned enough to live at home with his aunt and uncle and care what happens to their construction business."

"His uncle deserves to have his plans wrecked, since he never should have made them in the first place," Athena scoffed. "And Yannis has other irons in the fire anyway."

What did she mean about Yannis having other irons in the fire? Cara was about to ask when Athena grabbed her elbow. "Come. Walk me around the land."

The land was flat and easy for Athena to pass along. She muttered to herself, mostly imprecations against Yannis's uncle Gus. Cara didn't know the man well, but thought he'd been underhanded to go against a dead woman's wishes. She hoped Yannis didn't have the same questionable morality, although she couldn't imagine why that would be a problem. After all, they were just playmates for a summer fling.

Concentrating on her own thoughts and not paying attention to her steps, Cara stumbled. Fortunately she'd let go of Athena as she fell onto her hands and knees.

"Karoleena, are you all right?" Athena cried.

"Yes, yes, I'm fine." Cara looked down at the ledge of dirt she'd fallen off. They'd been walking on a higher part of the land and Cara had stepped into an indentation, not much lower than the rest, but enough to trip her up.

"As long as you are not hurt. Did you trip over something?" Athena brushed loose gravel and dust off Cara's knees, tsking as she went. "You are going to have some marks."

"The ground drops off here, so be careful." Cara wiped her palms clean on her denim shorts. Fortunately, there was no bleeding as the rocks had only scraped her skin.

Athena nodded and they went on, careful to avoid the drop-off. They came to an olive tree and stopped to rest in its shade. Athena looked back along the path they had taken and narrowed her eyes. "Do you see that, Cara?"

Cara stared at the sparse bushes and drooping trees that probably flowered in the spring. "It's very pretty, Athena. I can see why you wanted to build here."

She waved a hand. "No, not that—the lower ground you tripped on is a huge rectangle."

"Really?" Cara blinked and let her gaze travel along the path. It did appear to be a rectangular shape. She left Athena under the tree and walked the upper perimeter. "You're right!" she called. "It's almost as big as a football field." She continued to the end where the goalposts would stand. "There's a big mound up at this end. No, wait, I'll come help you."

Athena had pushed away from the tree and was speed-walking toward her. Cara met her halfway. "Careful, careful."

"Bah!" Athena ignored Cara's concern. "Show me what you saw." Cara followed as Athena hurried to eye the clump of shrubs raised up on a smaller rectangular mound. "Almost like an altar…" she mused.

"Did there used to be a church out here?" Cara asked. The *koura* or cathedral in Aphrodisias was several hundred years old and was in the center of the town. She couldn't see the locals coming all the way out into the hills to go to church.

"No." Athena shook her head. "Never a church…maybe a temple."

"A temple? To whom?"

The older woman turned and gave her a wide, calculating grin. "Aphrodite, of course." She burst into wild laughter. "*Kyria* Nomikou, you sly old lady, you left me Aphrodite's Temple, untouched and unexcavated. The archaeologists will swarm over this site like ants on honey. Oh, what can those foolish men say about this?"

Cara burst into laughter, as well. "You know Yannis and his uncle Gus will have plenty to say about this."

"I'll handle Gus, but I leave Yannis to you." She wiggled her thick brows suggestively. "Tell me one thing, *chriso*

mou, and I promise not to tease you anymore. Is Yannis
Petrides descended from Zeus? He looks like a man with
a long lightning bolt."

Cara sputtered, her cheeks heating. Athena hooted with
laughter. "Never mind, darling. Your face tells me everything I wanted to know."

"YANNIS, finish up in there! You're worse than the girls."

Yeah, right. Yannis had begun his shower a whopping
five minutes ago. He gave himself a final rinse and shut
off the water. Living with his uncle's family as if he were
still a kid was starting to get on his nerves, but at least it
was only for the summer until he went back to school.

He reached for a towel and started drying off. He didn't
know how Niko could stand living with his mother year-
round. Actually, he *did* know. Niko had free room and
board and then just went to a hotel with a tourist girl if they
wanted to have sex. Whereas Yannis, being the classy type,
fondled his own tourist girl in the water at a public beach
and then had rough, quickie sex with her on a cabana chair.
Or against an olive tree in his grandfather's vineyard. He
sighed. Maybe someday, they would actually have a bed.
At least she'd enjoyed herself, despite his almost animal-
istic response to her. Or maybe because of it?

He smiled at himself in the mirror and then reached for
his razor and shaving cream. No point in marking Cara's
delicate skin. He was about to lather up when his uncle
banged on the door again.

"Now, Yannis!"

"Fine, fine!" He wrapped the towel around his waist and
unlocked the door.

Uncle Gus rushed in. "About time. You look pretty
enough as it is."

"Thanks," he muttered. He shoved his gear back into the cabinet and rinsed the lather down the sink.

His uncle looked over his shoulder into the mirror, his black eyes crafty. "That redhead who drove Athena Kefalas to the job site?"

"Yes?" He raised an eyebrow, willing to be just as crafty as Gus.

"You know her?" Gus was just toying with him now, he could tell.

"Niko introduced us. I've run into her a few times."

Gus smiled. "Did she move to Aphrodisias to start a construction company? Because the boys said she met you after work at the job site. Are you showing her the *ins* and *outs* of our business?" Gus chortled and slapped Yannis on the back.

Yannis gave him a sour look. How many more weeks did he need to live here? He couldn't wait to get back to Ohio where his neighbors didn't know who he was sleeping with and wouldn't care if they did.

His uncle got serious with some effort. "Look, Yannis, I'm not asking to be nosy."

No, he was asking because he was a dirty old man.

"I'm asking because if this girl is a friend of Athena's, then she might, you know, *know* things about Athena, like is she going to give us more trouble about our Belgian villa project?"

"I'm sure she will, Uncle. The heirs basically welshed on the deal she had with their grandmother, so she has plenty to complain about."

Gus threw up his hands. "Yeah, yeah, yeah." He didn't want to be bothered with the ethics of the thing. That was the trouble with Uncle Gus. Yannis had plenty of experience with the building trades, having been around them his whole life, but he'd never gotten used to certain cutthroat aspects of the business. At least Yannis wasn't as naive as his father had been—his trusting nature had cost their family almost everything.

"So will you do it? Will you ask this girl some questions?"

"What?" Yannis jerked his attention back to his uncle.

"You know, take her out, wine her, dine her, learn what Athena is up to. As a favor for your uncle. And for the company." He reached for his money clip and pulled out some euros. "Dinner on me."

"Well…" Yannis didn't need the money, but enjoyed being on the turnaround side of his uncle.

Gus frowned and pulled out a couple more bills and shook them in front of Yannis's nose. "Think of your aunt. Think of your cousins. Even if she is a redhead, you can spend *some* time with her."

Annoyed by his uncle's backhanded insult to Cara, Yannis grabbed the money. "I'll see what I can do."

"Good boy. Now get out. You don't want to be anywhere around here. I had goat stew for lunch that didn't agree with me."

Yannis fled.

"HELLO, STRANGER." Emma lifted her sunglasses and peered up at Cara from where she reclined on a low-slung chair. "Did you have trouble finding me?"

"Not with that hot-pink bikini." Emma was turning into a beach bunny and had developed a pale golden tan, spending the past few days at the beach when Cara was visiting or plotting with Athena. Her evenings and nights were spent with Nick, sometimes at the villa, but they had grown more considerate than their first time there. "But why are you way over here? The beach is pretty rocky."

"I didn't feel like swimming and there were too many kids over there. I was reading and their ball knocked the book right out of my hands." Emma pointed to a thick, brightly colored paperback sitting near her leg. "How is Athena doing?"

"Fine. She had me looking up phone numbers for archaeologists who might be interested in the possible temple compound." Cara unfolded her own chair and arranged her towel on top.

"How neat! But don't archaeologists need permission from landowners to dig?"

Cara shrugged. "I tried to tell her that, but insignificant details like that don't concern her." She sat and smoothed sunblock over her skin, which had also darkened slightly since their arrival. The light tan looked good with her turquoise bikini and aquamarine belly ring. Maybe she'd get a matching ankle bracelet. Emma was wearing her pink one today.

Cara settled into her chair and closed her eyes. They flew open as several drops of icy water landed on her bare stomach. "Yikes!"

Emma was leaning over her, shaking her water bottle onto Cara. "Yikes, yourself. You don't get a nap until I hear what the heck you've been up to with Yannis."

Cara felt a flush that couldn't be explained away by a sudden sunburn.

"Aha!" Emma crowed, setting down her bottle. "I knew he had it bad for you as soon as he saw you in the taverna. So have you and he…?" Emma made a vague, fluttering motion with her hands.

Cara grinned. "Yes."

Emma leaned over and hugged her. "Tell me everything, you sly girl. When was your first time? Was it romantic?"

"Well, we left the taverna that first night—"

"You naughty girl! I should dump this water over your head for keeping it a secret for a week. I thought you were spending your free time with Athena." She shook the bottle. "But I won't, as long as you give me all the details."

"After the taverna, he took me on a scooter ride along the coast." Cara sighed at the memory. "The moon was full and all the stars were out. The breeze was blowing our hair as we drove, and the night smelled of flowers."

"Ohhh…" Emma sighed, as well. "Then what?"

"I wanted to go for a walk on the beach, and then we decided to go for a swim—"

"A skinny-dip?" she asked eagerly.

"Yeah." Cara blushed again. "And there we were in the ocean, and one thing led to another and we wound up on a cabana lounge chair… Oh, Emma, he was so hot and wanted me so much. I just couldn't help myself. I've never done anything like that before." Yannis just blew away all her inhibitions. She'd gladly accepted the risk of discovery, but knew somehow he'd never let anything bad happen to her. She'd never felt so safe with a man.

Her friend's eyes had widened. "In the water and on the beach? I promise, I will never order one of those Sex on the Beach drinks without thinking of you." She giggled. "And I thought Nick and I were daring, doing it on the floor."

"Um, yeah." Cara would never, ever admit to Emma she'd been an unwitting witness to that precious memory. "So, I don't know. It's been less than a week, and I can't think of anything but him. Every time I leave him, I count how long until I see him again."

"Have you told him you were married before?"

"No way. We haven't had the 'talk about our past love lives' conversation yet." And that conversation would be a long time coming, if she had her choice. Talk about a good way to frighten off a guy—she could just imagine that scenario. *Guess what, sweetie? I was married to a Greek man before we met. Who? Con Constantinos, that rich guy—you might have seen photos of him and his mistress in the tabloids.* Cara shook her head. "How about you?"

"Cara, I barely have any past love life. We just talk about our jobs, a bit about our families."

"That sounds cozy. Is Nick properly impressed with your academic achievements?"

Emma's eyes shifted to the side. "Well…"

"What?" Was Emma embarrassed about her math ability?

"I told him I was training to be a math teacher." Her words rushed out. "I didn't mention the bit about grad school."

"Emma! Why on earth would you keep that a secret? You teach advanced theoretical mathematics to graduate students. You were voted Graduate Assistant of the Year three times." Cara pursed her lips. "Is Nick one of those barbarians who is intimidated by smart women?" Like Con?

"Of course not! It's just a welcome change to meet somebody who wants *me*, not my brain." She shoved out her lips in a pout. "I'm tired of being a math geek, Cara. I want to enjoy myself, not make a decent guy feel stupid because I have a college degree and he doesn't. I want to be a bimbo this summer. Why should they have all the fun?"

It was hard to disagree. Cara wasn't exactly winning prizes for Most Honest Summer Fling, either. "Being a bimbo is overrated—you have to spend too much time on your hair and clothes, too much time worrying about being skinny enough." Too much time in the bathroom trying to get skinny enough to recapture her husband's wandering attention.

Emma's face softened. "Suffering from bulimia wasn't your fault. The new research shows real imbalances in hormones and brain chemistry. You should be proud of yourself for getting help and getting better."

She shrugged, still uncomfortable with discussing her past. "So this summer, you can be the math teacher bimbo and I'll be the…" Who would she be? More to the point, who *was* she? And how was she supposed to tell Yannis who she was when she hadn't figured it out yet? "I'll be the American college student who's met a really nice, hot Greek guy for a sexy summer fling." At least that was part of the truth.

"Sounds good." Emma gave her a relieved smile.

Cara remembered she'd discussed Emma's education with Yannis the first night they'd gone out together, and made a mental note to ask him not to mention it to Nick. "Oh, Emma, I almost forgot. Your academic advisor left you a message on my cell phone."

She sat up and frowned. "Oh, pooh. Sorry about that, Cara. I only gave her that as an emergency number. What did Dr. Gaithers want?"

"She wants you to call or e-mail her back to discuss your progress so far this summer." Cara eyed her friend. You didn't have to be a math genius like Emma to add one budding tan, one promising summer affair and one dusty laptop to come up with how much progress Emma was making on her grad work.

Emma rolled her eyes and popped her sunglasses back on. "I'll send her an e-mail today—no, wait, Nick is getting out of work early and we're taking the ferry to Mykonos for the weekend."

"Really? Your first trip together, huh." So far, Emma and Nick had mostly gone out for dinner and then back to the villa for sex. "Mykonos is fun—a real party town. It was built by pirates for their mistresses."

Emma giggled. "Really?"

"Yep. One writer wrote several hundred years ago that the women on Mykonos were more noted for their beauty than their chastity."

"Kind of like us," Emma chortled. "And it's about time."

Cara laughed and reclined into her seat. The late-afternoon sun relaxed her almost to the point of sleep. She wasn't sure how long had passed before Emma exclaimed, "Oh, my gosh!"

"What? What?" Cara sat up and wildly looked around. Emma slammed her chair shut and tossed her gear into her bag.

"Nick's going to come pick me up in an hour and I need to shower and finish packing." She slipped on her cover-up and sandals and started hiking up to the road. "I'll see you late Sunday, okay?"

"Okay. Have a great time!" Cara called. Emma waved and then scurried off. Cara settled into her chair again, but noticed Emma's paperback in the sand. She'd just take it back to the villa for her.

Brushing off the cover, she raised her eyebrows at the metallic-gold title—*Sins of Summer.* Intrigued, she flipped to the first page and started reading. The third chapter was particularly juicy, the glamorous heroine lounging around her estate in the Hamptons, spying on the half-dressed, well-built gardener. The hunky horticulturalist was preening at his boss's rapt attention when a shadow fell over the pages and Cara squeaked.

"Sorry, Cara, I thought you heard me coming. I saw Emma at your place and she told me you were here." Yannis bent down and kissed her. He must have come

from the job site since he wore his customary cotton T-shirt
and work boots. Today he was sporting khaki carpenter
shorts, his legs strong and brown under them. "My lazy
crew actually finished their work early. Good book?"

"I guess." She marked the page with her finger, slightly
embarrassed. "Emma forgot it earlier."

"Oh, right. Niko said they're going to Mykonos tonight.
His aunt has a nice couch for her to sleep on there."

Cara stared at him in horror. "Emma is planning a romantic weekend, and Niko's having them stay at his aunt's
house?"

"It's a big house," Yannis said innocently before bursting
into laughter. "No, he did get a hotel room. Not as fancy
as yours, but they probably won't catch bedbugs. I hope."

"Oh, you." Cara slugged him in the arm.

"Where did you leave off?" He plucked the book from
her, his eyes widening. "I leave you to go to work for just
a few hours, and you have to read this? I must not be doing
my job to satisfy you."

"What? What?" Cara grabbed the book and looked at
where his finger rested. The slinky heroine was seducing
the gardener in the middle of the lawn. "I didn't get to this
part yet."

Yannis read aloud over her shoulder, "'She licked her
suddenly dry lips as he unzipped his shorts. His magnificent purple manroot bulged—'" He broke off. "Manroot?
Is that what I think it is?"

Cara muffled her giggles unsuccessfully. "Exactly."

He shook his head and took the book from her. "All
those years of studying English and I never learned that
word before."

"Consider yourself fortunate."

"Skipping the manroot parts..." He grinned at Cara's

snort at his pun. "Ah, here we go. 'She was clad in the tiniest of bikinis, knowing his hot eyes would eagerly travel over her body—' How did his eyes get out of his body? Is that some American phrase?"

"No, just bad writing."

Yannis studied the book again. "'His callused finger traveled gently over her soft skin, as if amazed it was permitted to touch such lovely silkiness. He untied her bikini top and feasted his eyes on her bounteous mounds of pleasure.'"

Cara's giggles broke off when Yannis yanked the tie behind her neck, her top falling loose. "Yannis!" She pressed the cups against her breasts. "I didn't mean for *you* to feast *your* eyes."

"There's nobody around, and I want to see your bounteous mounds." He tugged the top free and tossed it to the sand behind him. "Show me, Cara *mou*. Then we can find out what happens next."

She slowly unfolded her arms, baring herself. She'd sunbathed topless years ago, but not recently; pale triangles of skin outlined the areas her suit usually covered.

"Nice, very nice." He nodded in approval and dropped the paperback on the sand. "But you'll burn quickly unless..." He picked up the sunblock and drizzled it over her breasts.

"Yikes, that's cold!" Her nipples immediately tightened, in reaction to him as much as the change in temperature.

"Not if you rub it in." With his hands he began massaging the cream into her skin.

She grabbed his wrist. "Yannis, I don't think we're supposed to do this here."

"What?" He gave her an innocent look. "Topless sunbathing is permitted on this end of the beach, and I'm just a good Greek host trying to keep a pretty tourist from getting sunburned."

Cara looked around. They were several hundred yards from anyone, being on the rocky end of the beach. She let go of his wrist and lay back on the chair. "Just so I don't burn."

"Of course." She squirmed on the chair as he took his time, his fingers leisurely slipping and sliding over her. "There's an art to this, you know."

"Oh, really?" Her breath was coming faster now.

"Yep." He nodded. "You have to be careful not to miss an inch of skin. Especially here." He caught one of her nipples between his slick thumb and finger and rubbed the peak. Cara's hips twitched. "If you were to get sunburned here, how would I suck on you?"

A moan escaped from her. "Yannis…"

"Shhh." He moved to her other breast, massaging and squeezing her. The ocean breeze cooled her skin, making her nipples even harder. "Roll over on your side."

She looked up at him in confusion.

"Face me." He grabbed her hip until she was lying on her recliner like a topless pinup model, her back to the rest of the beach.

"But, Yannis, I don't want to sunbathe anymore. Let's go back to my place. Emma will be gone by now."

"No, not yet. This first." Before she could protest, he drove a finger under the waistband of her bikini bottom and found her clit.

She tossed her head back as lust speared through her. He was slick from the lotion, and her juices made him even more slippery. She grabbed his forearm, intending to stop him, but he shook his head.

"Not yet. You need me right here, right now." He reached over with his free hand and flicked her belly ring.

"So sexy. This jewel is like an arrow on a map, pointing down to right where I want to be." He stroked her little knot of pleasure as it swelled under his finger. "Right here where you want me to be."

"Yes, Yannis," she panted. "Always."

He dipped into her passage and she contracted around him. "Do you remember when we were under the olive tree and I was licking you?" His expression was casual, as if she had just decided to roll over to chat with him, but his cock pressed hard against his fly and a droplet of sweat ran down his temple. "You were the sweetest thing I had ever tasted."

She groaned. "You, too," was all she could manage.

"Oh, yes. Your soft mouth on me drove me crazy, made me suck you harder. I only wished I could see your beautiful face, watched you crest and soften when you came."

Heat spread up into her cheeks at his sexy talk and his even sexier caresses.

"I'm going to take you home to your villa and soap you up in the shower. Your breasts." He stroked them, obviously enjoying how she shivered at his delicate touch. "Your ass." He cupped her there, pinching and squeezing. By then she was so aroused, she didn't protest at how anyone could see him. "And here, your soft copper nest. My cock wants to be *here*." He slipped his whole hand into her suit, working two fingers inside her with his thumb on her clit. "I'll spread your thighs wide on the bed and not let you up all weekend."

Cara bit her lip to hold back her cries, but his fingers just sped up. Her hips bucked on the lounge chair, making it squeak and sink deeper into the sand.

"Now, Cara *mou*, show me that beautiful expression I love to see, the expression that I alone can give you." He pinched her clit and she melted under his hands, her pussy wildly pulsing around his long fingers. He muffled her scream with a hard kiss, his own desire and frustration finally breaking free. He drove his tongue deep into her mouth, mimicking exactly what he planned to do to her once they were truly alone.

She clutched at his arms as the shock waves of her orgasm continued to ripple through her. He was her only anchor in the shifting sand, despite causing her torment. She broke away and gasped for breath. "Oh, Yannis, Yannis."

He pulled his hands free and she closed her eyes, slumping back on the chair. She felt a kiss pressed to her forehead and then heard the rustle of him undressing and the jingle of keys.

She turned her head with her last bit of strength and opened heavy lids. He had taken off his boots and shirt and set the contents of his pockets on top. "Yannis, honey, what are you doing?"

"Going for a swim."

"Oh." She sat up and groped for her bikini top. His blue gaze focused hungrily on her swaying breasts. "Maybe I should swim, too."

He shook his head. "Not unless you want me to strip off the rest of your suit and fuck you in the water. I'm so hard for you that I don't even care who sees."

"Oh." His blunt confession made a fresh wave of desire break over her. She shifted and licked her lips, trying to ease the renewed ache.

He groaned and swore in Greek. "Just…just…stay there. God, I hope the water's cold." He stood, his bikini briefs not disguising his arousal one bit. He sprinted to the surf and dived in. Cara thought she heard a yelp as he went underwater.

She rested on the chair, pleasantly drained. The heat of

the sun on her bare breasts was nothing compared to Yannis's touch.

After several minutes, Yannis climbed up the beach. When he saw she was still topless, he closed his eyes. "Get dressed so I can take you home. It's the last time you'll need clothes until Monday."

YANNIS RUSHED into his house and headed to his room to throw some toiletries and clothes into a bag for their romantic weekend alone at the villa. He hated to leave Cara even for a short time, but a toothbrush and some deodorant wouldn't be amiss.

He clattered downstairs to leave a note for his aunt not to expect him home, but found his uncle in the kitchen lighting a cigarette and rummaging in the refrigerator.

"Eh, look, it's the Invisible Man. Your auntie was beginning to wonder if you'd moved out without telling her." He wiggled his gray bushy eyebrows. "I told her I've been keeping you busy at the office."

"I've been busy at the job site, but we finished everything on your list. Tell Aunt Eleni I won't be home this weekend. You can call me on my cell phone if something comes up." Yannis plucked some olives from the dish his uncle held and headed for the door.

"Just a minute, young man." Gus waved his cigarette at Yannis. "I've been more than patient waiting for your report, but I need some information now. What did you find out from the American girl?"

Yannis wished he'd never accepted the old man's measly bribe. "I haven't found out anything. You can have your money back." He dug into his wallet to hand the wad of euros to his uncle. Unfortunately two condom packets fell out.

Gus eyed them with glee. "You're quite the man-about-town, Yannis. Maybe you should keep the money—just for supplies, if you know what I mean."

"First of all, Cara has not told me anything that Athena Kefalas hasn't told you straight to your face. Athena feels you cheated her out of the land and is no doubt plotting to get it back."

"I did not cheat anyone!" Gus's face reddened. "No signature, no deal. If you are going to be a builder, you are going to have to be more businesslike, Yannis."

"You mean ruthless," Yannis retorted.

"Bah! You are soft and sentimental like your father. That is why he chips stone in cold, rainy London and not here on Aphrodisias."

Yannis's face burned. "My father trusted his business partner. How was he to know that crook cooked the books for years?"

"He would have known if he had paid more attention to money. But no, your father is an *artist.*" It wasn't a compliment. "He was tied up in his architectural sculptures and never noticed his partner charging obscene amounts of money to their clients and giving your father a pittance. And even worse, misfiling taxes? Your father is lucky he didn't go to prison for tax fraud like his partner did."

Yannis gritted his teeth. His parents had moved to London for a fresh start after that humiliating time, and his father now worked for a famous architectural restoration firm. "My father is an honest man."

Gus had caught the underlying sentiment. "And I am not? Does my concrete work chip a year after I lay it? Do my foundations sag and the walls crack? Have any of my buildings ever come down during an earthquake?"

"No," he muttered. "But I won't quiz Cara about her friend's plans. It's not right."

Gus shook his head. "Not everyone sees right and wrong with your moral clarity, Yannis. I hope the rest of us do not disappoint you someday when we fail to live up to your lofty standards."

10

"PUT DOWN THAT FRUIT and come give me some of your sweetness." Yannis snagged Cara around the waist and gave her a long kiss, slipping a hand inside her terry cloth robe. Since she hadn't bothered to throw on any clothing for the past two days, he easily found what he wanted.

Cara dropped the melon on the countertop as he pinched her nipple just the way she liked. His own robe gaped open to reveal his brown, muscular chest. "You are insatiable. We've barely left the bedroom since Friday." Now they were enjoying a leisurely Sunday afternoon. "Haven't you gotten enough?" Despite her teasing words, she nudged his robe open and found his erection with her hand.

"Never enough with you, Cara." He jolted his hips into her grasp. "Hmm, this table looks sturdy enough."

Just then the phone in the living room rang. Cara ignored it, instead enjoying Yannis's velvety skin sheathing hard, hot flesh. He buried his face in the crook of her neck and murmured sweet nothings in Greek to her. He was becoming more and more affectionate with her, and Cara wasn't used to that. It worried her for a minute, but then she realized that of course he'd be affectionate, considering how often they were naked together.

"Mmm, *latria mou, hara mou,* yeah, that's it," he muttered as she cupped his balls. Now she was his darling, his joy? Cara mentally pinched herself for letting anything distract her from his pleasure. He had given her so much pleasure that he deserved one just for himself. It was no sacrifice considering how sexy he was.

Yannis groaned, his sac tightening in her hand as he ripped open her robe. He frantically stroked every inch of her that he could reach—her breasts, her belly, her back, between her thighs—but she ignored the familiar heat since she could tell he was getting close. She ran her tongue around his ear. "I'm in charge this time, Yannis Petrides, and you're gonna beg me before you're done. You're a bad Greek boy to let an American girl lead you around by your cock." She squeezed his shaft and it jumped in her hand. "And your balls, too." She slipped a finger behind them and he moaned. "Maybe I should be really bossy and tie you to my bed and suck on you till you come." She stopped moving her hands on him. "Or not."

"Cara, please!" His voice was a hoarse cry. "Now, now…"

Close enough to count as begging. She literally man-handled him until he threw back his head, his neck tendons straining, roaring, "Yes, yes, yes…" He exploded into her grasp, clutching at her as his orgasm ripped through him. She felt strong and powerful as he gasped for air, Aphrodite bestowing a gift of love on a mere mortal.

Love? No, she had meant sex, not love. Or even affection, but not love. She released him and he rested against the heavy wood table, his chest heaving.

"Oh, Cara, what was that?"

"A little hostess gift." Or was she still pumping him for info?

He looked confused, but then again, wasn't she? They

cleaned up and tried again with the food. This time when the phone rang, Cara answered it.

"Hello?"

"Hello, darling." It was Athena, speaking in Greek. "I called in a few favors and found one of the university archaeologists over on Naxos. She is coming tomorrow to evaluate if the land was an ancient temple of Aphrodite."

Cara was careful to respond to Athena's Greek in English. "What? I thought you were joking. How can you know what it is after thousands of years just by looking at it?"

"Ah, you're speaking English. Is Yannis there?"

"Yes." He was gathering items for their snack as if he knew what he was doing in a kitchen.

"Well, looking at it *is* the archaeologist's job. She grew up on Naxos and has always been fascinated by the ancient temples to the goddesses. And she is applying for tenure!" Athena finished triumphantly.

"Great." An ambitious professor would be Uncle Gus's worst nightmare. "And what about the owners?"

"According to Greek law, antiquities are government property. Whatever might be underground there belongs to the people of Greece, so that is protected land until the archaeologist says it's empty."

"But you don't think that."

"Of course not. Something is there, and Dr. Aristides is the woman to find out."

"If you say so." Geez, what had happened to her uncomplicated summer of sunbathing and swimming?

"It is not I who says so, but the government." Athena's voice came out a bit sharper than usual. "Pass along this news to Yannis."

Cara sighed. Caught in the middle again. "Fine."

"Come meet the professor tomorrow at ten. Then we can plan our next step. Goodbye, Karoleena." Athena hung up, doubtless to avoid any more protests.

Yannis had finished slicing up the fruit and had found some goat milk feta cheese and brine-soaked black olives. He was quite handy in the kitchen. His mother must have taught him some basic skills. "That was Athena?" he questioned.

"Yes." She picked up the bottle of strong red wine and filled two glasses. A bit of wine from the romantic vineyard might make the news go over better, although she doubted it. "Let's eat on the terrace."

"In our robes?" He looked down with mock horror. "Someone might get the wrong idea."

"No, they'd probably get the right idea." She drank half her glass and refilled it. "Come on."

He followed her outside, where the roses grew overhead on an arbor, muting the June afternoon sun and giving them some shade. He pulled two chairs close together and set the platter on a small mosaic table between them. "Nice day."

"Do you want to go out?" She bit into the salty, slightly sour feta and followed with a melon chunk.

"Are you kidding?" He gestured to their surroundings with his wineglass. "For once, we have food, we have a bed, we have a shower with plenty of hot water for soaping each other up. Why would I want to leave?"

She laughed and picked up an olive. He caught her hand and sucked it into his mouth, deliberately swirling his tongue around her fingers. "If only we didn't have a phone…" he mused.

"Oh, yes, that." Cara took a deep breath. "Something came up in regards to the property she and your uncle are fighting over."

"I should have told you he made the same request as Athena—that I pass along any information I found out. But I figured Athena can tell him herself. She's not shy."

"No, Yannis. This is serious and could change everything."

"Yeah?" He sat up straight, his mellow mood melting away. "What is it?"

"It's a historical site."

He shrugged and relaxed. "The whole island is a historical site. Aphrodisias has been continually inhabited for the past seven thousand years, according to the archaeologists who wander through every so often."

"It will block your uncle's plans for the near future. Maybe permanently."

He narrowed his eyes. "What do you mean permanently? He's counting on this for his business. He could be in trouble if it doesn't go through." Yannis threw up his hands in frustration and jumped up to pace back and forth on the tiny balcony.

Cara sympathized, but she knew Athena was right. "There's a very good possibility that it was once the site of the temple dedicated to Aphrodite."

"Oh, come on. There have to be at least six or seven supposed sites of that temple. The whole island was dedicated to Aphrodite. Does that mean we throw everybody off the island and leave it for the goats?" He dropped into the wrought-iron chair and drummed his fingers on the table.

Cara shrugged. "There's some compelling evidence. The property has been in *Kyria* Nomikou's family for hundreds of years and passed down only through the women. Athena says the old lady used to claim she was a direct descendant of the priestesses of Aphrodite."

Yannis stared at her and burst out laughing. "Really? She admitted that?"

"Sure, why not?" His snickers were starting to get on her nerves.

"Cara, sweetheart, in the old days the priestesses of Aphrodite were mostly professional lovers, if you know what I mean."

"You mean hookers? Call girls? Ladies of the evening?" she said sweetly, and had the satisfaction of seeing him choke on his wine in surprise. He *did* know quite a bit of American slang. "After all," she continued, "Athena says most of the men on the island claim to be descendants of Zeus despite their puny lightning rods."

He winced. "And I thought she was this sweet old lady who baked great cookies."

"Apparently she has a broader set of experiences than either of us thought." She dropped into the chair next to him.

"I guess. She spent several years in Athens keeping house for that rich cousin of hers, Con Constantinos."

Hearing her husband's name was a surprise, but then Cara had an even more horrible thought. "But you're Athena's cousin, too. Are you related to that guy?"

"No." He shook his head. "Athena was related to him on her father's side, and she's related to me on her mother's." He laughed. "Too bad, eh? Then I might have inherited some money from him when he died. Athena got a bundle, but that American trophy wife of his got the lion's share according to Greek inheritance law. Boy, was the rest of his family pissed off." He poured more wine. "Although my aunt said she was a pretty blond girl, so she must have kept him happy."

Cara wanted to throw up. She'd been called worse than a trophy wife by Con's family, the tabloids and Greek so-called "entertainment" television, but hearing it from Yannis was the worst. She forced her numb lips to say, "I heard of him. Wasn't there something strange about how he died?"

Yannis shrugged, unaware he was tossing bombs into her lap. "He supposedly had a heart attack in his long-term mistress's arms. Kind of young, but according to my aunt Eleni, weak hearts ran in the family."

Weak hearts and weak characters, too. Yannis was absolutely right. Con had collapsed on top of former Greek ballet star and long-term lover Clio Papadopoulos. A little thing like marriage to Cara had not even been a bump in the road of their affair. Like most ballet dancers, Clio had been tiny and slender to the point of emaciation, obviously what Con preferred in women since he had tacitly encouraged her own insane weight control methods.

Cara grabbed a huge hunk of feta off the plate and bit some off, chewing angrily. She slowed down when she realized she wasn't even hungry. So why would she eat? To spite a dead man? She sighed and set the rest down. No more eating to stuff her emotions instead of her stomach. It was time to come clean to Yannis about her past with rich, successful, cheating Con Constantinos. But he continued before she could open her mouth.

"Yeah, Aunt Eleni loves all those gossipy, celebrity magazines. That's all she and her friends talk about when they get together for coffee. Who's marrying who, who's cheating on who, who's getting a divorce."

"Really? She follows that stuff so closely?" If that was true, Cara didn't dare tell Yannis she was Con's widow. If the paparazzi discovered she'd returned to Greece, Aphrodisias would become hell on earth with dozens of scooter-riding photographers chasing her, Yannis, Emma, Athena and anyone unlucky enough to know her. She'd been chased enough to be seriously frightened many times, she and her security detail even crashing their car once. Having such a relatively small population meant intense media scrutiny for anyone in Greece with any kind of celebrity status.

He laughed. "She's always asking Athena what it was like to work for a real-life Greek shipping tycoon, but Athena never says anything."

Thank goodness for Athena's tight lips. "I don't suppose you know what happened to the American wife after he died?"

He shrugged, losing interest in what was obviously old news to him. "Apparently she went back to America a very wealthy woman. But that was several years ago. Hey, are you okay? You look kind of pale."

She touched her forehead, which had started to hurt from stress and upset. Hearing her previous life in Greece reduced to its sordid skeleton made her want to cry. American blond bimbo marries rich Greek shipping magnate, inherits half his money despite the loud protests of his relatives, and takes off for the States with her loot. Add to that the prospect of the paparazzi hounding her until she either fled again or went into hiding, and it was no wonder she'd had enough.

"I have a headache all of a sudden. I used to get migraines before, but I haven't had one in a long time."

"A migraine?" He stood up in alarm. "Do you have medicine for it? I can go get it."

"No, I don't have anything." She'd thought she'd had something with Yannis, but her past still interfered.

"Come here." He helped her to her feet and then swung her up into his arms.

"Yannis…" she protested, but he carried her into her bedroom where he undid her robe and helped her into a largely unused cotton nightgown. His touch was kind, but not sexual, his eyes full of concern.

"Climb in bed and I'll get you something for the pain."

"Okay." She blinked. The afternoon sun was sparking little haloes in her vision, and he shut the shades.

"I'll be right back, Cara *mou*. Just close your eyes and try to rest." He dropped his own robe and dressed.

"Yannis…" The lump in her throat was nearly blocking her voice. "I'm sorry."

"For what?" He bent and kissed her forehead. "You didn't give yourself a headache." He let himself out and she heard his steps clatter down the stone stairs.

But she *had* given herself a headache, one that had started when she met Con and had never totally gone away.

YANNIS HURRIED back to the villa with Cara's medicine. He quietly pushed open her bedroom door and found her sleeping. Despite the dim light, the tear tracks on her face were visible. His heart twisted. His poor Cara, in so much pain it made her cry.

He filled a glass with water and sat next to her on the bed. "Cara, I have your pain medicine."

She slowly opened her eyes and to his dismay, they filled again with tears. "Oh, Yannis."

"No, no, it's okay. The pharmacist says this will help." He fumbled the pills, but managed to hand her the right dosage. "Take these."

She sat up and swallowed the pills. "Don't leave me, Yannis."

"I won't." He couldn't. Maybe not ever. Not ever? His thoughts echoed through his head as he kicked off his shoes and lay down next to her.

He hadn't planned any of this when he'd come back to Aphrodisias for the summer. He'd wanted construction experience, some money for school and a summer at the beach.

Instead, Cara had burst into his life, first in the alley then again at the taverna, her personality as fiery as her luxurious hair. She had led him a merry chase before letting him seduce her—or had it been the other way around?

He grinned to himself. It didn't matter. What mattered was he couldn't get enough of her—had a hard time keeping his hands off her. More than that, he wondered what would happen once the summer ended.

He'd been too busy during school to date seriously, not letting his social life interfere with his career ambitions. But if there were a woman who could distract him, it was Cara.

He stroked her tumbled hair, hoping her headache started to feel better.

Her breathing slowed as she fell back asleep. He closed his eyes and inhaled the scent that was uniquely Cara's, a blend of sun, sea and her own honey-sweetness. As for what would happen to them after their Greek summer together, only the Fates could say.

"COFFEE, *chriso mou?*" At Cara's nod, Athena set a cup down on the small glass table in the garden behind her house. "I can fix you some lunch if you are hungry," she offered. The sun was high overhead, but they sat under an arch of purple and white bougainvillea shading much of the rays.

"Maybe in a little bit." Cara sipped her coffee and stared at Athena's garden. She'd slept late, not even waking when Yannis must have left the villa to go to work. What a Monday. She still felt slightly hungover from her migraine medicine, but the sound of water trickling from the copper wall spigot of the blue-and-white tiled fountain smoothed her fuzzy nerves.

Athena settled into the chair next to her. Today she was wearing a more modern outfit of khaki slacks and a white embroidered blouse and a sturdy pair of walking shoes. "Dr. Aristides arrived this morning on the ferry from Naxos. She brought some students and Demetria drove all of us to the temple property. We stopped for you, but Emma said you had a sick headache yesterday, so we let you sleep. The professor and the students are still there for a preliminary survey."

"What does the professor say?" It had to be good news for Athena judging from the broad smile on her face.

"'Very promising,'" Athena quoted. "She says the site is remarkably similar to a temple excavated down on Crete. That temple turned out to be gigantic and quite a find. Dr. Aristides will make a report to the Hellenic Ministry of Culture as soon as she finishes a preliminary assessment."

Cara stretched out her legs. The acidic coffee wasn't sitting well on her empty stomach. "What does this mean for your museum and Gus's villa project?"

"They are both on hold," Athena admitted. "A bit of a Pyrrhic victory," she said, referring to the ancient Greek battle where the victors were harmed just as much as the losers.

"You knew that would happen when you called in the experts," Cara replied.

"True." Athena reached over and pinched off a brown bloom. "But it is worth it to see the expression on that old goat's face when he finds out. Serves him right for being so underhanded." She smiled, her cheeks wrinkling into a fine net of lines. The tradition of revenge was alive and well on Aphrodisias.

"Well, the archaeologist has thrown enough monkey wrenches into the underhanded property sale. Even if Gus could buy the land, the excavation will take years, and what rich tourist wants to buy a fancy house next to a dig site? Your museum is in a much better position to eventually buy the land and incorporate any archaeological findings into its exhibits."

"Wonderful idea, Cara." Cara's stomach growled. "Eh, you haven't eaten yet today, have you?" Athena leaped up and soon returned with a tray of *spanikopita* squares, grilled bread topped with olive oil and salt along with the ubiquitous Greek coffee cups. "Eat, eat."

"Don't worry, Athena. I'm not going back to what I used to do." To prove her point, Cara bit into a *spanikopita*. The crispy phyllo pastry blended perfectly with the creamy feta cheese and mellow spinach.

"I know that, darling. You are not the same woman you were then. I think Greece has finally been good for you. And good to you."

Cara nearly choked on a stray phyllo crumb. "That's only because no one knows who I am—"

"Who you *were*," Athena rapidly corrected. "And that was never the true you in the first place."

"But Yannis knows about me." The remnants of her headache stirred at the memory.

Athena raised a brow. "Really? When did you tell him?"

"I didn't. I mean, we were talking about how you used to live in Athens and then he mentioned Con and his American widow."

"Oh. I see." Athena was obviously disappointed Cara hadn't taken the chance to come clean with Yannis. "So you told him nothing. You did not tell him how you left home at eighteen to get away from your parents' battles and worked your way up to sailing ships for the richest, most powerful people in the world. How you would have captained your own ship in just a few years had Con not swept you off your feet."

Cara shook her head. "I still don't know why Con singled me out. If I'd had my thinking cap on instead of being dazzled, I would have realized he was just playing me for a fool."

"Stop." Athena raised her hand. "You were everything Con wished he could be but wasn't—cheerful, humorous and liked for yourself, not your money."

"I never had any." Cara could finally muster up a weak smile.

"Constantinos had plenty of money, but he knew it was not enough. He envied the qualities that attracted him to you in the first place." Athena shrugged. "For him, it was easier to drag you down to his own misery rather than lift himself up."

"Really?" Con had envied *her?* Sturdy, redheaded sailor Cara?

"Really." Athena sipped her coffee. "I knew him since he was a boy. His father ignored him and his mother spoiled him—Con swung between thinking he was nothing and thinking he could do no wrong. Never any balance."

Cara sat back in her chair as she stared at a fat bumblebee drinking from a purple bloom. "Oh, Athena, why didn't he tell me any of this? I might have been able to do something to help."

She raised a thick dark brow. "What could you do? You could not starve away your spirit and give it to him, although he was willing to have you try. My darling, only *Theos* above can make a person whole, and Con didn't bother asking Him for help."

"I did," she admitted.

Athena captured her hand and gave it a squeeze. "As did I. But you know Greek men—they are stubborn as the goats and hard as the marble and nothing can make them change. What's done is done, *chriso mou.* You must look to the future, not the past. And your future is maybe here on Aphrodisias, eh?"

"You mean Yannis. I seem to have a tendency to fall for your cousins, Athena."

Her black eyes sharpened like a hawk that had spotted her prey. "So you have fallen in love with young Yannis."

"Love?" Cara clutched her *spanikopita,* feta and phyllo crumbs littering her lap.

"Yes, *love.* What is so bad about loving Yannis? He is a good boy, kind to that gossipy aunt and crook of an uncle." Athena helped herself to the grilled bread.

Cara jumped to her feet, food bits falling to the ground. "Yannis and I don't know each other well enough to even think of the word *love.* When I said I was falling for Yannis, I was just referring to our, um…"

"Passionate summer affair?" Athena interjected in a dry tone.

"Yes, that." Cara fought back a blush at the older woman's phrasing.

"Ah. And of course, you are a sophisticated woman who can have affairs of the body, but not of the heart. A woman who is only out for a hot time in the sack, as you Americans call it."

"Athena!" Cara just knew her face flamed as red as her hair.

"Pah!" Athena spat out. "You lie—not only to me, but to yourself."

"I am not lying," Cara insisted. "Yannis and I could never be in love, not once he knows who I am. He already thinks the worst of me—that I was a blond American bimbo who took half of Con's money—"

"You are no bimbo and Greek law stipulates that a widow without children inherits half the husband's estate. You know that. And by not telling Yannis important things about you, you have taken away his choice to decide who or what you are. You, of all people, who just now wished you had known more about your husband's past."

Cara sighed and slumped into her chair. "I should leave Greece before anyone gets hurt. I've only been dating him a few weeks—if I go back to Michigan now, he will have plenty of time to find somebody else to date this summer."

But the idea of Yannis embracing a sultry Greek beauty or statuesque Scandinavian jolted her stomach and almost startled a cry from her mouth. What if Athena was right? But she couldn't love Yannis after only a few weeks—could she? Athena compressed her lips so hard they vanished, and Cara could tell she was fighting back a retort. But when she did unclamp her mouth enough to speak, it wasn't what Cara expected. "Run away if you must, but at least stay for the big feast."

"What big feast?"

"Yannis's name day feast is Sunday, June 24, the Nativity of Agios Ioannis Prodromos, St. John the Baptist. Despite your merely casual feelings for Yannis, you would disappoint him greatly if you missed it. You know name days are much more important than birthdays here."

Cara did know that, and the Nativity of St. John the Baptist was a major holiday on Aphrodisias.

Athena continued, "His aunt and uncle are throwing a big party for him, and we are all invited."

"We are? Still?" Cara lifted an eyebrow. Athena and Gus were still tussling over the possible temple property.

"Of course!" She gave a belly laugh. "What's a Greek party without arguments? Everyone would fall asleep from boredom. Besides, you can meet his aunt Eleni, my cousin. She's a nice girl, even if all she thinks about is her hairdo, gossip magazines and what to cook for that bum of a husband. But she takes good care of your Yannis."

"He's not *my* Yannis," Cara pointed out yet again.

"Well, I don't see him trying to belong to anyone else, so whatever you do to the boy is certainly working."

The blood rushed to her face yet again. "Athena!"

"Ach, again with the blushes. Listen, *chriso mou,* I was married for twenty-five years and widowed for twenty. When we all lived in Athens, what do you think I did on my weekends off?"

Cara had never really thought about it. "Um, you wove tapestries?"

Athena roared. "I've never heard it called *that* before." She patted Cara's cheek. "No, my dear. I had lovers."

"Lovers?" As in plural?

"Of course. I did not die when my husband did, and there are plenty of kind, tender men who have lost their own spouses but do not plan to remarry." Athena gazed into the garden, a secret smile crossing her face. "So instead of wooing with a promise of marriage, they must woo with their skills in the bedroom."

Cara tried not to shudder, but it was as if her own grandmother was discussing her sex life. "Yannis is not wooing me."

Athena snapped back to the present. "You do not think so? Emma tells Demetria he brings you aspirin when you are sick, fixes food for you, takes you on long, long, *long* drives out into the country—" she wiggled her brows knowingly "—and you think this is not wooing? What do you want him to do—serenade you under your balcony with a bouzouki?" She broke into a famous Greek love song that of course ended with heartbreak and tragedy.

Cara wanted to pinch her. "You see? You see? Even the love songs know what's going to happen if I stay. I don't want to be wooed. I just want to go back to Michigan before anyone gets hurt." Especially her. Maybe she should leave as soon as possible, even before Yannis's name day. The next ferry for the mainland left Saturday, and she could be on it.

"Do you worry about Yannis being hurt or yourself?" Athena eyed her closely, as if guessing at her whirlwind thoughts. "Who will be hurt if you stay, and who will be hurt if you go?"

Cara made a helpless motion. It was too much to consider.

"Okay, okay, I do not mean to bully you. Maybe you need a break to clear your mind?" Athena thought for a minute and snapped her fingers. "Ah! The perfect thing."

"What?" she asked warily.

"My cousin Stavros owns a bus and drives tourists out to the more remote parts of the island. Let him show you the real Aphrodisias, the wild Aphrodisias."

"Why can't I drive myself?"

Athena shook her head. "Easy to get lost out there, have a flat tire. Stavros would be happy to do this for you. I'd go with you, but the roads are too rough for me." She grabbed her hip and winced, Cara thought, a bit theatrically.

"Fine. What is it, a half-day tour?"

"Exactly. How about Friday?"

"Friday, Emma is going on a day trip to Santorini. I guess Niko is showing her the remnants of the volcano there."

"Niko, eh?" Athena rolled her eyes. "That boy would date a goat if it wore a blond wig."

"Athena…" Cara had had much the same thought, but had never voiced it from loyalty to her friend.

"Your friend is much too beautiful and smart for him. And his mother…" The older woman shuddered. "She makes Jocasta look like a disinterested mother."

Cara snorted. Jocasta was the mother of the mythological King Oedipus and the inspiration for Oedipal complexes everywhere.

"And Emma, does she know you're considering leaving?"

"No, I haven't discussed it with her, but if I do go, I'll make arrangements to pay for the rest of her summer here."

"And you think she will use your money to stay when you go?"

Cara sighed. "No, I suppose not."

"Of course not. She is a good friend to you, and she will leave when you leave."

"Athena…" Cara could feel the guilt sweeping over her. Running away was bad enough, but to drag her friend with her?

"Eh, not to worry, Karoleena. Didn't you say Niko was distracting Emma from her schoolwork? It will do her good to get away from him."

"I don't like to manipulate my friends that way, Athena."

Athena's black gaze slid away from hers and she busied herself with stacking the appetizer plates. "Emma will work things out for herself. But let Stavros take you on a nice calm trip into the heart of Aphrodisias. The goddess will help you know what to do, especially if you ask her."

As far as Cara's love life was concerned, Aphrodite would either shake her head in disgust or hold her nose at how bad Cara was stinking things up. Cara didn't see how visiting the deserted interior of the island would help, but a half day out in the sticks would make little difference. "Okay, one short trip with Stavros. Then I have to go."

Athena bent down to kiss her on the cheek. "Stavros will show you a new side of Aphrodisias you've never seen."

EMMA KNOCKED on Athena's blue door and Demetria opened it. "Emma!" Demetria swept her into a big hug and cheek-kiss. "You just missed Cara. She is going to the beach for some fresh air."

"Is she feeling better?" Emma had worried over Cara's pale face and puffy eyes this morning.

"Nothing a snack and some coffee couldn't help. Eh, you want something to eat?" Demetria overrode Emma's polite refusals and shepherded her toward the kitchen.

Athena was talking on the phone in the hallway, not quite yelling at someone. Athena started slightly to see Emma and then she grinned. She hung up and Demetria said something to her in Greek.

"English, please, Demetria. It's rude to speak Greek in front of our American guest."

Demetria snorted. "Fine. What did Stavros say?"

"Yes, naturally. Especially when I told him I'd tell his mother if he didn't do it."

Emma looked between them, confused. Demetria wore a long-suffering look on her face, while Athena's expression could only be described as triumphant.

"If you're in the middle of something, I can just go meet Cara at the beach…" she offered, her dislike of conflict kicking in.

"No, no!" Athena caught her elbow with a surprisingly strong grip. "In fact, I need you to do a favor for me, as well. Come into the kitchen, and I'll tell you how you can help our friend Cara."

Curiosity won out over caution, and Emma let herself be towed into the kitchen like a rowboat on the ocean. She just hoped she wouldn't get pulled into a whirlpool.

"CARA?" Emma approached her friend, who was lying on the couch reading an actual novel in Greek. She didn't know Cara could read Greek, as well as speak it.

Emma was impressed. She could read individual letters thanks to her mathematical training, of course, but putting them all together was a totally different skill.

"Yes, Emma?" Cara looked up from what appeared to be a paperback romance. Perfect summer reading, even if in another alphabet. Previously, Cara had always disdained romance novels, saying they raised unrealistic expectations of what men were actually like. Emma had been sad to hear that, so Cara's change of mind was a good sign.

Emma sat next to her. "Are you enjoying our trip?"

Cara frowned, puzzled. "Sure. Are you?"

"Absolutely." Shoot, she wasn't doing this right. She wasn't tricky like Athena, but she'd promised the older woman to help out Cara. "I mean, is Greece okay for you?"

"Emma, why do you ask?" Cara closed the book and set it on the coffee table.

"Athena said you had some unpleasant times associated with Greece."

"Oh." Cara sighed and sat up. "What else did she say?"

Emma looked away and fidgeted. "That was about it."

"Right." Cara gave her a half grin. "Well, remember when I told you I was married before?"

"Yeah, that was a surprise." She thought she'd known Cara pretty well until then.

"My husband was a Greek guy. We lived in Athens for a few years."

Emma blinked several times. So that was how Cara understood Greek so well.

"His name was Constantine, and he was so charming, really smooth. At least until right after the wedding. Then Prince Charming turned into a frog. No, not a frog—frogs are kind of cute—a slug."

"I'm really sorry he didn't treat you well, Cara. When did you divorce him?"

Cara tipped her head and studied Emma. "Athena really didn't tell you everything, did she?" Without waiting for an answer, she continued. "I only discovered that Constantine actually had a heart when it gave out as he was fu— ahem, boinking his mistress. The scandal was all over Europe."

"He died? As he was, um…" Emma clutched her own chest in shock. She didn't know what was more horrifying—the actual death of Cara's husband or the sordid circumstances. "Wow, Cara, I am so, so sorry." She pulled Cara into a swift hug, patting her springy hair. "And yet here you are in Greece. You are a brave woman to come back again and face your past—"

"Emma." Cara's voice vibrated against Emma's shoulder. "Emma, I can't breathe."

"Oh, sorry." She let go, and Cara sucked in a deep breath. Emma had a horrible thought. "Cara, are you using up all your inherited money to pay for our trip?"

Cara flopped back onto the couch and guffawed. "Constantine was one of the ten richest men in Greece. Greek law dictates that childless widows inherit half the estate. So you see before you, sweet Emma, one of the richest women in Greece."

"No!" Emma's jaw dropped.

"Oh, yes. You know the old saying, 'If you marry for money, you earn every penny'? I married Con for love, but wound up paying through the nose." She looked away, obviously lost in unpleasant memories.

Emma's stomach contracted. Their vacation of a lifetime was subsidized by Cara's pain and heartache. "Yannis never mentioned any of this to Nick."

Cara's head whipped around from where she'd been staring into space. "Yannis doesn't know, and you and I aren't going to tell him. Do you know how awkward it is for a regular guy to date a superrich woman? Everyone assumes he's a gigolo and she's bribing him for sex."

"Oh, please, Cara, anyone can tell that's not true," Emma scoffed.

"Remember that Scandinavian princess who married her handsome, younger bodyguard? The paparazzi called them 'the Princess and her Pauper' and calculated how much money he would earn every time they had sex."

"That's awful." Emma couldn't imagine what kind of people would do something like that.

"The paparazzi would love to get photos of Yannis and me and write lies about us." Cara gave her a crooked smile. "You could pay off your student loans easily if you let them know I was back in Greece dating a cute guy."

"Forget it," Emma retorted. "I'll teach algebra to sixth graders before I betray a friend."

"And does Nick still think you're a middle school math teacher?"

Emma picked at the fringe on the couch's woven throw. "Well, yeah."

"Why haven't you told him?" This time, Cara's tone was curious, rather than condemning, so Emma thought first instead of being defensive.

"I guess I was tired of all the preconceived notions about math geeks, all the high expectations I carry throughout the school year. My professors don't mean to pressure me so much, but then they brag about me to their colleagues at other schools. And when I present at symposiums or write journal articles, I can just feel everyone waiting for me to fail. Nick, well..." She shrugged her shoulders. "He doesn't expect anything of me except to enjoy myself. It's a nice change."

"Emma, I had no idea you felt that way." Cara touched Emma's hand. "You should have said something."

"Like you told me about being one of the richest women in Greece?" Emma felt an embarrassed flush creep up her face. "And I made a big deal over treating you to that bikini when you could buy two of everything in the shop."

Cara squeezed her hand, startling Emma. Cara was a wonderful friend, but definitely not touchy-feely. Emma was always the one who initiated hugs and comforting pats. "Emma, you were the first person in a long time to buy me a gift out of the goodness of your heart." Cara's blue eyes filled with tears. "No strings attached, no expectations except to enjoy myself."

Emma's eyes blurred, as well, as Cara echoed her previous sentiments. "You and I, what a pair."

Cara nodded and swiped her eyes with the backs of her hands. "I know. It's like being back in Greece is stripping away all the bandages I slapped on myself over the years. I don't know how much more I can take before I'm completely raw." She shivered despite the warm evening air blowing through the French doors.

"Yannis would help you heal, I just know it."

Cara sat up straight, looking alarmed. "Swear to me you

won't tell him this stuff. He doesn't need to get dragged into my mess for what's only some summer fun."

"You should tell him at some point."

"Like you told Nick all about yourself?" Cara's moment of weakness was obviously over.

"Okay, Miss Smarty-Pants, let's make a deal. I'll tell Nick about my doctoral work if you tell Yannis about your late husband and your money."

"They'll knock each other over racing to get away from us," Cara warned.

"If they do, then good riddance!" Emma declared. "We deserve better. So do we have a deal for this week?"

Cara hesitated. "Leave that up to me, Emma. I'll figure out when."

"Okay, Cara. I promise. But I think Yannis would understand."

Cara frowned at her, and Emma subsided. Cara had potential happiness with Yannis within her grasp, but was afraid to reach out for it, thanks to a dreadful marriage. And all Emma had to do to help was go along with Athena's plan.

Any guilt about deceiving Cara flew out the arched, whitewashed window. That horrible husband of hers! He certainly hadn't deserved Cara's love and trust.

Emma shook her head. No wonder Cara was gun-shy, even with such a nice guy as Yannis. Nick couldn't say enough good things about him, and you'd have to be blind to miss how Cara looked at him, and vice versa. But she knew if she pressed the subject, Cara would just close up on her. "So, Cara, tell me about your paperback."

Cara glanced down at the forgotten book on the table. "Oh, yeah, it's called *Naked Model,* and it's lots of fun. Here, let me translate the good parts for you."

"Oooh." Emma sat on the couch next to Cara and folded her leg under her as she listened to her friend read.

Emma didn't think Cara realized how wistful she sounded as she read the falling in love parts aloud. But that was okay. Soon she and Yannis would realize they were meant for each other, even if they did need a little nudge from Emma and Athena.

YANNIS TAPPED on Cara's door after work and immediately swept her into his arms. She opened her mouth eagerly to his and clung to him as if she were stuck in an Aphrodisian riptide. He pushed her inside the villa and eagerly dipped his tongue into her honeyed mouth, her luxuriant hair caressing his cheeks.

He finally lifted his head to say, "Let's go to bed."

Instead of agreeing, Cara stepped away from him. "Yannis, I have something to tell you." She looked nervous, which was unusual for her. "This is so hard to say." She hugged her arms around herself.

He moved to hug her but she jumped back. "Okay, Cara." He lifted his hands. "You can tell me anything." Unless…was she breaking up with him? He really didn't want to hear *that*. He shoved his hands into his pockets. "If you don't want to go out with me anymore…" he began.

"No, not that. It's something else." She looked pale and kept clutching nervously at her waist. Was it possible? He rapidly counted back. Just a few weeks since they had begun making love together.

"Are you…" He gestured vaguely at her middle and trailed off. "Are we, um, expecting?"

"What?" Her eyes grew wide with shock. "Expecting a baby? No, of course not! Geez, Yannis."

"Okay, okay," he backpedaled, a weird sense of disappointment dogging him. Not that he had wanted to cause an accidental pregnancy, but still...the image of a little girl or boy with bright blue eyes and red-tinged dark curly hair lurked in the back of his mind. Yannis Petrides, who didn't even want the responsibility of a goldfish, mooning over babies? He rubbed his face. What was going on with him?

Her dry laugh surprised him. "After that notion, maybe my bit of information won't be so horrifying. Come sit before you fall over." Yannis sat next to her on the sofa, still anxious to hear what she had to say.

She took a deep breath. "Yannis, I was married before."

Well, that wasn't what he'd expected to hear. His Cara had been someone's wife? Been in his bed?

The words spilled from her now that she'd started. "I met him when I was very young, he was several years older and swept me off my feet and I loved him, but he didn't really love me back and it ended badly for both of us..." She trailed off, her shoulders slumping.

How could the man *not* love Cara? Outrage straightened Yannis's spine. She was utterly lovable. What if the fool realized what he'd lost and came after her again? Yannis wouldn't step aside for any man. "Where does he live now?"

She looked uneasy again. "He had a heart attack two years ago and died. Yannis, I'm a widow."

A widow? The only thought that passed through his stunned brain was that Cara was the sexiest widow he'd ever seen.

WITH HIS WIDE EYES and gaping mouth, Yannis reminded Cara of a fish that had accidentally jumped onto her ship's deck. "Yannis?" she asked cautiously.

"A widow?"

"Yes. I normally wear a lot of black." Her lame joke made him frown.

Cara walked to the balcony doors for some fresh air. Her honesty had gone over like a lead balloon. Well, better she find out his true colors now rather than later, when she'd gone and fallen in love with him.

Love?

"Cara?"

She nodded silently, still facing out over the town. It was that quiet, hot time of day when only the tourists wandered the streets and the locals were all home in bed for their afternoon nap, either sleeping or doing other things. Things she could be doing with Yannis, if it weren't for her conscience.

"Do you have children?"

Longing and loss slammed into her. Oh, she'd wanted them, but her poor body had known better. "No. If I had children, I would be with them, not fooling around all summer."

He came up next to her and took her shoulders. "Fooling around? Is that what you think this is?"

She looked up into his angry face. Good—anger she could deal with, having had plenty of experience with that.

"What else?" She forced herself to shrug, lifting his hands off her. So she'd be heading back to Michigan sooner than she thought. There was no way she'd tell him the full extent of her humiliation and notoriety. Yannis would pity her, and she didn't want his pity.

"What else?" he echoed. "Yeah, well, I guess you had some lost time to make up for, right?"

"Right." What she hoped was a smile curved her lips. "You're okay with that, aren't you, Yannis? My husband—" geez, she hated to refer to Con as that "—my husband was older and more interested in other things—" like his mistress "—so we rarely spent any time together."

"You should have told me before," he snapped. "I hate liars. I guess Athena and the whole rest of the island already know, and I am the last one."

"No, only Athena and Emma. Not Nick, not your uncle, if that makes you feel better."

He jerked his arm into the air in a typically Greek gesture of impatience. "It doesn't."

Another petulant Greek man to deal with? She didn't need that. "What's done is done. What are you going to do about it?"

"I don't know!" He was steaming mad.

"Then you should go until you decide."

That threw him for a loop. Greeks were used to shouting out their differences until they either got into a fistfight or made up. "I go, then! You think about anything else you forgot to tell me and I may listen. Or not." He strode to the door and noisily closed it behind him.

Cara hastily stepped back from the balcony so Yannis couldn't see her watch him hop on his scooter and roar away.

Another man gone. Did Cara have the knack or what?

11

CARA SHOULDERED her backpack and found the bus Athena had described waiting in the small ferry dock parking lot. The bus was painted in the cheerful blue-and-white colors of the Greek flag overlaid with the ever-present summer dust. She peeked in the open door.

"Stavros?" she inquired of the man in the driver's seat.

"Eh, you must be Miss Cara." Stavros looked like a Greek tourism poster, barrel-chested and with a luxurious black mustache. "Welcome to my bus. I take good care of you, or else Athena…" He shuddered theatrically and then gave a big belly laugh.

Cara laughed, as well, her first since her argument with Yannis. She hadn't heard from him for three days and hadn't called him, either, despite Emma's urging. She wasn't going to chase after a man who obviously wanted to stay away from her.

She and the driver chatted for a few minutes, Stavros showing her pictures of his plump wife and good-looking children, who would be finishing the Greek version of high school in the next couple years. Cara made a mental note to expand her secret scholarship fund to include his children.

"Okay, we go." He slammed the bus door and turned over the ignition, the bus roaring to life after a couple false starts.

Cara looked around. She was alone on the bus. "Stavros, where is the rest of the tour?"

Stavros shrugged. "We pick them up in a couple kilometers, miss."

"Oh. All right." Cara fell into a vinyl seat as Stavros gunned the bus forward. They jolted through town for a few minutes until Stavros yanked the wheel to the side and stopped at a corner near the swimsuit shop. He flipped open the door.

"Eh, come on up," he called to someone standing on the sidewalk.

A voice called in Greek, "Stavros, come into the office to talk about your remodeling. Aunt Eleni sent pastries again today."

Instead of a busload of tourists, Cara saw a familiar black head ascend the steps. "Yannis?" Cara leaned down.

"Cara?" He ran up the stairs into the bus. "What are you—oof!" Stavros stomped on the accelerator and Yannis staggered into the aisle. Fortunately he hadn't fallen out the still-open door.

Yannis pulled himself into the seat across from Cara and berated Stavros for his reckless driving before turning to Cara. "What are you doing here?" he repeated, looking suspiciously from Stavros back to her.

She couldn't very well say Athena was sending her on a pilgrimage to ask the goddess Aphrodite for help with her screwed-up love life. Cara figured love pilgrimages were off the itinerary, since she was officially swearing off men for the rest of her life. Was there an organization in Greece for not-quite-virginal vestal virgins? "Athena's sending me on a tour so I can see the interior of the island." Before Cara left on the ferry for Mykonos tomorrow, not that Athena knew she was leaving. She'd been careful to keep her reservations a secret from Emma, as well, who was still madly in love with Nick. Cara had paid rent for the rest of the summer and planned to leave a nice envelope of euros for her friend to use.

"A bus tour?" He looked puzzled. "I would have taken you anywhere you wanted."

That was the problem. He would have, but that would mean she would spend more and more time with him, and never want to leave him.

"Well, I know you're busy with your uncle's projects…." Her sentence drifted off as she realized that most likely wasn't the case.

He raised a cynical eyebrow. "Not as busy as I would have been if that land wasn't covered in a swarm of grubby archaeology students."

Cara nodded. Any kind of development was on hold until the archaeologist submitted her official report to the antiquities commission. "So you were waiting on the corner for a bus ride?"

"Athena said Stavros needed to talk to me about remodeling his kitchen."

They both looked accusingly at Stavros, who was studiously ignoring their conversation. Yannis raised his voice. "So, Stavros, you want a new kitchen? I have the feeling your wife doesn't know anything about that."

"Well, uh…"

Cara joined in. "I'll be sure Athena tells her what a nice surprise you have for her. I bet you want the very best— cherry cabinets, granite countertops, marble floors."

"And don't forget the stainless-steel German appliances," Yannis added with a touch of maliciousness.

The bus driver hunched his wide shoulders over the steering wheel. "Yannis, *parakaló…*"

"Don't you 'please, Yannis' me, Stavros. What's the deal?"

Stavros looked up in the wide rearview mirror, his eyes pleading. "All right, all right. Athena wanted to surprise the two of you with a romantic bus ride into the heart of Aphrodisias." Just then Stavros hit a large pothole, sending them practically to the ceiling. The bus backfired, the smell of diesel fumes wafting through the window. Oh, yes, this was the essence of romance.

Yannis scoffed. "Give me a break, Stavros. You have to go along with every foolish notion an old lady tells you?"

It shouldn't have hurt Cara to hear he didn't want to spend time with her, since that was what she had intended by leaving tomorrow—but it did hurt.

"No, no, I swear. I didn't want to fool you like this, but Athena threatened to call my mother if I didn't help her." He wiped sweat off his forehead. "Please don't tell my wife about a new kitchen. She's begging me to remodel and I just can't afford it now. The bus needs a new exhaust system, fuel prices are terrible…" He ran out of breath.

Yannis looked at Cara, who shrugged. Despite their previous argument, she couldn't blame Stavros—he was a victim of meddling as much as they were. "Okay, okay." Yannis added in Greek, "We all know how women can be, right, *philos?*"

Cara rolled her eyes quickly, but Yannis caught her. "Hey, you understood that?"

"A bit. *Philos* is 'friend', right?"

"Yeah, not bad." Yannis slapped Stavros on the back. "See how smart this lady is, Stav? Only on the island a few weeks and picking up our language like *that*." He snapped his fingers.

Actually, Cara felt more dishonest than smart. "I studied a bit before I came, but you all speak so quickly, it's hard for a beginner to understand." It had taken Cara several months of Greek lessons with Athena before she could begin to understand native Greeks speaking with each other.

The men laughed, Stavros finally relaxing. Cara wished she could. There was still so much left unsaid between her and Yannis. Fortunately it would be a short bus tour and she could probably avoid a heavy-duty conversation where they were forced to hash out their differences. She'd raise a cloud of Greek dust running away from the bus once they returned to the village. "We Greeks just have a lot to say, right, Yannis? That's why we talk fast."

Yannis stared solemnly at her. "And we want to make sure everybody on the island can hear what we have to say, that's why we talk loud." He leaned over to Cara. "But some people never learn how to talk about things at all." Cara froze at his cold blue gaze. The bus pitched again and Cara stared straight ahead, trying to endure the bumpy, smelly ride somewhere into Back of Nowhere, Aphrodisias.

STAV NEEDED TO BUY new shocks as well as an exhaust system. About an hour later, which seemed like six to Yannis's severely bruised ass, Stav pulled over in a small clearing. Yannis stood up and frowned. "What are we doing here, Stav? There's nothing around but some rocks and weeds."

Stavros shrugged. "Don't ask me. I've never heard of this place and neither have the other tour-bus operators. But Athena says there's a grotto if you follow the trail for a half mile or so."

Cara furrowed her brow, obviously expecting some well-marked pathway. Yannis grimaced.

"See that worn spot in the grass? That's the trail," Stav told them. It disappeared behind some boulders and then reappeared several hundred yards up the hill.

"Nice day for a hike, eh?" Stavros gave him a wide, tour-bus operator grin. Too bad the only tip Yannis had for him was one that involved vulgar anatomical possibilities.

But Cara was already moving toward the door. "Oh, stay with Stavros if you don't feel like hiking, I won't be long. You have the whole summer to hike, after all."

He frowned. It sounded as if she didn't plan to hike anymore during the summer. Maybe she didn't want him around and was dumping him with Stav. Well, that was too bad, since they had unfinished business. But she was already down the steps. He followed, half considering telling Stav's wife about her fake new kitchen anyway. "You're not coming with us, are you, Stav?"

"No, no. You know my bad knee." He vaguely gestured at his pant leg. "Too much for me."

"Lay off the baklava, and you'll move around easier."

His friend glared at him, his mustache twitching in indignation. "Enjoy your hike, Yannis."

"Thanks a lot." He clattered out of the bus and followed Cara up the goat path. She had shouldered her backpack and walked ahead without acknowledging him. The path was too narrow to walk next to her, but at least he consoled himself with a great view. Not the island of course, but Cara. Her legs were creamy-golden and disappeared into khaki shorts that cupped her ass just the way he wanted to.

Maybe this hike wasn't quite a loss. She reached a gigantic boulder and turned to wait for him. "Oh, you're coming with me. I guess you want to talk about what happened—"

He shrugged nonchalantly, as if finding out she'd kept large parts of her life secret from him didn't bother him. "You don't want to talk, I don't talk."

"Oh." She was puzzled. "If you don't want to talk, what do you—"

He cut off her words with a hard kiss, spinning her out of sight of the bus and pressing her against the warm rock. She clutched his shoulders in surprise, but quickly melted in his arms, as she always had. At least that hadn't changed. He pulled back from her soft lips. "Tell me you still want this—you still want me."

She was fighting some internal battle—he could tell by her furrowed brow and set jaw. With a sigh, she pulled him back to her and whispered, "yes," into the hollow of his throat.

Yannis shoved down the sweeping sense of relief at her yielding to him and focused on making sure she'd never regret it. He slipped a hand under her tight white T-shirt and his other hand unzipped her shorts.

With another couple motions, her shorts and panties were around her ankles, her front-close bra flapped open and her T-shirt was around her neck. Her backpack cushioned her skin from the rock's surface, which would be good when he pushed inside her.

He was mindless as usual around Cara, focusing only on sucking on her pretty coral-tipped breasts and massaging her hard little clit. Her juices dampened his fingers and her face tightened as she gave short breathy cries, panting his name. He slid down her body and parted her plump folds to lick her sweet button, and her cries broadened into a scream.

She slumped forward onto him, and he gladly bore her weight. His awareness expanded to notice his rock-hard cock practically bulging out the leg of his shorts and he was about to figure out what do about it that didn't involve a nonexistent condom when he heard a familiar and ominous explosion.

"Shit!" Why was Stav firing up the bus? Yannis yanked Cara's shirt down and shorts up and charged down the hill to the clearing.

"What the hell!" A pile of luggage sat on the ground, and Stav was pulling away. "Stavros, get back here!" But the man only waved before tooting the horn nastily.

Yannis gave him an obscene gesture that merely earned him a faceful of Aphrodisian dust and a diminishing view of the blue-and-white bus. Coughing, he turned to the heap of suitcases.

Cara picked her way down the last meters to the clearing, her cheeks still pink and her eyes still glassy from her orgasm. "Yannis, where is Stavros going?"

He shrugged helplessly. "I have no idea. Wait—" He pulled a folded note off the top bag. Cara yanked it from his hand and opened the paper. "Oh, I don't believe this."

"What?" He craned his neck to read over her shoulder. She hadn't fixed her bra yet, so he could see the tips of her nipples under her shirt. Forcing himself to concentrate, he read the note written in English. "This is Athena's doing?"

Cara pursed her lips.

Dear Cara, as a treat to you and Yannis, I have arranged a romantic, rustic weekend at Aphrodite's Grotto. These supplies include everything you need to have a wonderful time together. Emma and Eleni helped pack for you, so they know you are gone. Stavros will come pick you up Sunday in plenty of time for Yannis's party. I am sure you both have plenty to talk about. All my love, Athena.

Cara shouted into the quiet air. "Athena, I'm going to strangle you!"

"What? Why would she strand us in the middle of nowhere?" And worst of all, without condoms, no doubt. Yannis unzipped one duffel bag and found clean clothes. Another had a small tent, and in two bags were sleeping bags. A cardboard box held camping rations and water. "Give me your cell phone, Cara. I'll call one of my cousins to come get us." The faster they got back to town, the faster he could take Cara to bed and make her forget she'd ever loved another man.

"Here." She handed it to him and he pressed several buttons.

"It's not turning on, and there should be service even out here." He slid open the battery compartment and showed her the empty slot.

"Great, somebody removed the battery. Try yours, then." Cara sucked her lower lip into her mouth, looking worried.

He shrugged helplessly. "Niko asked to borrow it and then forgot to give it back." Yannis would buy Niko a huge beer as soon as he saw him again. He fought back a grin, knowing Cara was genuinely concerned. As far as he was concerned, stranding him in the wilderness with a beautiful woman deserved a nice thank-you.

"Forgot on purpose, I bet."

Yannis walked around the clearing, stirring up the settling dust. "Looks like we're here until Stavros comes back for us Sunday, but where are we supposed to camp? Here in the road?" He didn't much care as long as they had the tent for privacy.

Cara showed him the paper. "Here's a map at the bottom of the note to the grotto she was talking about. I guess there's a pond or something there."

"Okay." Yannis eyed the pile and lifted the tent and duffel bag. "This'll take more than one trip. Grab what you can manage."

"What do we do with the rest of it?" Cara lifted a sleeping bag in each arm.

He balanced his load and started up the trail. "If somebody comes by to steal it while we're gone, they can offer us a ride back to town."

YANNIS TURNED A CORNER and gave a low whistle.

"What?" His broad shoulders blocked Cara's view. "What is it?"

"Come see." He moved to the side and Cara saw what had elicited his whistle. It wasn't a pond, as she'd thought from the map. It was an ancient hot spring about the size of an American backyard swimming pool, the opaque water the color of expensive pale green jade.

Three walls of a marble bathhouse stood at one end of the spring, a small arched opening in the back wall illuminating the spring's smooth, glassy surface. "I hope they packed swimsuits for us," Cara muttered, still shaky after her abrupt capitulation to Yannis's caresses. Despite her amazing sexual release, she was not thinking kindly of Emma and Athena's stunt, obviously designed to make her miss her ferry reservation. Probably Athena's cousins ran the reservation office, too.

"I don't," Yannis replied with a grin. "I've never heard of this hot spring. The popular ones are down on the coast near the hotels."

"A real hot spring." Cara set down the sleeping bags and

wondered if they zipped together into one big bag. "We may as well stay right here. The tent can go on the flat area over there."

"Okay." He dropped the tent gear where she pointed. "I'll go get the rest of the supplies and then put up the tent." He went back down the hill and she unzipped the tent bag.

Piece of cake. It was a modern backpacking tent and didn't require a second person for setup. Within a few minutes, she'd popped up the tent, rolled out mats for extra padding, and zipped together the sleeping bags after some consideration. It would be foolish to think she could be alone with Yannis all weekend and not want to touch his beautiful body or watch his handsome face tighten as she touched him.

Being out in the fresh air had mellowed her panicky mood somewhat, the trickling of the springwater in the grotto soothing her nerves. She carried the duffel into the tent to find out what Emma had packed for a "romantic, rustic weekend." Flannel and silk?

She laughed to find that wasn't far off the mark. Emma had tossed in several slinky nightgowns along with clean underwear and rolled-up hiking socks, pretty much what she had expected. But on top of the socks was a flowery-smelling paper bag.

Curious, she opened the bag and lifted out a note. Underneath was a pile of freshly picked pink rose petals. Rose petals to strew on a sleeping bag? That was taking it a bit far.

She unfolded the note.

Dear Cara, the petals are for an offering to the goddess Aphrodite. Toss them in her spring and wish for your heart's desire. Love, Athena.

Cara sat back on her heels. Now that was just silly. Rose petals in water might make a nice bath, but they would never grant her heart's desire. She shook her head and stuffed the note back into the paper bag. Rose petals aside, she hoped Athena had packed more toiletries than that to keep her smelling nice this weekend.

Yes, she'd even packed Cara's toiletry case, which bulged at the seams. Hoping it contained her deodorant and toothbrush, Cara unfastened the case and a mountain of condoms fell out on the sleeping bag.

A delighted whistle came from behind her. Cara shifted around to find Yannis rubbing his hands together. "I didn't think there were that many condoms on the island. Remind me to buy Emma a white wine when we get back to civilization."

Heat crawled up her face. "Maybe they're from Athena."

He grimaced. "I wouldn't be surprised, but at this point I don't care." He swept the packets off the sleeping bag save one, which he held up invitingly. "It would be rude to let these go to waste."

Cara just couldn't resist him—she knew that now. "We certainly don't want to be rude." She pulled her shirt and loose bra off in one swift motion, enjoying how his nostrils flared at the sight of her bare breasts. She shimmied out of her shorts and underwear and kicked off her hiking boots. "Wanna go for a swim?" She walked toward the water's edge, as she heard his clothing and work boots hit the ground.

"No, but how about some skinny-dipping?" He swept her up against his own naked body and tested the water with his toe. "Perfect." He carried her into the spring, the warm water lapping around her bottom. He stopped and slowly sank them both until they were shoulder-deep, sitting side by side on a built-in marble bench below the surface.

Cara sighed and closed her eyes, the heat relaxing muscles she didn't realize were tight. It was like being in a hot bath, but more slippery and buoyant from the mineral content. She rolled her shoulders and neck. "Oh, that's lovely."

"Yes, you are."

She looked at him in surprise, his blue gaze intent on her face.

"Always, to me." Yannis continued, "When I kiss you here." He kissed her lips gently. "And here." He gave her little kisses over her cheeks. "And here." He kissed the column of her neck. "And when I touch you here."

She felt the ripples of his hand moving through the water and then he cupped her. "Your plump breast filling my hand, reacting as I play with you."

Cara swung her leg over his lap to fully face him. He quickly found the juncture of her thighs. "And here—the sweet place I need to be." He pulled her hand down to his cock and to her surprise, he was already wearing a condom. He must have put it on when he undressed. "Let me come in you, sweet Cara."

Her answer was a sweet kiss on his lips. He caught her around the hips and eased into her. They both sighed as he sank deep, reaching her inner core he had just barely teased behind the boulder a half hour ago.

"Yes, Yannis." Using the bench for leverage, Cara rose and lowered herself onto him. Her movements were slow and purposeful as the warm water ebbed and flowed where they were joined. She took the time to smooth back a stray glossy curl from his brow. To kiss his forehead, and to draw patterns in the black hair that cushioned his gold medallion—Agios Ioannis Prodromos, of course, St. John the Baptist, whose feast day she would celebrate after all, before leaving Aphrodisias.

She shook her head.

"What, Cara *mou?*" His glazed-over eyes hadn't missed her hesitation.

"Nothing." She moved faster on him, determined to make their time in the spring a memorable one. Religion was quickly forgotten and the sheer pagan nature of the place took over. Yannis dug his fingers into her butt and thrust up into her.

His lips captured her wet nipple as it bobbed out of the water, his hard suction washing down to her clit. He let go of her for a second, and she frowned down at him.

He grinned up at her. "Mmm, salty. Like some other places I like to lick." He stroked her tiny knot of nerves between them and Cara felt herself swell into his touch. She yanked his head to her breasts, muffling his self-satisfied chuckle.

His stubble skidded over her wet flesh and she dug her fingers into his slippery shoulders at the sweet friction. The merciless water caressed every inch of her outer being while his cock glided deep inside her. Her emotions were not neglected, either, thanks to the sweet things he was murmuring to her in Greek, half of which she missed because of the growing roar in her ears.

Suddenly her orgasm rushed over her like a dammed river breaking its banks. "Oh, Yannis, Yannis," she cried, the turbulent water washing over where his cock pleasured her.

"Cara, Cara *mou,* lovely Cara," he chanted, diving into her again. His beautiful face, so much like a classical statue, took on an expression that was all man as he groaned his pleasure at being inside her.

The water gradually calmed around them, and Yannis raised his lips for a kiss. "Ah, Cara, what you do to me."

"And you, too, Yannis." So they nestled still joined while the sun shone through the arched window and cast flickering patterns on the jade-colored water.

12

CARA COLLAPSED next to Yannis on a blanket at the edge of the spring. "Oh, Yannis, that was wonderful." Yannis had spent a long night in the cozy tent pleasuring her and they had stoked up with a Saturday-morning breakfast of protein bars before running back to the spring. Their quick cleanup had turned into a slow, sensual exploration half-in, half-out of the spring. She was his water nymph, his insatiable muse.

"Well, Cara, you make me crazy for you." Yannis shoved his hand through his wild tangle of curls. He really needed to find a comb, but didn't care a bit at this point. Cara leaned over and kissed his forehead.

"Is that a bad thing?" she asked coyly, running her hand down his belly.

"I am a satyr around you. You look at me and I harden." He gestured down to his erection, which never seemed to go away when he touched her. Or was near her. Or even thought of her.

"A satyr? I saw one of those painted on a vase in Athens. He actually had a wineglass balanced on his erection." Cara reached for a water bottle and pretended to set it on top of him.

He sat up in protest, automatically raising his hand in self-protection. "Hey!"

"All right, all right." Cara giggled and set the bottle down. He snuggled her onto his shoulder and stroked her silky back. They were under a small tree that wouldn't afford them much shade soon once the sun was overhead. He needed to rub some sunscreen onto the pale triangles usually covered by her bikini. She had loved it before when he massaged her breasts with the slick lotion....

"And what do you think your aunt and uncle will say about you disappearing for the weekend?"

Okay, now his erection was subsiding. "I am a man. I answer to no one but myself." He winked at her to let her know he was joking. She seemed touchy about the macho aspects of Greek culture.

"And I am a woman. I answer to no one but myself." She gave him a haughty look.

"Except Athena." He kissed her shoulder.

She made a growling noise. "She's gone too far this time."

"Okay, *not* Athena." He laughed but then grew serious. "I have an idea. Just for now, why don't we answer to each other?"

"EACH OTHER?" Cara wasn't sure what he meant. Answer to each other? She gave him a puzzled look and then re-alization dawned and she bit her lip. She'd gone from self-reliance as a single woman to utter dependence on her husband and then back to a shaky sense of independence. Yannis's suggestion was something new.

"Yeah, each other." He gave her a quick smile. "I look out for you, and you look out for me. These hills are pretty wild—you never know what could come roaring out of them—minotaurs, centaurs, cyclopses—"

"Goats, donkeys, rabbits," she interrupted, trying to avoid his real question.

It didn't work. "So what do you say, Cara *mou?* Will you protect me from the wild bunnies?"

"Okay, Yannis. And will you protect me from…" She was about to say "myself," but knew that wasn't true anymore. The only danger she posed to herself was letting her heart get broken.

He was waiting for her to finish her sentence, so she tried again. "Will you protect me from any feral goats?"

"Absolutely." He kissed her, but not before she saw a flash of disappointment in his eyes at her hesitation. She hated to be the one who put it there, but she didn't know what else to say.

She sighed as his breathing slowed. It was simple for him. He got up every day, went to work and came home to his doting aunt. Replace his aunt with a wife in a few years and his life would continue on, probably much like his uncle's—tied into the island's rhythms and cycles, adjusting to the times, but remaining essentially the same.

A rose-scented breeze wafted to her. Those rose petals again. Yannis had mentioned the scent in her luggage last night, but she'd told him it came from a potpourri sachet. He'd nodded uncomprehendingly, obviously writing it off as some girlie thing.

Her heart's desire. No, she wouldn't wish for something like that when she wasn't even sure what it was. Yannis shifted under her, his big, warm hand coming up to rest on her shoulder. Cara buried her face in his neck, inhaling his salty male scent, the firm muscles of his chest cushioning her breasts. Even in sleep he was sexy, his penis still half-hard from their lovemaking.

Oh, who was she kidding? *Yannis* was her heart's desire. It would be crazy to wish for him, knowing what a jinx she would be for him or any man.

But the beautiful grotto smelled like a rose garden in full bloom, stronger and stronger until she had to see just what kind of rose petals Athena had packed.

She slipped reluctantly from Yannis's embrace and tiptoed to the tent. The paper bag still sat in her duffel. She couldn't smell the petals until she opened the bag, and they were wilting and turning brown around the edges in the summer heat.

It wouldn't hurt to throw them in the spring. At least she and Yannis might have a colorful swim. She scurried back to the pool.

Boy, that rose smell was everywhere. Maybe there was a wild thicket of roses over the hill. She opened the bag and tossed the few handfuls of petals onto the water, their bruised and fading surfaces contrasting sadly with the vibrant green water.

Just then, Yannis murmured in Greek, "Cara, come back to me."

Embarrassed, she spun around and his sleepy smile undid her heart. *Oh, I wish this could never end.* The thought popped into her head before she could help it.

So be it. She'd wished for lots of things that had never come to pass, and a few sickly rose petals wouldn't change that losing streak.

Yannis must have dozed a bit, thanks to his long night, since the sun was at a higher angle when he opened his eyes again. Cara slept tucked into his chest, but he could see the pinkness starting on her skin. He wasn't exactly accustomed to nude sunbathing, either, and wasn't eager to find out if certain areas burned or not. "Cara, wake up. You need some sun lotion."

"What?" She tipped her face up to him, her eyes heavy

with sleep. Her tongue came out to moisten her plump lips and he groaned. She gave him a knowing smile and leaned over to run her tongue over his mouth. He opened eagerly and let her nibble and suck at his lips, finding her nipple with his fingers and playing with it until it swelled and peaked under his fingers.

He went to roll her under him, but she stopped him. "Wait, Yannis. I want to please you." She pushed him onto his back and moved over his thighs. Her breasts swayed tantalizingly, their coral tips darkening with arousal as she reached for the water bottle.

He was hard enough to support the bottle by now, but fortunately she didn't try that. "Lie back. I'll clean you." He hesitated, but wanted to see what she had in mind. She grabbed a clean towel from their interrupted bath and poured some water on it. He hissed in shock as she dabbed his shaft and head, wiping every inch with the cool cloth. She moved down to his balls, cupping and lifting them until they tightened dangerously.

He moaned and called out her name, grabbing at her breasts, her ass, her clit, wherever he could reach. He was so crazed with lust he was about to lift her and plant her on top of his bare cock, protection or no.

She must have been aware how close he was to the edge since she moved back from him. "And now for a rinse." Her voice was unsteady, but her movements weren't as she squeezed the cloth over him, the water soaking his entire groin and running down into the blanket under him. He'd never felt anything like that before, and his cock agreed, turning purple in the sunlight.

"Nice and clean." Cara tugged at his hands until he struggled to his feet, guiding him over to the pool.

"Cara, what are all these flowers?"

She turned to see what he saw and she gasped.

The water's surface was entirely covered in rose petals—red, white and every shade of pink.

"I, um, tossed a few into the water—you know, for a romantic effect," Cara explained.

"It's very romantic." He wondered briefly how on earth Athena had packed several pounds of petals without him noticing them, but then their sultry scent buzzed through his brain. "Are we going for a swim?"

Cara blinked and turned to him, her blue eyes hazy with desire. "No, I am." She tugged him down to sit on the marble tile surrounding the spring, his feet dangling into the hot, flowery water.

Then she did the unexpected and slipped into the spring, gliding to face him.

Her red curls floated behind her, her breasts peeping out of their floral blanket. He couldn't see her lower body, and for a crazy minute, she was a real water nymph emerging from her spring to ease his poor mortal pain.

But then she opened her hot, sweet mouth to enfold him and his pain spiked into agony. She sucked at him as if he were wild honey, his foreskin slipping back and forth under her tongue as she reached the exquisitely sensitive tip underneath. He clenched the side of the pool until his fingertips went numb.

Her motions were slow and leisurely due to the water, and for one horrible second, she even stopped. He thrust into her mouth and groaned. Her rosy lips widened into a smug smile around him.

"Cara!" He wrapped his hands in her hair, trapping her in the juncture of his thighs. "*Parakaló*, Cara *mou, glykha mou, thea mou...*" He was calling her his sweet, his goddess, all the fine and good things she was. She sped up at his plea, her slippery fingers tickling and pressing his balls, cold against the marble.

Her eyes were closed and she made little hums of satisfaction, buzzing his cock until he thought he'd scream. He was dizzy with lust, drunk with desire, drugged with lechery, as if he were that satyr at an orgy. But the only one he wanted was Cara. He looked down at her beautiful face and rich hair and couldn't last a second longer.

His climax exploded through him, drawing up from his toes to his cock and pouring into her magical, mystical mouth. He spasmed over her and his feelings flooded out of him, as well. "Oh, Cara, *eime erotevmenos mazi sou, eime erotevmenos mazi sou,* Cara." He loved her—he loved her. It had hit him with all the force of his orgasm—he *did* love her, crazily, passionately, tenderly. He'd loved her ever since he'd found her crying in her sleep from that headache.

She pulled back from him, her eyes wide at his outburst. Thankfully she didn't understand much Greek, or else she'd totally freak out. He hadn't planned to fall in love with her, but how could he not? She was perfect for him— smart, beautiful, funny. He decided not to tell her in English yet, so he gave her a bland look and slipped under the water next to her. "Hey, you. Come here."

She was still looking at him warily as he tugged her close. "What were you telling me, Yannis?"

"Well, *'glykha mou'* is 'my sweet' and *'thea mou'* is 'my goddess'. That's all."

"Oh." Cara relaxed at his casual approach and went into his embrace. That wasn't all, but it was enough for now.

YANNIS KISSED CARA'S FOREHEAD, his lips warm and sweet on her skin. Her limbs were heavy and relaxed from the spring, and she floated in his strong, brown arms for several minutes. With her cheek resting on his chest, she listened to the gradually quieting thump of his heart. It still amazed her that she had such an effect on such a sexy man as Yannis, but his response to her was unmistakable.

But Yannis couldn't *possibly* love her. It had only been a couple weeks since they met, and her own husband hadn't loved her even after several years. She sighed in self-pity and then frowned at herself.

"Tired?" He had mistaken her sigh for a yawn.

"What?" She looked up into his heavy-lidded blue eyes. "Maybe a little. We *were* up most of the night."

"I'll take you to bed for a nap."

Cara yelped in surprise as he wrapped his big hands around her waist and lifted her out of the spring to set her on the cool marble edge where he'd just sat. Her nipples tightened as the breeze skimmed her skin.

Yannis noticed, too, leaning forward to capture one in his mouth. She yelped again, this time in delight, as he sucked her deep, flicking her with his tongue. She threaded her fingers through his slick, dark curls, water beading up on his smooth back like diamonds in the morning sun. "Oh, Yannis," she whimpered. He was an assault on the careful walls she had built around her, cracking them gradually every time they made love.

He looked up at her with his devilish grin and let go of her nipple. "You'll like this even better." He slid his open mouth down her belly. She cried out as he unerringly found her clit with his tongue, darting and licking the slick nub. He moved his mouth over her lush, damp folds and rubbed his stubbled cheeks slowly over her tender skin, despite her attempts to urge him on.

He started murmuring in Greek as he stroked her clit

with his fingers. "So sweet, so hot, I die for the taste of you, the scent of you, finer than wine…" His sexy words faded into appreciative groans as he dived back onto her with his mouth. Cara loved hearing the secret things he spoke to her, and she swelled under his tongue, spikes of sensation reaching deep into her pussy. She grabbed his slick shoulders in a futile attempt to drag him out of the water and into her, but he easily resisted her efforts. "No, no, Cara, let me please you."

Oh, he did please her, especially when he licked her with long, strong strokes reaching deep inside her. She squirmed and wiggled on the marble trying to ease her ache. He knew exactly what she needed before she knew, sliding first one finger and then a second where his tongue had just darted into her.

She immediately shuddered around him, and he stopped licking her clit long enough to give her a satisfied grin. "More?"

She shook her head. "Too much, too much."

"Not with me." He returned to his task, this time gently wiggling his fingers back and forth until he hit a magic spot she hadn't known existed until he'd found it. His lips captured her clit in delicate suction and the terrible, delicious tension spiraled throughout her.

She stared down at him in dazed fascination, his black head brushing her red curls, his sun-darkened hands gripping and spreading her pale thighs wide to receive him.

She was a marble goddess worshipped by her mortal lover, a stone object gradually coming to life under his ministrations. Her fair skin flushed from her belly up to her breasts, her nipples darkening and jutting even more. She cupped her breasts and tentatively brushed her thumbs over their tips. It felt so good that she pinched herself. A hedonistic cry escaped her lips. How had she never experienced this before?

Startled, Yannis looked up at her, his perfectly shaped mouth dripping with her juices. She fisted her hand in his curls and dragged him up to her by his hair. She wanted to experience everything in their wild place of love and crushed her mouth to his.

She could smell and taste herself on his firm lips, but it was arousing, not distasteful, to have the same sensations on her mouth as on her clit. To know that he had created this response in her and they both fully enjoyed it. His hot skin slipped over hers, her nipples catching in his chest hair. He worked his fingers inside her again and she suddenly needed his attention back there.

She shoved his head back between her thighs and fondled her breasts again. She thought she heard a muffled chuckle, but was too close to coming to notice much but his and her touch in union. Locking her ankles around his neck, she rocked back and forth against his sucking, lapping touch. When he scraped her clit with his teeth and the last bits of her stony facade cracked away, her passion for him burst free as she writhed under his mouth and hands. "Oh, Yannis, Yannis…" She trailed off into a wordless cry. Sweet shards of desire pierced her whole body and she shook in his embrace.

After an eternity of pleasure so intense it bordered on pain, she pressed a kiss to his head. He tipped up his face to hers. "Thank you, Cara *mou*."

"For what?" She should be thanking him for how she felt.

He lifted her around the waist and helped her slide into the soothing water of the spring. "For being here with me. I've never enjoyed anything like our time together." He nuzzled her hair.

"Thank you, Yannis." His sincerity and honesty touched her, yet saddened her at the same time. He deserved somebody equally sincere and honest, and once she left, he'd find somebody much better than she.

13

YANNIS SET the last of Cara's camping luggage in her living room. Cara dropped her backpack on the couch and stretched her aching spine. "Oh, that feels good. The bus ride back from the grotto wasn't any smoother than the ride there."

"Don't do that unless you want me to stay." His gleaming gaze was fastened on how her breasts jutted out when she arched her back.

She giggled. "Haven't you had enough, Yannis?"

"Of you? Never." He caught her around the waist and nuzzled her neck.

That sounded suspiciously romantic, so she edged out of his embrace just as Emma came out of her bedroom. "Hey, I thought I heard voices. How was your trip?"

"Into the back of beyond? Where my cell phone battery was mysteriously missing?" Cara tried to sound censorious, but failed.

"I'll let the two of you catch up." Yannis tipped up her chin and kissed her lips. "I'll see you tonight at the party, Cara."

"Okay," Cara replied. She couldn't resist seeing him again as soon as possible.

"Emma, you did a great job packing." He winked at them both and headed out.

Emma turned to Cara. "What did he mean, I did a great job packing?"

Cara's face heated. "All those condoms, probably. Where on earth did you get so many? There had to be at least twenty."

Her friend's eyes widened. "I only had two to put in there. Athena must have…ewww." They both groaned and Cara flopped down on the orange couch.

"Em, I really should chew you out for going along with her plotting, but that woman's a force of nature."

Emma collapsed next to her. "Like the volcano that destroyed Santorini. Or the earthquake they think sank Atlantis."

"Only more troublesome." They looked at each other and laughed.

"Come on, Cara, didn't you have a nice time up there? Athena said you and Yannis needed to be alone."

"That place was about as alone as you can get," Cara allowed. "But yes, we camped next to an ancient hot spring, swam, slept, talked…" Talked, but not about the biggest thing he'd let slip, not knowing she understood his every word of love.

Emma patted her hand. "It sounds fabulous. I wish Nick and I could have more time alone, but his mother always worries if he stays out too much."

Cara nodded, but didn't believe that was his mother's motive. As if Nick's mother didn't know exactly where he was, on such a small and close-knit island? Ha.

Yannis had said his parents wouldn't be at his party, since they couldn't leave London because his sister had just had a baby. Not that she wanted to meet his parents or have him meet hers—she still planned to leave Greece as soon as the next ferry docked. He was a nice guy and didn't deserve the trouble she could inadvertently cause him.

And if Yannis *did* think he was falling in love with her, her sudden departure would cure him of that.

She reached up to push a curl off her forehead and grimaced. "Ugh. The hot spring was great, but the water was full of minerals. I think my hair is calcified by now."

Emma jumped up and extended a hand to help her off the couch. "Hop in the shower. The party doesn't start until after dark, so there's plenty of time for you to even take a nap." Emma stood back and crossed her arms over her chest. "Hmm, you do look pretty tired. Did the crickets keep you awake all night?" she teased.

"Something kept me up all night, but it was bigger than a cricket," she joked back.

"You know, Cara, I think the Aphrodisias effect has done you a world of good. Before we came, you were quiet and wore black all the time. Now you're laughing, wearing bright colors, enjoying yourself."

Emma was too polite to mention Cara's torrid summer affair, but they both knew what she meant. "Are you having a good summer, too, Emma?"

Emma hugged her enthusiastically. "Oh, yes, Cara, thank you. I never would have been able to stay on Aphrodisias for the whole summer if you hadn't treated me. I would have missed all of this—the beautiful island, the beach, Nick…" She finished with a blush.

Cara almost changed her mind about leaving. She knew Emma's conscience wouldn't let her stay if Cara left, even if Cara paid for the rest of the summer's stay. Maybe Cara could lie low in Crete for a week or so to try to put her head together.

"And you never would have met Yannis." Emma smiled at her. "I think he's falling in love with you."

"You do?" Cara's insides chilled. "Why do you think that?"

Her friend shrugged. "Just women's intuition. Don't you think so?"

"No." Cara turned on stiff legs and headed to the bathroom. Yannis hated liars, he'd said so himself. And while she'd told him the partial truth about Con, she still hadn't fully opened up to him. "He doesn't know me well enough to love me," she called to Emma. And if he *did* know her better, he would never love her.

CARA PARKED Athena's compact car in front of Yannis's aunt and uncle's house. She'd never been there before, but judging from the four hundred or so people milling around, she figured she was at the right place. They lived a short distance from town in a typically cubic, whitewashed house. Lights blazed from all the rectangular windows, and Greek pop music blared from jumbo speakers set up in the yard.

Athena had assured her that the excavation was in the hands of the government now, and Uncle Gus had thrown up his hands in typically Greek fatalism at the delay of his deal. Athena had extended him the proverbial olive branch and connected him with another of her relatives who had a nice parcel of land for sale, so everyone was happy.

"This looks like a pretty fancy party. Are you sure we don't need to bring any birthday presents for Yannis?" Emma looked at the small box of pastries from the local bakery.

Cara shook her head. "It's not his birthday, and Athena says around here people just bring some sweets or wine for a name day party." She lifted a bottle of local ouzo. "We've got both covered."

"I suppose you can always give him an extra-special present later. I asked Athena if I could sleep at her house tonight. You know, just to give you guys a little more privacy."

"Oh, Emma, you don't have to do that—"

Emma held up her hand. "Really, it's not a big deal. I tossed an overnight case into the back of the car. Athena will give me a ride back to her place and you and Yannis can hang off the chandelier for all I care."

Cara laughed and shook her head. Emma had done her own share of blossoming during their trip. While Cara had her doubts about Niko's motives, he seemed to be helping Emma lighten up and enjoy herself after years of study. "Come on, let's go find the guys."

They walked up the yard past men poking at half a dozen sides of lamb and kabobs the size of fencing rapiers over a flaming fire pit. The men looked up and stared at Cara and Emma in the typically blunt but not rudely sexual manner of Greek men. Cara barely noticed it anymore, but Emma twitched uneasily at being the center of attention.

"We just walk in?" Emma asked as they approached the wide-open front door.

"Who's going to hear the doorbell if we ring it?" Cara pointed out as she entered. "The women are in the kitchen, so we'll take the food there."

A burst of high-pitched laughter guided them to the kitchen at the back of the house.

The laughter stopped as soon as Cara and Emma entered, mostly teenage girls and young women sitting around. The Greek women wore their most fashionable clothes and frequently shook out long, straight layers of dark hair. Cara looked good tonight, too, her square-necked sundress the color of ripe cantaloupe, its straps crisscrossing a mostly bare back. She'd even bothered to straighten her hair for the first time in a long time.

"Hello," Emma said awkwardly. "Has anyone seen Yannis?"

"Which one? There are eleven here," one of the teen-agers answered, her friends snickering. One particularly snotty-looking girl made a crack in Greek about stupid, fat American women.

The "stupid" crack bugged Cara the most. She turned and gave the mouthy one a hard glance. "Yannis with the blue eyes. *My* boyfriend," she answered in perfect Greek, publicly calling him what he really was. Her first boyfriend in ages, but much more. "Isn't he handsome?"

The women looked at her in surprise, but most of them nodded in agreement. One petite brunette announced, "If he weren't my cousin, I'd go to bed with him in a second!"

"That never stopped you before, Angelika!" her friend catcalled among a chorus of hooting. Emma looked ques-tioningly at Cara. Cara gave her what she hoped was a re-assuring glance.

Emma looked over Cara's shoulder. "Oh, see, here's Yannis," she said in relief.

Cara spun around. Yannis stood at the back door, a curl tumbling down his forehead, his smile widening as he took in her appearance. He moved quickly toward her and pulled her into a deep kiss in front of everybody.

She was embarrassed to be the center of attention, but the magic of his embrace immediately blocked out every-thing else.

He finally pulled away from her. Ignoring the whispers and giggles, he stared at her. "You straightened your hair." Yannis stroked it as if he'd never touched it before. "It's so soft and smooth. And long." His eyes heated, and she knew he wanted to incorporate her temporary look into some bedroom games.

"I had some extra time to blow-dry it and, well, I wanted to take a nap and I knew sleeping on wet, curly hair was a bad idea."

He threw back his head and laughed. "You're so honest, Cara." She flinched, but he didn't notice. "Come on and meet my aunt Eleni. Theia Eleni! Meet Cara—she's my American girl I told you about."

Aunt Eleni came out from the pantry with a platter of stuffed grape leaves. She was short and plump with elaborately teased black hair and heavy makeup. "What, Yannis?" Her smile faded as she saw him with his arm around Cara's shoulder. His aunt obviously knew of Cara's connection to Athena and her roadblocks to the construction company. Despite Gus's pleasure with his new building site, Eleni held a grudge. That was okay. Cara was protective of Yannis, as well, although he'd never understand why.

After introducing them, Yannis steered her out into the backyard. More barbecues were flaming along, the men drinking and poking at the meat, tiki torches shining off their beer bottles. Yannis greeted them cheerfully, but didn't stop to talk. "I want to show you something." He stopped on the far side of a big equipment shed.

"What? Your tools?"

"One of them, if you're a good girl." He kissed her hard and long, his lips and tongue making her forget half the island was fifty feet away.

He couldn't stop touching her hair. "You look blond in this torch light—almost like another person."

"Blond?" She patted her hair nervously. She hadn't worn straight, blond hair since Con died, partly to take back her real self and partly to confuse people about her former identity.

"Don't worry, I like your hair the way it truly is." He leaned closer to whisper. "All those red ringlets to sink my fingers into as I sink into your body." He sucked her earlobe and she shut her eyes at the hot, wet sensation.

He palmed her breast through her dress and her eyes flew open. "No, Yannis, you can't. Most of your family is right around the corner."

"Doesn't a man deserve a special treat on his name day?" He leisurely found her nipple and teased it into a hard peak. "It would be a treat for you, too."

It sure would, Cara knew. Every time they had sex, it just got better, deeper and emotionally intimate on a level she'd never experienced before. As if making love with Yannis was her refuge. But she caught his stroking hand and pushed it away just the same. "Your special treat will have to wait until there aren't three hundred people within a hundred yards. Now let's try some of those lamb kabobs. I haven't eaten grilled lamb in years."

"Okay, okay." He relented good-naturedly. "Food first, then our other appetites later."

Cara let him guide her back to the party, their fingers entwined as if they were a real couple. She fought back nerves. If it took such self-control just to remove his hand from her breast at a busy party, how could she ever bring herself to leave him?

"MORE *TORTA?* Or *elliniko?*" Eleni hovered over Cara, offering her more cake and coffee as several women sat outside in the garden after the main meal was consumed. Yannis was off with the men, where there was raucous laughter and a lot of clinking of shot glasses likely filled with ouzo or retsina. With a small smile she realized she trusted him enough to know she wouldn't feature in any stories.

Thanks to Eleni's searching looks, Cara was antsy and didn't need any more caffeine. *"Oxi, efkhareestó."* Rats, she'd slipped back into Greek when she'd said "no, thank you" to the food.

Eleni nodded and went back to whisper to her friends. Cara looked for Athena, but the older lady was sitting with her friends in the living room. Cara sipped at her bottled water, wondering who to chat with. The younger girls only spoke Greek, and it was way too late for Cara to reveal her language skills. She sighed and stared over the torch-lit garden as a Greek dance mix played in the background. It was the same song that had played at the disco the first night she had met Yannis—the pop paean to summer sluttiness. Especially if you were a foreign girl wearing a tiny bikini and prone to spring-break-type public drunkenness according to the music video she'd seen on Greek TV last week.

The younger girls giggled at some of the risqué lyrics as Eleni and her friends frowned in disapproval, casting sidelong glances at Cara. Was it possible they recognized her? Would they pump Yannis for details and possibly give her away? She set down her water and went looking for Emma.

Emma was coming out of the bathroom, her cheeks and lips flushed pink.

"What's up, Em?"

Emma grabbed her hand and dragged her to a relatively quiet corner outside the front door. "Nick just left to visit his uncle Ianni's own name day party. But before he went, we had a *talk.*"

"What did you *talk* about?" she asked, laying the same significant emphasis on the verb.

"Us." Emma was practically giddy with excitement.

"And the two of you are…?"

Emma took a deep breath. "I'm taking some time off school to stay here on Aphrodisias with Nick."

Cara narrowed her eyes. "How much time?"

Emma looked cagey. "I don't know. Maybe a semester, or two. Or a couple years."

Cara's jaw dropped. Emma was less than a year away from earning her Ph.D. from one of the best universities in the world. "Are you crazy, Emma? You're going to throw away your whole academic career for some guy? What are you going to do with a half-finished grad degree in theoretical mathematics on this tiny island? Bookkeeping? You don't even balance your checkbook half the time."

"Nick makes a good living, and we're talking about getting married." Emma stuck her chin out. "Until then, we could live with his family."

"You haven't even *met* his family!" And she knew what they thought of Emma, if they thought of her at all. Cara shoved her hands into her apparently blond, straight hair and tried to keep from pulling out large chunks.

"Don't do it, Emma. You don't know how these people think. His mother will hate your guts and his family will never accept you."

Her stubborn friend shook her head. "They'll come around."

"Emma, this isn't *My Big, Fat Greek Wedding.* They don't want you. You're smarter than all of them put together and here's the big point in neon lights—you are *not* Greek." Cara knew she was starting to lose it, but couldn't help herself, blood roaring in her ears. "Even if Niko somehow grew a pair and married you against their wishes, he would never stick up for you. Greek men are like that. Just look at me—do you think my loving Greek husband ever took my side? Hell, no! His family called me the vilest names possible while Con fucked around on me and nobody ever said boo."

"Cara, it's not the same." Emma extended a calming hand, but had a frightened expression. "Cara…"

"What? Don't you want to know what it's like to marry a Greek man?" She was shaking by then.

"Your husband was a Greek man?" Yannis had come around the house from the backyard.

Cara immediately spotted his blue eyes wide with shock. "I was foolish enough to fall in love with him, or rather who I thought he was."

Just then Yannis's Aunt Eleni barreled out of the house, Athena close on her heels and yelling her head off. "It's true, it's true!" Eleni yelped in Greek. "This girl, she is Karoleena. It's the hair—blond, straight hair!"

"Shut up, Eleni!" Athena shook her fist at Yannis's aunt, but Cara shook her head.

"What girl is Karoleena?" Yannis looked puzzled.

"Oh, I forgot, you were at the university in Ohio during her great scandal and didn't see the photos. They were all over the magazines and television."

"The university in Ohio?" Cara turned to him. "You went to school in Ohio?"

"He still does," Eleni continued. "Top of his class in architecture."

"You're speaking Greek. Very well." He gave Cara a narrow glance.

"And you're a university student less than two hundred miles from me?" At least Cara hadn't been the only close-mouthed one.

"She ought to speak Greek well. I spent years teaching her," Athena bragged. "Karoleena can speak, read and write almost like a native."

Cara grimaced. Bad timing.

"You understood everything I said to you." He was obviously remembering how he'd told her he'd loved her, but in Greek only.

She went to Yannis. "Remember the American blond trophy wife who had the 'good luck' to have her husband die while he bounced around on his mistress? The one who took half his money and went back to the States a wealthy woman?" She spread her arms wide. "Here I am. Heavier, healthier and definitely not a blonde."

Yannis stared at her as if she'd socked him in the gut.

"You see? You see?" his aunt shrilled. "She used her poor, dead husband's money to ruin your uncle's construction project. All for some stupid women's museum."

Athena started shouting at the woman in Cara's defense. Yannis ignored them and spoke to her. "Is it true? You are Karoleena Constantinos?"

"I used to be. After Con died, I took back my own name. And my own life."

He seemed too shocked to take it in. "I don't believe this. After all you and I... You couldn't even do me the courtesy to tell me your whole story. No, it is bits and parts and half-truths until the only way I learn about you is from other people." He shook his head. "Why couldn't you tell me?"

"Yannis, you don't understand. If people had known I was here it would have wrecked everything. I couldn't let anything wreck you, too."

"I am not some weak little boy to be wrecked, Karoleena." His face hardened until he appeared much older. "I am a man—but obviously you do not think so."

Before she could stop him, he hopped on his scooter and gunned the engine, driving into the night.

"Yannis!" She ran after him and looked back at Athena

for advice, as always. But Athena was lost in the crowd, fascinated and drawn by the noise and spectacle.

But Athena didn't hold answers for Cara—Cara would need to find them on her own. She had leaned on the older woman for years in order to survive in her gilded cage.

Con had built her gilded cage, but Cara had walked in and locked the door of her own accord. She could have left him when she discovered his fifteen-year affair, could have avoided falling into bulimia, could have confided in Athena and her family and gotten help. It was time to stop blaming her own disasters on other people and fix her own damn life.

What did she want with her life?

Yannis. Just as she'd wished at Aphrodite's grotto while tossing those petals. She loved Yannis, shaking in the dark with that monumental self-discovery. She wanted him in her life. Not to be her whole life, since she'd learned that painful lesson, but to weave him into her existence.

Despite his youth, he was a real man, not a boy. She should have told him everything and not tried to put him in his own gilded cage, an unwitting toy for her to take out and play with on her vacation.

She'd existed in a drab world of gray skies and black clothing until coming to Aphrodisias, and it was as if she were Dorothy stepping from Kansas into the Land of Oz. Magic happened here, too—hadn't she seen for herself how a handful of dried roses had bloomed over a whole pool? Talk about stopping to smell the roses. She was ready for love, ready to live her life again, ready for a loving life with Yannis.

But she couldn't explain all of that to him if she couldn't find him. Ignoring the stares and pointed fingers starting to aim in her direction, Cara ran to where the scooters were parked and picked one that didn't need keys.

Jabbing the push-button ignition, she swung her leg over the seat when the engine turned over. A cry went up from someone in the crowd, probably the scooter's owner, but Cara roared into the street and away from the party.

"Whoa!" The scooter wobbled a bit underneath her and she forced herself to concentrate on driving for a minute. It had been years since she'd driven a scooter, but it quickly came back to her.

Now, with the motorbike under control, she needed to find Yannis. It was only a short distance to the beach where they'd first frolicked in the ocean. She pulled into the parking lot, but it was empty. He probably needed more time to cool off, if he even stopped anywhere. She thought for a second. She didn't know all his haunts around the island, but one came to mind. She gunned the engine and hoped she could find it in the dark.

"Son of a bitch!" Yannis punched the old olive tree's trunk and then immediately wished he hadn't. His knuckles were no match for something that had withstood two thousand years. He paced around the tree, blowing on his lacerated skin.

The pain was slight compared to his heart. Stupid, stupid Yannis. Looking back, there were all sorts of clues that Cara had been keeping secrets from him. How she had learned Greek so quickly. How she was supposedly a college student but had plenty of money for what even he could tell were nice clothes and jewelry in addition to a whole summer's stay on an expensive Greek island. How Athena treated her like a second daughter but was unusually closemouthed about Cara's past when she gossiped about everyone else.

"*Gamoto!*" He let loose with a blistering string of

Greek curses, mostly aimed at himself. What a fool he was. What an utter fool to fall under her spell like a sailor lured onto the rocks by a Siren. Lured by her radiant smile, her sun-red hair and her luxuriant body, but bound by what he thought was her growing affection for him—or even love.

Just like that first night after the discotheque, he was her lovesick pet goat led around on a string. He howled his pain and rage up at the merciless full moon, just another witness to his stupidity and foolishness.

CARA SLOWED the scooter as she crested the hill leading to the old olive tree. At first she didn't see anyone there, but a dark figure separated from the black, shadowy trunk.

"Cara?" Yannis shaded his eyes as her headlight illuminated him.

"Hello, Yannis." She came to a stop and gingerly got off the scooter. "I'm sorry I ruined your name day party."

"And you rode all the way up into these dark hills to apologize for that?" he scoffed.

"That and other things," Cara admitted. She hoped her skirt concealed the shaking of her legs.

"Yeah? Like what?" He obviously wasn't going to make it easy for her, and she couldn't blame him.

She clasped her hands behind her back to keep from reaching out for him. He'd rebuff her anyway. "Like not telling you that I was married before, and to whom."

"I find all of this incredible to believe, so let me understand this. You, Cara Sokol, are actually a widow. Okay, you told me about this before, and I was sorry for your loss. And now you *finally* tell me the rest of it—that you are the widow of Constantine Constantinos, one of the richest men in Greece. You inherited a million dollars from him, but are pretending to be an American university student. Why?"

"I'm just as much a college student as you are, Yannis. When were you going to tell me you weren't just a construction foreman? Didn't your aunt say you were top of your class in architecture somewhere in Ohio?"

He shrugged. "That's right. I go to Ohio State University in Columbus. I don't think much about school during the summer, and once we got involved I obviously didn't think about it at all."

Cara winced at his sarcasm. But if he was young enough to still be in college… "How old are you anyway?" she demanded. God, what if he was nineteen? Had she fallen in love with a teenager?

"Twenty-four. I'm finishing my master's degree."

Her sigh of relief was audible in the darkness.

"Why? How old are you?"

"Twenty-eight."

"Ah, an older woman. But not as old as your late husband."

Since he'd brought Con up, she took the opening. "No, I was twenty-two when I met Con, and he was thirty-six. He wanted a wife to produce an heir to his shipping empire, and I wanted a loving husband. Neither of us got what we wanted."

Now that she had found Yannis, the adrenaline surge receded and she sat under the olive tree before her legs gave out.

"Why are you sitting? I didn't ask you to come here, and I don't want you to stay here on my land."

She put her hand on the ancient tree trunk for support and inspiration, silently begging for the words to make him understand, if not forgive. "I want to tell you what happened, and why I was dishonest."

"You know, my family was almost destroyed by lies.

My father had to leave Greece to find work once his cheating business partner wrecked their reputations. I swore I'd never let the same thing happen to me. I didn't have to tell you Gus wanted me to pass along information about the land deal, but I did, because I didn't want any dishonesty between us. And now I find the woman I— Never mind. I don't want to listen to any more lies."

Cara put her hands on her hips. Had he almost said the woman he loved? She stomped over to her borrowed scooter, pushed the ignition button and sent it roaring into a thorn bush, where the motor choked and died. Now she was stuck there until he either listened to her or left her. "I can't keep you here, Yannis. You can race back to town, back to your party, and tell everyone what a deceiving bitch I am. I'll go pack and leave on the ferry tomorrow."

"Crazy! You're crazy!" He walked toward his scooter, and for a long, long minute, she thought he was going to do exactly that. But he made an angry gesture at the machine and stormed back to her. "And what kind of man would I be, eh? To leave a woman alone in the dark out in the country with a broken scooter she probably stole and has no idea how to drive?"

Cara had managed okay, but he was right about the theft.

He went on, "So you tell me what you have to say, and then we both go back to town."

"Thank you, Yannis."

"I don't need your thanks, *Karoleena*." He leaned nastily on the Greek version of her name. "Unless you want to thank me for all the pleasure I gave you?"

"You got plenty of pleasure of your own, buddy, so don't look for a thank-you card from me!" He'd finally goaded her into losing her cool.

He gave a short chuckle. She took a deep breath and started telling him how she had been a crew member on a charter on Corfu and Con had been a guest of the ship's owner. Tanned, athletic Cara had caught handsome Con's eye and he had bowled her over with his rich worldliness and protestations of love. He'd even insisted on calling her "Karoleena" to give her a sophisticated air.

After a whirlwind courtship, Con married her on his own private island and settled her there with Athena to look after her. Cara took a deep breath before the next part of her story. Yannis's face was set into deep lines, and she was unsure what he made of her.

"So Con headed back to Athens after our honeymoon. I stayed with Athena, who tried to ease me into Greek life. She taught me Greek, not knowing I'd read the tabloids that said that Con was seen at various parties with his longtime companion, Clio Papadopoulos. 'Companion'— at least that's what the Greek dictionary I checked said. 'Mistress' would have been more accurate."

Yannis had been standing unnaturally still and burst into motion, pacing back and forth over the packed ground. "Why didn't you tell me who you were when we were talking last week about Constantine—your husband," he said with a grimace. "Oh, I understand—right before you got your migraine. Was that a pretense, too?"

"No. It was a shock to hear what you thought of me."

"You?" He threw up his hands. "I was talking about some woman my aunt read about in those tabloids. How was I to expect the most infamous widow in Greece was the woman I was sleeping with?"

"And that is exactly why I didn't want to come back. If it hadn't been for Athena being so sick I never would have set foot in Greece again." Cara faced him. "Con picked me as a baby-maker. I was young and healthy, and his mistress was infertile, so she didn't ever expect him to marry her. I didn't get pregnant right away, so he went back to Athens for business and pleasure. Once I found out about his infidelity with Clio, there was little pleasure from me. He promised me several times that he'd ended his affair, but he couldn't keep away from her."

"He preferred someone over you?" Yannis sounded outraged, which was encouraging.

"I still thought I loved him, so I did my best to draw him back to me," she admitted. "I returned to Athens, I straightened my hair and dyed it blond, lost a terrible amount of weight and made myself sick in the process. I stayed out late partying and generally made a fool of myself." She shuddered at her past desperate behavior. "The paparazzi stalked me and one even rammed into the side of my car. In fact," she continued, "when Con died, his family wanted to disinherit me but couldn't. And they treated my husband's mistress as the grieving widow, not me. She couldn't inherit his fortune, after all."

"But you risked coming back to all that? Why?"

"I came for Athena. But I stayed...for you."

"Me?" He straightened up from leaning against the olive tree.

"Yes." Risking the paparazzi was small potatoes compared to what she was risking now. She stood, drawing strength up from her legs like a tree's roots. "I stayed for you because I fell in love with you."

"You don't love me. You wanted a hot Greek guy for the summer, and you got him. Now you can write a nice paper for your English class called, 'Who I Did on My Summer Vacation.'"

Cara winced. His cynicism was out of the ordinary for

him, but not unexpected. "I am sorry for deceiving you. I was a coward for too many years, but meeting you, being with you, *loving* you, forced me to change. To be brave." She stepped forward, pressing her body against his. He tried to move away from her, but the olive tree was at his back and to her advantage. "Oh, Yannis." She twined her arms around his neck. "Yannis *mou, latria mou, fos ton mation mou.*" She told him all the endearments he'd used with her. *"Eime erotevmeni mazi sou."* I'm in love with you. She pressed kisses over his face, continuing to tell him of her love for him. *"S'agapo, Yannis."* Somehow, it was easier to spill her heart to him in his native language.

"You really do speak Greek well." He kept his hands at his sides, but his breathing had sped up.

Encouraged, she kissed his mouth. "These lips will not lie to you again, Yannis. I promise."

He grabbed her shoulders and held her away from him. He stared deeply into her eyes, seemingly intent on arguing more, but then blurted, "Oh, hell," and dragged her close. He lowered his face to hers. *"Cara mou, eime erotevmenos mazi sou.* I love you, too, Cara, despite your million dollars."

"More like twenty million," she muttered just as he was about to kiss her.

"Twenty?" He pulled back, clearly surprised. "Are you joking?"

"I'm trying to give it away, I swear. You know those anonymous Aphrodisias islander scholarships your cousins won?"

"You?" He started to laugh. "Now my uncle really will have a fit."

"I'll send Stav's kids to university, too, if they want."

He cupped her cheek. "Hmm. I guess we do owe that

guy a favor for stranding us at Aphrodite's Grotto. It's a magical place."

Cara shook her head. "The magic was with us all along."

"Yes." His eyes glittered in the moonlight, wild and deep with passion. "You and I."

This time, he actually did kiss her, and she clung to him under the ancient olive tree, the tree that had sheltered two millennia of lovers. It knew its job by now, its leaves whispering songs of love to the man and woman who stood entwined in the shadows of its branches.

Epilogue

"I'M NOT SURE how you're going to carry me over the threshold with this setup." Cara stood with her hands on her hips and stared at the cozy pop-up tent set in Aphrodite's Grotto. Stavros had once again dropped them off at the Grotto, this time willingly and without threat of blackmail. Athena had cut back her meddling with the locals now that she had a whole crop of new people from the university excavation team. More often than not she was found bossing around the student workers, dust covering her black dress as she strode through the dig site. Once the dig was finished, the women's museum would be built nearby to house all the unearthed Aphrodisian temple artifacts, including a beautiful small bronze statue of the goddess carrying of all things, a rose.

"Oh, yes, your quaint American wedding custom." Yannis came up behind her and nuzzled the back of her neck.

"Right, like Athena and your aunt rolling half a dozen local babies over our sleeping bags to ensure our fertility *wasn't* a quaint Greek wedding custom?" Once Aunt Eleni saw how well Gus's new Belgian villa development was selling, she'd forgiven Athena and Cara for ruining the deal Gus had tried to ruin in the first place. After all, what was a little wheeling and dealing among family now?

His white, flashing grin still made her weak in the knees. "Don't worry, I brought plenty of antifertility charms, if you know what I mean." He slipped his hand down to cup her ass. "Want to try one out?"

She spun in his embrace and wrapped her arms around his neck. "You know I do." She gave her husband of one day a sweet, long kiss, hardly believing that two years had passed since their first hot, sexy summer on Aphrodisias. So much had happened. Emma had lived with Niko and his family for a few disastrous weeks that summer before returning to grad school. It had been so bad that sweet, good-natured Emma had learned the Greek curse for the Evil Eye from Athena and used it on Niko's mother as she packed her bags and left. Niko finally got his own place, where he picked up blond tourist girls to his heart's—or some other body part's—content.

Emma had been in fine spirits at Cara's wedding, bringing along her current boyfriend, a mountainous Scot with a Ph.D. in theoretical physics. When he wasn't playing rugby or looking longingly at Emma, the two lovebirds had in-depth conversations where Cara only understood the words, *if, and* and *but*.

Cara and Yannis had both graduated from school and were looking forward to new jobs, dividing their time between Aphrodisias and Athens, Yannis as an architect and Cara as a translator and English teacher. Athens finally felt safe to Cara now that so much time had passed, even more so with Yannis at her side in their cozy apartment.

But the magic island of Aphrodisias would always be their true home. Cara slipped out of his arms and picked up a bouquet of red, white and every color of pink roses specially chosen for a special place. She carried the fragrant bundle to the small alcove behind the spring where a statue of the goddess of Love had once stood—maybe even the small bronze she'd soon see in the museum. Cara laid the flowers on the marble niche, and the summer breeze stilled, the birds quieting in the trees.

"Thank you," she whispered, blowing a kiss. The wind picked up the scent of roses and swirled it around the grotto as Cara returned to her husband, Yannis, hand-delivered seemingly by Aphrodite herself. With more than a little help from Athena.

* * * * *

YOU LOVE
ROMANCE?

WE LOVE
ROMANCE!

Printed by RR Donnelley at Glasgow, UK